13

FRUIT OF THE LEMON

Faith Jackson has set herself up with a great job and a brilliant flatshare. But her relations with her overbearing, though loving, family leave a lot to be desired, especially when her parents announce their intention to retire back home to Jamaica. Perplexed, even furious, Faith makes her own journey there, where she is immediately welcomed by her Aunt Coral, keeper of a rich cargo of family history. Her aunt's compelling storytelling unfurls a wonderful cast of characters from Cuba, Panama, Harlem and Scotland in a story that passes through London and sweeps over continents.

Books by Andrea Levy
Published by The House of Ulverscroft:

NEVER FAR FROM NOWHERE
SMALL ISLAND

ANDREA LEVY

FRUIT OF THE LEMON

Complete and Unabridged

CHARNWOOD
Leicester

First published in Great Britain in 1999 by
Review, an imprint of
Headline Book Publishing, London

First Charnwood Edition
published 2006
by arrangement with
Headline Book Publishing
a division of Hodder Headline, London

The moral right of the author has been asserted

Extract from 'Lemon Tree' by Will Holt reproduced
by permission of Campbell Connelly & Co Ltd
and TRO Essex Music Ltd, London

British Library CIP Data

Levy, Andrea, *1956 –*
Fruit of the lemon.— Large print ed.—
Charnwood library series
1. Women—Black—Great Britain—Genealogy—
Fiction 2. Jamaica—Fiction 3. Large type books
I. Title
823.9'14 [F]

ISBN 1–84617–122–9

Published by
F. A. Thorpe (Publishing)
Anstey, Leicestershire

Set by Words & Graphics Ltd.
Anstey, Leicestershire
Printed and bound in Great Britain by
T. J. International Ltd., Padstow, Cornwall

This book is printed on acid-free paper

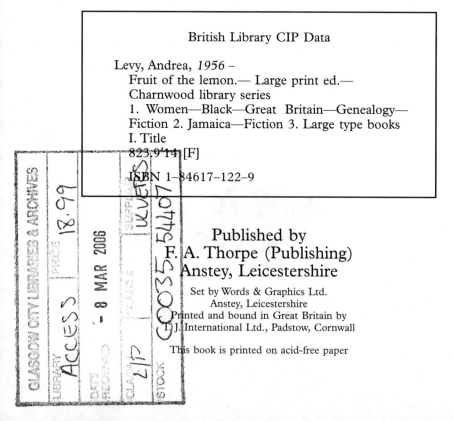

In memory of Mary Pat Leece
'Nor can I forget'

Acknowledgements

I would like to acknowledge the assistance of two books in my research: *History of Jamaica* by Clinton V. Black and *Caribbean People* (Book 3) by Lennox Honeychurch.

I would also like to thank Gill Lipson, Michael and Max Munday for providing me with a quiet place, Amy Levy for understanding, Albyn Hall for listening and Bill Mayblin for everything.

Lemon tree very pretty
and the lemon flower is sweet
But the fruit of the poor lemon
Is impossible to eat

Will Holt
Lemon Tree

Fruit of
The Lemon

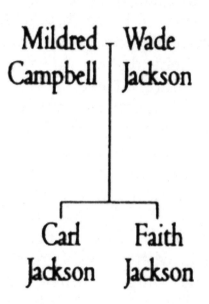

'Your mum and dad came on a banana boat,' that was what the bully boys at my primary school used to say. The boys with unruly hair, short trousers and dimpled knees that went bright red in the cold. 'Faith is a darkie and her mum and dad came on a banana boat.' They'd walk round behind me in the playground, pushing and pulling at each other's home-made knitted grey-with-a-green-stripe V-neck jumpers, until I began to cry or my friends told them, 'Oh no they never. Leave her alone — just shut your gobs or we'll tell Miss.'

So it was a bit of a shock when Mum told me, 'We came on a banana boat to England, your dad and me. The Jamaica Producers' banana boat.' The little white boys were right. I thought of the song we sang in music and movement. 'Hey mister tallyman, tally me banana.' The song that made the boys nudge each other, point at me and giggle behind their hands when the teacher wasn't looking.

'Where did you sit on this boat?' I asked my mum.

And she laughed. 'It was a proper boat with cabins and everything. Even had a dance every evening and we took it in turns to sit at the captain's table. What, you think we sit among the bananas?'

I didn't tell her then but, yes, that was exactly

3

what I thought. My mum and dad curled up on the floor of a ship, wrapped in a blanket perhaps, trying to find a comfortable spot amongst the spiky prongs of unripe bananas.

I remembered the illustrations of slave ships from my history lessons. There was the shape of a boat with the black pattern of tiny people laid in rows as convenient and space-saving as possible. It looked like an innocuous pattern. A print that could be repeated and transferred to cloth to make a flowing skirt. Slaves in a slave ship. We had to write essays telling the facts — how the slaves were captured then transported from Africa to the New World. We drew diagrams of how the triangular trade in slaves worked, like we drew diagrams of sheep farming in Australia. I hated those lessons. Although there were no small boys laughing and pointing, I felt them. 'Your mum and dad came on a slave ship,' they would say. 'They are slaves.'

My mum and dad never talked about their lives before my brother Carl and I were born. They didn't sit us in front of the fire and tell long tales of life in Jamaica — of palm trees and yams and playing by rivers. There was no 'oral tradition' in our family. Most of my childhood questions to them were answered with, 'That was a long time ago,' or 'What you want to know about that for?' And if Mum ever let something slip — 'You know your dad lived in a big house,' — then I was told with a wagging finger not to go blabbing it about to my friends, not to repeat it to anyone.

As I got older Mum began to throw me little

4

scraps of her past — 'I met your dad at a bus stop,' — which I would piece together like a game of Consequences I used to play as a child — fold the paper and pass it on — until I had a story that seemed to make sense.

My mum and dad met one very hot afternoon in the parish of St Mary in Jamaica. Mum was then Mildred, the youngest of three sisters from the Campbell family. The family lived on a farm in St Mary. 'Not like farms you know,' Mum told me, 'it was just some land but we grew all sorts.' They grew oranges, bananas, paw paw, sour sop and coconuts. There was even an ackee tree but they kept that fruit for themselves. The other fruits were sold in a tiny shop that was run by my grandmother. My grandmother was 'tall'. My grandfather was 'a clever man and very hard-working like your dad'. There were other relatives around but they were, 'Yes, well, I can't remember them all just now.'

Mum kept a goat and the goat ate everything. You could make Mum's chest quiver with laughter for several minutes if you just said the name Columbine — which was the name of her goat and unfortunately my middle name. 'But I loved that goat, why shouldn't I call you after me goat, Faith?'

My grandfather, as well as working on the farm, also mended shoes. 'Every time I hear a

5

tap, tap, tapping, I think of me dad mending his shoes.' My grandmother made dresses which she sold in the shop. 'Lovely dresses with lace and frilly skirts. Not like the drab things children wear now.'

Mum had to look after chickens on the farm while her sisters, evidently, lazed around all day looking in the mirror.

Her teacher at school was from Scotland. 'A lovely woman — she used to go red in the sun — we thought she would explode like a melon. We called her red ant.' At school Mum learnt about England, 'the Mother Country'. Trafalgar Square, Piccadilly Circus, Buckingham Palace. She learnt the names of all the cities — London, Manchester, Birmingham — and had to know by heart what each of the cities produced. Sheffield for steel, Newcastle for ships, Nottingham for lace. Her teacher taught her all about snow, how it was white and cold and that if you licked something that was frozen your tongue would get stuck to it and the fire brigade — in their red engines with the clanging bells — would have to come and prise you off.

Mum's school burnt down one night and everyone came to watch the fire. Mum stood in her nightdress clinging to her school friends as the flames gobbled up the building. 'I never seen anything like it before — there was nothing left — the fire just go out 'cause there nothing left to burn. From that day I scared of fire.' She had to go to a makeshift school after that where all the classes were in one room together and she could

6

hear what everyone else was supposed to be learning.

Mum wanted to be a nurse. 'Well, all the girls wanted to be a nurse,' she said. 'There wasn't much else but being a nurse. Although me sister wanted to be a teacher.' She went to Kingston to train at a hospital. 'They were strict, it was worse than being at school and we were grown women by then.'

It was around this time she started to dream about going to England. She wanted to get away from 'everyone knowing me business — telling me what to do'. She wanted to see all those places she'd learnt about, Trafalgar Square and Buckingham Palace. She wanted to work for the National Health Service. But she could not afford the full fare to England and at that time, she could not get an assisted passage on a ship unless she was married.

Then one hot day — 'I was perspiring and I could hardly breathe in it was so hot. You children don't know that sort of heat,' — she was waiting for a bus with her friend Violet, when she met Wade.

Wade, my dad, was the oldest son of the Jackson family. He had a younger brother called Donald and the two brothers grew up in St Andrew. 'I don't remember much about when I was a child,' Dad told me. 'We played and that. We must have played, you know.' He must have gone to school. 'Yes, of course I went to school, I just can't remember much that happened — was a long time ago, Faith.' And after school he started to learn bookkeeping. 'It was a bit boring but . . . you know.' His parents had their own business importing haberdashery. Wade's father was 'ohh . . . a very strict man'. His mother was 'oh . . . you know'. Wade got a job working for Tate & Lyle in the accounts department but then he gave up the job to work for his father. But his father was 'a very strict man', and Wade was not happy. Then one day as he was walking down a road in St Mary he met Mildred at a bus stop, standing with a girl he knew.

As the story goes, Wade nodded at Violet and then smiled at Mildred. The first thing Mildred noticed about Wade was that he was not shorter than her. 'Every man I meet look me straight in the chest except your dad.' The first thing he noticed about her was 'she was tall'. They talked at the bus stop for a long time about 'this and that . . . not very much . . . I don't remember now'. But by the end of the conversation Wade had arranged to see Mildred again.

Mildred was very impressed with Wade. His brother Donald had been in the RAF and was living in England. She also liked the fact that 'he had a spark about him, your dad, a twinkle in his eye'. Wade thought Mildred was 'well, she's your mother, of course I thought she was pretty, Faith!'

They began courting and after only a few months decided to get married and go to England. They had to save up money for the passage. Wade's father promised to give him some money and Wade did everything his father requested for several weeks but in the end his father only gave him a few pounds. 'He was very upset, your dad. He never really forgave his parents. But you see they didn't want him to go.' So Mildred had to borrow money from her parents, 'and they didn't really have it to give'.

Both the bride and groom wore white to the wedding. And, my mum and dad agreed, 'it rained all day'.

Then Mr and Mrs Wade and Mildred Jackson set sail for England on the Jamaica Producers' banana boat. The bananas, evidently, were kept in the hold of the ship. Mildred and Wade watched them being brought on board. 'The tallyman,' Mum told me, 'slice off the top of the stems of the bunches as they take them in. Then him count the little stubs he just sliced off and pay the farmer. Quite interesting.'

The ship sailed for two weeks. And every night they went to the ballroom and danced to a live band. Dad was not a good dancer. 'I could do it, mind, but . . . you know.' So Mum was often partnered by an Englishman who explained many British customs to her as they waltzed and quick-stepped. 'He taught me a lot, that man.' Dad smoked on deck while the Englishman, Mr Thomas, explained that it was polite to arrive at dinner parties five minutes late, that men should remove their hats when inside a building and that milk should always be put into tea last.

The ship finally docked at West India Dock on Guy Fawkes' night. As the ship pulled into its berth, Mildred and Wade heard the pop and whistle of crackers and saw fireworks lighting up the sky. Mum explained, 'At first we didn't know what it was for. In Jamaica you only get fireworks

9

at Christmas. Your dad thought it might have been a welcome for us, having come so far and England needing us. But I didn't think he could be right. And he wasn't.'

On the instruction of Mr Thomas — 'He was a gentleman, that man,' — they got a taxi to Ladbroke Grove where they met Dad's brother Donald. 'I remember that taxi ride. England looked so grey and all the time we riding along my nose was running and there was steam coming out my mouth from the cold.' Donald had said that the newly-weds could live with him until they got themselves fixed up. He lived in one room in a large dark house. In all the other rooms lived white women with blonde hair, who were, as Mum put it, 'ladies of the night'.

'I never thought English people lived like that,' Mum told me. 'One room and we had to share the kitchen and bathroom down the hall with all these women. And they were nice enough but in Jamaica I never saw many people with blonde head and to this day I always think women with blonde hair are ... you know.' Dad's first impression of England was that it was 'oh ... very cold'.

Wade fixed up a curtain in the room and Donald lived on one side of it while he and Mildred lived on the other. 'I ask you, I never thought I'd end up living like that in England.' Mildred did not like living in this one room with two men. 'They thought I was there to serve them.' Donald was a bachelor and persuaded Wade to go out with him nearly every night to

10

the West End; Trafalgar Square and Piccadilly Circus.

'It was not every night, Mildred.'

'It was every night, Wade, and you just leave me in the stinking room and expect me to clean everything up for you.'

Wade found a job with his brother, working for a builder. He started off 'just carrying things — you know'. But after a short while he began to paint and hang wallpaper. Mildred found a job in a hospital although not as a nurse but as an orderly: 'Skivvy at home, skivvy at work. What a disappointment.'

After about six months of living like that, 'I wanted to go home,' Mum said, 'I never thought England would be like that but we didn't have the money.'

Then Donald left. He went back to Jamaica where his father had promised him a better job with more pay. The curtain came down and, 'your dad was quite nice without his brother. It was his brother that turned his head.' Mildred began to train as a nurse. 'Oh, it was lovely.' Meanwhile Wade continued to learn painting and decorating, going to college one evening a week to get a qualification 'with certificates and everything, Faith'.

Mildred then got pregnant with my brother Carl and when he was born — 'Oh, he was a lovely little thing with little dimples. Everyone said, what a lovely little boy, and he made all these little noises and when he smiled everyone said how he was going to break girls' hearts when he grew up. Me little, little baby Carl,'

— the room became too small. Wade worked long hours — 'I had to provide for me family, Faith,' — from six in the morning until after nine at night. And Mildred was left in the room with Carl, who had to be watched all the time because of the paraffin heater, the stairs and all the blonde women. Then the day Mildred found out she was pregnant with me — 'Oh, I was so sick,' — they also found out that they had to leave the house because the landlord wanted to sell it.

The council put Mildred and Carl in a halfway house with other homeless families, while Wade found himself digs in a hostel for men, where he shared a room with nine others and took his belongings away with him every day. Then I was born. 'That labour nearly killed me — you were a big child.' They lived like that for six months with Wade only seeing Mildred and his children at weekends. 'Those days are best forgotten, Faith. Best forgotten.'

Then the council found us all a flat in Stoke Newington. 'It sounded a posh place, Stoke Newington,' Mum told me. 'But I was shocked when I see it. I never thought English people lived like that.' The flat was on a small estate and inside the tiny flat every wall was painted dark brown. But Dad started work on it as soon as we moved in. He stripped off the brown walls and painted them pink and blue and hung hand-tinted photographs of me and Carl on the wall. 'He never sat down, your dad,' and soon it was 'lovely inside'.

We lived in the flat for ten years. When Carl and me came home from school — 'You see you come home together — you hear me, nah' — we had to tell our next-door neighbour we were at home then let ourselves into the flat and watch television until one of our parents came back. 'Latchkey kids! Cha! Let them mind their business. You were not latchkey kids.' Then Mum became a district nurse and got a new dark blue uniform and learnt to drive. 'I pass that test first time. Your dad took two goes.' And Dad started to work for himself, taking on jobs for people who knew him as a conscientious worker. Soon he bought a van with the company name on the side in blue letters: 'Wade's — Painting and Decorating of the Highest Quality'.

Then Mum and Dad bought the house in Crouch End with money they had saved in a post office account. 'No more handouts for us. We make our own way now.' And when Mildred and Wade closed the door of their house for the first time, they both hung their heads and shut their eyes in prayer. 'We finally arrive home,' they said.

Part I

England

1

My parents' hobby was collecting empty boxes. They'd been doing it for years. Brown cardboard boxes mostly. Fyffes boxes that used to contain bananas from the Caribbean; packets of Daz boxes; toilet-roll boxes; Wagon Wheel packet boxes; unspecified boxes; thick double-lined boxes; stapled up on the bottom boxes; small handles cut out the side boxes; supermarket boxes; greengrocers' boxes; stationers' boxes.

My mum was the greatest gatherer. She'd come back from the shops with the groceries inside her brown plastic shopping trolley whilst balancing two, sometimes three, empty boxes on the top of it. My dad and she would discuss the merits and weaknesses of each box brought into the house. 'You see, Wade, what took my eye is that it has a strong bottom that sort of interlocks.' Or, 'But, Mildred, I don't think we can have a use for a box six feet long and only eight inches wide.' My dad would store any new boxes in the small cellar of the house with mathematical precision — boxes in boxes all standing on black plastic sheeting to keep out the damp.

It started when we moved from our old council flat to the house in Crouch End. My parents had to 'pay good money' to rent boxes from the removal company to place in all our 'nick-nacks and paddy-wacks'.

17

'Crooks,' my mum had said as she and my dad watched the brick-shit-house removers in dirty jeans take back all the boxes when we had finished with them.

Just after that the first box came. It contained the new television. My brother and me watched *Dr Who* in glorious living colour as my parents cooed over the box. The next one was oblong and had 'Hoover' written on the side. 'You never know when a box will come in handy,' my parents would say. 'You just never know.'

The day I moved out of home Dad struggled into my room with several of his very finest 'double-strength even got a top' boxes. 'I've got bags,' I said, showing him a suitcase and piles of well-used, screwed-up plastic carrier bags. He looked at me like I was no child of his.

'Bags,' he spat, 'things get mash up in bags, Faith. Bags break. They not strong. You need a box.' He then banged the bottom of the sturdiest one. 'Strong,' he added, as he picked up a plastic bag from the bed, unravelled it and punched his fist straight through the bottom. He then sucked his teeth. Point made, no more words necessary. I took two of the boxes and he left a happy man.

I thought I'd have hardly anything to put in them. At that time I was leaving behind my childhood. Leaving behind my student days. I had lived at home all through my art college life. The grant authority had ummed and ahhed for months before they decided my parents didn't live far enough away from the college to warrant them giving me independent status. And for four years I had had to juggle late-night parties, sit-ins and randy boyfriends, with 1940s Caribbean strictures. 'Faith, you see you in by eleven — Faith, you can bring a nice girl back with you if she's clean — Faith, I don't want you messing around, you have plenty time for fun when you're older.'

All I had to take were my duvet; my alarm clock with the bells on top and a clanger that whizzed so fast that I cut my finger every time I turned it off; several assorted empty tins that looked pretty and were given to me as presents so throwing them out as useless junk felt like betrayal; various bottles of hair oil called things like 'Sta-soft-fro-curl!' or 'Afro-sheen-curl' that I never used but thought I might; a record player and a pile of dusty dog-eared records ranging from *The Sound of Music* and *Oliver* to Tamla Motown's Greatest Hits in many volumes.

The boxes soon filled up and I had to ask my dad for some more. He looked at me and sucked his teeth then started to moan that I was 'taking all the good boxes'.

'You offered!' I shouted, then added, 'What do you need them for anyway?' At which my dad did the strangest thing. He blushed. Then silently gave me three more boxes. But as I left the cellar he said, 'Don't come askin' me for any more.'

I was moving into a short-life, shared house with friends — two men and a woman. I had thought I was reassuring my mum when I lied a little and said my new flatmate was a young woman. But instead she had said, 'A woman. Be careful of living with women.' I had then looked at her and smiled. I had tipped my head to one side and explained to her that 'nowadays, Mum, women have different relationships with each other. Nowadays', I'd elaborated, 'women support one another — they are sisters.' To which my mum had butted in saying that the worst women she had ever lived with were her sisters and that if women started behaving like sisters then God help the world. She then looked to the portrait of Jesus on the wall and apologised, 'Excuse me, Lord'. And went on telling me about the handfuls of hair she used to find in the bedroom she shared with her sisters in Jamaica, pulled out of a head during one of the many sisterly fights. And how her big sister Coral once punched her so hard that the sweet she was sucking got stuck in her throat. Her mother, apparently, had to grab her by her feet, turn her upside down and slap her on the back until the sweet popped out.

'Be careful of living with women and thank God you only have a brother,' she'd finally ended.

My brother Carl said, 'So you moving in with a bird, then?' as he helped me carry my boxes to the back of his van.

'No, a woman actually,' I said pointedly.

'Wos a matter with calling her a bird?'

'Birds,' I said, 'have wings. They fly. They sit in trees and tweet. Women don't.'

'Bird not good enough for you an' all your women's libber friends now? So what do you birds call blokes then?' my big brother asked with a broad goading grin.

I did not respond. Not immediately. Because

20

when we were young Carl came home one day and insisted that from that day on he wanted to be called by his middle name, Trevor. They used to tease him at school. Carl was an unusual name in the schools of North London. There were no other Carls and boys used to walk behind him in the street shouting his name or calling him Carol, among other things. So Carl became Trevor and from that day he would answer to nothing else. It took Mum, Dad and me months to remember. Months of calling out, 'Carl, dinner's ready,' only to hear him say, 'I don't know who you mean, my name is Trevor.' But eventually we all got it.

Then Trevor left school and started work driving a delivery van for a textile company. After two weeks he decided that Trevor no longer suited his image. He wanted to be called Carl again. Carl, he decided, had a certain *Superfly*, *Shaft*, don't-mess-with-me-I'm-a-black-man message. He deployed the same tactics: 'Trevor, who's Trevor? Never heard of him.' Until he was once again Carl.

So I didn't have to say anything about birds. I just smiled and said that we call blokes Trevor and he shut up.

My dad stood by the door to watch me take the last bits of my belongings out of the house. He had hedge clippers in his hand and he stood in front of the perfect clipped privet hedge in the garden, pretending to cut at stray leaves, like a barber clipping over the top of a well-cut head of hair. Then my mum came out wearing pink rubber gloves and carrying a duster and a can of

Mr Sheen which she sprayed onto the front door and began to wipe at vigorously. They needed something to do as they watched me leave.

It wasn't how they would have liked their only daughter to go. They would have preferred to see me swathed from head to toe in white lace, with hand-stitched-on pearls and sequins. Standing in between my bridesmaids — one my age and two little ones — dressed in lemon-yellow satin with white lace trim. Our skirts ballooning out in the sun as I stood with my back to them ready to throw my bouquet into the cheering, laughing crowd. My new husband — a Christian with family from Jamaica or one of the 'small islands' — watching on in a dark suit with wine-coloured cummerbund and a frilly shirt. Then the two of us moving happily down the human arch of men standing holding paintbrushes aloft like swords.

'Marry a decorator like your dad and you'll never have to worry about paint,' Mum had always advised. Every year she steeped several bags of dry fruit in rum ready to make a wedding cake at a moment's notice. And every year she looked at me accusingly as she tipped out the jar of alcoholic sultanas and currants and made another Christmas cake instead.

'Ah Faith, what can we do with you? You just go your own sweet way,' my parents had both decided a long time before. 'Your own sweet way.'

2

I was alone in the house the day my dad made his surprise visit to me. Lying on the settee enjoying my last days before I had to start a new job. I saw him standing in the doorway of the front room and I looked up unsurprised, saying, 'Hello, Dad.' Until I began to realise that it was in fact unusual, very unusual, for my dad to be standing in any doorway in that house.

'How did you get in?' I said, struggling to get up.

He held out a key in front of him as he grinned and said, 'I found this in the door.' He was looking around, 'You must be careful, anyone could have come in. It was lucky it was me.' He gave a strained chuckle. 'Could have been a burglar or anyone. You're lucky it was me and not some madman. Ha ha.' His mouth laughed but his eyes stayed their what-time-d'you-call-this stern. 'You must remember to take it out of the lock, Faith.'

I took the key from him muttering something about being grateful and forgetful and promising to be good, as I scanned the room for anything that would shock him. The ashtray on the coffee table was not only full but choked with roaches — the cardboard remains of several joints rolled the night before and smoked in quick succession in the hope of getting some small 'buzz' out of Mick's homegrown, but which instead sent us all to bed with rasping throats and headaches. But my dad was too busy looking at the dark green walls to notice.

'You like this colour?' he asked, his top lip curling.

'It was here when we came,' I told him. He nodded then looked round at the double doors that divided the front room. He ran his finger down the mottled pink paintwork. He frowned. 'You wan' me paint it for you? I could bring a few of the boys and we could . . . '

'No thanks, Dad,' I interrupted, 'we'll do it ourselves.'

'Suit yourself,' he said, looking up at the cracked ceiling. He knocked one of the walls with his knuckles and looked surprised. 'Umm, quite solid.'

'What are you doing here anyway?' I wanted to know.

'Well, I thought I give you a little surprise. I was just having a walk. We finish early today, so I thought I'll just go for a walk. And I find myself passing here.'

My dad liked to walk. He would set off from our house in Crouch End returning several hours later with tales of the lovely boat he saw on the River Thames. 'Thought I'd give you a little surprise.' He smiled. 'You goin' to show me round?'

I tried to stay looking pleased but I knew I was being spied on. I could hear my mum: 'Go on Wade, go up and see what she up to. You could say you just passing. You always just passing. Just go and see nah.'

24

My dad stood in my new front room ready to report back, 'Mildred, the walls are green and the doors are pink — the child gone mad!' But worse he would soon be reporting, 'But wait, Mildred, you tellin' me she told you her flatmate called Marion?' He would soon be anxiously saying, 'Cha. Mildred, the child is sharing a house with grown men. Is there nothing we can do?'

Marion was my friend. We had met on the foundation year at art school in London. At the time I was being followed round by a boy who was pale, skinny and underdeveloped and whose name I can't remember, but who had a crush on me. I knew the only reason he fancied me was the thought of the look on his parents' faces if he took a black girl home to meet them. He liked to think of himself as a rebel and I was the only black girl on the course. He fancied me and Marion fancied him, for some reason. So she would turn up wherever we were saying, 'Oh hello, I didn't know you were going to be here.' Marion was completely undeterred by the boy's lack of interest in her. When he would say, 'Not you again,' she would smile and offer to buy him a drink. I began to admire Marion. She was like a boxer — punched and staggering but still coming back for more. After a while we became friends. Even after she left art college saying it was too boring and took up her place at the University in Norwich which was saved for her by three A's from school A levels. We used to meet in the holidays and spend days in Marion's parents' house, discussing the strange habits of the middle-class people we met and drinking Coca-Cola with ice cream.

Marion collected old boyfriends. She had lots of them who all remained friendly with her. 'They're just so relieved they're not still going out with me,' she would say wistfully. Mick was one of them. He had found the house and needed people to share it with him. It was a house that was waiting to be converted into flats by the council. But there was time between buying the house and 'doing it up'. So they let it out to Mick for six months. Mick felt sure it would be empty for longer than that. 'They'll need loads of money to do this place up — it'll take them years. No sweat,' he told everyone. His friend Simon had put down for one of the four bedrooms and Marion and me talked our way into the other two. We had a meeting in a pub before we moved in and giggled our way through several halves of lager until we'd convinced ourselves that we could all be happy together.

My dad started to look at the mantelpiece in the room, not touching anything but straining his neck round to read a moving-in card Simon had been sent by his mother. He then looked at the wooden floor, tapping a floorboard with the heel of his shoe. He was about to turn his attention to the coffee table when I said, 'Well, come on then, I'll show you round and then we can have a cup of tea.'

'I not stopping long,' Dad smiled. 'I have to see a man about some bathroom tiles.'

Dad followed me through the house.

'How's Mum?' I asked.

'Oh busy, busy, busy.'

'And Carl?'

'Oh, you know, you know.' It occurred to me then that I had never really spent any time alone with my dad. He was just part of Mum. Mum did all the talking and Dad looked absent-minded until called upon to say, 'You heard your mother nah.'

'This is the kitchen.' Dad stood still in the doorway, moving only his head to look around. Then he saw the sink and walked slowly towards it. There was washing-up piled on the draining board. 'I'm going to do it,' Mick had said the night before, 'I know it's my turn, it's just that I'll have to buy a plunger for the sink. The water won't go down.' The sink was blocked with something mysterious and was full of fetid brown water with grey scum floating on the top. Mick had pulled a face and stuck his hand down into the water and wiggled his finger in the plughole. And Simon had untwisted a wire coat hanger and stuffed it down the hole. When he pulled it up again it had a squelching potato skewered to it. We had all clapped and Simon had taken a small bow but the water level remained the same. 'We need a plunger,' Mick decided.

'You need a plunger,' Dad told me. He looked around the sink and then at me. 'You have one?'

'No — but we're getting one today,' I told him and quickly changed the subject. 'Come and look at the garden.' Dad had trouble turning his head away from the sink — every time he went to move towards me his head would snap back

27

onto the trouble spot, trying to find a new solution. 'Or caustic soda,' he added.

The moment I opened the double door and stepped in the garden I regretted it. The garden was a mass of uncultivated, uncared-for weeds. Apart, that is, from the extremely neat, lovingly tended row of Mick's home-grown marijuana plants which were swaying gently in their pots.

'Actually there's nothing much to see out here,' I said, as Dad began to peer out over my shoulder. 'It's a lovely house, isn't it?' I said, shutting the garden door. Dad turned round too quickly and tripped over his own foot. 'Georgian, you know, beautiful, bit run-down but nice.' He straightened his jacket and stared back at the spot where he'd stumbled. 'Oh yes, they all lovely,' he said, then added, 'from the outside.'

I showed him my bedroom next. I was sure about my room. I knew it was clean and tidy with the bed well made. Because I loved it. I was so proud of the beautiful room with its large wooden shuttered windows that ran from floor to ceiling and looked out onto wrought-iron railings and the street. The walls were white and the sun came in through the window for most of the day and shone on the bright pink duvet cover on my bed. I had spent days stripping the fireplace, taking off the hardboard that covered it. Revealing the black cast-iron insert and scrubbing down the grey marble surround.

'You could cover that up, Faith,' my dad said, pointing to the fireplace. 'Stop the draughts getting down. Bit of hardboard.' He walked across to it and put his hand up the chimney.

'Feel the draught. You should cover that up.' I nodded. He leant down and looked into the grate. 'Old-fashioned things,' he concluded. Then he got up, brushing his hands together and muttering.

In Marion's room Dad said, 'What's that on the bed?' Her bed was a mattress on the floor. 'Is it some sort of rope?'

'No, it's . . . ' I hesitated. 'It's the sheet, Dad.' Marion's bed was so dishevelled, the bottom sheet was so twisted that it looked like a curl of grey rope running down the centre of it. As Dad went in closer to have a better look I saw two flaccid condoms near her pillow. I quickly took a jumper that was lying on a chair and threw it across the room so it arrived before my dad and landed gracefully over the contraceptives. I smiled when he looked at me. 'Would you like a cup of tea now?' I asked.

Dad was as compliant as a dog as I led him back to the living room. He looked puzzled as he settled himself down onto the settee. 'But Faith,' he said, 'this is a big house. You tellin' me it's just you two girls in it?'

I went into one of my elaborate lies. I had become skilled in these from years of answering the 'who, why and where were you last night' questions. I told him that we two women were going to have the house to ourselves but that in the end it was so big that we would not have been able to heat it properly because it would be too expensive for just the two of us. I stopped.

Usually any form of financial prudence would make my dad nod with approval but he stayed as blank as a professional poker player. 'So . . . ' I was using my hands too much, waving them around like a liar. 'So it was Marion's idea, not mine, to get in these two . . . ' I fumbled for the right word. Men sounded too sexual. 'Boys.' I paused for a reaction. Dad continued to look at me, his eyelids heavy and tired. 'Not boyfriends or anything,' I added quickly. He looked smaller. He used to take up so much space in my childhood. Any room could be filled by his broad shoulders and rumbling voice. But his head looked small and wizened like the clay shrunken head ornament my parents kept on the wall at home — the one that I was always too scared to touch. Then I realised Dad was slowly sinking further and further into the settee. His knees were getting gradually nearer to his chin. Mick's sofa did that to people. Unless, like Mick, you always lay on it in a reclining position. Dad began to notice and started fumbling around like someone trying to get free of quicksand.

'I can show you their rooms if you'd like?' I asked, going over to him. I held out my hand for him to grab before he disappeared completely into the upholstery. 'It's a bit old,' I explained. He waved my hand away, wordlessly twisted himself round and levered himself off the piece of furniture like a toddler. He straightened his jacket as he got up then looked back at the settee.

Dad had only said, 'What a lot of stairs,' by the time I opened the door to Simon's room. My smile was beginning to ache around the back of my ears.

Simon's room was public-school immaculate. Ready for inspection by the housemaster at any time. His shoes were in a neat row with the toes all just sticking out from under the bed.

'A musician,' my dad said in a tone that implied drug taking weirdo.

'No, a solicitor actually, Dad.'

He looked round the room again. 'Doesn't look like a solicitor's room.' I wondered what a solicitor's bedroom should look like. But Dad was right, Simon's room had nothing of the law about it. There was an electric piano, two guitars on stands, a wall of LPs, two huge Tannoy speakers, a 'NASA control' of stereo equipment and a bed. Simon was a reluctant solicitor. He worked a few days at a law centre but laughed if you asked him for his legal opinion on anything. He spent his evenings locked away in his room playing his musical instruments into a reel-to-reel tape recorder. Then he made us all listen, 'without laughing', to the tinkling tunes.

I was tired and thankful that my dad shook his head when I said, 'You don't want to see the other bedroom, do you?' I'd remembered Mick screaming that morning as he stepped out of bed onto a slug that had crawled in through the garden into his basement room and I was scared what I might find. Mick was a teacher at a run-down Further Education college and his bedroom was a dark, damp pit. We had all stared open-mouthed at Mick as he decided that that was the bedroom he wanted by choice. 'It's near the kitchen and the bog, so it's handy for a piss and a pint of water in the night,' was his

31

reasoning. Passers-by would look down into his room from the street. 'Oh look, Jeremy, this one's really in a state,' someone had said once. And as Jeremy looked, Mick had showed him the two naked cheeks of his bottom.

My dad refused a cup of tea but guzzled down a glass of water like a man who'd just crawled through a desert. He wiped his hand across his face then looking straight at me said, 'Faith, you see you always covered up.' I only managed a feeble 'What?' before he carried on. 'You must wear plenty of clothes all the time. Don't go round the place half-naked. You hear me? There are men in this house. I was a young man once and I know. So you must keep your door shut and always make sure you have on plenty of clothes that's buttoned up.'

I was about to respond to the stricture as I always had in the past. My hands began to make their movement onto my hips. My breath came fast and deep. I was about to shout that it was my life, that I could do what I want. That they shouldn't interfere. That they should just leave me alone. When I realised I was in my own house now. And that what I really wanted to do was laugh.

So I nodded and I think I even said, 'Yes. Thank you.' Which made Dad look at his shoes, embarrassed, and mumble, 'Well, good, good, Faith. Yes, good girl, yes. I know you a sensible girl, Faith. Good.'

When he stood up to go I was overcome by excited relief which had me saying things like, 'Come back any time . . . bring Mum . . . bring

Carl ... ' I skipped to the door as my dad followed me through the hall, feeling the wall every so often with his hand, once more engrossed in the decorations.

I opened the front door and Simon stood, key poised, in front of my dad looking startled and so terrified that he gave a little scream. 'Oh sorry,' Simon said, beginning to laugh. He held his chest and blew out a breath, 'I thought you were a burglar — sorry.' He laughed again, 'You gave me a fright.' He held out his hand for my dad to shake. 'Simon,' he stated. Mick was behind him holding up a black rubber sink plunger in the air.

'This is my dad,' I explained.

Mick pushed through the door saying, 'We've worked that one out.' Simon smiled at Dad, 'It's nice to meet you, Mr Jackson,' and Mick said, 'Hello.' Dad had to duck out of the way of the sink plunger as Mick waved it about explaining, 'I'm going to fix that sink if it's the last thing I do.'

'Are you just leaving?' Simon said, looking first at me then Dad. I nodded but Dad just stared, expressionless, at the two men, looking them slowly up and down as they walked on through the hall. 'Bye. Nice to meet you,' Simon waved as they disappeared down the stairs.

I held the front door open and my dad stepped out but then stepped back in and asked, 'Faith — your friends, any of them your own kind?'

I wasn't sure what he meant.

'What? From college?' I asked.

33

'No, no, I mean any of them ... any of them ... ' He looked around himself to see if anyone was listening then whispered, 'Coloured?'

And I said without thinking, 'No. Why?'

'Oh nothing ... I just wondered ... I don't suppose you meet ... with college and everything ... I don't suppose.' He trailed off without finishing. I didn't ask him to explain. I didn't ask him to finish what he was saying. I didn't want him to. He took a breath then tapped the lock on the door. 'Remember to take out your key next time, Faith.' He smiled with a simultaneous frown. I watched him walk down the street, his stooped back getting gradually smaller. I lifted up my hand and as if he knew, in that second he turned round and we waved.

3

I was hopelessly early for the first day of my new job. But I didn't care. I stood and savoured the sight of the awesome building. The brick-built citadel of entertainment, resting resplendent in the middle of a wasteland. The Television Centre.

I smiled at the guard on the gate and wondered if he was wondering whether I was someone famous. I flashed my temporary pass like so many celebrities would be doing that day. Security gates are a great leveller.

I had got no sleep the night before and by the time Simon had woken me with a mug of tea and a piece of rather high-baked toast at six-thirty in the morning, I had worked out twenty-four different permutations of outfit I could wear that day. There was a sign pinned to the back of the front door that said, 'Good luck Faith', in large green letters and scribbled in blue at the bottom Marion had added, 'Bring us back an actor'.

'The duties of the job,' they had told me at the interview, 'would be to make sure that all the costumes are properly labelled and ready for the productions.' I had had to shake my head energetically when they wondered out loud whether a job like that would be beneath a woman with my qualifications — whether someone with a degree in fashion and textiles could get enough job satisfaction from such a post. I nearly laughed — if only they knew the tedium of the job I had just escaped.

I was one of the lucky ones, I had been told, because I had been offered my first job at my degree show. My tutor had decided that it was something to do with my being black and everyone else on the course being white.

'Your work has an ethnicity which shines through,' she told me. 'A sort of African or South American feel which is obviously part of you. Don't you find that exciting, Faith?' As I was born and bred in Haringey I could only suppose that I had some sort of collective unconscious that was coming through from my slave ancestry. Or perhaps it was that I was just better than everyone else. But whatever it was, Olivia sought me out at my degree show and offered me a job.

My mum had been standing with me. She'd worn a hat, a black hat with small black flowers and a rim that turned up at the front but down at the back. She stood by my exhibition clutching her handbag to her, looking at my work, nodding and saying, 'You did all this yourself, Faith? Very nice, very nice.'

She had avoided the man with the tray of white and red wine, preferring to pretend not to see him than to have to tell him that she didn't drink. When he finally got her attention she had said, 'I have one, thank you,' and vaguely waved her hand around. Dad had not been able to come to the private view as he had had to tile a bathroom in Finchley.

Olivia cut in front of Mum to talk to me and

36

as she stood between us smiling, I could see Mum staring at Olivia's hat in wide-eyed disbelief. Olivia had an upturned-multicoloured raffia bin on her head at the time. As she introduced herself and shook my hand the little beads that fell from the rim of the bin onto her forehead knocked against each other and sounded like chattering. 'I love your work,' Olivia told me. Then offered me a job designing textiles as her assistant.

The job had started out extremely well. 'Faith, can you go to Milan now?' were Olivia's opening words on my first day at her Chelsea studio home.

'That's a good job,' my brother Carl had conceded.

'Wow — you lucky thing,' from Marion.

I really thought I had landed on my feet. I could see myself as a sort of textile trouble-shooter. Travelling the globe to wherever fabric needed me. A lunch in Paris, dinner in New York sort of person. A change of knickers in my handbag, sort of life.

But after I got back from Milan, the real job started. This consisted of a whole week spent sitting on a stool in front of an old table loom, passing a shuttle through the open threads of a warp, then changing the lifting pattern with the levers on the side and passing the shuttle back the other way. As I did this Olivia would waft about the room, chat to her international clientele on the telephone, lunch in Knights-bridge and sit in the garden developing her tan. When I had finished the sample fabrics on the loom, Olivia would cut them off, stick them on little bits of card and call them her own.

It was what I had been trained for — it was weaving as I had done at college. Except there was no one else to talk to — no gossiping in tea breaks and laughing over *Woman's Own* magazine. My days were not broken up with lectures on Fortuny or Art Nouveau. It was just day after day of smacking a raddle against a newly made weft and listening to Radio Four.

'I may as well be packing pencils in a factory,' I complained to Marion.

Then one day I got to work early and caught Olivia standing by the door wearing a silk kimono, kissing a man whose hands were wriggling inside the wrap of the fabric. As she turned round startled, her breast slipped out. I stared momentarily at her porcelain-white tit with its tiny pert pink nipple. It was like catching the Queen, knickers down, on the toilet. I found it hard to look her in the face after that. And she, after suffering my embarrassed mute sullenness for a week, packed up two weeks' wages in a window envelope and sacked me.

'What am I going to do?' I moaned to Marion. My working life was over at the age of twenty-two. I couldn't tell my parents about the sacking because the day it happened I went home and Dad proudly presented me with an awful, silver briefcase.

'We saw this and thought it would come in handy, Faith — for your new career,' he had smiled. I had taken it enthusiastically saying it was just what I needed and continued to leave the house every morning as usual, swinging my businessman's case with a smile. But instead of a job I went round to Marion's and sat on her bed, thumbing copies of *Draper's Record* and typing letters to would-be employers on her portable typewriter.

One of the letters was to BBC Television. I was surprised when I received a letter back from them inviting me to an interview for a job in the costume department. And I was 'over-the-moon, cock-a-hoop, open the champagne, yes, yes', ecstatic when I got the job.

'We get you that briefcase just in time, Faith,' my parents declared, when I told them their only daughter now worked in television.

The reception at the television centre had a bank of televisions along one wall. I sat and watched several different test cards while the clock edged its way nearer to the time I had to present myself at the third-floor costume department.

The third floor was a long corridor, dark and muffled with carpet. There were doors, lots and lots of brown doors all with rectangular black plaques with white numbers on. As I scrabbled in my handbag looking for the letter so I could memorise the room number I needed, a man who read the late-night news hurried past me. His shirt tail was hanging out of the back of his trousers and he ran with the gangly movement of tall boys in school playgrounds. I smiled in case he looked back at me but he disappeared through a door.

The corridor was eerily empty. Then I heard

the sound of tinkling cups and saucers and saw a woman in a small room filling a tea urn with water from a metal jug. I asked her if she knew where Room 3203 was and she pointed helpfully and said, 'On the left, brown door with a number on.' I thanked her anyway.

I eventually found it and pushed gently at the door. I wasn't sure what would be behind it. Whether the room would be full of famous actors all being raucously pushed and poked into costumes, like a dressing room at a pantomime. But the room was empty of people. It was large and airy with windows all along one wall. Along all the other walls were rails and rails of costumes. Huge dark red brocaded capes and sparkling doublets looking unruly and heavy alongside khaki green uniforms with brass buttons. Prim floral print dresses neatly in a row behind a line of skinny dangling pale blue tights with gold and silver paste jewels encrusted up the legs.

'Are you for me?' a voice behind me asked. I turned round and a tall man with a black moustache momentarily opened his eyes wide in surprise. He then grinned a smile that looked like it had been rehearsed in a mirror.

'I've come for the costume . . . ' I started before the man said, 'Then you are for me.' He held out his hand for me to shake. I went to take the gloved hand but the man tutted and withdrew it. He began removing the glove by pulling on each finger in turn. I stood with my hand out feeling ridiculous. He finally removed the whole glove with a sweeping flourish and shook my hand. 'Henry,' he said. 'I suppose I'm your boss, although we don't like to think we have bosses here.'

I stood still in the middle of the room watching while Henry took off his coat. He unbuttoned it carefully then put it on a wooden hanger, flicking at the lapels and shoulders before placing it into a cupboard. He then got the coat out again and twiddled with one of the buttons, pulling at a thread. While I, not knowing what else to do, stared. He put the coat back in the cupboard and locked it with a key which he took out of the lock and placed in his trouser pocket. When he looked at me again he gave a little jump and bit his lip, which made him look like a little boy not a middle-aged man.

'Oh, look at me — I've forgotten all about you already. I've had such a morning — you wouldn't believe it. But come and sit down.' He indicated at a table which had three chairs around it. I went over and sat in a chair.

'Not there, dear,' Henry said. 'That's my seat.' I got up and moved to the next chair.

'Well, you could sit there but I'm sure Madam would have something to say about it.' I moved along to the other chair and looked at Henry — there was nowhere else to go.

'That's a good one,' he smiled. 'That's where Evelyn used to sit. She's the one you're taking over from.' He sat in his chair and leant forward as if he was going to tell me a secret. 'She's gone to work in production,' he whispered. 'For the kiddies' programmes. She was a high flyer, that one. I could tell the moment she walked in. I

41

knew she wouldn't stay here.' He leant back. 'They all start here but they want to do something else really. They think of it as just a foot in the door.' He folded his arms and stared at me. 'I expect you want to direct, don't you?' He held his head back and roared an open-mouthed laugh. I smiled. My fantasy was more that I would be standing in the lift — a director comes in — stares at me for several minutes — then tells me that I must be in his film, that now he has seen me no one else will do. And I would be whisked away from the costume department to a life of celebrity. But as I watched Henry laugh, I felt stupid.

'What's your name?' he asked but carried on, 'Listen to me rabbitting on. Still, you'll have to get used to it. I hope you aren't going to be so quiet. You have to learn to speak up for yourself in this place.' He looked at me and I stared at him. After a while Henry said, 'Name?'

'Oh, sorry — it's Faith.'

'Faith — oh, very virginal. Faith what?'

'Jackson.'

'Well, Faith Jackson, welcome to the madhouse. I'll run you through what we have to do here, then we'll get a cup of tea. Her Highness should be in by then and we can introduce you to everyone. We're like a family here, Faith,' he said. Then pointing a finger which made it sound like a threat, he added, 'We take care of one another.'

Henry took me through the procedures, explaining what door the costumes came in and the door by which they went out. How we had to

42

make sure that the clothes that came in matched the delivery docket and the clothes that went out were all present and correct. It was our job to go through every article and garment that came in and describe it. Henry demonstrated by standing next to a rail which had a long robe on it. He lifted up the costume so I could see it properly and in a deep Shakespearean voice began, 'Red velvet overcape with diamanté trim.' He moved on to the next garment, ostentatiously holding it up like a magician's assistant showing the crowd. 'Gold and red striped doublet with matching codpiece.' He worked his way along the rail fingering each item, feeling the fabric and searching for distinguishing marks. Then pausing, he lifted his head as he composed his description, and delivered it.

Until he suddenly stopped. 'Oh, you have to be so careful. Look at this,' he said beckoning me over. 'A hood.' I looked at the garment in his hands and nodded but I was not quite sure of the significance. Henry soon explained. 'Now, I didn't say *with a hood*, and it's detachable.' He clutched the hood to his chest, rolled his eyes and carried on. 'This hood may have come off during filming and the costume might have come back to us sans hood and we wouldn't have known because we didn't describe it when it came in. And that, my dear, is when the shit would hit the fan.' Henry breathed out still holding his chest. 'We have to be very careful.'

I followed him back to the desk where he showed me the typewriter and explained that we would take it in turns to type down the descriptions in carbon-copied triplicate to be filed later.

'I can't type,' I admitted.

'Two fingers, dear,' Henry said, wiggling his two index fingers. 'It's not bloody Pitmans — you'll soon be as fast as me.' Henry then recapped, walking round the room pointing, 'In here, out there, blah blah — now what else?' He held his forehead, 'I'm all at sixes and sevens today — of course — I forgot.' He beckoned me over to him, 'Come here, Miss,' he smiled. He lifted the back of the army uniform and pointed. 'Labels — we have to write little labels and stick them in each costume. Then we check them against the typed sheets when they come back and we can see if anything is missing. It's not a beautiful system but it works.' He twitched his eyebrows up and down several times.

'Is there anything else?' I asked.

Henry threw his arms into the air. 'She wants more!' he shouted.

A young woman came in eating a huge doughnut which was squashing against her cheeks as she pushed it into her mouth.

'You'll get fat,' Henry said when he saw her. She took the doughnut out of her mouth, chewed, and with a mouthful said, 'Oh, shut up.' She had sugar and little bits of jam all round her cheeks. 'Morning, Henry,' she said, showing us the chewed doughnut in her open mouth.

'Oh, she's such a lady,' Henry said to me. 'Lorraine, this is our new girl. Our new girl, this is Lorraine.'

'Oh hello, you just started?' Lorraine said, in a

44

high shrill voice that made my back teeth tingle. She wiped the back of her hand across one of her cheeks then the palm across the other and held out the hand for me to shake. I shook it. It was sticky. Henry tapped my shoulder, 'Sugar?' he said.

'A bit sticky,' I laughed, discreetly wiping my hand down my trousers.

'No, I mean in your tea, dear — do you want sugar? I'll buy you a tea today although I won't be making a habit of it.'

'Oh, Henry,' Lorraine said, flicking his shoulder. 'You make such a fuss.'

'Don't touch me with your filthy hands, Miss,' Henry jokingly sneered as he went out of the room.

'He's an old fusspot, but we love him,' Lorraine grinned, then added, 'Well, most of us do anyway. Has he been showing you around?' She giggled like a little tinkling dinner bell and stuck the doughnut back into her mouth. She chewed it impatiently, waving her hands up and down to try and hurry herself. 'I got you down to come today. Faith, innit?' she eventually said, breathless. She sucked on each of her fingers in turn, 'I'm the secretary.' She giggled again. 'Dogsbody actually. I always say secretary but . . . ' She rolled her eyes. Her hair was mousy and lank apart from where an old perm still clung on frizzing to the ends. I smiled at her. 'Oh, don't look at me,' she said covering her face with her hands. 'I've just remembered I've got no make-up on.'

'You look fine,' I began when she suddenly

45

said, 'My boyfriend's coloured. His name's Derek. I live with him and his family. They're ever so nice. Although some people are prejudiced, aren't they?' I was silent.

A man came in wheeling a rail of costumes.

'Oh no, they've arrived,' Lorraine said. She went to the door. 'Henry, they're here,' she shouted.

'Where do you want them?' the man asked me.

I looked around. I looked for Lorraine who had walked off into an office that was behind a glass screen.

'I don't know,' I said. Another man and another rail came in and stopped behind the first man who said, 'She don't know where she wants 'em.' A young man ran in the door, stopped in front of me, panting, saying, 'I need the *Prime Time* rail — which one is it?' I looked around. 'I'm not . . . ' I began as the man with the rail said, 'Here, I asked her first.' And the young man answered, 'My need is greater, Norris — which one?'

'I don't know,' I admitted and the man blew out his breath.

Lorraine stuck her head out of the office, holding a mascara brush. 'Leave her alone, she's just started. Henry'll be here soon.'

'We'll leave the rails here, you can sort them out later, love,' Norris said. He pushed the rail in front of me and the other man started bringing in rail after rail full of leather lederhosen and green jackets. I started to pull the rails further into the room, twisting them round, pushing

46

them to the side so they would all fit in. The young man from *Prime Time* started looking at the spangly tights and saying, 'These must be for me — are they done?' But then finding himself trapped behind the ever-increasing loads of German clothing he yelled, 'Help! I'm drowning in boys' trousers.'

And as Henry walked in the door he spilled his tea. 'Five minutes I'm away and it's pandemonium!'

4

'The thing I don't understand,' my brother Carl wanted to know, 'is how you've meant to have left home, right. But how you seem to be back here every minute looking for something to eat?'

He had interrupted me. I was telling Mum about my job. Mid-flow about the weatherman who had asked me to pass the salt to him in the staff canteen. 'You know the one, Mum, with the bald head and moustache.' I was also, at the time, looking through the kitchen cupboard for the Fondant Fancies. 'Tell me Faith, have you seen that nice man who introduces *Songs of Praise*? He's a lovely man. So clean,' Mum was asking when Carl butted in, 'Don't you have food in your house?'

He was waiting with his feet up on a chair for Mum to put the Sunday dinner of chicken and rice on the table. The only movement he made was to gently tap his cigarette on the side of the ashtray. I didn't answer him. I'd found the Fondant Fancies. I opened the box, took out the first one that came to hand and pushed it whole into my mouth.

I had wanted to add Fondant Fancies to the house shopping list, but Marion said they were revolting and that we should eat something more healthy, something more brown not fluorescent pink. Mick didn't like sweet things and Simon had never heard of them and suggested the

48

sickening Battenberg instead. But I could carry on eating Marion's indigestible macaroni cheese with undercooked greens, Mick's egg and chips and Simon's shepherd's pie soup, if I knew that I could go home to my mum and dad's, binge on chicken and eat a Fondant Fancy whole whenever I got desperate.

I opened my mouth and quietly showed my brother what I was chewing.

'Faith, lay the table for me, nah,' Mum said.

'Ask Carl.'

'No.'

'Why not?'

'Because I ask you,' Mum stated.

'But you always ask me and I don't even live here any more.'

'Just lay the table, Faith,' Carl interfered.

'And you can shut your gob. Bloody men.'

'Oh God,' Carl said crossing himself, 'I've started her off.'

'Carl,' Mum snapped, 'don't speak of the Lord in that way.'

'It's not fair, Mum, he never does anything.' It didn't come out as I had wanted it to. I said it too high and petulant, like a spoilt little girl. What I had wanted to say was that my brother Carl had never, as far as I could remember, cooked a meal. If he went to make even a simple piece of toast Mum would shake him off the grill and finish watching it brown for him. He had never consciously washed any plate or saucepan. 'Leave it, son,' Mum would say, 'Faith can do it later.' He had never cleaned a room because Mum decreed that, 'Men can't see dust.' Carl had never washed a garment because, 'Washing is a skilled job', according to Mum. I used to question my parents, 'How come you never ask Carl what time he's coming home?' or 'Why don't you ever want to know where Carl has been?' And to all the questions I got the same answer. 'He's a man,' they would say, which was meant to explain it all. 'He's a man.'

'You're such a lazy bastard,' I whispered to my brother and he smiled at me, showing me the two dimples in his cheeks. His charming cheeky smile that made my mum giggle no matter what he had done.

'Let's face it, Faith,' Carl said, spreading his hands and shrugging, 'I've got to have a fault otherwise nobody would believe I was real.'

★ ★ ★

I knew something was odd at home when, after we had eaten our dinner, my dad followed my mum, Carl and me into the living room to sit down. This usually did not happen. Dinner was just an interruption from my dad's jobs around the house. On Sundays after church Dad was always fixing, painting, adjusting or mending. He was always, 'in the middle of a job', that required his full, silent concentration and a monkey wrench. If I ever asked him what he was doing he'd say, 'Fixing something, so don't come bothering me now.' If I ever asked him what he was fixing he would say, 'I thought I told you not to come bothering me when I'm fixing.' He would change ball-cocks, rewire light fittings, put

50

up shelves, clear gutterings, ease windows, plaster walls and mend electrical goods with a tiny soldering iron that required him to put on his reading glasses, which he had mended across the nose-bridge with a fat lump of sellotape.

But this was not the only strange thing. It used to be strange for us to go into the living room at all. It was always kept for best with Mum's carefully embroidered runners on the sideboard and school photographs of Carl and me smiling and showing our teeth in various stages of hideous development. When we were little my brother and me had a game — we would see who could sit in the living room the longest before they got scared that they would be caught and snapped at to 'Get out of there child!' On my turn I would sit perched on a chair, feet in position, ready to run, while the eyes in the portrait of Jesus on the wall stared and convinced me I was committing a sin. Carl always won and I got called 'scaredicat'. Now we were adults, however, we could go in the room any time we pleased, our parents convinced that we would no longer damage one of the glass ornaments or spill our tea on the furry fireside rug. But as I walked into the room I saw six, maybe seven of my mum and dad's boxes piled up in a corner. My eye was drawn to them because they were out of place and nothing was ever out of place in that room. The boxes were also full, sealed across the top, bottom and sides with wide brown tape.

'What are these doing here?' I asked, going over to them. I turned round and watched as

Dad looked at Mum, Mum looked at Carl, Carl looked at Dad and then back at Mum. But nobody looked at me.

'What's going on?' I looked at them all one by one. Then another strange thing happened: my dad spoke first.

'Sit down, Faith,' he said. He began to finger the knuckles on his hand, feeling each one in turn. He used to do this when it was time to discuss the 'could do better' bits in my school report. I began to get scared.

'No, I won't sit down.' I wasn't sure why I said that but I felt like someone in a film who was about to be told something that would make them scream and pull at their hair. Unfortunately everyone else sat down and I had to stay standing. Nobody spoke so I placed my hands on my hips.

Dad started, 'Your mum and me,' then faltered. He began again, 'Me and your mum,' and stopped. He went back to, 'Your mum and me.' I looked at my mum who was looking at her knees and pulling imaginary hairs off her skirt, while Dad continued to stutter his various permutations. He was onto, 'We,' when I said, 'What?'

Carl's lighter clicked and he blew out cigarette smoke. Mum said, 'Carl, don't smoke those filthy things in here.' And Carl, instead of leaving to drag on his fag in the privacy of any other room, stumped it out in the ashtray and stayed sitting. That made my knees feel very weak and I had to sit down.

'Come, Wade,' Mum said, looking impatiently

at my dad who had still not completed a sentence.

'Your mum and me are thinking of going back home,' Dad said finally.

I thought of our old council flat where Carl and me had grown up. Although we had lived in Crouch End for years, it was the crumbling flat in Stoke Newington that I thought of as home. The blue door with the silver number twenty-three and a knocker that could be heard anywhere in the flat. With the drainpipe in the bathroom, where bathwater from the flats above could be heard rushing through. My bedroom with its council-pink walls and tiny bed where I put my discarded teeth under the pillow and the tooth fairy would replace them with a sixpence.

I thought in that moment that my parents had somehow lost all their money. That Mum was having to leave her job as a district nurse; the old folk cured, the district cutting back. That Dad's business — which he had built up so carefully with sixteen-hour days, including Saturdays and Sundays, and evenings spent writing invoices in his best handwriting in a little blue book — had after all gone bust. I thought they were having to move out of the house. The house in a proper street that they were so proud of they sent pictures of it to relatives with invitations to come and stay.

'You going back to the flat?' I asked.

Carl sniggered and I knew I was wrong.

'No, Faith,' Mum said. 'We're thinking of going home to Jamaica.'

And my reaction was, 'For a holiday. Fantastic! How long for?'

'Not for a holiday, Faith,' Dad said hesitantly. 'Your mum and me are thinking . . . ' He held up his hand, 'Only thinking, mind, of going back there to live. To get a little place and live.'

I stared at my dad and thought about Fondant Fancies. My mind involuntarily remembered the price of them and I worked out if I could afford to buy my own. I looked at Carl as he tapped his fingers on the chair, desperate to get to somewhere he could smoke.

I went to smile but I couldn't. 'Going home to Jamaica,' I eventually said. I had then intended to say, 'Fantastic! I can come and visit,' but instead I said, 'Why?'

'Your dad and me are getting old now,' Mum started, 'and we feel that you and Carl are grown-up, so we can go home and . . . '

I'd stopped listening. Because what I meant by why, the question I wanted answering was, why Jamaica? Why is Jamaica home?

I knew my parents had come from there. I knew we had relations there. And the odd family friend would go out to visit the island, bring us back strange fruits and talk about back home. But what Mum and Dad really loved was snow and cold evenings after shopping, when we would all sit round a coal fire and eat muffins and drink cups of tea whilst watching Cilla Black and arguing over whether she could sing or not. My mum's mantra had always been, 'You couldn't get this in Jamaica.' Everything from our automatic washing machine to the chunks of peanut brittle she loved to suck — they were all things enjoyed here and denied there. Dad would never talk about Jamaica, just telling me it was a long time ago when I asked him about his growing up — his mum and dad, his tooth fairy. They had never been back to Jamaica. At holiday times they had never stared yearningly at the atlas and wished they could afford to go to the Caribbean. They had looked at the Shell road map of Britain and decided Scotland looked nice or Wales sounded like somewhere to visit. And they always ended up on the church holiday trip to Devon because they liked to eat scones with jam and clotted cream.

'No. Why Jamaica?' I interrupted too loudly. I was angry, for some reason.

Mum looked at me with her mouth open and the deepest crevices of a frown on her forehead. But she didn't speak. Nobody did. I thought I'd got them — foiled them with a faultless logic.

'Because we from Jamaica, Faith,' Dad said quietly.

'So?' I said.

'Don't be so childish,' Carl said.

'I'm not being childish!' I stood up and looked down at the three of them. 'All I want to know is why you want to go and live there all of a sudden.'

'It's not all of a sudden,' Mum said. 'We've been thinking about it for some time now. You children are grown-up and . . .'

'But Faith,' Dad interrupted, 'it's nothing definite yet. You don't have to fret. We just thinking that . . . '

'You've packed boxes,' I said.

'Grow up,' Carl said.

'You shut up — I wasn't talking to you.'

'Calm down, calm down, child,' Mum said. She stood up and put her hand on my shoulder. Dad looked up to the ceiling pretending he had spotted something that needed his attention. Carl lit a cigarette and nothing was said this time. I sat down. Mum sat beside me and put her arm round my shoulder and tapped me like I'd just fallen over.

'Try not thinking of yourself for once,' Carl said. 'I know it's hard.' And Mum hushed him with a flick of her hand.

I looked at the boxes and began to work out how many boxes there were in the cellar and how long it would take my parents to fill all those boxes and wrap the tape round them. And whether once they were full, they would all fit in the living room. It was very quiet, apart from Carl sucking on his cigarette and tapping it on the ashtray.

'When are you going?' I eventually asked. Mum and Dad spoke together in a fast flurry of, 'We don't know . . . nothing definite . . . it may all come to nothing . . . won't be for some time yet . . . don't worry about it . . . not right away . . . plenty to do yet.'

'Did you know about this?' I asked Carl as Mum and Dad were still speaking.

'Yeah,' he whispered. 'What you making such a fuss about?'

'Carl, leave your sister,' Mum said as Dad was still saying, 'We may not go . . . it may come to nothing . . .'

'Will you sell the house?' I asked, but I didn't get a reply.

'Listen, Faith,' Mum said looking excited. 'Your dad has some other news for you.' She smiled into my face then nodded over at my dad. 'Wade, tell Faith.'

Dad looked suddenly animated like he'd seen an old friend across the room. 'Oh yes,' he chirped. I didn't want to hear anything else. I wanted to go and sit in my bedroom. The bedroom with council-pink walls.

'We have a little bit of money now, so we thought we could buy you a little car like you always wanted.'

My brother rolled his eyes and said, 'You don't have to do this,' as Mum hushed him again with her hand.

I had to breathe in hard. It occurred to me then, as my parents smiled at me, willing me to be excited about the prospect of a car, that at that moment I could have asked for anything money could buy and I would have got it. My parents always bought their way out of bad feeling. I got thirty pounds when Dad didn't make it to my college private view — sixty pounds for the first holiday they took on their own.

Soon everyone was talking about the new car — even Carl. Discussing what colour would be nice and the best make for a reliable second-hand model. And I began to think — as I looked between them, nodding my head at the copies of the *Evening Standard* dumped in my lap with little red circles round 'Ford Escort, only one lady owner' — I began to think that I had just dreamt that my parents had told me they were leaving me to live in another country.

5

It was an ordinary Sunday afternoon at the house. Marion was standing in the middle of the living room. Her head was wrapped in creased silver tin foil because she was dyeing her hair with henna and didn't want to drip the brown mud onto everything. She was standing in front of the television trying to explain to us all what had happened on the first day at her new job as a clerk at a solicitors'.

'So they showed me this bathful of files,' she was explaining. 'They told me to file them. It was a bathful. I'm telling you a *bathful* of files. An actual bath in a bathroom ... Is anyone listening to me?'

Most of us were trying to see round her, watching the last minutes of *Star Trek*. Mick had his feet on the coffee table and an ashtray balanced on his chest that he was flicking one of his thin and pathetic hand-rolled cigarettes into. He was not bothering to listen to Marion and only shouted, 'Klingon!' when Marion had, as an attempt to get attention, stood in front of the television. I was sitting on the floor with my back against the radiator. I'd just had a few puffs of a joint that was being passed round. I last saw it being held in tweezers by Rob who complained that he always got the hot end and that next time he wanted it just after it was rolled.

Rob was a friend of mine originally although

he had gone out with Marion. I first met him at college. Then one day I saw him in a pub and we talked. He kept a constant eye contact with me that made me want to blink for him and was smiling with keen interest at everything I said when suddenly Marion appeared. And I swear, or at least this is how I remember it, she was flying through the air, head first parallel to the ground. Rob was the most fanciable man in the pub and I was never any competition for Marion when she was on heat. Rob and Marion went out together for a few months and then it was over. Marion was packed in by Rob on the southbound platform of Highbury and Islington tube station. 'I wouldn't mind but he went off with my ticket,' she moaned. I had had to listen to hours of Marion's tearful account of the break-up and join along in the mantra that all men are bastards. But he still came round the house — now part of Marion's collection of old boyfriends — and often mooned around me. But I could not break the unwritten code, 'Thou shalt not go out with thy friend's old boyfriend, especially when thou hast agreed that he is a bastard'.

Philippa was there, sitting with her knees up next to her chin, flicking through a copy of *Spare Rib* but with her eyes on the television. She had started life as one of Mick's girlfriends. Then, the only sight I used to catch of her was as she wafted through the kitchen after making a mug of the revolting Barley Cup. But since they had split up she had become a more regular feature of the house, much to Marion's disgust. 'The woman is certifiable — a complete and utter head-case,' Marion would say.

Philippa only ever wore black and white. Even her flat, Mick told us, was decorated only in black and white. 'They are the only colours I feel comfortable in,' she once explained. But then Marion pointed out to her that neither black nor white were colours. 'They are the absence of colour,' she smugly told Philippa in the hope that she could humiliate her. But Philippa seized upon this and used it to further her enigma, 'I don't wear colour, I only wear its absence,' she started to declare. And Marion would roll her eyes and spit, 'She thinks it makes her sound deep.'

Philippa and Marion did not get on. Not for the obvious reason that they both shared the same old boyfriend but because one day Philippa had insulted Marion's cooking. She had likened Marion's macaroni cheese sauce to wallpaper paste. 'Although,' she added, 'the paste tastes better.' Philippa had then laughed and so had myself and Mick — more out of embarrassment than humour. Philippa was, I later found out, unused to other people actually laughing at her jokes and proceeded to lay it on much thicker. Marion's greens were like wallpaper, that sort of thing. Until Marion told her to shut up. Philippa then lectured Marion about how incorrect it was to tell another woman to shut up. Something to do with the fact that men had used the silencing of women to oppress us over the years. So Marion told her to 'fuck off' instead. It was whilst Philippa was telling Marion that she was childish that Marion leapt for Philippa's throat. As Philippa backed away Marion scratched her down her face. I jumped up and held Marion back while Mick looked horrified and then began to suppress a laugh behind his hand. Marion was red-faced and raging but then turned round to me, sank her head onto my shoulder and began sobbing, muttering incoherently and pointing at Philippa — like a two-year-old. Philippa then started telling Marion that she was disgusted with her for scratching her face. Not because the three red weals were beginning to seep blood and look very painful and sore but, 'because a punch would have been a more appropriate response'.

Philippa left after Marion and Mick screamed at one another for about an hour. Marion saying that she didn't want 'that fucking cow' sitting round in her house and Mick yelling that he would have anyone he liked around. I didn't take sides. And after a few weeks of cooling off Philippa was back.

On the other side of the double doors that divided the living room, Simon was teaching his friend and fellow alternative cabaret performer, Duncan, the guitar chords and words to a song Simon had just written. It was something about a crèche and quiche although I couldn't hear the words very well because of the television and Marion. Simon and Duncan were downstairs because when they were learning a song together they kept time by banging their feet down hard on the floor. They had started rehearsing the song in Simon's room which was above the living room. They had been banging their feet with a regular thud, thud, thud, for about five minutes when a glass on the coffee table began to move by itself. We all watched its slow progress across the table top like we were in a seance. Eventually it came to the edge of the table and fell off onto the floor. It was then that Mick called up to Simon and Duncan to 'Shut up'. It stopped for about thirty seconds then started again. A small piece of ceiling plaster then landed on the coffee table. Mick went upstairs and we heard his muffled, irate voice interspersed with the loud clear words of 'fucking', 'banging' and 'stop'.

I offered Simon and Duncan my room at the top of the house to practise in. But the front room window started to shake violently with the vibrations even though they were two floors up. They then tried the solid floor of the basement kitchen but kept getting disturbed by Marion mixing henna and looking for tin foil. Mick's room had bad acoustics evidently and Marion's room was 'too disgusting, thank you'. Next door in the living room all we could hear was the strumming of the guitars and, 'G flat. No, G flat. Oh for God's sake, can you play the bloody guitar or not?' And the thud, thud, thud, on the carpeted floor was bearable.

The house was always full of people. It was unusual to have an evening where just the four of us sat around. And it was an impossibility to get the house to yourself because before long several people would come in, pass cans of beer round and ask 'What's on the telly?' or 'What's going on?' Even if I was in my room being alone, I would hear the doorbell ringing or the front door banging or feet running up the stairs or people calling out or knocking on my door asking me if I wanted a drink or a cup of tea, to meet someone or to see something or to go down the pub . . .

And it was into the living-room that my brother Carl now walked. 'Faith, your phone is permanently engaged,' he said. He stood large and dark in the doorway to the room, jangling his van keys in his hand. For a brief moment as he stood looking around the room at my friends I saw my brother as a stranger. A tall man in faded jeans and a brown scuffed leather jacket. A big man — with a brown complexion that was pock-marked round the temples from adolescent acne. A black man with a round head of afro hair that was too long so the back ended in a hard wedge on his shirt collar instead of tapering into his neck. When Carl was young he was in the church choir. Age ten in his red and white cassock with his sweet soprano voice and big brown eyes, everyone said he was like an angel. Then as he got older, muscular and his voice croaked deeper, they all thought he came to resemble the devil.

'Carl, what are you doing here?' I said. He was out of context.

'Is there something wrong with the phone?' he replied. Rob sat up a little and looked to where his foot was pressing the phone and lifting the receiver just enough to make it inoperable. 'Ooops.'

Carl looked down at me and then flicked his

head which was, I knew, my cue to move. 'This is my brother Carl,' I told the room. Rob swung his legs off the settee and indicated for Carl to sit down. But Carl lifted his hand and said, 'I've just come to get Faith.'

As he did Simon and Duncan began singing the chorus of their song very loudly in the other room. 'Three wankers in a boat, there were three wankers in a boat.' Carl looked to where the singing was coming from then back round the room and into Marion's smiling face.

'Do you remember me, Carl? Marion. We've met a few times', she said, forgetting that her head was a silver pointed dome. Carl looked at her straight-faced and said, 'You haven't changed a bit.' At which Marion touched her head and laughed. Carl almost smiled but instead sniffed the air four times then looked at me again. I pulled Carl into the hall.

'What are you doing here?' I said, when I thought I could not be overheard. Carl smiled for the first time and said slowly, 'What are *you* doing here?' He handed me a newspaper where a red biro circle had been carefully drawn around an advert for a Renault Five.

'Well, why didn't you phone me first?' I asked.

Carl rolled his eyes, 'That's where I came in. We've been trying to get hold of you for . . . ' he looked at his watch, 'for bloody ages.'

The advert said the car was green. 'It's green,' I said, 'I hate green.'

My brother blew out his breath, 'Beggars can't be choosers.'

'I'm not begging.'

'Look, Faith, I'm not here for the benefit of me health. Do you want to go see it or not?'

'I'll give it a ring,' I said.

'Don't bother.' Carl lit a cigarette. 'Dad's phoned them already. It's all sorted out.'

I began to protest. I wanted him to know — I wanted my mum and dad to know — I wanted the whole world to know that I didn't need them to do things for me, that I could do it myself. I was mid-flow — 'I'm twenty-two years old, I've got a job and my own home and . . . ' — when Carl tutted and said, 'Get your coat,' and walked out to his van.

★　★　★

There was something about being in Carl's van, any van that Carl had, and he had had a lot over the years — Mercedes, Bedford, Escort, Luton, Transit — once I got inside my brother's van, it always felt like I was going on an adventure.

When I was at home studying for my A levels, Carl would turn up during the day saying he had to go to the country. Anywhere that wasn't London was the country to my brother — be it the leafy Cotswolds or Birmingham — it was all the same, it was all the country. 'You wanna come?' he'd ask. I'd take all my books — my Shakespeare and Jane Austen, my Gombrich *Story of Art* and climb into the van. I'd sit with the books on my lap and Radio One on the van radio and we'd drive out singing along to the top ten, eating our way through a family bag of Opal

Fruits, until the scenery got green. Then Carl would sigh, 'Ahh, this is the country — you can tell by the pylons.' And whoever spotted them first would shout, 'cow' or 'sheep' or 'look over there, a horse'. And we'd point out little cottages that we liked the look of and say, 'One day when I'm rich I'll buy that one.'

'I'd really like to live in the country,' Carl once confided in me. 'Somewhere in a little village with a little friendly post office.'

After he'd delivered what had to be delivered, we'd drive back taking as long as possible. While we were in the van the country always looked so charming. Miles and miles of picture-book pretty that reminded me of trips to the seaside with Mum and Dad. 'England is lovely — when you get out of the filthy city, England is a lovely place,' Mum always said.

Occasionally we used to stop, to get out of the van with the aim of running through a field or paddling in a river. But we were always greeted with fences and gates and barbed wire. And we never knew how to actually get onto 'that green and pleasant land'.

Carl tapped me on the head as I settled in my seat. He always did that when I got in his van. 'Holland Park,' he said. 'A bird named Charlesworth.'

I didn't know many of the songs on the radio — only the golden oldies, but Carl tapped out the rhythm of every song on the steering wheel as we went along. And there were only screwed-up, discarded wrappers in the Opal Fruits bag.

'What do you think about Mum and Dad?' I asked him.

'They're all right,' he grinned.

'You know what I mean. What do you think about them going to Jamaica?'

Carl shrugged and didn't say anything but he continued tapping the steering wheel long after the record had finished and the DJ had started talking.

'Where are you going to live when they go?' I asked after a long pause. Carl smiled and looked across at me for an alarmingly long time considering we were moving through traffic. 'Don't worry about me, little sis. I've got plans.'

I knew better than to ask Carl what his plans were. Since I was little my brother had plans. Big ones, small ones, I never knew. They were just plans, that were going to get him out of any dead-end situation or past any insoluble problem. When Carl said he had plans what he really meant was . . . end of conversation.

We pulled up outside a huge house in a street full of houses that looked like they were made from cream-coloured icing sugar.

'Bloody hell,' Carl said, ducking down low so he could see the whole house out of my window. He looked at a bit of paper. Then up the road and back.

'Is this it?' I asked.

Carl rolled his eyes and said a reluctant, 'Yeah.'

As we got out of the van I saw a green Renault Five. 'That's probably it,' I pointed. Carl went over to the car and began looking inside, pressing his hand on the side window as he peered around the whole interior. He then got down on his hands and knees and began looking underneath.

'It might not be the right one, Carl.' He got up brushing dirt from his hands and looked up and down the street.

'Must be — it's the only one here,' he said. 'What d'you think?' He walked round to the other side of the car as I began to imagine myself as a motorist — free to roam with the wind in my hair. 'It's nice,' I said. Carl was pressing his head up against the window shielding the light with his cupped hand on his forehead.

'The gearstick is on the dashboard,' he told me. 'But they're easy to get used to.' I looked into the car to see what he was talking about, when a man called down from the window of the house opposite. 'Excuse me, what are you doing round that car?'

I looked up at the man and smiled. 'We've just come to look at it — it's for sale.'

While I was speaking, Carl kept his head pressed firmly on the car window and hissed at me, 'Don't tell him — nosy bastard. Let him mind his own business.'

'Do you know the person whose car it is?' the man continued.

'We're just going inside,' I said, and then I whispered, 'Come on, Carl, let's go and ring the bell.' Carl moved on to the back of the car and began looking at the exhaust pipe.

'Come on, Carl,' I pleaded.

'Does the person who owns the car know what

you are doing?' the man called.

'Tell him to mind his own business, nosy git,' Carl said from the ground.

'Let's go now — come on. It might not even be this car.'

'Excuse me, Miss . . . Miss . . . I asked you a question.'

Carl deliberately began to take his time.

'Excuse me, I don't want to have to call the authorities but if . . . ' the man was saying. I smiled up at him, 'We're just going to see the owner now. We've got an appointment.' I walked off to the house number and Carl followed, sending the man a V sign over his shoulder.

We went up the steps and I rang the bell. As we waited for someone to come I looked at Carl slouching against the freshly painted pillar, with a surly look on his face. I wanted to be like Mum whenever she took my brother and me on a visit. I wanted to be able to say to Carl, 'Stand up straight, take your hands out of your pockets, nah. And smile when the lady comes to the door. Don't give her big lip. You behave now — you hear me?'

The door was opened by a small white woman whose long dark hair was greasy-flat on her scalp and whose fringe totally obscured her eyes. She wore a flowing Indian print skirt the flounce of which was tamed by a thick arran jumper that ended at her knees. Her shoulders were rounded as if permanently huddling from the wind. Mousy, Mum would have called her.

'Miss Charlesworth,' I said, in my best 'I've-got-a-degree' accent. She smiled using all

70

her teeth. But her smile got fixed on her face as she looked between Carl and me several times. I said, 'We've come about the car.' But she didn't respond. I began to wonder whether my brother and me on her doorstep may have put her into shock, when her lips began to close slowly over her dry teeth.

'Oh yes,' she said, 'I was expecting . . . ' but her voice trailed away. 'Jackson, is it?' She grinned again, this time just at Carl who nodded back at her.

'Is that the car down there?' I asked her.

'Yes, I'll just get the keys,' she said. Then added, 'I'll just have to shut the door because I've got a cat and I wouldn't like him to get out into the road. So I hope you don't mind but I'll just shut this door and get the keys and join you down by the car, if I may.'

As the door shut Carl rolled his eyes with a weary look. 'She thinks we've come to mug her,' he sighed. I shushed him and we went and waited by the car. The man appeared in the window again but was silent.

The woman held a beige mac round her as she ran towards us with the car keys. We all stood looking at the car as she explained, 'I've had it for a very long time but I've just got a job away from London so I'll be commuting more and I thought I'd treat myself to something a little bigger. It's been a good car for me. Suited me very well and is mostly very reliable.'

'Does it start all right in the mornings?' Carl asked.

The woman looked at him startled, as if she

didn't expect him to be able to speak. 'Oh yes, well, most mornings. I mean there are always those odd wet mornings . . . ' she went on addressing me, 'when it won't start. But I think all cars are the same in that respect.'

Carl went to the front of the car and got onto his knees again.

'Does your husband know a lot about cars?' Mousy asked me.

'Oh, he's not my husband, he's my brother actually,' I said. The woman nodded again but was staring intently at what Carl was doing.

'The car's for me,' I smiled, trying to get her attention. The woman nodded but stayed watching Carl.

Then for some reason I added, 'I work in television, you see.'

The woman slowly turned her head round toward me and gave me a genuine smile which made her look almost pretty. 'Television,' she repeated. 'How interesting. What do you do there?'

'I'm in the costume department.'

'Really, how fascinating.' Carl was now bouncing his bottom on the bonnet of her car but the woman was oblivious. 'Do you design the clothes?'

Oh what the hell, I thought. 'Well, on some productions,' I lied.

Carl came and stood by us.

'Can we take it for a drive?' he asked Mousy.

She looked up at him. 'Of course.' She started fiddling with the lock and asked me, 'Have you worked on anything I would have seen?'

'Probably,' I said.

'Who's driving?' she asked, opening the door. Carl said, 'You drive, Faith.'

'I can't,' I tried to whisper to him. 'I haven't driven a car for ages. You drive.'

'It's you who's getting the car,' he said too loudly. I smiled over at the woman who was waiting for us to decide. 'I can't drive, Carl,' I hissed. I pictured myself cornering on two wheels as Mousy and Carl covered their faces.

I got in the back of the car while Mousy settled in the front and Carl got into the driver's seat. 'Not a lot of room for transporting costumes in here,' she joked. I laughed politely while Carl was looking under the dashboard, sliding things and opening the ashtray.

'I don't suppose you've ever met Tom Conti, have you?' she asked me. Carl momentarily stopped what he was doing. He frowned — first at Mousy and then at me.

'I haven't had to do his costumes but I have sat next to him in the canteen.'

Her mouth opened and she made a small whimpering sound. 'Really,' she breathed. 'Tell me, is he as gorgeous in real life?' Carl adjusted his driving seat and the driving mirror. He wiggled the gearstick which was a metal handle with a green knob on the end that stuck out from the dashboard.

'He looked quite shy actually,' I told her. Mousy stared at me for a little while with the vacant adoration of a fan, then seemed to shake herself.

She had just begun to tell Carl where to put

the ignition key when he started the engine, pushed the car into first gear, wound down the window, put his elbow on it and drove off.

He went so quickly that I was thrown against the back of the seat. Mousy turned her body suddenly round to the front and stared at the passing road with wide eyes. Carl pulled the gear stick round — in and out, up and down. He began moving the steering wheel left and right quickly so the car made jerking movements. Mousy was gripping her seat. Her knuckles were pressing through the skin of her hand. I was about to tell Carl to slow down when he turned a corner and began to cruise down the road at a gentle speed. Then he suddenly stopped and Mousy and me were thrown forward. Mousy turned to Carl, her mouth open in a silent scream. But Carl just nodded to himself then started moving off again. This time driving slowly and carefully through the traffic. After a few minutes Mousy let out a long breath and her chest and shoulders collapsed back into their huddle.

'Do you know where you are going?' she squeaked at Carl. He didn't answer but then the icing-sugar houses came into view.

'Oh,' she said with surprised relief, 'back again.'

Carl pulled the car into the kerb. 'Not a bad little car this,' Carl told Mousy. Then he smiled at her showing both his dimples.

Mousy invited us into her home which was just a small flat tucked in the corner of the enormous house. Carl sat down in the middle of the sofa and spread his arms out along the back, as I leant forward smiling at Mousy and listening to her tale of when she first got the car.

'I was so scared to drive it that I could feel it going up and down in the drainholes as I passed over them.' I laughed. 'But I shall be sad to see the car go, it's been a good friend to me.'

Suddenly Carl leant forward and said, 'So how much do you want for the car?'

Mousy looked at him and said, 'Five hundred pounds,' very clearly.

Carl tipped his head to one side and said, 'Now five hundred is what it says in the advert. But what I want to know is what you actually want for the car.' I tried to get Carl to shut up — to shut up and just give her the money.

Mousy looked at Carl and he smiled at her again.

'Well, obviously, five hundred pounds is what I want,' she said.

'So,' Carl said shifting in his seat so he was looking directly at her, 'if I said,' he smiled again, 'four hundred and fifty, then you would tell me to take a running jump.'

'Well, Mr Jackson . . . ' Mousy started.

'Yes, Miss Charlesworth,' Carl said with a grin. Mousy blushed. Carl was staring into her eyes.

'I think I'd like a little more than that,' she giggled.

'Well, let's see. You tell me what you want.' Carl leant even further forward.

Mousy laughed. 'I want . . . ' she began,

looking in the air. 'I want four hundred and ninety-five?'

'Now is that a question or a statement?' Carl laughed.

'It's a fact,' she tittered.

'Well, if it's a matter of fact — I've only got four hundred and fifty-five,' Carl grinned.

This went on for about ten minutes. I sat a dumbfounded spectator. Finally Mousy decided with a schoolgirl giggle and much patting of her greasy hair and fondling of her own cheek and neck, that four hundred and sixty-five pounds was a fair price considering, as Carl had pointed out, that the car was green and a little low on petrol.

'It's a deal then,' Carl said and held out his hand which Mousy shook. He then put his hand in the top pocket of his shirt and pulled out a wodge of notes, and began counting the money into Mousy's hand saying, 'Ten, twenty, thirty . . . ' while Mousy looked up at him. She handed me all the paperwork but asked Carl, 'Would you like a cup of tea?' And Carl said almost graciously, 'No, we'd better be going.'

★　★　★

As we walked down to the car I looked out for the man in the window. Carl looked up too and said, 'Shall we put a brick through the windscreen — make his day?' I screamed no and Carl rolled his eyes and said, 'Joke.' I patted the top of the car. 'All mine,' I said excited. 'Thanks, Carl.' Then Carl threw the car keys at me. I looked at them and realised I would have to drive the car back — Carl had to drive his van.

'I can't, Carl, I can't. I can't drive it. I can't. I haven't driven in ages. I can't drive all that way. Not on my own. I don't know the way. I can't, Carl, I can't!'

My voice was getting dangerously shrill, when my brother rolled his eyes and held out his hand for the keys — 'Get in, little sis.' He drove me home, parked my new car outside my house. And as Marion ran out of the door screaming, 'Is it yours, Faith? Is it all yours?' Carl returned to Holland Park on the tube to pick up his van.

6

'I don't have to work here. I do it because I like to. I don't need the money,' Henry told a costume designer who sat by his side eating a cheese roll. He told me this nearly every day of our working life together. And Lorraine would mouth it behind his back when she heard him telling anyone else. The designer looked politely interested and nodded, saying, 'Fantastic, Henry. I knew you were fantastic.' Henry blushed a little.

'You are making a real mess of that roll,' he said. 'It's all over you.' I knew Henry would have loved to get the clothes brush out of his cupboard and brush down the designer, sweeping the crumbs into his cupped hand and placing them in the bin. But Henry knew the pecking order. He could do that to me and did nearly every morning. But a designer? Henry spoke to everyone with a varying degree of poshness depending on job and status. From delivery man to dresser he used the ordinary suburban-street: 'Just put it over there.' Designers got: 'If you could just place it over in the corner.' While the head of wardrobe received the full Windsor Royal: 'If you would be so kind as to leave it my staff and I will deal with it as soon as is convenient.'

'I must tell you what happened to me yesterday, Henry,' the designer was saying. He

78

was square-jawed-handsome with dark hair and a thick black moustache. He offered me one of his crisps as Henry began to look impatient for his story; sitting up straight-backed in his chair with his hands resting neatly in his lap. 'I'm all ears,' Henry prompted.

'I was in this toilet,' the designer began. Henry looked across at me then back at the designer. He threw a message to him with his eyes that I wasn't supposed to understand.

'No, Henry, it was the gents in John Lewis.' They both smiled at me and I smiled back.

'Go on,' Henry said.

The designer leant closer to Henry and whispered, 'I had a bit of a shine so I thought I'd put some powder on my face.'

'Oh, don't mind her,' Henry erupted. 'She lives in a house with some very odd people.' He crossed his eyes teasingly at me and I poked my tongue out at him as the designer was saying, 'So I thought I'd go into the cubicle, as you can imagine, for a bit of privacy. Well, there I am balancing the compact on the toilet-roll holder, trying to see into the silly little mirror. The next thing I know the compact falls on the floor and rolls into the next cubicle.'

Henry threw his head back and started to laugh loudly.

'No, wait, Henry, you haven't heard it all yet.'

Henry put his hand over his mouth to stop himself but his shoulders still twitched. He leant towards the designer.

'I got on my hands and knees,' the designer went on, 'to get the thing back. Well, there it was in the other cubicle resting between a pair of rather butch-looking feet.'

Henry flapped his hands in the air: 'Oh, this is good,' he giggled.

'So I put my hand under to grab the compact.'

Henry screamed, but the designer went on, 'There was powder all over his shoe.'

'Stop, stop!'

'So being polite I wiped some of the powder off his shoe before I grabbed the compact.'

'What did the man say — what did he say?' Henry began wiping his eyes with his white handkerchief.

'I don't know, I got out of there quick, Henry,' the designer said. 'I suppose it's not every day that a hand comes under the toilet while you're in the gents and starts brushing face powder off your foot, but what's a girl to do?' He took another bite of his roll and stood up. I smiled. But Henry's mouth was gaping open. His face was red and he did not breathe in for several seconds — like a toddler about to scream. When he finally let out the laugh it was so loud that it brought Lorraine out of the office.

'What you laughing at?'

'Tell her, tell her,' Henry panted at the designer. 'Tell her please, she'll love it.'

'What?' Lorraine asked.

'Sorry. Got to run, Henry — I've got Nigel Havers at two o'clock.'

Henry let out another loud shriek as the designer disappeared out the door. 'I love that man,' he said wiping tears from his eyes. 'He's so nice and such a good designer. The best. Award-winning.'

'What — tell us?'

Henry tapped his chair for Lorraine to sit by him. Then he recounted the designer's tale with a few hyperbolic adjustments. The boots became black Doc Martens. The compact was gold and valuable. The man grunted when he saw the powder all over his shoe — that sort of thing.

'I can tell you like that one, Henry,' Lorraine told him.

Henry loved stories. He reserved the seat by him for people who wanted to tell tales. And they'd come from all over the department. Henry had nicknames for everyone — I was 'El professor' because I had a degree. As people approached he would call out their name. 'Well, if it isn't 'the Welsh dresser'' or 'here comes 'la plume de ma tante''. Then he would sit comfortably and they'd begin. It was mainly the dressers who came and they usually ignored me. But I would listen attentively to the stories of life on the studio floor: of the actress who sweated so much her costume had to be dried after each take; of the singer whose wife could make executives cry; of the magician whose hair lived in a box, or the actor who liked to show everyone his willy. And I enjoyed everything vicariously, like a poor relation. If the story was good Henry would pat their arms saying, 'You're joking. Stop. I'm not sure I want to hear this.' If the story was boring he'd stand up and find work to do.

Henry liked to hear about my shared house and when I had something to tell him he would beckon me over to sit in the chair even though he could hear me just as well from my seat opposite. I would exaggerate Marion into an adorable untidy slut and Mick into a dopehead. I told him the story about Simon. How he had woken in the night after a rather drunken evening and thought he was at home with his mummy and daddy and believed that he still kept a potty under his bed. Simon then went pee-pee in his potty only to wake the morning after to find that he had pissed into his shoe. Henry made me bring a picture of Simon in to show him. He pointed to his shoes in the photograph and laughed for about ten minutes before deciding, 'Well, he looks a nice boy for you, Miss. What's the matter with you? Ask him out. You're footloose.'

We worked shifts with long days on duty and the next day off. In the mornings Lorraine, Henry and me would sit at our table eating doughnuts and listening to Lorraine as she told us another story about her boyfriend's family. 'I mean his dad's lovely, really, but he's got this temper and when he shouts I can't understand a word he's saying. It just sounds like a load of bwuba bwuba. Something like that. And he looks frightening, this big black . . . sorry, Faith . . . coloured man. I don't mean to be horrible but . . . '

Lorraine's boss would come in saying, 'Morning, Henry,' and he would look at Lorraine and me and say, 'And morning, *les girls*. How are *les girls* today?' Lorraine would then go reluctantly into her office where she opened the mail and ordered taxis.

When the costumes started arriving, Henry and me would get to work. I liked typing better than describing. Usually I would describe a garment and Henry would type down something completely different, saying things like, 'Well, I just thought my version was a little more accurate, because what you described as trim is, in fact, a peplum.' When I was typing I could stop Henry for minutes at a time as I waited for the Tippex to dry on an error. It was blissful silence and sometimes I did it just for the power to shut Henry up.

At lunchtimes I went to the canteen with Lorraine. Henry never went. 'It's full of weathermen with bad haircuts,' he said. But in the canteen I could queue up for my pork chop with two veg behind Queen Victoria and in front of Gandhi. It was in the canteen that I really knew I worked somewhere potentially glamorous. It was in the canteen that I could overhear the lunch-time conversation of Jonathan Miller and Judi Dench and then recite it at home round the dinner table as if it had been said to me. In the canteen I could sit and listen to Lorraine's endless beauty problems — whether to have her legs waxed or spend the money on a colonic irrigation — whilst keeping my eye on the movements of Noel Edmunds.

And when I could I would go to the viewing galleries high above the studios and watch what was going on down below. I'd catch unfamiliar scenes from familiar programmes — the children's programme with the presenter who sat

83

in the middle of a hissing and growling cat and dog trying to keep them apart and shouting, 'Oh, fuck this.' And the singer who sang, 'Jump down, Jimmy jump, Jimmy jump down,' while being swallowed up in a fog of dry ice, while the director shouted, 'Where she's gone — where the hell has she gone?'

My job had slipped into a routine which I refused to think of as dull. But on my tube journeys to work I began to wonder — as they had enquired at my interview — whether the job was beneath a woman with my qualifications. There was a notice board that advertised all the vacancies at the television centre. Producers, editors, researchers, cameramen, floor assistants: the self-important people who talked loudly in corridors and looked through you blankly when they passed. I'd ask Henry what the jobs involved. And he always answered adding 'glorified' before his description. Researchers were glorified busy-bodies, floor assistants were glorified dogsbodies. 'Don't run before you can walk, Miss — you'll only be let down,' he advised me.

* * *

Then one evening Lorraine and I went to see them recording *Top of the Pops*. I used to watch *Top of the Pops* with Carl when we were young. We would bet on what was going to be number one that week and the loser had to dance round the room to the music. Not watching *Top of the Pops* became our rite of passage — a signal to

84

each other that we were growing out of the childish world — moving into an adult world where things did not have to thump and swirl to keep our attention.

The doorman, who was a friend of Lorraine's, looked me up and down suspiciously but then nodded us in and onto the studio floor. The studio was filled with young girls. I felt old, like a parent come to watch a school show. Most of the girls had drooping shoulders and looked mildly sedated. They wore their best jumpers and skirts and shifted from foot to foot, obeying the order which was to dance. There were only one or two boys and they looked around themselves constantly — red-faced and embarrassed. They were herded, shuffling, over to the stage that held a group. The music bellowed from speakers all round the studio. And the singer of the band sang, sweated and strutted — her hair dyed blue and a guitar with no lead slung low on her body — while the girls in the audience looked up at her, swaying politely. Then a band full of young men dressed in dark glasses and mohair suits mimed with golden saxophones, swaying in time, jumping up and fooling around. And the audience of girls stared almost motionless. 'Can you look like you're enjoying it,' a voice ordered them over the speakers. At which a few of the girls smiled while others started to wiggle their hips.

Some dancers danced in costumes I recognised and I said out loud, 'I put labels in those,' and then felt embarrassed. We went before the recording was over — before Henry could start to complain. As we slipped out of the studio door past the guard, who looked relieved to see us leave, the compère shouted, 'Are you having a good time?' but none of the girls in the audience appeared to answer. As we walked back along the corridor I asked Lorraine, 'What do you have to do to be a dresser?'

'Just apply,' she told me with a shrug.

'I might do that,' I said.

'Yeah, that's a good idea, you're wasted with Henry.'

I smiled to myself. She was right. I was wasted sticking labels into costumes. I was wasted. I should be down among the action. I should be on the studio floor — with the lights, the camera, the actors. But Lorraine carried on speaking, and in a tone of voice that could have been explaining the filling in her sandwich, she added, 'But they don't have black dressers.' I stopped walking and looked at her. It took a while for her to realise I wasn't by her side. 'Oh sorry,' she said, 'I don't mean to be horrible but it's just what happens here. Haven't you noticed there aren't any coloured people dressing?'

No, I hadn't noticed.

Lorraine was still speaking. 'It's just a couple of the managers. I overheard them saying that they didn't think the actors would like a coloured person putting their clothes on them. Henry said, 'What if the actor is coloured?' And that's what I said, because some of them are now on television, aren't they? I didn't say it to them 'cause I only overheard it. But that's what I said to Henry and he agreed. It's not right.'

My hands began to shake.

'You should try though, Faith. You'll probably be all right because everyone likes you.'

I stared at her.

'You're not upset are you, Faith?'

I shrugged.

'Oh, don't be upset. You're not upset, are you? You shouldn't let them upset you. You're not upset, are you? Don't let them upset you. They're not worth getting upset about.' And Lorraine carried on insisting until she thought she had made me smile. 'Don't be upset, Faith. Don't be upset . . . '

7

'It's foolishness, Faith, just foolishness. You must take no notice of their foolishness. You're an educated woman now. They can't mess with you. It's just foolishness.' Mum sat close in front of me with her hand resting lightly on my knee. She had, as usual, asked me to tell her all about my new independent life. 'Me daughter a young woman.' We had gone through everything. Yes, I cleaned out my bedroom regularly. Yes, I eat properly. Yes, we paid the bills on time. Yes, I only had to do my washing and no, I didn't have to clean up after those two men.

'And that good job of yours?'

I told her I wanted to be a dresser. I explained what the job involved.

'Wait, you tellin' me these people can't put their own clothes on their back. Is grown people we talking about?'

I told her about the rails of costumes, the quick changes, the corsets. That the actors needed to be shown the right costumes and how to wear them properly.

'Seems odd to me that grown people can't dress themselves. Little children, yes. I had to do that for you at the ballet shows. Remember the tutus? But grown people! You sure you want to do that job?'

'Well,' I interrupted, 'someone told me they don't employ black people as dressers, anyway.'

88

Mum sat back from me like she'd just seen fire coming from my mouth. A look momentarily appeared in her eyes that was close to sadness. A look that pleaded, 'you can hate me but please love my children.'

Then she sat forward again. 'It's foolishness, Faith, just foolishness. You must take no notice of their foolishness.' But as she looked closely at me I could feel her mentally combing at my 'too long and a little fuzzy' hair, straightening it, cutting it short, neat. Taking off my jeans and tee-shirt and dressing me in a knee-length skirt with a nice white button-up cardigan and placing a copy of the New Testament in my hand, so I would look more . . .

'You're respectable, you're from a good home and you're educated. You must let them know these things. I know you don't like going to church now, but you could let them know that . . . '

'Why should I?' I shouted, which surprised me as much as it surprised my mum. She wanted to give an answer but said instead, 'Faith, that is no way to talk to your mother. I'm just saying . . . I'm just trying . . . It's for your own good.'

'I'm sorry,' I mumbled. She sat up straighter and accepted my apology with a nod then began, 'There are laws now, you know. When me and your dad first came to this country . . . '

As she spoke I noticed the boxes in the corner of the room. There were three more than last time, although one of them was still open. Sticking out from the top of it were the four legs

89

of a ceramic horse that used to sit on a shelf in our old flat. I hadn't seen it in years. I used to pretend to ride it when I was little, sitting on its back and dragging it under me as if it were taking me for a gallop. 'That is a precious thing not a toy,' Mum used to shout. 'I didn't bring that all the way from Jamaica to have you sit on it and break it up.'

Mum was still talking, telling me something about prayer when I went over to the boxes and pulled the horse out. She stopped and watched me.

'Remember that?' she asked, 'I brought that horse all the way from Jamaica. I don't remember who give it to me now but that horse been everywhere.'

'And now it's going back,' I added.

Mum stood up, brushing down her skirt. 'Well, better get on,' she said, 'your dad will be wanting something to eat soon.'

'Why don't you want to live here any more, Mum?' I asked quietly. She shut her eyes for a second and took a sharp breath then smiled and said, 'Who say we don't want to live here? We just thinking. Thinking this, thinking that. We're always thinking me and your dad. Thinking, thinking, thinking. We're just thinking,' she finally sang, like a little girl playing a teasing game.

The phone rang and she picked it up before the first ring had completed. 'Oh, one, nine, six, five, six, seven, nine, one. How may I help you?' she said steadily into the receiver.

I put the horse down on the floor. I didn't want to put it back in the box, scared of what else I might find in there, waiting to emigrate.

Mum held her hand over the phone mouthpiece. 'Can you go and get your brother?' She smiled conspiratorially, 'Tell him it's a woman.' I went to the door and yelled, 'Carl, phone.' And Mum, still holding the phone, shouted at me in a whisper, 'I could have done that myself, child. Go and get him. You want the whole street to know you want him? I don't know, Faith, I thought you were growing up. You don't change.' I instinctively tutted and rolled my eyes then walked out into the street to get my brother.

Carl and Dad had their heads inside the engine of my car. When I had first got to the house, Dad asked me with a grin, 'How's the new car?' I said it was wonderful and then in passing mentioned that I thought it might be pinking — that was that the engine didn't stop immediately when you turned off the ignition. I had learnt the term and symptom from Carl along with several others like slipping clutches, binding brakes, faulty tappets. I also began to mention that the fan seemed to screech on a high setting, when I noticed my dad reaching for his glasses and looking around, presumably for his monkey wrench.

'Leave the car, Dad,' Carl said quickly. 'I'll look at it later.'

'Son, I'll just go and have a little look . . . ' Dad began.

'Dad, leave it. You don't know anything about cars.'

Dad then looked incredulously at Carl — stuttering and blinking until he managed to say, 'I had a van since before you were born and I keep that van in good working order without you.'

'Like the time you tried to change the clutch?' Carl reminded him. Even I remembered that. Dad coming in the house after being under his van for several hours, carrying a large lump of metal and saying to Carl as matter-of-factly as he could, 'So tell me, son, whereabouts this bit go now?'

'That was just one time I have a bit of bother,' Dad answered.

'Dad, I'll look at the car in a minute.'

'Wade, listen to Carl nah,' Mum added and Dad frowned with the betrayal of it. He stood in the middle of the room looking at each treacherous member of his family in turn. Then said, 'I'll just go and have a quick look,' and walked out with Carl running out after him shouting, 'Oh bloody hell. This is your fault, Faith.'

I flicked Carl on the head with my index finger. 'Phone,' I said. He swatted me off and hit his head on the bonnet. I laughed. Carl didn't. I called after him, 'Oh, by the way, it's a woman,' which made him move faster.

'D'you know what's wrong with the car?' I asked my dad. He didn't answer, he was in deep concentration. I asked again and he said, 'Mmmm.' I looked at the mucky black engine.

Dad was gently tapping the different parts of it, one after the other, with a spanner. He was listening carefully, nodding his head slowly like a doctor with a stethoscope. I watched him for several minutes but then I became aware that he had no idea what he was listening for.

8

Marion had a way of knocking on my bedroom door — she used her tapping knuckle to push the door open. She would be inside, still knocking but asking me if it was all right for her to come in. If it wasn't for some reason, she'd put her hands over her eyes and continue knocking until I told her it was.

She threw herself onto my bed. 'These bloody jeans, Faith. They won't do up.' I watched her for a few minutes — desperately breathing in, sucking in her cheeks in the hope her hips would follow, trying to hold the sides of the jeans with one hand whilst pulling at the zip with the other. It was hopeless. But Marion was not about to give up. She changed position — on her back, on her side, kneeling.

'Have you thought of getting a bigger size?' I finally asked her.

'It's just stuck. You have a go, Faith.'

I got on the bed and straddled her legs. I tried to pull at the zipper but it was slimy with Marion's sweat. I grabbed at the zipper through my tee-shirt but it still wouldn't move. Flesh was holding it back. I pulled harder and Marion screamed, 'Fuck,' as the teeth of the zip nicked her skin.

I gave up. 'Wear something else.'

We both sat back on the bed, spent with the

effort. She pouted like a little girl, 'I haven't got anything else.'

'Wear something of mine.'

Marion huffed and started at the zip again. 'Just hold the edges, Faith, and I can do it up.' I held the edges, resting the top of my head on Marion's chest. The zip began to edge upwards but I started to laugh.

'Don't, Faith, you're making me laugh.' The zip suddenly sprang up to the top.

'There!' she said triumphantly holding out her arms. But as she breathed out the zip slowly began to undo from the bottom. We both watched it gradually open with a quiet metallic rasping. Marion's stomach poked its way through, reclaiming the gap like rising bread dough. Marion tutted, 'It's bloody broken now,' and left the room with her bottom lip sticking out.

We were getting ready to go out to see Simon and Duncan, alias The Members, perform one of their first gigs at a pub called the Crown and Castle.

Marion came back in my room carrying a bundle of her dirty washing. She threw it on the floor and knelt next to it. She sniffed at each item and made two piles. 'Right,' she said, pointing to the smallest pile, 'these aren't too bad.' The other pile she pushed away with her foot as she held up a tee-shirt and a boiler suit looking for stains.

I heard Simon's footsteps running down the stairs. When Simon ran down the stairs the house tended to shake.

'Oh God, listen to him,' Marion said. 'He's been up and down to the toilet about seven times the last ten minutes. He's driving me mad.' She stepped out of her jeans and pulled on the blue boiler suit. It was so crushed that it had the texture of dried cod. She opened her arms with a flourish. Simon walked up the stairs and shut his room door behind him. 'What do you think?' Marion asked.

'Aren't you going to iron it?'

She brushed at the front of the suit with the palms of her hands. 'It'll drop out before I get there.' And Simon clomped down the stairs again causing my door handle to rattle.

'Again!' Marion shouted, 'He's turning inside out.'

I waited until he came out of the bathroom. 'Simon,' I called, 'why don't you use your potty?'

'Oh yeah, very funny, Faith,' I heard him mutter as Marion and me laughed.

★　★　★

I took Marion in my new car to her parents' house. For some reason Marion wanted her dad to come with us. 'He said he was interested,' Marion told me. And when I asked her what he was interested in — was it the comedy or the cabaret circuit? Marion replied, 'No, he's interested in my life.'

I was not used to having passengers in my car with me. I'd managed to avoid it up until then. I preferred to make my, oh-God-not-another-right-hand-turn noises with no witnesses to stare and tut. Mick came with Marion and me but as we pulled up in front of her parents' house he said, 'I'd better stay here.' Marion agreed adding, 'Yeah, my gran hasn't forgiven you yet.' And Mick shouted down the street after us, 'Forgiven me for what? What have I done?'

Marion's parents' home was a tall terraced house in a part of Holloway that estate agents had optimistically started to say was 'going up'. It was the most dilapidated house on a street of dilapidated houses. The front bay window was held in place by a wooden buttress of thick struts and beams that were angled down into the front garden. There was subsidence in the bay and the council had ordered Marion's dad to fix it before the bay fell out onto passers-by. Her dad did not have the money to fix it so he applied to the council for a grant. The council refused. Her dad then told them that in that case the house would just have to fall down. So the props came from the council and were wedged into place. They had been there for years. Marion's dad was a builder.

The hallway in the house was dark. The walls still carried the original Victorian wallpaper — brown and dirty with age. Some patches of wall plaster were gone, revealing the thin slats of wood used to partition the rooms in the olden days. There were no light switches, just wires that fell out of the walls and the only light came from a fanlight. But as you went up the stairs and opened the kitchen door everything changed.

The kitchen was brand new. A large light airy room fitted out with wooden cupboards and work surfaces in slate grey that matched the floor tiles, the double oven and the large fridge-freezer. There was a shiny chrome double sink with taps that worked with levers like in a hospital. A dishwasher, a washing machine, a tumble dryer and even a microwave oven. And separated from the kitchen area by a breakfast bar with two wooden stalls was the dining room with a pine dresser, a pine table and six chairs. It was cosy and warm and always smelt of fried bacon. The kitchen had been completed by Marion's dad in a frenzy of activity to celebrate the death of their sitting tenant. He was an old man, bought with the house, who had occupied the middle room for over fifty years. He used to frighten Marion and her two sisters whenever they passed his room by opening his door a little and hissing at them. Marion and her sisters called him Mr Fartface. And when he died they all danced round his empty room.

Marion's mum was standing by the cooker when we went in. Marion's mum was always standing by the cooker. I once walked straight past her mum in the street and she had called after me saying, 'Faith, it's me! Marion's mum. Don't you know me?' And I didn't tell her then but I didn't recognise her without her cooker near. Marion's grandmother was sitting at one end of the table eating a sandwich and her grandfather was sitting at the other reading the sporting section of the paper. This grandmother, however, did not belong to the grandfather. They were both widowed but one was Marion's mum's mother and the other was Marion's dad's father. They both lived in flats in houses that were on the same street as Marion's parents: her grandmother lived three doors down on the ground floor and her grandfather lived four doors up on the top floor of a house that belonged to Marion's grandmother's sister.

Everyone looked up as we walked in.

'What d'you want?' Marion's mum smiled. 'Whatever it is I haven't got it and you can't have it.'

'Well, if you haven't got it I obviously can't have it, Mother,' Marion replied.

'You know what I mean — you can't have whatever it is you want,' her mum explained playfully.

'No, I know because you just informed me that you haven't got it.' The smile on her mum's face faded as she said, 'You're too clever for your own good sometimes.'

'But surely it's good to be clever,' Marion retorted as she opened the door of the fridge.

Her mum then looked over to me. 'Faith, come in, sit down. D'you want a cup of tea?' she asked.

'Charming. Don't I get offered one?' Marion said.

'You're no guest,' her mum told her. I said I didn't want a cup of tea or a sandwich or a biscuit or a Coke. 'What about a jacket potato, Faith? Won't take me a minute . . . ' Marion's mother was saying as Marion's gran looked at her and said, 'What are you wearing, Marion? You look like such a scruff.'

99

'It's the fashion,' Marion said looking down at her boiler suit.

'It ain't the outfit, darlin' — it's the way it looks. Can't you run a bleedin' iron across it or something? State of ya. Christ Almighty, Margy, look at the state your daughter goes out in. She needs to run an iron across that.'

'It'll drop out,' Marion said, as she bit into a pork pie she had found in the fridge.

'You know your trouble, girl?' her gran went on. 'You're bone bleedin' idle. You always have been. You're spoilt. Get an iron across it. I wouldn't be seen out dead with ya in that.' Her gran looked at me, 'You gonna go out with her looking like that? You look so nice, Faith. You always look nice, Faith. You take care of yourself. It's her — Madam — bone bleedin' idle. You wanna get an iron across that. Margy, get her to get an iron across that.'

Marion rolled her eyes and blew out her breath. 'Where's Dad?' she asked her mum. Her grandad turned the page of his newspaper and sniffed loudly. And her grandmother answered. 'He's out looking for that sister of yours. That Trina. She's done another bunk 'cause she's in trouble up to her ears again. You're all bleedin' hopeless. And I know why — you're spoilt, the whole bleedin' lot of ya.'

Marion's mum whispered to me and Marion, 'I think she's somewhere in the house but you know what she's like — she won't come out.'

'Did you call her?' Marion whispered back and her gran said, ''Course she bloody called her — what d'you take us for? You think we're all bloody stupid 'cause you've been to some university. She ain't gonna answer — little madam. I'd take a strap to her, that's what she needs. You should take a strap to her, Margy — you're too soft with her, that's why she's gone to the bad.'

Marion pulled at my arm to leave the room with her. 'Let's go and find her,' she whispered in my ear.

Marion and her two sisters, Trina and Kirsty, had a bedroom each at the top of the house. All the bedrooms had been renovated into rooms you might see featured in a magazine. Sunken lighting, fitted wardrobes, sink units with vanity areas and stage-dressing-room lights, fitted carpets, venetian blinds. Each bedroom contained the same items but in different permutations depending on the layout of the room. But now, Marion's room only held her mum's sewing machine and a dog basket.

Marion kicked open Trina's bedroom door, went straight over to the wardrobe and parted the clothes. And there was her sister sitting in the cupboard with her knees up round her chin.

'Oh God, it's you! Don't tell 'em you found me,' Trina said, looking up at us.

Marion stood to her full height and folded her arms. She was the oldest sister — six years older than Trina, and seven years older than Kirsty. 'What are you sitting in there for this time?'

'He's doin' his nut,' Trina started, then she saw me. 'Oh hello, Faith. How are you?' she smiled. 'Marion says you work in television now.' I nodded as Marion shouted, 'What are you hiding in there for?'

Trina looked back at her sister and rolled her eyes. 'I had a fight with some wog at school. Stupid coon spat at me and pulled me hair. So I hit her.' Then Trina looked back at me. 'Here, Faith, do you see anyone famous when you're at work?'

'Is that all or is there something you haven't told me?' Marion asked.

'Well,' Trina carried on, 'the stupid bag headmistress calls me into her office and says she's gonna get Dad to come up to the school. And I said to her, don't do that 'cause I'll get fuckin' killed. And she says to me that she has to for my own good. And I explained to her that if my dad had to come up the school again I would get killed. But she says it's her duty. So . . .' Trina began to laugh, 'I turned over her desk. Tipped the whole fuckin' thing onto the floor. Everything went everywhere. She was so shocked — you should have seen her fuckin' face. Then I legged it. I would have stayed out but it's too fuckin' cold. Here, Faith, have you ever seen that actor who'sin that thing on telly — you know the one?'

I sat on the bed and looked out of the window.

'Trina, you're going to have to face him sometime,' Marion told her. But Trina just said, 'Here, Faith, can you get us a job on the telly — 'cause I reckon I could do that.'

And then there was shouting downstairs, 'Where is she? She come in yet?'

'That's Dad,' Marion said evenly. 'Come downstairs. Don't you think you've put him

102

through enough today? Just come down and sort it out.'

'Piss off,' Trina said and shut the cupboard door.

Marion's dad was standing by the dresser drinking a cup of tea when we walked back in. I thought he was going to shout but he looked up at Marion and said, 'Hello, love.' Then he folded his arms, 'What d'you want? Whatever it is I haven't got it and you can't have it.' And Marion laughed and hugged her dad. 'Oh, at least one of my girls is all right,' he said, patting her back. Then he looked at me, 'Faith, how are you? Long time no see since you moved into that house of yours. I miss you round here eating us out of house and home.' He winked at me. 'You look nice too, Faith. We all goin' out tonight on the razzle?'

Marion's gran started on at Marion again about ironing her clothes, as her dad asked, 'You seen that sister of yours, Marion? She's in trouble. I've had to go up the school again. She went and clocked some darkie. And this coon's mum and dad come up the school wanting to see Trina. They said she'd been bullying their daughter. Now their daughter is a great big, six foot bloody gorilla and Trina, as you know, is only little. I had to laugh at that. Trina bullying that bloody great thing. But then they starts shouting in my face that I don't know how to bring up my kids properly. I thought that's bloody rich comin' from a coon.'

Marion's gran butted in, 'What they bloody talking about? You know how to bring up your

103

kids — you don't need no bloody help from no nig-nog.'

Marion looked briefly at me, smiled and shrugged a little as her dad carried on. 'Then the headmistress tells me Trina turned her desk over onto the floor. I said to her, 'Give over.' Trina's only little and she could not tip up this huge bloody wooden desk. I'd be hard pushed to tip that desk up and I'm a grown man, I told her.' He looked at me, 'You all right, Faith, you're ever so quiet? You wanna cup of tea? Margy, get Faith a cup of tea.'

'No, thank you,' I said.

Then Marion made a little excited jump in the air. 'Look, I've got an idea — let's just go out and forget everything for tonight. She'll be back and you can sort it all out tomorrow. Don't let it spoil tonight. She'll be back.'

'I know and I'm going to kill her when I see her. Why can't all my daughters be like my lovely Marion?'

'You wanna take a strap to them all,' Marion's gran began. 'They're all useless.'

'Oh, she's off — time to leave,' Marion's dad said, rubbing his hands together. Kirsty, Marion's other sister, came in the kitchen. 'Perfect timing,' her dad said. 'We're off now, darlin', to see a cabaret or something . . . '

'I ain't goin',' Kirsty said.

'Yes you bloody well are, my girl,' her dad said, pointing a finger. 'And don't go looking to your mum 'cause you're coming with me.'

'I'll stay here.'

'Oh yeah, do I look like I just got off a boat?

Soon as I'm out that door you'll be off meeting them bloody boys. I've told ya — you're coming with me tonight.'

Marion looked at her sister. 'You'll like it, Kirsty — it's comedy.'

'I'll go with Mum.'

'You're not coming with me,' her mum said. 'I want a rest from the lot of you.'

'Mum's going out with her sister,' her dad went on. 'Gran and Grandad are going home — I hope.' Marion's grandad coughed and spat into his handkerchief. 'And you're comin' with me. Ain't she, Faith?'

'We can go in Faith's car,' Marion said, and her dad laughed.

'No offence, Faith love — but women drivers . . . '

Marion put her hands on her hips and said, 'What are you talking about — women can drive perfectly well and you know it. That's a terrible thing to say.'

'Oh, listen to her. I'm sure they can, love, but not with me in the car. I'll take me own.'

'Oh honestly, Dad, I wish you wouldn't say things like that. You know it upsets me. Women are just as capable as men. I don't know why you say it. Well, if you're driving you can't drink then. Promise me.'

Marion's dad held up his hands and said, 'What d'you take me for, love? Not a drop of alcohol will pass these lips.'

Marion went in the car with her dad and sister. I went back to Mick in my car with Marion's mum calling out of the window after me, 'Don't be a stranger, Faith — it's always lovely to see you.'

★　★　★

'Nice of your old man to get you this car,' Mick said, as I sat in the driver's seat and he looked for the ashtray. I shrugged. He lit a cigarette as I drove and started to tell me about a UFO he had seen. The unidentified flying object was a green cigar-shaped light in the sky. It seemed to stand still for several minutes but then moved very quickly leaving a streak of light in its wake. It was not a bird because birds do not glow in the dark. Not a plane either because they have smaller lights, and, Mick told me, it was too low and big in the sky and it wasn't the right colour green — the UFO was more of a phlegm green.

'It was incredible. I wasn't the only one who saw it. Philippa saw it too and some people standing near us. Everyone was looking at it. But the funny thing was, Faith, it wasn't reported in the papers.' He then went on about how in America, evidently, these things are sighted all the time but the government hushes it up for some reason.

'What reason?'

'They don't want to cause mass panic. They've got captured space ships and everything in Arizona.'

I nodded with the intrigue and wonder of it all. Then I asked innocently, 'When did you see the UFO?'

Mick got quite animated and began, 'I

106

remember it well because it was Guy Fawkes' night . . . ' I then had to pull the car over to the side of the road because my laughing was making my steering erratic and dangerous and I could not see properly through the tears in my eyes. But Mick kept protesting, 'It wasn't a firework . . . it was not . . . they don't make fireworks that look like that . . . '

★ ★ ★

The Crown and Castle pub was old — all Victorian brown wood and frosted glass. The Comedy Cabaret, as it was billed, was upstairs. Downstairs was filled with ageing couples, sitting at the tables in silence, occasionally sipping from the drinks in front of them whilst staring transfixed at the flashing lights on the slot machine. They all looked totally bored but would go home believing they'd had a great night out.

The upstairs room should have had a smoker's cough — the nicotine smells seemed to puther out of the walls and ceiling. The windows were open but this just allowed carbon monoxide into the mix.

The stage was only elevated about twelve inches off the floor. There was no curtain. There were no wings. I had fantasised about going backstage to congratulate Simon and Duncan in their dressing room with flowers and a, 'Darling, you were wonderful.' But a damp towel and packet of smoky bacon crisps in the gents' bog looked more befitting. All the tables around the room had a bistro-effect candle and an ashtray on them. Mick began pulling several tables together right at the front.

'Don't go so close, we'll put him off,' I said.

'Good,' he said.

The room filled up very quickly. People passed round flyers showing who was on that night. I hadn't heard of anyone, although Mick assured me that one of the comedians had been on the telly. His name was biggest on the flyer. Simon and Duncan were very small towards the bottom and their name got mixed up with the designer and typesetter, which unfortunately made it read, 'Designed and typeset by: The Artists Members'.

Marion arrived. Her dad told us all to, 'Call me Fred,' and her sister Kirsty looked round the room and said, 'Gor, what a dump.' Philippa came and sat at our table with Rob, who was wearing a black beret, and so did Marion's newest 'friend' Jeremy, who liked to say, 'Wink, wink,' instead of hello.

Marion's dad insisted on buying everyone a drink. I found it hard to call him Fred. I had known him for too long as Mr Cooper Marion's dad.

'It's Fred, Faith. Now what are you having? . . . Shall I make that a pint, stop me having to go up again? . . . Go on, I'm sure a big girl like you can manage a pint . . . Jeffrey, oh pardon me, Jeremy, what can I get you, son? . . . Get off, that's a poof's drink . . . I'll get it if you want but I'll have to walk with me back against the wall . . . Mick? . . . That's more like it, a man after me own heart. Shandy, sweetheart and your usual,

108

Marion? . . . Are those two with us? They look like they're from outa space.'

Marion's little sister looked self-consciously around with the expression of the newly bereaved. She was trying, like most adolescents, not to draw attention to herself but in the carefree atmosphere of the room, she was as vivid as a zombie at a wedding.

The acts were introduced by a dishevelled, grey-haired man who assured us that he had scoured the land for the talent we were about to see. 'You will be witnessing the finest that alternative comedy can muster.' In fact, Simon had told me that at his audition the man had looked at them through bleary eyes and said, 'You've got instruments, you can sing on key, I almost laughed. You're in.' He had had a long day, Simon explained — the act before had spent half an hour trying to make him laugh by sticking his fat belly into a plastic washing-up bowl and standing up straight with the bowl still attached.

The first act was a comedian. He was dressed in a donkey jacket and wore glasses. He pulled the microphone off its stand and then started. He ranted for about twenty minutes hardly pausing to take breath. He covered everything, from British Rail to men's obsession with women's tits. Someone from the back shouted, 'Shut it, wanker,' and the comedian said, 'Oh. Oh. Very clever heckle. Shut it, wanker. Well, that's put me in my place,' and carried on regardless. He then turned his wit onto Margaret Thatcher and the room convulsed with cheers and whoops and hollers. And Marion's dad could be heard saying to Rob, 'But to be fair . . . I mean I like a joke but you have to give Maggie her dues,' while Marion rolled her eyes and slid herself further under the table. Mick and me stood up to applaud him at the end but the people behind told us to sit down. And Marion's sister stayed straight-faced throughout.

The next comedian read a poem he had written about Vanessa Redgrave. When anyone laughed he told them to fuck off and stuck his two fingers up at them — except that it was very funny. Then came the man with the washing-up bowl. As he sank his belly into it, Marion's sister could be heard howling with laughter and everyone, unfortunately, stared at her.

'And now, new faces to the circuit but I'm sure you'll be seeing a lot more of them. The Members.' Simon came on squinting into the lights. He saw us all at our table but looked away quickly. Duncan sat on a stool while Simon went to his keyboard. He had to twiddle a lot of knobs very quickly; on the synthesiser and the tape recorder. I could see his hand shaking. Mick grinned, with an expression caught between a proud parent and a taunting sibling. And Marion was explaining to her dad, 'They're not. They've both got girlfriends. Anyway, so what if they are. Honestly!' I looked round the room and saw Duncan's girlfriend sitting at another table. She leant forward and gave me the thumbs up.

Simon looked different on stage. At home the most I usually saw of him was in the kitchen in the mornings. He would schlep into the room in his brown towelling dressing gown that was too small — the sleeves ended near his elbows and the hem just about covered what it should, until, that is, he bent over to get the milk out of the fridge. His hair usually sat up straight which made his head look like a coconut. He would pat it down when he saw anyone but it would always spring back, defying gravity until water was applied. His eyes were always red and puffy, like a toddler woken from an afternoon nap. And he had an annoying habit of slapping his dry lips together while he waited for the kettle to boil.

But as he pulled the microphone to him on stage I could see what attracted so many women into his room at night. It was his dark beard and moustache that was shaved close to his chin — his bum fluff he called it. And it was his green eyes with long dark lashes that made him look as if he was wearing make-up, like a girl. He and Duncan were dressed in old brown suits which they had bought from a shop in Greenwich — suits like my dad used to wear with wide trousers with turn-ups and double-breasted jackets. They reminded me of grown-ups.

Simon's familiar tinkling music began playing. Mick made a small groaning noise and I slapped his leg with the back of my hand. The music got quieter as they stood dead still at the foot of the stage. They then started doing sketches, pretending to be different characters as the taped music changed and acted as backing.

They were trendy lefties leaving a benefit for El Salvador, passionate that something should be done about the situation in South America. 'I feel very strongly about this. *Someone* should do something.' They were in the army performing gun drill when a soldier asks why men never hugged each other. 'What are you, private, some sort of shirt lifter?' They were a vicar and an aristocrat in a village who thought they were being invaded by Russia, only to realise they weren't Russians but Americans. 'We're not being invaded, Vicar, we're being liberated.' They sang about trendy art galleries that nobody went to unless they wore arty glasses, and pop groups with stupid haircuts.

At the end Mick and me stood up to applaud again and no one asked us to sit down. Marion stuck her fingers in her mouth and let out a loud whistle. Then Marion's sister called us all, 'bloody trendy lefties'. Mick sat down next to her to deny the tag — telling her earnestly about his working-class upbringing, his lack of money. 'And,' Mick finally concluded, 'I wasn't even breastfed.'

The last act was introduced as a poet. Everyone cheered as the poet walked on the stage.

He was black.

Marion looked at me and winked. Suddenly, as I looked up at this black poet I became aware that the poet and me were the only black people in the room. I looked around again — it was now a room of white people.

I became nervous waiting for the poet to start. I was thinking, 'Please be good, please.' The poet became my dad, my brother, he was the unknown black faces in our photo album, he was

112

the old man on the bus who called me sister, the man in the bank with the strong Trinidadian accent who could not make himself understood. He was every black man — ever.

'Me first poem,' he began in a Jamaican accent, 'is about those upholders of law and order, me friends the police.' He had long dreadlocks that flowed and swayed round his waist. I looked at my feet.

He was a dub poet and the poems had a strong beat as if accompanied by music. His first poem was about his fantasy of kicking a policeman back after the policeman had kicked him. People started to laugh and clap. All the poems — about the law, about his mum, about smoking weed — made people cheer. Hecklers only called, 'yeah'. And I slowly began to look up.

'This me last one,' the poet said and Marion's dad said, 'Good,' loud enough for people around to look over at our table. He was sitting back with his arms folded and a smirk on his face that I recognised from teachers at school when they were waiting for the cheeky kids to be quiet. He rolled his eyes at Marion and she looked momentarily over to me to see if I had seen. The poet went off waving.

'God, Faith, my dad!' Marion said as she followed me to the toilet. A band was playing on stage. Two of the instruments were huge metal dustbins and the sound of them thrashed and crashed even through the double doors to the toilets.

'I wish he hadn't come.' She rolled her eyes

and looked at me. 'He didn't like that last act,' she went on. 'He'd liked everything else though.' She became sheepish. 'He can be a bit like that. A bit . . . racist.' She stopped then turned and looked at me in the mirror. It was my turn to speak but I didn't, so she carried on.

'I said to him, how do you think it makes Faith feel — I mean, he's so insensitive. He just said, as usual, 'Oh, Faith's different.' And I said, 'No she isn't. Faith is my best friend and she is black.' But you see it's a cultural thing . . . '

Whenever Marion talked about her white working-class origins — her extended family who had all lived in the same street for generations — everything they said, everything they did was a cultural thing. Something that belonged to their way of life — like an instinct. I had known Marion's family for years. I liked them. I envied Marion that she had a gran and grandad and aunts and uncles and sisters and cousins. On my birthday I always got a card with a bunny on it 'from all the Coopers of Holloway'. And at Christmas I'd eat prawns with pickles and hokey-cokey with them all. But when they looked at me — as I stuck my right leg in, my right leg out, in out, in out and shook it all about — I always wondered who they saw.

'Not that being a cultural thing makes it all right,' Marion carried on. 'But that's why I asked him to come tonight. Broaden him and my sister out a bit. My family are very close. Working-class families in this country have traditionally been close. He says he wants to see the sort of life I lead now. So they want to change. They like you

Faith. It's a matter of educating them.' My heart was thumping very loudly in time with the dustbins in the band. 'I am forever battling with them. But they've just grown up with this.'

'Yeah, all right, Marion,' I suddenly snapped, 'I don't need a lecture today.'

She looked startled but carried on. 'I mean my dad's not bad, it's just . . . '

'A cultural thing — I know. Can we change the subject now, please?' I said.

There was silence then Marion said, 'I think we should talk about it, Faith.' She wasn't going to shut up — I hadn't smiled and forgiven her yet. In her strident Marxist phase she assured me that all racism would be swept away after the revolution. As a feminist we were all sisters — black and white.

'I mean,' she went on, 'these things can be so easily internalised and I wouldn't want you to. I mean as a woman in this society I think I know how you must feel. I can understand that you might be angry by what you heard in my house today, for example. It's going to take time but the working classes are already forming allegiances with a lot of black organisations . . . '

'Oh shut up Marion!' I shouted and walked out of the toilet.

9

The hallway was different at my mum and dad's. The brown wood table that almost blocked the way was gone. In its place stood a brown wood chair which had a leather seat that was cracked with age and speckled with mildew from its days in the cellar. There was a pile of dusty shoes under the chair. They were mine. My old brown suede platform zip-up boots that still had the stain from the steak and kidney pie I once drop-kicked onto them. Black leather things I'd worn to school, some platform cork clogs and a pair of white plimsolls that had the names of the entire double-winning Arsenal football team written on them, for some reason.

'Are these going to the church jumble sale?' I asked Mum.

'No!' she said, flaring her nostrils. 'They don't want shoes. I don't know how people give their old shoes. Who wants old shoes? Old shoes are old because they're broken-up things.'

'Pardon me,' I said, surprised by her attitude. All my cast-off things since I could remember went to the church jumble sale with a, 'What one person throw away is another person's treasure, Faith.'

'I wanted to know if you wanted to keep them,' Mum enquired. I laughed. 'Well,' she said, producing a black bin liner out of nowhere like a magician, 'I'll put them in the bin then.' As I watched her stuffing the items into the bag with no ceremony or nostalgia, I suddenly wanted to grab them back and hug them to me. But I didn't.

There was a pile of Carl's dog-eared magazines, on photography, boats, motor racing, even some on stamp collecting. They were testament to the many hobbies my brother had tried to pursue. There was also a drawing from his schooldays. It had on it 'Trevor Jackson Class V C', and it had been marked by the teacher. In one corner in faded red ink I could still make out, 'D — see me.'

I remembered the drawing. The task was to draw an orchestral instrument and to name all the parts. My brother drew a triangle. He had marked 'steel triangle', 'handle' and 'steel thing for hitting'. And as an inspired thought he had marked the gap in the triangle with an arrow and the word 'gap'. He was genuinely shocked at his teachers, 'D — see me', and brought the drawing home to show Mum and Dad for some sympathy at the injustice. Dad lectured Carl for several days on the need to take his schoolwork seriously and Mum told him that he should have drawn a violin, a cello, a trumpet, a flute, anything but a triangle. 'You'll never make anything of yourself with that attitude,' they concluded. But my brother never really understood what was wrong.

'Don't throw this away,' I told Mum. She looked at it then sucked her teeth.

'But it's rubbish. I can't go keeping all your old things.'

'It's our history,' I told her. She laughed and

kept repeating, 'history' under her breath whilst shaking her head and stuffing more things into the bin liner. I grabbed Carl's drawing before it was screwed up and gone for ever.

'Is that Faith?' Dad said coming out of the front room. He smiled at me so expansively that I saw teeth I had never seen before. Then he looked me up and down, 'Oh, you're lookin' . . . ' but didn't finish the observation.

'Oh yes,' Mum said, 'we have a guest, Faith.' Dad opened the front room door wide.

'You remember Noel, Faith?' he asked.

A young man stood up from the settee. He quickly wiped his hand across the top of his head, then, grinning, he held out his other hand for me to shake. His dark skin glistened around his forehead where he was beginning to sweat. He looked like a man uncomfortable in his dark blue single-breasted suit. He put his hand up to his shirt collar to release it a little, grimacing like a gargoyle for a second as he adjusted the tie's stranglehold on him. As I shook his hand he began to look familiar. It was Noel. Noel, my dad's workmate. I suddenly felt silly shaking his hand — I had known Noel for years.

'Noel,' I shouted, 'I didn't recognise you.' I giggled.

'He look different, don't he, Faith, when he's all clean up.' I went to nod but felt embarrassed talking about him like that to his face. But Noel did look different.

The Noel I knew was always covered in dust. When he moved dust would billow from him like a dirty old settee. His face was always caked in it

— his chestnut-brown complexion given the pallor of tan suede by it. His hair made grey by it, like an actor made-up to be an old man. Noel rarely came into the house but when he did he left dusty, size-ten footprints over the carpet and Mum would sweep them up with a dustpan and brush muttering, 'Noel! How the man get so dusty?'

Noel always wore overalls. They were white once but had become psychedelic from the paint that had splattered on them over the twelve years he had worked for my dad. They were baggy on the leg and a little too long so that when he walked he tended to trip up every few steps. Rather than take the overalls up, he had incorporated the trip into his walk and could do it without spilling or dropping anything.

He had started as an apprentice. A friend from church had offered Dad her son. Noel had come to this country from Jamaica at the age of nine. Until then he had been living with his grandmother in Spanish Town. By the time Noel came to the airport — a little boy in a man's suit — he didn't know his mum, he hadn't seen her for eight years. 'He's had a hard time,' his mum pleaded with Dad, 'but he's a good worker, Mr Jackson, a good worker.'

Dad had always thought that Carl might join his business. He had even made plans to have, 'and Son' added on the side of the van. But Carl showed no interest or aptitude. And when one day he put the tall ladder inside the van, instead of on top, ramming it in with a final push that jettisoned the top of the ladder through the windscreen, Dad finally gave up on his idea of founding a painting and decorating dynasty. Noel entered the profession with such enthusiasm that Dad said he liked to think of Noel as an honorary son.

I looked at this cleaned-up version of Noel and realised for the first time that he could only be a few years older than me. I had always thought of him as someone who came over on the banana boat like Mum and Dad — a middle-aged apprentice who still lived with his mum. But it was just the dust that aged him.

'Sit down now, Noel,' Dad said. And Noel sat down.

'Faith, you sit here,' Dad ordered.

'Do you remember this picture, Dad?' I said, showing him Carl's drawing. He looked at it. 'Not really,' then added, 'but show Noel, Faith.'

'What?' I said, looking over at Noel.

'Would you like to see the drawing, Noel?' Dad intoned, as if Noel had problem hearing. He then nodded his head until Noel nodded back. I handed Noel the picture and he studied it, tracing the line of the triangle slowly with a movement of his head.

'Faith did that when she was a little girl,' Dad grinned.

'No I didn't, it was Carl.'

'Oh,' Dad said grabbing the picture from Noel's hand and throwing it onto the table, 'I thought it was yours.' Mum and Dad stood side by side smiling at me and Noel.

'You remember Noel, Faith?' Mum repeated.

And I began to feel uncomfortable.

'Yes I do,' I said, getting up.

'Where are you going, Faith?' Dad asked.

'I'm just going to the kitchen.'

'Wait — I'll get it,' Dad said, going to the door. Mum came over to me and pushed me gently down onto the settee. She sat beside me and gave a little laugh. 'We'll stay and talk to Noel.'

Dad was frowning, 'What was it you say you want from the kitchen?' he asked me but I just said, 'Nothing.' So he sat down too.

'You know, Faith,' Dad began, 'Noel has made some plaster cornice by copying the original. The woman whose house it is say she can't tell the difference.'

'That's good,' I said.

'Faith works in television,' Mum said, leaning towards Noel.

'Oh,' Noel said, nodding his head.

'Noel, do you like to watch the television?' she asked.

'Oh yes, Mrs Jackson.'

'Now Noel,' Mum said, 'you call me Mildred.' Noel nodded.

'Cornice is very hard to copy. It's a skilled job,' Dad went on.

'Faith, tell Noel what things you have worked on. He may have seen them.'

'Well, I work on a lot of programmes,' I said.

'He's going to try a centre-rose next,' Dad was saying.

'Do you like *Doctor Who*, Noel?' Mum said. Noel nodded.

'Cornice can make some nice money. It's a

121

skill you see,' Dad continued.

'Faith, tell Noel about *Doctor Who*.' I stared at my mum.

Dad was still speaking, 'It not like that rubbish you get in the shops. People pay good money for a nice job. And Noel is very good.'

'Wait, Wade,' Mum said, 'Faith is just telling Noel about her job.' They all waited for me to speak.

'I just check in all the costumes.'

Mum sat nodding her head and Noel smiled.

Then she began again. 'Faith was telling me, Noel, that they have a coloured person on *Doctor Who*.'

Noel said, 'Oh.'

'It's not *Doctor Who*,' I corrected. 'It was *Blake's Seven*.'

'Well, tell Noel about this seven . . . what-you-call-it.'

'There's nothing to tell!'

Mum looked lost for words. She looked over to my dad who gladly said, 'I'm lucky to have someone as good as Noel on the cornicing, otherwise I would have to buy the rubbish from the shops. And it's not good.'

'That's great,' I said. 'Shall I make a cup of tea?' I was desperate.

'Oh, of course,' Mum said. 'Mind my manners. Mark you, when I lived in Jamaica you don't offer a drink until someone been in your house for a long time. You remember that, Noel?'

Noel smiled and nodded politely but did not look convinced. I stood up.

'No!' my parents shouted together. Then Mum

carried on, 'I'll make it. You stay and talk to Noel.' She walked to the door and as she opened it she turned around and said, 'Wade, could you come and give me a hand?'

Dad looked briefly shocked but then complied with a little laugh, 'I leave you to tell Faith about how you did the plaster-work, Noel.' He tapped Noel's shoulder and waved his hand at him as if to hurry him along. Noel smiled and nodded but didn't say anything.

He sat forward in his chair and ran his hand across his head again. Then he settled — his arms resting across his knees. He would have looked relaxed if it were not for his right leg which was twitching up and down very fast. I suddenly felt very sorry for him.

'So Noel,' I started. 'Do you like working with my dad?'

'Oh yes.'

'You've been with him for a long time.'

'Long time.'

'Do you enjoy decorating then?'

'Oh yes.'

'You must see a lot of my dad.'

'Oh yes.'

And then I gave up. 'I'll just go and see what's happened to that tea.'

Dad was sitting by the table staring into space when I went into the kitchen and Mum was putting away washing-up. They looked up startled. Dad then grabbed a cup and began waving it in the air as if he was doing something useful.

'What is going on?' I asked them.

'Nothing, nothing, nothing, nothing,' they said between them.

'I'm just bringing the tea now, Faith. Wade, pass me that cup. It's boiling now. You go back and talk to Noel. Don't leave him on his own. Wade, get me some more cups, nah.' Dad got up and looked around him, momentarily unable to locate cups in his kitchen. Mum pointed.

'Why is Noel here, Mum? Are you trying to . . . ' I couldn't bring myself to say it — it seemed too ridiculous. I could not say matchmake.

'No, no, no, nothing like that. You hear that, Wade, ehh. No, nothing like that, no no, no . . . ' Mum protested too much.

'But,' Dad added, 'Noel is a decent man.'

'Ahh, let me tell you something, Faith,' Mum began. 'You know Carl has a new girlfriend? Ruth her name.' She paused a little, saying, 'She nice enough.' Then she sniffed and began adjusting the waistband on her skirt. 'But every time she ring he just seem to jump up and run to her. I tell him slow down. Don't make her think you're too keen. Sometimes tell her, no, you can't come. But he doesn't listen to me. She has him right where she want him.' She pressed her thumb down on the kitchen top with alarming violence. 'Just like that,' she said doing it again. She looked up at me and sighed, 'But it would be good to see you two settled before . . . ' and stopped herself. 'Wade, take the cups in, nah.'

Dad pulled my arm as we returned to the front room and whispered, 'Did Noel tell you about his ceiling work?'

124

After an hour of sitting in the front room with my mum, my dad and Noel, after an hour of answering polite questions — 'Faith, tell Noel . . . Noel, tell Faith . . . Did you know Faith . . . ? Did you know Noel . . . ? — Carl walked in. He did not stay long. He opened the sitting room door, looked at me then at Noel. He shut the sitting room door and then began to laugh uncontrollably.

Noel left soon after that. He looked at his watch, bit his bottom lip five times, ran his hand across his hair and then stood up.

'You off now, Noel?' Dad asked and Noel nodded.

'Is that the time?' Mum said. 'Time just fly by when you chatting away.' Mum restrained me at the front door and made me watch Noel get into his pale blue Ford Escort. 'Wave, Faith, wave,' she ordered, before she let me go.

10

'It's Faith *Columbine* Jackson? Columbine, that's a strange name. Where does that come from?'

I didn't tell them that I was named after my mum's goat. They didn't look the sort of people who would understand. 'It's an old family name,' I said.

The two men in front of me were sitting behind a regulation desk made of brown teak with black metal legs. The desk had mounds of paper that formed an undulating hilly range between me and them. They had introduced themselves at the start of the interview, holding out their hands in turn for me to shake. One rather clammy gentle shake from Mr Reeve. The other firm and slightly painful from Mr Williams.

Mr Reeve was familiar to me. He was Lorraine's boss — 'Morning *les girls*' — and, I now realised, my boss too.

'He has responsibility for our bit, though he never bothers me, Miss,' Henry had told me before the interview. 'But be nice to him though.'

Mr Williams wore a grey suit that coordinated precisely with his grey hair. His glasses had split lenses and as he moved his eyes would get smaller or bigger depending on which bit he was looking through. He was a middle-manager and I had seen him before moving quickly down the corridor holding a bit of paper.

'Oldest trick in the book, Miss,' Henry told me. 'The bit of paper makes him look important. But he's just a spare prick at an orgy.'

'Where do your parents come from, Faith?' Mr Williams asked.

'The Caribbean.'

'But you,' he said turning over my application form. 'You were born here. And I see from this, you have a degree in fashion and textiles.' He looked up at me. 'Well done,' he said and Mr Reeve nodded too.

'So Faith, down to business. Why do you want to be a dresser?'

I was not as prepared for that particular question as I had thought. I considered the options. 'Tell them you want to better yourself,' Henry had told me to say. Or, I want more money, I want to meet famous people, I want a challenge. Or there was always Carl's idea, 'Tell them the truth, Faith. That you're just doing it to piss them off.'

'I want to work more directly in the making of television programmes,' I said.

One of Mr Williams's eyebrows rose above the rim of his glasses. 'You do realise what the job would involve? I mean, you won't be producing programmes just yet.' Both men chuckled at the little joke.

'Have you had any experience of dressing?' *Les girls* asked.

'No, but I'm sure I will be able to pick it up.'

'It's not quite as simple as it may seem,' he carried on.

'Even so, I'm very confident that I could do it.'

127

'But you've had no actual experience.'

Only twenty years of it. Every day. Sometimes twice a day since the age of three. Shoelaces took a little bit longer. But my speciality are knickers and vests.

'No. But I do think I could do it.'

'Can you tell me what you think you would have to do?' *Les girls* then sat back in his chair and folded his hands across his lap.

'Mainly to make sure the actors have the right clothes for the scene and that everything is present and correct. And then to help them into the clothes and make any adjustments that might be necessary.'

'That's the simple version,' *les girls* responded. 'It is, unfortunately, a little more complicated than that.' He did not elaborate but sat looking at one of his fingernails.

Mr Williams then spoke, 'Perhaps you could tell Miss Jackson what the other duties are.'

'Of course,' *les girls* said, sitting forward again. 'Firstly you would have to make sure that all the costumes are ready for each scene. This involves you working with the designer or the designer's assistant — if there is one on that production — so you know what is needed for what or which scene. Secondly, you would have to make sure that all the costumes are in good condition. This could involve you in some sewing or ironing or other duties of that sort of character. And thirdly and lastly you must then dress the actor or actress or indeed performer. This obviously means communicating with them.' He nodded and sat back.

128

'So are you clear about that, Miss Jackson?' Mr Williams asked. And I said, 'Much clearer now, thank you.'

'You're sure you know what you will be letting yourself in for,' he added, as *les girls* muttered, 'A little more to it than you thought, eh Faith?'

Mr Williams studied my application form again then, frowning, said, 'Forgive me, Miss Jackson, but don't you feel that you may be a little overqualified for the job of dresser?'

'I see it as a progression,' I began. 'Sort of getting to know all about costume in TV.'

'So,' he said shifting his weight onto his elbow. 'So you wouldn't see this as a long-term commitment to dressing?' He sat back with a slight smirk on his lips. His expression looked as if he'd cornered me, as if this was not an interview but some sort of sport. He looked as if he might say, 'Aha gotcha!'

'Basically, I'm very interested in gaining experience in all aspects of costume design and television production,' I replied with a smile.

They both began to write on the sheets of paper in front of them with *les girls* surreptitiously looking over at Mr Williams's paper like he was in a school exam.

'If I can just go on to the report we have for you from your present employment as a wardrobe assistant,' Mr Williams said. *Les girls* started to cough into his hand and look out of the window. I sat up in my seat. 'The report is on the whole very good. It says you are a good worker and have excellent timekeeping — well done. That you have picked up the job very well.

And blah, blah, blah. But it also says here,' he went on, 'that you are rather slow.'

I jumped. I know I jumped because I banged my elbow down hard on the arm of the chair and it caught my funny bone and the pain was stinging through me as I said, 'Slow?'

'Yes, slow. When you walk.'

'I'm sorry?'

'Well, over to you, Lionel,' Mr Williams said to *les girls*. 'It's been Mr Reeve's job,' he went on, 'to observe your performance over the months you have been here.'

'Well, not just mine,' *les girls* corrected. 'Your colleagues, Henry et al, have given me some feedback as to your progress.' He began to go red which sent the acne scars on his face into relief. He avoided my eyes, looking at the desk, my application form, at Mr Williams, at his fingernail. He began repositioning a small metal calendar; making it straight along the edge of some paper that was lying on the desk. 'And it was felt that you tended to walk rather slowly.'

My mouth opened. I had intended to say something but nothing came out. *Les girls* stayed looking at the calendar which was now nice and straight. 'It has been commented on and I must say observed that you walk very slowly.'

'When do I walk slowly?' I finally asked.

'Well, if, for example, you're asked to get something or to look at a costume, you walk slowly over to it.'

'I don't think I do,' I said, looking at Mr Williams who was watching the exchange.

'Do you feel, Miss Jackson, that you don't

130

walk slowly?' he asked.

'Yes, I don't.'

'Could it be, Miss Jackson, that you don't *realise* you walk slowly.' They both nodded.

'I didn't know I had to walk fast.'

'So you do admit that you walk slowly.'

'No. But I can walk faster if you want,' I said trying to stay tactful. 'How fast would you like me to walk?'

Les girls shifted on his seat and said, 'It's not so much the speed as the attitude to the job.'

'But I thought the report on my work was good.'

'It is, on the whole. It's just that there is the problem of your walking pace.'

'But if someone had said that I should have walked faster, then I would have started to walk faster.' Then I stopped and sat back on the chair. I went to fold my arms but checked myself and made an embarrassingly elaborate arm movement instead — all elbows and wrists. 'But it's ridiculous. I don't walk slowly.'

'Well, let's move on. One of the other things it says in the report,' Mr Williams started, 'is that you have a tendency to be argumentative.'

'No, I don't,' I snapped, before I realised what I had said. Both men looked at me with 'see I told you so' expressions. I took a breath. 'Could you elaborate on that, please?'

Les girls's head gave a little swagger of the righteous. 'Well, you have been observed arguing with your work colleagues. Sometimes quite vociferously.' I had to think. Did he mean my 'arguments' with Henry? Arguments like whether

131

children's drawings could be as powerful as a Picasso, with Henry saying 'No they can't,' and me saying, 'Yes they can.' Or whether last summer was hotter than this. No it wasn't. Yes it was. Or if a Big Mac was nicer than a quarter-pounder with cheese?

Mr Williams was speaking. 'It would be important to be able to get along with people as a dresser. You have to work very closely with actors who can sometimes be quite temperamental.'

'I think I can get on with people very well. If the arguments you are talking about are the ones with Henry . . . ' I tried to explain. But *les girls* cut me off saying, 'You need to be outgoing and friendly.'

I sat forward. 'May I ask a question, please?' I said. They both looked puzzled — questions from the candidate always came at the end of the interview. But they waited politely for me to start.

My lips began to quiver as if I was about to cry. I was scared they would see that. And I was frightened that my voice would come out as a tremulous whisper as I said, 'Someone told me that you don't like to have black people dressing. Is that right? Because you have no other black people in the department . . . '

'Let me stop you there, Miss Jackson,' Mr Williams said, with his hand outstretched like the traffic police. 'It is really not a question of that.' He shifted on his seat. *Les girls* leant forward to me, 'Who told you that?' But Mr

132

Williams started again, 'There is no discrimination going on in this department. I think you may be getting a little sensitive because of all the things that have been said and I can understand that.' He tried to smile.

'But who told you we don't like coloured people here?' *les girls* said again. Mr Williams carried on, 'We don't have coloured people in this department because, up until you, we have not had a suitable candidate. But if a suitable candidate were to apply, they would be treated the same way as everyone else. As indeed you were, Miss Jackson. There is absolutely no question of racial or any other prejudice going on here. And I think Mr Reeve would agree with me on that.' But *les girls* was too busy looking at me. 'Can I ask you again where you heard this rumour from, Faith?'

This time there was a silence. 'I just heard it,' I said looking between them. 'And I can see there are no . . . '

'Well, let me put your mind at rest once more, Miss Jackson,' Mr Williams started again. 'Every applicant in this department is judged on merit and merit alone. I can't think who could have said a thing like that, but let me put your mind at rest that nothing of that nature has gone on or will go on in this department while I am here. I must assume that you did hear this . . . '

'Even though you won't tell us who said it,' *les girls* added.

'I must assume you did hear it. But let me tell you again that nothing, nothing like that goes on in this department . . . ' He was rambling,

133

repeating his assertions as the stuffy, soporific room began to crackle with the accusation and denial. And *les girls* kept muttering, 'Now if you told us who said it we could . . . '

★ ★ ★

'You didn't!' Henry kept saying. 'You didn't say that! You didn't! Oh my God!' He put his hand over his mouth. 'Well, I bet the shit really hit the fan.' And he laughed. 'Then what happened?'

'They asked me a few more things about getting bloodstains out of clothes and how to iron grosgrain.'

'Oh, they always ask those — that's nothing new. And then?'

'And then it was over,' I said.

'And are you our new dresser, Miss?'

'I don't know, they'll write to me they said.'

And he laughed. Henry found my interview funny. He found it very, very funny.

11

Simon was whittling a carrot with a bread knife. He was sitting at the kitchen table in his apron — a gift from his mother, wipe clean and illustrated with British birds — and he was sculpting the carrot so that it would fit into an old electric fire with the carrot replacing one of the orange bars. He looked up when I walked in and nicked his finger with the knife. He swore, stuck his finger in his mouth and asked me how my interview went. I just shrugged. I was more interested in why he was whittling the carrot and spraying the kitchen with little orange shavings. He was about to explain when Marion could be heard screaming, 'Just do it, Mick!'

She then thudded down the stairs and erupted into the kitchen. She was red-faced and puffing and ran to the garden door ignoring Simon and me. She yanked at the door but it was locked. 'Where's the fucking key?' she shouted at no one.

'In the lock,' Simon told her quietly. He shrugged as we both watched Marion fumble with the key and pull at the door. Suddenly Mick was flying across the kitchen and pushing the door shut. Marion opened it again. Mick slammed it closed. Marion wrenched it open. Mick stood in the doorway holding onto the door. This created a gust of wind that sent the carrot droppings fluttering like confetti round the room.

'Just bring them in from the garden,' Marion screamed into Mick's face. 'What is the bloody problem?'

'They're all right — no one can see them,' Mick shouted.

'I'm not losing my job because of you — you bastard,' Marion yelled.

'What are you talking about? You are being so fucking stupid.'

Marion turned to me and Simon, 'Can you hear it?' We both looked at her as she went on, 'The helicopter — can you hear it? There is a police helicopter flying over our house . . . ' And Mick butted in with, 'She thinks they're looking down at my pot plants. Can you believe it . . . ? She thinks that's why they're flying about.'

I laughed at that. Even from a very close distance Mick's marijuana plants looked so straggly and weedy in their five little pots that it was hard to tell if they were plants at all — in fact it was hard to tell if they were a life form. Simon said, 'I can't hear anything,' and started whittling again while Mick let go of the garden door and pleaded with me, 'Tell her, Faith. Tell her she's being bloody stupid.'

But Marion quickly nipped through the garden door and threw one of the plants into the kitchen. It landed with a crash — the pot shattering into pieces, spilling the earth out over the floor and leaving the harmless green leafless twig in the centre of the mess.

'For fuck's sake,' Mick snapped. He pulled

136

Marion into the room by her jumper sleeve. But Marion struggled from his grip and got outside again. I could hear the dull intrusive drone of the helicopter as it circled. It was now probably watching Marion and Mick tussling in the garden. I said, 'Oh, stop it, you two,' like I always said when Marion and Mick were having one of their spats. And Simon said a sudden, '*Voilà!*' and held up the electric fire to show me the carrot fitting neatly across the bar. Marion was kicking out at the four remaining pot plants as Mick was dragging her backwards into the kitchen. He locked the door, put the key in his pocket and he and Marion stood looking at each other — panting.

'All you had to do was bring them in, didn't he, Faith? Tell him,' Marion said.

'They cannot see them,' Mick intoned. 'They are not interested in them. They would not waste their money on a helicopter to look at them. Will somebody tell her.' And Simon said, 'Actually I can hear a helicopter now,' and I mimed at him to shut up.

Mick bent down to pick up the remains of his plant, 'Are you premenstrual or something?' he asked. Marion then took the longest loudest deepest breath and shouted, 'Old sperm!' into Mick's face.

'Will you shut up about old sperm,' Mick huffed and Marion started taunting, 'Old sperm, old sperm, old sperm, old sperm . . . ' She ran out of the room giggling with Mick following behind shouting, 'I have not got old sperm.'

For a moment it was quiet and Simon asked,

'Old sperm? What's she going on about?' I told him about the article Marion had read in a magazine which warned of the health risks sperm could present to men as they got older. Mick had taken great offence as Marion suggested that that was Mick's problem and that he should have his sperm checked for signs of ageing. And Simon was just asking, 'Why? . . . Why? . . . What does old sperm do?' when Marion came thudding down the stairs again. She ran into the kitchen and started jumping on the poor plant which had been left lying in the debris on the floor. She was crying. 'Bastard.'

Simon sighed, 'I'm going to my parents this weekend, do you want to come, Faith?'

'Bastard, bastard, bastard!' Marion ran out of the kitchen again and slammed the door.

'It's in the country,' Simon went on. 'It's quiet. There's loads of room. My parents are going away. I fancy some peace and quiet.' The house shook as Mick banged up the stairs yelling, 'Stupid cow,' and Marion shouted, 'And you're a wanker!'

'Do you want to come, Faith?' Simon asked quietly.

Marion came back into the kitchen. 'I hate him. I hate him!' She was crying and sniffing and wiping the back of her hand across her face. 'I hate him, Faith — he's a bastard . . . he's a pig . . . he's a . . . I hate him, Faith, he's a . . . '

And I looked at Simon and said, 'Yeah, I'll come.'

12

The village in which Simon's parents lived was, he explained, 'Quintessentially English.'

'What does that mean?' I asked. He thought I meant the words not the meaning and went into a long explanation about it being a typical form . . . a manifestation . . . the embodiment of the quality . . . and ended by saying, 'Oh, you'll soon see.'

It was off the main road, past a row of cypress trees, down a long lane that meandered along the edge of fields, past a pub and over a small stone bridge. As we drove along Simon pointed things out to me. Over there was the tree he fell out of and broke his collarbone. Over there was where he played Pooh sticks with his friends. There was his riding school and the river he learnt to row on. And, 'you see that barn — that's where I had my first sexual experience'.

'Hoot as we round this bend,' he told me. 'It's very dangerous and few people do.' I hooted and there it was. Simon sighed. 'Every time I come back it looks more beautiful.'

The village reminded me of a model village that used to be in our park in London. Carl and me used to go there with Mum, lean over the railing and point out the shop and the church and the village green. And when Mum wasn't there we would climb over and walk among the little thatched houses, feeling like giants. Careful not to step on the village pub or cattle trough. Eventually the little model village had got vandalised. Kids from around came and threw stones at it and stole the little buildings. And someone knocked off the church steeple and trampled the nave into little pieces which were then used to smash some nearby windows. I always thought that model village was a reconstruction of how England used to be — like the caveman dwellings or Viking settlements we learnt about at school. But there it was again, around that bend. The village green with perfect lush grass sitting in dappled light, little thatched houses with windows and doors that looked too small, the pub, the post office, and the steepled church surrounded by yew trees and teetering grey gravestones.

'It doesn't look real,' I said.

'I know. Now you see what I mean?'

It also looked deserted to me. 'Where is everyone?'

Simon pointed out two people talking in front of a post-box, someone on a bicycle with a dog running alongside and several bobbing heads through a window under a sign that read Lillian's Tea Shop. And the people, I was surprised to see, were smaller than the houses.

'My parents live just outside the village.' He directed me down more lanes where the trees joined branches across the road.

'Dingly dell!' I shouted. On our trips in the van Carl and me always shouted, 'Dingly dell!' when we passed under the canopy of trees into the dark light.

'Sorry?' Simon asked.

'Dingly dell — the trees going over like that. It's all dark and my brother and me call it . . . we call it . . . ' and Simon frowned as I said, 'dingly dell.'

The house was at the bottom of a drive. I said, 'Wow!' involuntarily when I saw it. 'Isn't it beautiful!' Simon said. He was pleased with my reaction.

It was made of brick with doors and windows and a roof like most houses. But it was big — a mansion to anyone from a terraced house. And perfectly symmetrical. Like the architect had only designed one side then blotted the other half on to the plans. There were pillars on either side of the door and a large long stained-glass window above it. There were no buildings to the left of it or to the right. Only trees, flowering bushes and variegated shrubs that seemed to cradle the house like a cupped hand. 'Were you brought up here?' I asked. But Simon was too busy to hear me.

'There was a tree there — where's it gone? And the bench has moved. Oh look, the shed! I said not to put it there. I said you'd be able to see it from the drive. It looks so small now. I used to think it was huge when I was little. I used to bicycle up and down here and I thought it was a real adventure — it was such a long way. It's funny, isn't it? It just seems like an ordinary house now.' Then he shouted, 'Shit!'

'What?'

He pointed over to the right. Down a little drive, in front of another building that looked

141

too big to be a garage but obviously was, were two cars. A sleek black BMW and a little white nondescript thing. He looked at me and his face was a deep bright red.

'My parents are still here,' he said, getting out of the car. As his feet hit the gravel path, a dog rushed out from the front door of the house. It had a long white shaggy coat and looked like a chiffon blur as it ran. It jumped up at Simon, whimpering and licking his hand. It rolled on the floor in front of him and jumped up again, dribbling strands of saliva from its mouth, as Simon said, 'Hello, Milly. Hello, girl. How's my little Milly,' in a baby voice. Then a woman came out of the house with her arms outstretched.

'Darling, I thought it was you. Now don't be mad with us but we couldn't go. And I tried to telephone you but we couldn't get an answer.'

She had grey hair waved into a neat style, reminiscent of WRAFs in Second World War films. And she was dressed in flowers — a floral patterned blouse with a different patterned floral skirt and a beige cardigan resting over her shoulders. She looked like Simon — the same slim frame and the same green eyes. Her face looked used to carrying an easy smile but she didn't have stubble.

'Darling.' She was in her early sixties. 'Darling, don't be cross with us. We haven't ruined your weekend. Have we ruined your weekend?' She put her arms round Simon very gently and kissed him on both cheeks. Then stood back and adjusted the cardigan on her shoulders.

'Milly, down Milly. She's so pleased to see

you, aren't you, Milly, little girl? You're pleased to see your Simon. You miss your Simon, don't you?' Then she added, 'It's your father.'

'What's happened?' Simon said looking to the house.

'Don't get worried.' She looked at his hair and began to push it away from his eyes. Simon backed away a little. 'It's getting long,' she said. 'And is that a grey hair I see on my youngest son's head?'

'Ma, what's happened to Father?'

'He got tired from gardening,' she said, in a manner like she had said it all before. 'And I told him . . . ' she carried on. Simon sighed.

'I know. I told him, 'Don't overdo it before a journey'.'

'So what happened?' Simon was irritated.

'Well, he got exhausted and couldn't face going away. I know . . . but . . . anyway . . . ' She began looking around and in the window of the car. 'Did your friend come with you, Simon? I'm dying to see who my son lives with.'

And suddenly I became mouth-dryingly apprehensive. Scared. Scared his mother would look at my face, gasp for air whilst grabbing her pearl necklace, then hit the gravel in a faint, like a giant discarded bouquet. I opened the door and stood up.

His mother opened out her arms and looked to Simon for an introduction. 'This is Faith, Ma,' he said.

'Faith,' she said, walking around to me. 'I am really pleased to meet you. I wish I could say I had heard all about you and your other flatmates, but my son, I'm afraid, takes after his father and does not go in for gossip.' She kissed me on the cheek and the dog began to lick my hand.

'I love it, don't you, Faith?' his mother asked me. And I must have looked confused. 'Gossip. Do you like gossip, Faith?' I nodded.

'Good, because we can gossip and the men can do whatever it is that men do.'

Simon asked, 'So you're here all weekend, are you?' But his mother carried on talking to me. 'I have actually got no idea what it is that men do, have you, Faith?' And she began to laugh.

'Ma, will you be here all weekend?'

'Oh darling, don't say it like that.' She slipped her arm through mine. 'You'd think he didn't like us.' She patted my hand. 'But I'm sorry we've spoilt your weekend.' Then she slipped her other arm through Simon's. 'Couldn't you just pretend we weren't here?'

Suddenly loud booming music came shattering through a window. I was ready to run. Birds took flight from the trees. And Simon looked at his mother who said calmly, 'Shall we go and say hello to Pa?'

As we walked into the house Simon mouthed, 'Sorry,' at me behind his mother's back. I shrugged.

'Pa, do you have to play that thing so loud?' Simon's mother shouted. Simon's father was sitting in a chair with his eyes shut and his feet up on a footstool. 'Got to play Shostakovich loud, Old Thing, otherwise there's no point.'

He opened his eyes and saw me. He looked

like he'd stepped out of the plains of Africa after a hunting trip. A white man who would have tales to tell of his time in Kenya. He was even wearing a safari jacket and had large whiskers on his cheeks. His head, however, was almost completely bald and burned a painful shiny bright red on top. But as he stood up unsteadily out of his chair I noticed that he was also old and frail. He stood up like a man who had once expected to stand six foot high but was now only just taller than me.

'This is Simon's friend, Pa, Faith. She lives in the house in London.'

'How do you do, Faith.' He shook my hand. 'Is Simon here?' he asked as Simon stepped forward.

'Simon, good to see you.' Then father and son shook hands.

'Sorry we're still here,' Simon's father said, as he slapped his son a few times on the back. He looked between Simon and me. 'I expect we'll spoil it for you. We always do. Can't do a thing right when you get to my age.' He hit Simon's back again then began to cough.

'Sit down, Father,' Simon said, helping him back into the chair.

'Good to see you, Faith. Nice to have some young people about the place. What's happened to the music?'

'It's on, Father.'

'I can't bloody hear it.' He leant round Simon, 'Ma, turn it up again. I can't bloody hear it.'

'Let me sort out our guests first, Pa,' Simon's mother said. 'Now we've put you both in our old

145

room. Is that right?'

'No, Ma,' Simon said quickly. 'Faith and I are not . . . ' He ran his hand through his hair, embarrassed.

'Oh God!' his mother said. 'Did you hear that, Pa? They don't sleep in the same room. We thought we were being so modern.' Simon smiled another sorry at me as his mother said, 'Oh well, you in your old room, darling, and Faith can have Sarah's room.' And his father complained, 'Have you turned the music up yet, Ma? I can't hear a bloody thing.'

There were a lot of rooms in Simon's parents' house. Lots of tall rooms with several windows that looked out over the garden and the fields beyond. There was a morning room, a drawing room, a dining room, a music room, a family room, a study. There were several bedrooms and an awful lot of bathrooms. Simon showed me the interesting architectural details in each one. The stained-glass windows, the architraves, the inglenook fireplace.

He pointed out portraits of his relations. 'This is my great-grandfather who designed the house, that's on my mother's side . . . The paintings there, there and there are of my father's parents' parents and their grandparents and interestingly enough they were painted by my great-great — I lose count to be honest — but an old uncle anyway who became quite famous — we sometimes have to lend the pictures out for exhibitions. These model ships in the cases were made by my maternal grandfather and the model train engine at the back was made by his father.

It's a replica of the first engine on the Carlisle to Settle railway.'

The house was also furnished with antiques. Old furniture passed down from generation to generation. Everything seemed to have been someone else's once. And most things, Simon would tell me, were 'priceless'.

Simon showed me into my bedroom. It was a pretty pink room with three rag dolls on the bed and miniature painted portraits in gilded frames on a wall. 'My mother painted those. She's very good. They're on ivorine. They used to use ivory for these sort of portraits but you can't nowadays.' He looked carefully at each painting. 'There's me as a little boy, my brother Giles, and Peter and the little one is Sarah. That's my grandfather and grandmother. And those two Victorians are my great-grandparents on my mother's side.'

He also pointed out the other things his mother had made. She did needlepoint. 'That cushion over there and that wall plaque, Ma did those.' She quilted bedspreads. 'They're wonderfully warm.' She threw pots. She made her own jam, chutney and wine. She arranged flowers for the local church and was at that moment hunting for sloes for her famous Christmas recipe sloe gin. 'And oh yes,' Simon added, 'did I tell you she was a magistrate? Chair of the bench.'

Simon's bedroom still had the musty sweaty smell of adolescent boys. 'It's a bit like a museum in here. Ma wants to decorate but, I don't know, I'm just not ready to . . . ' his voice trailed away as I looked at the family tree which was carefully plotted along one wall — calligraphed in paint.

'Is this your family?'

'No,' Simon laughed. 'It's our royal family. It took me ages to do it. I had to ask permission from Pa to draw on the wall. He used to be very strict. He used to pull fuses out when my friends came round if they made too much noise. Plunge us all into darkness. He's mellowed since he's retired,' he added wistfully. 'It goes back to Ethelred the Unready.' I looked at the last entries. 'You haven't got Lady Diana Spencer,' I said. Simon looked momentarily concerned but then laughed, 'And I couldn't give a fuck.'

We had tea in the dining room. The table was laid with a blue and white teaset — the pattern of which appeared to depict a country scene by a river with a kneeling woman about to be attacked by a madman. And there were warm scones with home-made damson jam and cream. The tinkle of the cups on their saucers reminded me of the teas I made for my dolls in my bedroom. My little set was pink but whenever I played with it I somehow imagined myself in a situation just like this.

Simon's mother apologised for there not being any clotted cream. 'They ran out at the village shop.' And Simon's father mumbled, 'Not the same with this awful whipped stuff — air most of it.' Then he fell asleep, almost mid-mouthful. His chin slid onto his chest and he began to make a low growling noise. His hands, which were spreading a scone at the time, slowly landed on the plate in front of him — his index finger rested, dipping obscenely into some jam. No one else seemed to notice and carried on eating — even the dog continued to look up at him expectantly. And Simon's mother leant over to me and said, 'Now the one thing Simon did tell me about you is that you work in television. How fascinating that must be.'

After tea Simon's mother asked, 'Simon, darling, why don't you take Faith for a walk?' I was comfortable on the sofa — warm and full of baking. I was tired out from tea where I had sat for some minutes with the teapot poised above Simon's mother's cup, wondering how to get her attention. I felt self-conscious calling her Mrs Wyndham among the Ma's, Pa's, darlings and Old Things that were being said round the table. Luckily several 'umm-err, umm-errs' later she told me to call her Margaret. Simon was reading the paper and Pa was sitting in his armchair with his legs on a footstool, head back, snoring evenly. The dog was leaning against my leg, resting its chin on my knee, asleep. And I was just wondering whether it would be impolite to shut my eyes too.

'Would you like to go for a walk, Faith?' Simon's mother asked.

'Where to?' I said.

She laughed. 'That's what Pa always says, where to. He doesn't like walking. Never has. Simon, are you taking Faith for a walk?'

'I could show you the countryside, I suppose, if you want,' Simon said vaguely. 'It's quite pretty.'

'You don't mind if I come, do you? You don't mind an old woman playing gooseberry, Faith?'

'Ma!' Simon snapped, 'I told you . . . '

'Oh sorry,' his mother said, grinning at me. 'Well, in that case you won't mind me coming.'

I got my coat and stood by the door waiting for them. They both emerged together from a side room. They were dressed in identical dark green coats. Simon's mother was wearing a floral headscarf which was tied in a knot under her chin and Simon was wearing an old flat cap that matched his coat. And on their feet they both wore huge brown lace-up boots with thick socks and trousers that tucked neatly into the socks' woollen folds.

'Oh dear, Faith, have you not brought any walking boots?'

'We weren't planning on walking,' Simon answered for me.

'Well, let's find you some wellingtons at least. It's very muddy out.' Simon's mother showed me into the little room. Along one wall was a line of wellingtons that reminded me of the cloakroom in my junior school on wet days. They were different colours and sizes and above them was an array of coats — green ones, brown ones and even one in yellow PVC. And resting over them an assortment of hats and scarves.

'Simon, help Faith, darling. I'll get the dog and say goodbye to Pa.'

I looked at Simon's hat and laughed and he took it off and put it in his pocket. By the time Simon's mother came back I was properly dressed. I had wanted to wear the yellow PVC coat but Simon told me I would frighten away the birds. He selected a brown anorak instead. No wellingtons fitted me so I chose the pair only one size too big. Simon squashed a blue woolly pom-pom hat onto my head then stood back and laughed. 'You'll do,' he said.

I started out very well, striding alongside Simon and his mother. They walked very fast and with purpose as if we were actually going somewhere. They took me through fields that went up, down and around. And I joined in with Simon's mother's conversation — yes, the country was so much nicer than the filthy city — the air was cleaner, the people friendlier — no, the city was certainly no place to bring up children — while Simon kept saying, 'That's ridiculous — what rubbish! Oh honestly, Ma.'

I threw a stick for the dog who fetched it back barking and panting for me to throw it again. And every so often Simon's mother held up her binoculars and whispered, 'Faith, quick, in the trees, can you see it?' And I would look up to where she was pointing and say, 'Oh yes,' at nothing at all. She picked wild flowers, collecting a bunch and telling me their names as she did. She stuck a flower in my pom-pom hat and turned me round to Simon and said, 'Doesn't she look exotic?'

And as people passed us in a meadow, at a stile, down by the river, or over a little bridge, they smiled and said hello and good afternoon.

'It's a sort of tradition when you're on a walk,' Simon explained. 'When you meet someone you greet them.'

'It's just to show you're friend not foe,' Simon's mother added. So I said hello and smiled and nodded at everyone who passed us by. And I thought of Carl and our trips in his van searching for the countryside. I wanted so much for him to be here with me. So I could show him that at last I had finally found the countryside and that the land was indeed green and pleasant.

We had been walking for about half an hour when I began to get tired.

'Are we nearly there yet, Simon?' I whispered. He smiled and put his hand on my shoulder as his mother said, 'Oh look. Faith, up there. It's a jay, I think. Simon, did you see it? Look, the blue feathers on the wings as it flies.' She handed me the binoculars. And again I scanned the sky and treetops and saw nothing.

'It was beautiful,' I said.

We started to go uphill. Simon and his mother managed to stride on like they were still on the flat; lifting their legs as if no extra effort were required. And they began talking about Simon's career.

'I'm not really interested enough in the law.'

'But Simon, darling, can you make a living from singing?'

'I don't know. But I enjoy it.'

'What about the bar? That's more interesting. Let me call Andrew for you. I'm sure he could fix you up with something.'

'I'm not ready yet, Ma.'

'Well, you know you just have to say, darling, don't you? He's known Pa for years . . . '

Then I began to lose their conversation as the

gap between them and me widened. I was lagging behind but only the dog noticed. She started to run between us. Standing in front of me, rounding up her flock like a sheepdog. Simon and his mother were quite a way in the distance before they realised I was not with them. Simon waved, 'Are you all right?' And his mother called, 'It's very muddy, you must be careful, Faith.'

I was breathing too heavily to call back but I managed to wave away their concern. But my feet were sinking. With every step the mud seemed to reach further up my wellington boots. I was making very slow progress. The dog had given up on me and decided to stay with the fittest. And Simon and his mother talked as they waited.

Then I put my left foot down into the mud and as I lifted it out again the earth held my wellington and my foot came out of the boot. It was too late for me to save my poor flimsy socked foot and it splattered down into the oozing earth making the sound of a wet fart as it went. I was then a little stuck. I had two feet in mud and one was not in a wellington. The wellington was stuck behind me, sticking out of the mire. I could hear Simon and his mother's conversation coming on the breeze — 'Cabaret, darling? You can't be serious!' — as I made my manoeuvre to grab behind me for the boot. I pulled at it, lost my balance a little but luckily saved myself by landing on my hand. My cold soggy foot came out of the mud with a loud sucking sound. I lifted it and placed it back in the empty boot. And the mud squelched up from the inside and oozed over the rim of the wellington.

Simon and his mother were looking up into the sky pointing at a hovering bird when two people passed me. It was a woman and a man kitted out with rucksacks and sturdy boots with maps in plastic bags round their necks. I smiled at them and said hello. They looked at me but did not respond. I felt like I had one ordinary leg and one made of concrete. I had to consciously stop myself from walking in circles. Then I had to negotiate a stile while Simon and his mother looked on.

'Do you want some help, Faith?' Simon called.

And I thought, Oh God, please dear Lord, and shouted, 'No. I'm fine.'

My cement foot did not want to clear the top of the stile. It merely whacked against the wood each time I lifted it. In the end I had to grab the wellington boot with my muddy hand to lift it those extra inches. Then a man approached me near the stile and he didn't say hello either. He stared at me instead, turning round to look long after he had passed. In London the tradition would have been to ask him what the fuck he was staring at. But I wasn't in London.

'There you are,' Simon's mother said when I finally caught up with them. I was trying not to pant.

'I've suggested we go to the pub,' Simon told me with a wink. 'It's just down there.' He pointed at a nearby smoking chimney pot.

There was a notice outside the pub. 'Please

remove muddy boots before entering.' 'Bloody hell,' Simon laughed when he saw my foot which was so caked in mud that it looked like I still had a boot on.

'Would you like to take your socks off as well, Faith?' Simon's mother asked. I said no. I already felt absurd walking in a pub without my shoes.

As I opened the door and stood in the doorway my eyes caught the eyes of a man sitting at the bar. He had on a tweed jacket and he watched me with an expressionless face as I moved into the pub. I felt other eyes looking at me but I could not see them. And I thought the place hushed. I looked down and tried to hide my muddy foot behind the clean one.

Then Simon was behind me, rubbing his hands together vigorously. 'Right, what can I get you? The bitter here is wonderful.' He spoke very loudly — the whole pub could hear him. As his mother came in a man called, 'Margaret.' She smiled and went to him, shaking hands and nodding to a couple on her way.

'Right, let's find a seat,' Simon said, looking around. The pub room was just a little bigger than an ordinary living room and it had a low ceiling. Simon's head seemed to touch it and he had to stoop to avoid the beams and horse brasses. There were no vacant tables but he saw spaces.

'Do you mind if we just perch on the edge here?' he asked the people who were already at the table. It was two women and a man. One of the women inspected me as Simon ushered me into the seat. 'Go round there, Faith, I'll get another chair for Ma.' The woman began to move along the bench seat when I got close to her.

Simon rubbed his hands again. He still hadn't moderated his voice to the little room and almost shouted, 'Bitter? Half, or can you manage a pint? Or shandy if you want. The cider is good actually, Faith. Or would you like wine?'

And I said, 'Half a shandy, please.'

And he said, 'Sorry?' cupping his hand to his ear. Everyone was staring at me now — they had perfect reason to.

'Shandy — a half,' I said a little louder. Simon put his thumb up and said, 'It's a great place, isn't it?' as he went to the bar.

I avoided eye contact with anyone and feigned interest in the wall of photographs that was behind me. But out of the corner of my eye I could see the woman still looking me up and down. I could hear Simon's mother laughing. The old photographs on the wall all seemed to be of the pub. All taken at different points in the pub's history. Most of them were in black and white — with farmers, women in long dresses and men in uniforms with bicycles and pints of beer in their hands.

'It's a terribly old pub. It goes back to Tudor times, I think,' Simon told me as he put my drink in front of me. 'The photos are fantastic, aren't they?' He stayed standing, pointing at the pictures over my head and telling me, 'This was the pub during the Second World War — this was the First World War and this one goes back even

156

further. You can see the old costumes. And all the men have got moustaches in this one.'

He beckoned me to stand up. 'Oh Faith, look at this farmer, he's incredible. Look at him, look what they used to wear.' I didn't move. 'Faith, stand up, you can see it better. Just look at him. He looks a bit like Mick. Oh God, Faith, look at this. It's fascinating — the place is absolutely steeped in history. That's what's so great about these old English pubs.' But I didn't dare to move. His mother came to our table with the man she had greeted.

'Now isn't this a coincidence? I was just telling Simon about you, Andrew, and here you are. You remember my youngest son Simon?' she asked. Simon shook the man's hand.

'He's the old friend of Pa's I was telling you about. Andrew's a barrister. Andrew Bunyan. He owns the old cottage.'

'Oh yes, hello sir. Are you here for long?' Simon said, standing straight and formal.

'I like to try and come up as often as I can at weekends. It's not always possible to get away though. And who is this?' the man said, grinning at me.

'Faith,' Simon and his mother said in unison. Everyone sat down around me.

'And whereabouts are you from, Faith?'

'London,' I said.

The man laughed a little. 'I meant more what country are you from?' I didn't bother to say I was born in England, that I was English, because I knew that was not what he wanted to hear.

'My parents are from Jamaica.'

157

'Well, you see, I thought that,' he began. 'As soon as you walked in I thought I bet she's from Jamaica.'

'Just my parents are,' I added but he went on.

'I've just come back from there myself. Have you ever been there, Margaret? It's a wonderful place. Isn't it, Faith? Absolutely glorious. We were there for three weeks, got a real feel for it. Lovely place, lovely people — despite what you hear. We had a wonderful time.'

I smiled. Simon was about to speak when the man carried on.

'I must tell you this story . . . Faith, isn't it? This will make you laugh, Margaret. Very funny story this.' He adjusted himself on his seat and began. 'My last name is Bunyan. Not a common name you'll agree — especially when it's spelt with an A. But there I was, in Jamaica and there is this chap who ran a sort of boat hire thing for the tourists. He had those plait things. What are they called?' He looked at me.

'Dreadlocks,' I said reluctantly and Simon rolled his eyes at me.

'Dreadlocks, thank you. Down his back to his waist. And black . . . black!' He looked around himself for something that was as black as this man. 'Darker than you, my dear, if you'll pardon me saying. And his name — and this is the funny part. His name was Winston Bunyan.' He sat back and laughed. Simon and his mother smiled politely.

'Winston Bunyan! Can you believe it? I couldn't. How did that happen? I had my photograph taken with my arm around him. Me

158

and my brother Winston.'

He laughed again. 'What do you think of that, Faith?' he asked me. And because he asked me I said, 'Well, the thing is, that would have been his slave name, you see.' Then before I really knew what I was saying I'd said, 'Your family probably owned his family once.'

The man blinked hard. Simon spluttered a laugh into his drink. And I giggled a smile at Mr Bunyan. But he still stared at me like I'd just spat in his face.

Simon's mother quickly intercepted with, 'Did your wife go with you on this trip, Andrew?' But the man, still looking at me, stated, 'No! My family never had connections like that in Jamaica. My family were not in that sort of business. I have no family connections in that part of the world at all.'

Then he took a breath and got confident once more. He began to smile again. 'No. You know what it was? A wayward vicar. That's what we all think. We had a lot of vicars in our family. Some vicar just going round sowing his seed. Producing lots of little dark babies. That sort of thing happened all the time.' He laughed. 'Oh yes, that's what it will be. The Reverend Bunyan. The randy Reverend Bunyan.'

He stood up and grabbed his gin and tonic. 'It was lovely to see you, Margaret. Simon. Do give my regards to Mr Wyndham — Guy. I must come up and visit sometime.' And he nodded at me. Simon made a face and crossed his eyes behind the man's back as he turned to leave. And I took a long gulp of my shandy.

'Help me in the kitchen?' Simon's mother asked me when we got back to the house. Simon said, 'Well, what are you cooking?' But his mother said, 'Simon, darling, why don't you go and talk to Pa? He'd love to hear all about your career.'

He looked suddenly nervous. 'I thought you just said you wanted some help in here?'

'But Faith can help me, and you men can chat,' she said.

'I thought you women didn't believe in that sort of stuff any more,' he huffed as he left the kitchen.

'Oh dear,' his mother smiled at me. 'But it can't be helped, I want to talk to you.' She opened the fridge and handed me a large pale uncooked chicken. Then she began moving round the kitchen; pulling dishes out of cupboards, vegetables from wire trays, string and scissors from drawers and asking me, 'Whereabouts in Jamaica are your parents from?'

I followed her movements still holding the bird and saying, 'My dad's from Kingston. My mum I'm not sure — from the country somewhere.'

'And how long have they lived here?'

'Since the late forties,' I said then added, 'but they want to go back to live.'

'Really.' She took the bird from me and handed me some string. 'When are they going back?' I watched her stuffing sweet-smelling grey goo into the bird.

'It's nothing definite,' I said, 'they're only thinking.'

160

'Do you have a big family in Jamaica?'

'I don't know.'

'Are your grandparents still alive?'

'I'm not sure. I don't think so.'

'Do you have a lot of aunts and uncles?'

I began to feel ridiculous when I had to say, 'I'm not sure.' So I added quickly, 'I have an aunt there.'

'And what does your aunt do?'

'I don't know really.'

'And do you have cousins?' she asked.

'I think so.'

'How many? Lots? One or two?'

'I'm afraid I don't know much about them.'

'String.' I was puzzled. She nodded at the string in my hand and held her hand open. I passed it to her. She began to tie up the chicken's legs with fast precise movements.

'Have you ever been to Jamaica, Faith?'

'No.'

'Well, it will be wonderful for you to be able to visit. Aren't you curious to go?'

I shrugged.

'Where are your parents going to settle when they go back? Have they got a house?'

'I don't know.'

'Will you miss them when they go?'

I didn't answer.

'Scissors.' I handed them to her like I was a nurse at an operation. She clapped her hands on the bird's breast. 'Poor old thing,' she said then looked at me. 'That was a silly question. Of course you'll miss them.' She handed me back the scissors. 'I'm sorry I ask so many questions. I

161

used to be in intelligence during the war and I've never got out of the habit.' She began washing her hands.

'You were in intelligence?' She smiled at me when she could see I wanted to hear more. 'I used to train girls to go to France. This is occupied France,' she winked. 'They made me because I was fluent in French and knew the country backwards.'

'I saw a series about that on the television.' I remembered watching it — the heroic female spies on their bicycles — and Carl saying, 'This can't be true. It's too dangerous for a woman.'

'Yes — I helped them out with that. Gave them a few facts. And who knows, maybe one day I'll tell the full story.' She put her hands on my shoulders and said into my ear, 'If they let me that is. If it fits with their official version of the truth. Right, put that bird in the oven, my trusty assistant.'

As I picked up the chicken she said, 'You were quite right, you know, Faith.'

And I had to ask, 'Right about what?'

'What you said in the pub to that awful Andrew Bunyan.'

I was embarrassed. I looked at my feet. 'I'm sorry about that. I think I upset him.'

'Of course you upset him. But you were absolutely right. That is exactly how people got their names in the West Indies and you were right to say so. He asked you and you were right to say what you did. I thought it was very brave.'

I could not think of anything to say. There was a silence and we looked at each other. Then I remembered the bird I was holding and I opened the oven. A gust of hot air hit me.

'Right,' she said. 'Potatoes.' She slapped her hand on her mouth. 'I haven't got any.'

'I'll go and get some for you?' I offered.

'Would you, Faith? That would be lovely.' She went to a walk-in cupboard and opened the door. She walked straight past the shopping bags that I could see clearly on the back of the door. I thought she hadn't seen them and plucked one off ready. But at that moment, as I held up the tartan mesh bag, she turned round and held out a large garden fork to me. We looked at each other again.

'The potatoes are still in the ground, Faith, at the bottom of the garden,' she explained. And when I just stared at her, wide-eyed, not moving, she called out, 'Simon, darling! I think Faith needs your help.'

13

The letter came through the television centre's internal mail. At the time I was sitting at my desk typing a full and complete description of World War One army uniforms. 'We are pleased to inform you that your application for the post of dresser has been successful.' I yelped and Henry said, 'Well, there you go, Miss. Congratulations.' Then he added, 'That was a bit of a storm in the proverbial teacup, don't you think?'

Lorraine jumped up and down, clapping her hands quickly then hugging me, making sure not to smudge her make-up on my clothes. 'Oh you see. I knew Lionel was a nice man really. I mean, he can be a bit fussy. But I knew he wasn't prejudiced. He loves animals.'

When I got home Simon was just leaving — his bags packed and waiting in the hall, his face scrubbed, his beard trimmed to stubble and his hair washed and wet at the edges. I hadn't seen him much since we got back from the weekend at his parents' home. He had spent most of the time away. 'Gigging,' he said. 'Touring. Playing to sometimes — oohh, thirty people — in Nissen huts all over the country.' I missed him.

It was hard to describe the atmosphere that had settled over our shared house. Strained perhaps — in the way an elastic band is strained when it is stretched so taut that you get scared it will snap and ping painfully into your eye. Charged maybe — with a current you cannot see, taste or smell, but which would, if you touched it, throw you bodily across the room. When Marion and Mick were in a room together they would huff and puff. Mick, in the kitchen, would do more washing-up than he had to, and blow out so much breath in the process that I worried he might hyperventilate. Marion's favourite was to rattle an empty box of Bran Flakes and snort wind down her nostrils, like a raging bull. They huffed and puffed so much wind between them that they created a house mistral that blew the atmosphere through every corner and crevice. And when the wind passed over me, it made me shiver.

'Where are you going this time?' I asked Simon.

'Manchester and sunny Hull. It's all glamour, Faith.'

When I told him that I got my job he put his arms around me and hugged me to him. He smelt of Palmolive soap and his hair that fell on my cheek smelt of baby shampoo. He kissed me softly and quickly on the lips. 'When I get back,' he said, 'we can go out and celebrate?' He looked into my eyes.

'Yes, great,' I said and he smiled.

'Promise?'

Mick wasn't in — he didn't come home for days at a time. Marion was in her bedroom. She was lying on the floor with her legs pointing straight up into the air, listening to an exercise tape. 'I knew you'd get the job,' she said nonchalantly. 'You're lucky, I wish I had a good job. I hate that job of mine.' I tried to get her to have a girly giggle with me, like we used to at her parents' house with Coke and ice cream. I mentioned the possibility of me dressing Jeremy Irons. But she just said, 'I hate him. He reminds me of Simon.'

'What's wrong with Simon?'

'He's too English for me. But you like that sort of thing, don't you, Faith? Public-school boys. They're all emotional cripples taken away from their mothers too young — I've seen what it does to kittens.' She began rewinding her exercise tape, moaning. 'She keeps saying let your legs drag across your face.' Marion demonstrated how her legs could get nowhere near her face even when she bent her knees.

So I tried engaging her again with, 'Well, it's good that after all that I got the job.'

To which she replied, 'Can you drag your legs across your face?'

'No,' I said, 'but I could drag my legs across your face, if you like.' And I left slamming the door.

I did not see the man outside my parents' house, didn't notice him at all, standing across the road taking a photograph of it. A man in a neat suit who looked like he'd know how to use a Corby trouser press. He wrote something on a clipboard and then got into a shiny red car. His aftershave, however, hung around for a bit before it followed him.

I thought the silhouette on the glass panel in the kitchen door was Mum. But when I opened the door saying, 'Mum, what was that man doing outside?' I caught Carl ferociously kissing a woman. They sprang apart with such force that they ended up on opposite sides of the room.

'Bloody hell, it's you! What you doing here?' Carl said.

I was about to say that I lived there but realised that I didn't. The woman stood looking at me. I looked at her and smiled. She looked at Carl, then back at me. I looked at Carl, then back at her. We both looked at Carl as he sat down and started to light a cigarette. We sat down. He was not going to introduce us.

I had never actually met a girlfriend of Carl's before. He had them. Lots of them. I'd answer the phone to a tearful female saying, 'Can I speak to Carl, please?' Or a feisty, 'Carl, is that you?' And he'd lift up the receiver, flick his hand at me until I moved away and only speak when I was well out of earshot. I had seen women sitting in his van when he had run into the house to pick something up. I had even seen him once on Holloway Road, walking with his arm round a woman dressed in white. But as I called out his name they disappeared and he swore he never saw me. 'I never saw you, Faith — cross my heart and hope to die.'

But he never brought anyone home. Not, that is, since the age of twelve, when Angela from the church came round for her tea. Carl and she had held hands at the church jumble sale. Mum decided that Angela was: 'A lovely girl. Such a nice girl. A real decent girl. What a lovely girl.' She spent the next six years asking Carl about

Angela. 'What happened to you and that lovely girl?' And Carl would roll his eyes and plead, 'I only held her hand once. I was twelve, Mum!' Angela eventually got married to a trainee manager from Safeway. And Mum scolded Carl with, 'You let a good woman go there, son. That could have been you.'

'You must be Carl's sister,' the woman eventually had to say.

'Why — she don't look like me,' Carl butted in.

'I didn't say she did.' She looked at Carl with a flirty teasing grin. 'But she has to be someone and you're obviously not going to tell me. I'm Ruth.'

'I'm Faith. Are you going out with my brother?'

'I'm introducing you — if you don't mind,' Carl was saying. 'Faith, this is Ruth . . . '

We paid no attention to him. 'Afraid so.'

'Haven't you got enough problems?' I said. She laughed, and patted Carl's head. Carl looked between us, tutted loudly and flicked ash into the ashtray.

Ruth was not pretty. She wore glasses that sat low down on her nose and looked like they constricted her intake of air. She kept pushing them back up but they would gently slide back down. But she had beautiful skin. Rich brown like a freshly dropped conker — smooth and perfect. As if it had been stretched over her face by an expert who laid flat all the under-eye bags and puffy bits.

'Have you seen Mum?' I asked. Ruth put her

hand on my brother's leg and squeezed his knee.

'She's around somewhere,' Carl said, looking at Ruth. They both began to giggle.

'What's so funny?' I asked.

Carl looked at me as if he had forgotten I was there. 'Oh, it was something we were . . . ' He looked at his girlfriend again, raised an eyebrow and said, 'Don't forget bananas.' And they both laughed, for some reason. Ruth had a dimple in one of her cheeks which made her look strangely similar to Carl when she laughed. I felt unwanted and was about to leave the room when Ruth said, 'Carl tells me you work in television.' She had strange eyes that were brown but a pale watery brown.

'Yes. Oh Carl, I got that job,' I said. I thought he would be pleased but he just said a half-hearted, 'Oh.'

'Don't get too excited,' I said.

Ruth looked between us. 'What job is that?'

But Carl answered. 'She wants to put people's clothes on their backs for a living.' Ruth looked at me frowning for an explanation.

I was not going to let my brother upset me. 'It's called a dresser and you have to . . . you have to . . . ' The job description sounded ridiculous as it formed in my head. I phrased it carefully. 'You have to make sure the actors have on the right costumes for the scene.'

'Like I said,' Carl sneered. 'A bit like being a servant — I couldn't do that . . . '

I put my hands on my hips and started with, 'Oh yeah, and who the bloody hell was going to ask you to do it?' And ended by saying, 'I worked

169

hard to get that job. I'm probably the first black dresser they've had.'

Ruth's head snapped round to look at me. 'What do you mean?' she asked.

I was relieved to be able to talk about Lorraine, the rumour and the interview with someone who tutted at all the appropriate moments. And sighed and rolled her eyes and said, 'Really?' indignantly and, 'That's terrible!' with force. When Carl started sniggering she even told him to shut up. Then as I paused momentarily for breath, Ruth began. 'They shouldn't be allowed to get away with something like that. They think — these white men — that just because we're black, we're stupid. They think they can treat us like dirt.'

'I know,' I said.

'I mean, did you report them?'

'Report them?'

'Yes, did you complain about your treatment?' I just stared at her. 'Did you complain to the union or higher managers? Or better still, actually, you should write to the Commission for Racial Equality. No, hang on, have you talked to Equity, the actors' union? Tell them what's going on. See if you can get some sort of action going.'

I said quickly, 'But the thing is, I got the job in the end.'

'Yeah,' she went on, 'but why did you get the job?' She looked between Carl and me and I thought she wanted an answer.

So I said, 'Because I'm good?'

'No,' she said forcefully. 'It's just to shut you up. It's tokenism. It's what they do. How many other black people are working there? None, I bet. So they just employ you and then they can say, yes, we have a black person. And they carry on discriminating just the same. You really do have to do something.'

I looked at my feet and muttered, 'But I may have got it wrong.' But it didn't matter — she wasn't listening.

'We can't let this keep happening to us. Black people must stand together.'

'But I got the job.'

'That's not the point. Don't you understand? If it's not you it will be the next black person. It will be someone else. We're talking about European oppression here. Hundreds of years of oppression by white people that shows no sign of stopping. Black people have to fight. We have to struggle against this. All of us. Together. It's political — it's black against white.' My brother began to nod. I didn't know where to look as Ruth talked into my face, locking her eyes onto mine. 'It's racism, you were the victim of racism, Faith. Those white men have not done you a favour . . . ' Carl was staring at his new girlfriend with unguarded admiration, looking her up and down. And, as she was speaking, I noticed that she had a very long, skinny body. Luckily for her her arms were in proportion, because if she had my arms, she would never have been able to wipe her arse. Then she stopped. There was a silence and I said, 'Yeah,' before Ruth carried on with, 'You really cannot let it go at that, Faith.'

I was curious about Ruth. She was too intelligent for my brother. 'What job do you do?'

I asked her quickly.

She sat upright, taking the cigarette from Carl's hand and dragging on it. She handed it back saying, 'I work for a sex education project. We go round to youth clubs and schools. Outreach work. Just teaching young people about . . . ' She bobbed her head from side to side and she and Carl said, 'Sex,' together.

I felt sick.

'Where did you meet?'

Carl looked sheepish. Looking around the room trying to find a way to change the subject. Something was embarrassing him.

'We met at evening class,' his girlfriend told me.

'Carl — at evening class?' I said slowly.

Carl coughed into his hand as Ruth said, 'Yeah, he's doing . . . ' Then she stopped herself. And Carl said with a forced bravado, 'Yeah, well, I'm doing photography.'

'A level,' Ruth added.

'You're doing an A level,' I yelled at Carl, as Ruth said, 'And I'm doing black women's studies.'

I stared for a very long time at my 'in his mid-twenties and taking his first exam' brother. 'Since when?'

'You don't know everything about me.'

'An A level. You're doing an A level. In photography?' I found it very funny.

'He's very good,' Ruth said.

'Do Mum and Dad know?'

'Oh, shut up, Faith,' Carl said, picking up his jacket. 'Come on, Ruth, let's get out of here.'

172

'Have you got a camera?'

'Shut up, Faith. Just shut your gob.' Carl watched me laugh for a little then said, 'Oh, by the way, Noel has been asking after you.'

'Nice try,' I teased.

Ruth looked between Carl and me. She had no idea what was going on. Then Carl tapped Ruth on the shoulder. 'My mum and dad are trying to pair Faith up with my dad's workmate.'

'Yeah, yeah, yeah,' I said. 'So tell me about your photographic inspiration.'

But Carl carried on, 'I told them not to bother because Faith doesn't go out with black men.'

I was stunned into a straight face. Ruth looked slowly over to me with a contemptuous pity that made me want to slap her perfect cheek.

'My sister,' Carl carried on, 'lives in a house full of white people. She doesn't really like black people.'

The muscles on my face were rigid — I must have looked close to tears. I couldn't think of a word to say. I wasn't sure I had the evidence to deny it. 'Bye, Faith,' Carl sang.

And as they left Ruth said, 'Nice to meet you, Faith,' then added, 'Perhaps you need to spend some more time among your own people.'

★   ★   ★

'Is that woman gone?' Mum whispered, as she came into the room.

'Who? Ruth?'

Mum nodded.

'Don't you like her?' I asked, enthusiastically.

173

'She nice enough. It's just . . . ' she stopped herself and sniffed.

'What?'

'Oh nothing. It's not up to me.'

'Well, she's a bit . . . ' I started.

Mum needed no further encouragement to take over my theme. She was animated. 'It's just she has all these ideas. And she putting them in Carl's head. He was all right till he met her but now he keeps telling me we should be doing this and we shouldn't be doing that. He keeps telling me I'm black. And as a black person I should do this and I shouldn't do that. And I say, I know I'm black, Carl, and so are you and so is your sister and your dad. And he says, no, we are Black.' She waited for me to explain it to her. But I couldn't so she carried on.

'This girlfriend of his, you know what she tell me today? Just before you come in. I know you come in but I didn't want to stay in the kitchen with them. So I was showing the man around.'

'What man?' I asked, but Mum just waved away my enquiry.

'I didn't want to stay with them because she saying to me that I have the triple yoke. Now let me get this right.' She began to enunciate very slowly. 'I have the triple yoke of oppression on my shoulders. Yeah, that's what she say. The triple yoke of oppression.' She folded her arms. 'What you think of that?' I opened my mouth to ask what it meant, when she carried on, 'I tell her, I have no chip on my shoulder. She say it's not a chip, it's a yoke.' She stopped for a deep breath. 'According to her, I am a poor black woman. And I tell her enough of the poor. Your dad and me work very hard. And the good Lord bless us. We not rich people but we not poor.' She sucked her teeth and muttered, 'Poor black woman. The girl don't know she's born. I know poor. I know what is poor. And you know what else? This will make you laugh, Faith.' I doubted it very much. 'I making roast lamb with roast potatoes and mint sauce. She ask me where is the rice and peas. I say I fed up with it, and she tell me I should be proud of me black food. Your dad nearly choke.'

Dad came in as if on cue.

'You call me?' But Mum was oblivious.

'The woman won't even let us eat what we want. And it's your dad's favourite.' She stopped for breath sighing heavily and looking to my dad. 'Ruth, it's Ruth we talking about, Wade.'

'She still here?' Dad whispered. He looked around himself like a stalked deer.

'Is all right,' Mum said. 'She's gone now.' And Dad let his shoulders droop. 'And you know what else, Faith?' Mum carried on. 'She and Carl are getting a place together.'

I was astounded. I had to catch a breath. 'Carl's leaving home?'

'Yes. She and Carl are getting a flat. They are going to live together, they tell me. And maybe they will get married later, so they say. That is how you young people do it in this country. But we are going to meet her parents. They are coming here. What day is it? I can't remember now. But they are getting a flat together. Mark

175

you, I am pleased that your brother is settling down. Ehh, Wade?'

'Are you going to sell this house?' I asked.

'What?' Dad said.

'I am saying to Faith,' Mum interrupted, 'that we are pleased Carl is settling down at last.'

'Oh yes,' Dad said.

Then Mum asked, 'Is Noel coming in for a cup of tea, Wade?'

'Mum!'

'What, child?' she said, frowning at me. 'Tell Noel that I have the kettle on for a cup of tea.' Dad went to leave the room. I called him back and he stood looking at me waiting for me to say something. So I said, 'Who was that man outside the house?'

'What man?' Dad said. He sounded like an old hammy actor. 'Did you see a man, Mildred?'

'Oh, that man,' Mum said, as if it was nothing to talk about.

'I'll just go tell Noel to come in for some tea,' Dad said.

'No,' I said, firmly.

'He's cleaned himself up,' Dad told me.

'Was he an estate agent?' I asked them both.

'Who, Noel?' Mum laughed.

'Are you selling the house?'

'Noel's never been an estate agent,' Dad said and went on, 'Shall I tell him to come for some tea?'

'No, Dad.'

'What?' Mum said, 'You don't want me give Noel a cup of tea? Wade, tell Noel he can't come in for a cup of tea because Faith won't let him.'

176

'No, don't say that!' I could imagine Noel standing outside the door with his cap in hand, shifting from foot to foot, looking at the ground, waiting to be allowed in, like some step-and-fetch-it. 'Of course he can have a cup of tea,' I said to them both. 'It's just that I know what you're doing. And . . . ' I hesitated, 'and I have a boyfriend.'

Mum looked at me interested. 'You have a boyfriend?'

'Well, not exactly. Not yet. It's just someone I like,' I admitted to Mum who said, 'Wade, tell Noel to come in for a cup of tea.'

Dad left the room and I remembered the reason I had come to see my parents. 'Mum, I got the job. The one I wanted — as a dresser.'

'You see,' Mum said, nodding her head slowly. 'What did I tell you? What you heard was foolishness. They cannot mess with you. I knew you would get that job.' She fluttered her hands in the air with excitement. 'Everything is working out just fine.'

Dad came to the door with Noel who tripped into the room and fell into the nearest chair. 'You know me daughter, Noel?' Dad asked and Noel replied, 'Oh yes.'

14

'Well, Faith, I'm afraid it really is out of my hands,' *les girls* told me. 'There are not a lot of productions going through at the moment and the ones that are all want experienced dressers — so I can't send you as you've only been doing the job for two weeks.'

'Three,' I corrected him.

'Two . . . three . . . whatever. The point is that you have had very little experience. But as soon as something comes up that you would be suitable for, then we will send you straight down.'

Henry had told me to complain to *les girls*. 'I don't know how he thinks you're meant to get the experience, Miss, if all you do is sit in pool counting the hairs on your palm.'

Sitting in pool is what dressers did when they were not working on a production. They didn't send you home or tell you not to come in because we had to be prepared. At any moment Richard Briers might have trouble getting out of his tights or twenty German extras might get the zip caught in their lederhosen. We had to sit and wait.

'I've been in pool for weeks,' I told Lorraine.

'Oh, don't worry, something will come up soon. Do you wanna read my magazine?'

I had sat in the dressers' room and read *Woman's Own*, *Woman*, *Woman's Realm*,

Cosmopolitan, She, Honey. I knew all about skincare routines for combination, dry and oily skin. I knew the handy hints for keeping underwear together in the washing machine — just pop them into a pillowcase! — and I promised myself I'd try something sparkly to brighten up my evening wear. I had counted all the windows opposite — going up, going along, horizontally and diagonally. I watched cars bringing in celebrities and politicians, and I timed how long they took to get from the car to the door. Politicians won. I read books, I did crosswords and I even took up needlepoint.

'What on earth are you doing that for, Miss?'

'I'm bored, Henry.'

And as I sat watching the other dressers come and go, I had to stop myself from thinking. I had to stop myself from thinking that the reason I was not in the studio dressing rooms, prodding and poking actors into their costumes, was because . . . 'Let me assure you now, Faith, that there is absolutely no question of racial or any other prejudice going on here.' I had to stop myself from thinking that because — 'Nothing like that goes on in this department. Never has and never will.' I had to stop myself thinking before I heard the voice that said, 'They should not be allowed to get away with this, Faith — these white people. You really should do something. You are a black person — you must fight it.'

Then *les girls* finally said, 'I've got something for you, Faith. It'll last a few days too.' He put his arm on my shoulder and smiled. 'You've been very patient. It's in studio three.'

It was for children's TV. I was shown into the dressing room. Along one wall was a rail with costumes, but the costumes only hung down a foot from the top of the rail. Children, I thought with dread, or maybe it was the seven dwarfs. I was then introduced to my actors. One was a big teddy bear called Alfred and the other a gangly rag doll called Molly. They were the children's favourites evidently. Each week the perky male and female presenters, dressed in their bright dungarees with cheery smiles and exaggerated movements introduced the dolls.

'Let's see what Molly is wearing today.'

I had a list. On Monday Molly was a nurse. 'Oh Molly, you're a nurse today. Can you take my temperature?' And Alfred was her bandaged patient. On Tuesday she was a witch. 'Molly is going to put a spell on Alfred today, girls and boys.' And on Wednesday she was medieval — waiting to be rescued from a green fun-fur dragon by Alfred in his cardboard armour.

Henry laughed himself red. 'Well, you can't complain now, Miss. At least you're being a dresser.'

15

It was three men running that I saw first. Out of the corner of my eye — only registering their speed in my vision. But then I saw Simon chasing them. I turned my head to get a better look and a bald man hooted and gave me a V-sign. I stopped the car to watch.

Simon gave up the chase. Twenty Marlboros a day had him leaning heavily on his knees, panting like an athlete. I got out of the car and called out to him. He didn't hear but started to walk in my direction. Then I realised where he was making his way to. A black woman was standing in the doorway of a bookshop. She looked composed, although she had a startled stare — like she'd just won the pools and couldn't quite believe it. But sliding slowly down one side of her face were several strings of blood — thick, bright red blood. I stood in front of her and asked, 'Are you all right?' and felt stupid when she collapsed down onto the ground. Not in a faint but vertically — as if her knees finally decided not to support her. She landed sitting.

'Fucking hell, Faith! Fucking hell! Did you see them? Jesus Christ. Look at her. Are you all right? Fuck. Did you see them? The bastards. Fucking hell. I can't believe it. Fucking hell. Jesus Christ!' If it was a film I would have slapped Simon round the face at this point. But it was a Friday afternoon in Islington and people

181

were coming up to stare.

'What's happened?'

Simon ran his hand through his hair frenetically. Then he exhaled and said, 'Come on, let's get her inside.'

The woman began saying, 'I'm all right. It's all right,' as we helped her up. A man with shabby stained trousers came up to us carrying a can of lager which slopped its contents over his hand as he stood swaying. 'What's wrong with her? What's a matter with her?' He offered the woman the can of lager but Simon pushed it out of the way.

'I'm only tryin' ta help, ya cunt,' the man said. Other people slowed down, stretching their necks to look, as the swaying man shouted, 'What youse lookin' at, ya bastards?' As we moved into the shop the man tried to follow. 'Leave her, see. Come on, love. Leave her, ya cunt.' Simon pushed him out of the door — 'Don't touch me, ya bastard. I'll stick one on ya — ya bastard,' — and locked the door behind him.

The street noise suddenly went. We were in a bookshop, the three of us. A woman with a bleeding head, a panting, furious Simon and a terrified me. The moment was so intense that it felt like there was no other world but this. A red mist hung in the air — it was impossible to take a deep breath without choking on the heavy pear-drop stench. The shop had been sprayed with angry red paint. And all over it said NF, NF, NF. The red paint was over the walls — over the spines of books — arcing down the shelves and along faces on posters. Over the till and paying desk. Down round the children's corner — over the display of alphabet bricks and across the little seats. Round the racks of greetings cards. A swirling hate of NF NF NF Fuck Off.

Books were strewn over the floor and an unmistakable stench of piss came from somewhere. A half-full bag of shit was splatted on the table — while the other half of its contents slid down the bookcase of gay and lesbian books. And the black and Third World fiction was spray-painted with 'Wog'.

'Call the police,' Simon ordered me, then asked the woman, 'Is there a phone in here?'

She pointed over to the pay desk and said a feeble, 'I think I'm going to pass out.'

Simon sat her on a chair. He knelt down in front of her. 'Your head doesn't look too bad, I've seen worse.' He gently pushed a handkerchief over the wound and the woman flinched. 'Sorry,' he said as the white cloth seeped red with her blood.

The phone had a shaft of paint across it on its way to finishing an F. The receiver was sticky. My hands shook as I dialled and I had to ask Simon, 'What services do we want?'

'Shit, I think she's going to faint,' Simon said as the woman slumped forward in the chair.

'Police and ambulance,' I said into the receiver. He caught her and pushed her back. They wanted to know the address but all I could do was mumble the directions from Highbury Corner.

'They're coming,' I said, as I put the receiver

183

down. My hand was stuck to it. I had to hold it down with my other hand and pull it away with a force that left some of my skin behind.

Simon had taken off his coat and put it round the woman. His white handkerchief was red. 'Have you got anything I can put on her head?' he whispered. I took off the blue scarf I had round my neck and Simon pushed that onto the woman's gash which was still running trails of blood over her eyes and down her nose. She noticed and fainted forward onto Simon again.

'Let's get her on the floor.' He held her gently and laid her down like she was a baby in her cot. My scarf had gold lurex stripes which looked ridiculously exotic against her bleeding head. She was small, very petite, and her face was probably pretty when not the flat colour of brown stone with black sunken eyes and streaks of blood congealing like toffee all over it.

It wasn't until the police came — until a car screeched up outside with its blue lights flashing, sirens shrieking and two big tall men who ran whilst putting on their hats came banging at the door ready to smash it in if they had to — that I found out what had happened.

'Christ Almighty — you've been done. No need to ask who did it,' one of the policemen said. Another car came up. Another blue light, another siren and more men. And soon I lost count of the people who came in. Fussing over the woman, standing guard on the floor, shooing people away with, 'There is nothing to look at.' Talking into radios and wandering round the shop telling each other what they should do.

Simon and me moved closer together and I held his hand when it shook as he told the police, 'I was just coming into the shop. I opened the door and I saw one of the men hit her with a bar or something, and the other two were just doing this,' he said pointing at the mess. 'They saw me and just sort of ran up to me. I thought I was going to get hit but they just pushed past me and ran up the street. I chased them. They were laughing. But then I lost them.'

I became aware that my hand was stuck to Simon's as the officer asked me, 'Do you work here, miss?'

'No.'

'Did you see these men, miss?'

'Not really. Only running down the street.'

'Could you recognise them again?'

'I didn't see their faces. But they had green jackets.'

The policeman was unimpressed and asked Simon, 'How about you, sir?'

Simon hesitated for a moment. He pulled his hand off mine and ran it through his hair. 'Yeah, I'd know them again.'

'Well, between you and me,' the policeman said, 'we know who they are, we just need someone else to tell us.' He looked between Simon and me. 'You two know each other?'

'We live together,' Simon said and the policeman's eyebrows rose slowly up his forehead.

'All these leftie bookshops are getting done,' the policeman went on. He had a sneer in his tone. 'They say they're National Front but they're not, they're just a bunch of thugs.'

'Same thing, isn't it?' Simon said, but the policeman didn't appear to hear and carried on saying, 'We've told them not to have people in the shop on their own. One woman like that on her own. I mean, they're just asking for trouble.' Simon rolled his eyes at me when the officer wasn't looking.

My head was hurting like it had come out in sympathy with Yemi. That was the woman's name, which I learnt from the ambulanceman shouting, 'Okay, Yemi, we're going to take you to hospital now,' as if she had gone deaf or stupid.

The policeman wanted to know Simon's telephone number at home. But Simon could not remember it. 'It's ridiculous. I just can't remember. It's just gone. I'm sorry. Sorry.' He had to ask me. The police officer said he'd be in touch as we left. Simon smiled and nodded like he was accepting an invitation to a party.

The drunk man was singing, 'Oh Danny boy,' outside the shop. Serenading a policewoman who was looking at him saying, 'Are you going to move along? I'm not going to ask you again.'

And as we walked up the road, Simon yelled, 'Fucking shit — this is surreal.'

16

Everything seemed so normal when Simon and I got back to our house. Washing-up piled by the sink, a greasy carton of old pizza on the table next to several mugs with dregs of coffee in the bottom, most of the lights on in the house, music playing, cigarette smoke in the air and Mick standing at a sink wearing Simon's bird apron, washing a jumper and slopping water all over the kitchen floor. It was sedate and ordered.

'Bloody hell, what happened to you?' Mick asked. He saw the red paint over the back of Simon's coat, in his hair, over my hands and by now my face. 'Is that blood?' he wanted to know.

'I don't know, it could be,' Simon said.

The story sounded different when Simon retold it. It gained more menace with hindsight. It was now a fact that three men walked into a bookshop in daylight and hit someone over the head with a blunt instrument because they didn't like them. It was real. Not something skipped over in the local paper or tutted about at the dinner table.

I interrupted the story twice. 'She was a black woman,' I said. Simon had just called her the woman who worked there. Twice I had to tell them that the woman that was struck on the head was black like me. And both times Simon and Mick had looked at me and nodded.

'Bloody hell,' was all Mick said when Simon had finished.

Marion came in, looked at Mick, went to leave but then saw Simon and me. 'Bloody hell!'

Simon had to tell the story one more time — three men walked into a bookshop, sprayed it with paint and shit, and hit a woman over the head with something blunt.

'The woman was black,' I said again, as Mick stated, 'The National Front.'

'Did you see it, Faith?' Marion asked.

'Not the attack,' I said, 'but I saw the shop and the woman . . . ' But Marion had turned to Simon, 'You actually saw them hit her?'

Simon's hand shook as he lifted his cigarette to his mouth — he couldn't hold it steady. Marion put her hand over his to support it. 'I think you're in shock. Sweet tea is what you need,' she said looking closely into Simon's face. 'Mick, put the kettle on.' Mick began to protest but then reluctantly filled the kettle.

'I'm going to have to identify them,' Simon said. He looked at me then he slumped forward onto his hand, 'Jesus fucking wept.'

Marion put her arm round Simon's shoulder. His coat was sticky with paint. 'Oh, get your coat off, Simon.' Marion stood up behind him and gently took off his coat. Then she ran her hands over his hair. 'There's paint all over your hair — at least I think it's paint.' She lightly ran her fingers into his hair like an indulgent parent then smelt her hand. She then put her hand to Simon's nose, 'Is that paint? I can't tell any more.' Simon held her hand to his face.

'It's all over my hands,' I said quickly to Marion. 'It was everywhere. You should have seen it. It was awful. There was shit and piss and . . . ' But Marion was too busy with Simon, 'So what did the police say?'

'They want me to go with them to places they know the National Front will be. And I am supposed to look into their faces and see if I can identify them.'

And Mick said, 'Don't worry — they're just a bunch of thugs.' He said it as if just a bunch of thugs couldn't hurt you. As if just a bunch of thugs couldn't make you change direction in the street or take cover in a shop until they passed.

'Yeah, I know, that's what the police said,' Simon told him.

'They threatened to firebomb our college once,' Mick went on. 'They sent all these warning letters saying the college was full of lefties and Pakis and that they were going to close us down. But all they did was break a few windows.'

All my flatmates laughed. Just break a few windows, that was all a bunch of thugs could do.

'Anyway,' Mick carried on. 'Why were you chasing them? What were you going to do if you caught up with them?' They all laughed. Carl once came home with bruises on his eyes, his face, his arms. The bruises took weeks to heal and turned bits of his skin blue. He never told anyone what happened.

'Fuck knows!' Simon answered and Marion put her hand on his thigh. She leant her head close to his, 'Do you want me to run you a bath?'

189

Mick put four mugs of tea on the table and three white hands and one black stretched forward to take them.

'Do you want sugar in that tea?' Marion asked Simon. 'It should be sweet for shock. I got a first aid badge in the Brownies — have I ever told you?'

Mick was telling Simon, 'There's a network of National Front around here, so I've heard,' while Marion took one of Simon's hands and turned it palm up.

'There is paint all over you. We should wash it off before it dries solid.'

Then my flatmates were giggling. 'Don't let them know where you live . . . you better wear a mask, Simon . . . or a white sheet with a hood . . . what if they follow you home? . . . you'll have to go to court . . . stand up in a witness box with them all staring . . . does that make you a grass, Simon? . . . we'll have to live behind the shutters . . . I think it makes you a grass . . . we'll have to move . . . '

But then I tipped my cup of tea slowly over the table. 'Will you all just shut up. Just fucking shut up. It's not funny!' And there was complete silence as they stopped and stared at me.

I left the house.

★ ★ ★

I went home. I went to my mum and dad's house. I went, as Ruth had suggested, to be with my own people. I wanted to curl up small in my mum's lap and have her stroke my hair. I wanted my dad to say, 'Don't go frettin', Faith, we'll protect you.' They would understand how I felt — black on the outside and cowardly custard-yellow on the inside.

'Is that you, Faith?' Mum said, coming out of the living room. She shut the door behind her. She was all dressed up — her best paisley blouse with shell buttons, her navy pleated skirt, and her hair freshly rolled stiff and crisp. 'We weren't expecting you. Did you say you were comin'?'

'No, I just . . . ' I began as Dad came out to the door. He was dressed up too. Best unsaggy cardigan, beige slacks. 'Oh Faith, we weren't expecting you,' he said.

'We have guests. They have . . . ' Mum started, but Dad looked at me, 'Faith, you have paint all over you. You been decorating?'

'No I just . . . '

'Go and wash and clean yourself up, child,' Mum whispered. 'We have guests. Go and smarten yourself up, then I suppose you'll have to come and join us.'

I went to the bathroom. Marion with Simon? Ruth was right, I thought to myself. Simon and Marion? Ruth was absolutely right. What it all comes down to in the end is black against white. It was simple. It was so simple.

The paint wouldn't come off my face with soap and water. I had to scratch at my skin. Pick away at it with my fingernail. It became sore and tiny flakes of red paint floated on the surface of the water in the bowl.

Carl and Ruth were walking into the front

room. Carl saw me and said, 'What you doing here?'

'I just . . . ' I began. But they both looked anxious and polite and strange voices were coming from the room — introduction noises and nervous laughs. Mum grabbed one of my hands. She inspected my fingernails before saying, 'And this is my youngest, my daughter, Carl's sister, Faith.'

I was introduced to four white people. A woman, a man and two children who were obviously twins. They've come to buy the house, I thought. They've come to take over our house. The white people were sitting uncomfortably squashed together on the settee.

'Faith,' Mum began, 'this is Ruth's family.'

I thought I'd heard wrong but Ruth was nodding. She took over the introductions. 'This is my mum and these are my little brothers. And this is my dad,' she said, quickly correcting with, 'my stepdad.'

'I suppose,' her mother said, 'these two tots are Ruth's half-brothers but we don't like to say that.'

Mum whispered to me, 'Don't stare!'

Ruth's family were white. Her mother was white, her brothers were white, her stepdad was white. Ruth was black. It was simple. Ruth was black and all her family were white. And I said, 'How did that happen?'

Ruth's parents laughed politely. Ruth sighed, Mum hit me hard on the leg. Dad said something about tea and Carl tutted.

'My actual father is from Guyana,' Ruth

began. Her mum took over, 'I met Ruth's father when I was quite young. He was a student but he couldn't stay in this country. After Ruth was born I married and . . . ' she trailed away and Ruth said, 'I don't see my real father.'

I couldn't look into her eyes. It was simple. I felt dizzy. It was so simple. I ran.

★   ★   ★

There were noises of sex coming from Marion's bedroom — grunting, moist slapping, panting. Simon's bedroom door was open but he was not in it. I sneaked on tippy-toe into my room. I didn't want anyone to see me.

The streetlight was shining a yellow glow into the room. It was too bright, too light. The window let in too much life. I closed the wooden shutters and the curtains until it was so dark I could not see where I was stepping. I got into bed. But as my eyes adjusted to the dark I could see my reflection in the wardrobe mirror. A black girl lying in a bed. I covered the mirror with a bath towel. I didn't want to be black any more. I just wanted to live. The other mirror in the room I covered with a tee-shirt. *Voilà*! I was no longer black.

Marion was coming to a climax. Breathing deep and loud, faster and faster, getting higher and higher until she stopped with a faint sigh. I put my head under the covers.

I don't know how long I stayed like that. I don't know how long I was in bed. Marion came in. She wanted to talk, 'Oh Faith, I've got some news for you.' But I turned over and told her I was sick. I don't know how long she stayed for, but I know she left. Then she came back saying something about work. The puppets — the puppets needed me. Who would dress Alfred and Molly today, boys and girls? Not me. They didn't want me at the television centre. And I wanted to be wanted. I liked to be liked.

Simon came in — I think. He sat on the bed — he sat by the bed. He brought me a bowl of chicken soup which he promised he had not made himself. He asked me what was wrong. He pulled the towel off the mirror. I had to put it back when he left. I had to put the towel back and the bowl of soup outside the door.

'Are you ever getting up, Faith?' Mick asked. Evidently, *les girls* wanted to know when I would be back at my job. They wanted to know what was wrong with me. They wanted certificates from a doctor. 'You'd better do it, Faith, or you'll lose your job,' Simon told me.

I don't know how long I stayed there. I heard rain hitting the window and sometimes a shaft of light as fine as a pin would dart into the room. But it could never get me. I was safe.

Then there was Mum and Dad standing large and out of place in the room. Wringing their hands, looking around, tutting and shaking their heads.

'That nice boy Simon contact us. He told us . . . ' Mum hesitated. 'He told us you were not well.'

'I'm all right,' I told them.

'You don't look all right, Faith,' Mum told me.

'Flu,' I said. 'I have the flu.' Mum produced a thermometer from her pocket like a wand.

'You have no temperature, child.'

Dad pulled back the curtains and opened the shutters. The light dazzled my eyes. Mum was crying. I looked at her blinking at the light. And Dad stared at me intensely. He wanted to know how I could be fixed. They wouldn't leave me alone.

'Why you cover all your mirrors, Faith?' They wouldn't let me be.

Simon brought us all a cup of tea. He smiled and winked at me as he left. And as I sat up Mum and Dad brought chairs close to the bed. They sat down. 'We have been thinking, me and your dad,' Mum started. 'We have been thinking that what you need is a little holiday.'

'We have a little money put by . . . ' Dad butted in.

'We have been thinking that your auntie in Jamaica would like to know you. And we have been thinking that now might be a good time for you to go and visit with her.'

'For just a few weeks,' Dad added.

'For just a few weeks, yes. And it would be a good chance for you to see Jamaica. You could write to her . . . '

'I don't need a holiday,' I said.

'Oh Faith,' Mum said. She started crying again — her eyes magnified through the tears that spilled onto her cheeks. 'Please, please. Your dad and me . . . We can't stand to see you like this.'

'Is it because we said we were going away?' Dad asked.

'Oh Wade, don't start with all that now. We would never go anywhere unless you were happy. You know that, Faith. Please take the holiday.'

'I don't want to go to Jamaica. It's too far. What's wrong with Spain or somewhere?'

'No!' they said together. Then Mum pleaded, 'Please go to Jamaica.'

'Why,' I asked.

'Because it might help you,' she said.

'Why?'

And Mum said softly, 'Child, everyone should know where they come from.'

Part II

Jamaica

17

The luggage ramp was little more than an old conveyor belt which moved painfully slowly up a slope. Behind a door I could see men throwing the luggage — their hands caught in mid-air for a moment before the item landed on the belt and began its wobbly journey upwards. I waited for my suitcase but there didn't seem to be any bags, just box after box after box. Some of them were tied with string, some were bursting at the seams with their contents indecently revealed; a shoe, the brim of a hat. The ramp squealed as if powered by disgruntled pigs. An insistent noise that rose above the shouts and clatter of the people all around me, people pushing me to get to their boxes, hauling them off with grunts and wheezes. Speaking fast and loud in patois. Kingston airport was the noisiest place I had ever been.

I had been on the aeroplane for twelve hours but that included the hour stopover I had to make in Miami. In that hour, I had collected my case from an efficient, silent carousel which swept round in a circle, gliding its cargo with interlocking technological precision to waiting hands in a cool air-conditioned room. I went through Customs — standing in a long queue until it was my turn to step over the 'Don't step over this line until it is your turn' line.

A woman with heavy eyelids looked briefly at

me then at my passport. 'What is the purpose of your visit to the United States?' she asked.

'I'm not coming to America,' I told her.

She stared at me with a don't-mess-with-me-I've-got-a-gun look. 'Then what are you doing here?' she asked. I explained that I was getting a connecting flight to Jamaica. And she must have heard some annoyance in my voice because she said, 'You have to go through Customs if you're setting foot on American soil.' She sounded like Peter at the Pearly Gates checking no sinners were trying to get into heaven. And she stamped my passport with aggressive unconcern and told me to have a nice day.

I was halfway through the lounge making my way to the Jamaican Airlines check-in when I saw them. Shabby-looking people. Shabby-looking black people, with men dressed in baggy trousers held up at the waist with belts. With jackets that from a distance looked smart but close up were stained and torn. Women with huge bottoms in tight-fitting skirts with no tights and sandals on their feet. And flowery print blouses that strained across their breasts. There were only about twenty of them but they looked so out of place in the plush setting of an American airport. They looked too poor to fly. And they were checking in cardboard boxes onto the airline's weighing scales. Boxes that my parents would have discarded as too flimsy and thin to have been of any use. They talked in patois. A language all of its own but with the occasional word that a woman like me who had grown up around the Jamaican accent with its 'nah man's and 'cha' and sucking of teeth, could be lulled into thinking I might understand if only I listened harder or they would speak slower.

I was about to hand my ticket to the officially neat woman behind the desk when a young woman pushed in front of me.

'Where's this flight go from?' she asked in a south London accent. The woman behind the counter looked at the ticket, consulted a screen, looked at a clock and then said, 'I'm afraid the flight has gone.'

The south London woman's eyes opened wide. 'What?' she shouted. Then she turned round and in a voice louder than the tannoy announcements yelled, 'Oh no, Mum, the flight's bloody well gone!' A scream came from somewhere near a hot-dog-on-a-stick stall and a woman the shape of a pear came thudding through the crowds to the desk. The young woman's hands gripped her hips as she told everyone that she had to get to Jamaica to see her relations, that her mum was going home, that they couldn't have missed the flight as they had only just landed in Miami, while her mother trembled and sobbed. It appeared that their travel agent had booked them onto a flight to Jamaica before the flight from England had landed. A feat not even the most ingenious of Afro-Caribbean women could perform, as the young woman pointed out loudly.

A security guard was called. He stood by the women listening to their complaints intently like he had the power to do something about them, while the woman behind the desk consulted books and schedules. The women were then told that if they would get to the back of the queue they could get on the next flight. The older woman thanked everybody, including me, wiping a small white hanky across her eyes as she did it. The younger woman said, 'I should bloody well think so. Cha,' and went to the back of the queue sucking her teeth.

The pilot of the Jamaican Airlines flight was a woman. As she made her announcements about the weather conditions, a woman sitting opposite me across the aisle punched her fist in the air and shouted, 'Yes, mam,' and 'Tell it sister,' like she was listening to a preacher. When the pilot finished the woman clapped her hands and enthusiastically nudged the man sitting next to her saying, 'A woman — oh boy, a woman — yes sir — a woman!'

When he didn't respond but just continued trying to open the wrapper on the cake we had all been given to eat with our rum punch, the woman slapped his arm with the back of her hand saying, 'Women can fly Jamaican planes, Errol. You see women fly Jamaican planes.'

To which Errol said, 'Oh hush, woman.'

It was dark by the time Jamaica came into view through the airplane window. A small island glittering beautiful, like a tiara on the dark sea. My first view of the island my parents had left thirty years before. The place in the photographs in our tatty brown album. From high above, the island looked silent and quiet.

'Can you fasten your seatbelt,' a stewardess said to me in a broad Jamaican accent. I looked up at her. She was white. Completely white. Blonde hair, grey eyes — no stray African genes in her. 'Your seatbelt — could you fasten it?' she instructed as I stared at her for far too long. 'We're landing in Jamaica now,' she added with a smile.

The woman across the aisle from me clapped again when the plane landed and came to a stop. 'Errol,' she said, 'Now just tell me that wasn't the best landing you ever had. The smoothest landing you ever had and a woman do it. Oh boy. Yes sir. This is Jamaica.'

Kingston airport was so alive, so noisy it was hard to imagine that I would not have heard it from up in the plane. The large arrival lounge was packed with black faces. Everywhere I turned — black faces. Black faces of people in uniforms. Black faces waiting for luggage. Black faces behind counters. Counters to change money, counters to find luggage, counters to check bags and boxes. Everyone moving, walking with purpose or drifting around, staring or searching, standing, shifting from foot to foot. And screeching, shouting, talking, whispering like a crowd scene in an epic film where the director had just called, 'Chaos!'

I felt out of place — everything was a little familiar but not quite. Like a dream. Culture shock is how the feeling is described. A name made up by someone with a stiff upper lip who wanted to deny the feelings of panic and terror. The feelings that made me want to run for a corner and cover my head with my arms and scream for my mummy. I stood by the conveyor belt watching the boxes, sweating in the musty heat with my English woollen jumper sticking to my body — worried I would not survive this.

'You wan' me find your bag, miss?' a voice said. A man was smiling at me. He looked like my brother Carl, except for the shirt. Carl would never wear pink.

'Bag always get lost in this place. Me find it. What your bag look like? I go see for you.' An image of my bag came to me, the last time I had seen it as it was thrown violently against a wall in Miami airport. I was pleased that someone had come to help me. Anyone. I said breathlessly, 'It's blue and grey, from flight 267 from Miami.'

He smiled a broad white span of teeth. 'I go find it, miss. I know di airport. Bag get lost all di time. Not like America,' he smiled at me again. 'I find it. I bring di bag.' He didn't seem to want to go. He stood staring into my face smiling but moving his eyes to look over my shoulder every few seconds.

'Thank you,' I said. 'It's grey and blue and it was on flight 267 from Miami.' He went away for a few minutes, then came back and stood close in front of me. 'I see di bag, miss. You wan' me bring it?'

I was relieved. 'Where?' I asked him.

'All di bag,' he told me, 'they all there. You wan' me bring it?' He held out his hand, low down near his waist and looked at me. 'Gimme two dollar,' he whispered.

I began to understand. 'No', I said, 'you bring the bag and I'll give you two dollars.' I smiled at him. I thought, I am from London, I know a hustle. You can't pull one over on me.

The man leant close to me. His breath smelt of tobacco. 'Come, me no like that. Me no hackle. Me no t'ief. Me find your bag. You wan' me find your bag? You gimme dollar.'

He began to speak very fast and I began not to understand everything he was saying. I tried to move out of his eyeline. To turn my body round away from him. But he followed me, pushing his face close to my ear, talking fast like a machine gun firing. I could feel his spittle pricking my cheek. He smelt damp. I tried to walk away but he grabbed my arm firmly, 'Gimme two dollar. Gimme two dollar. Me bring di bag.' I told him to leave me alone, but he stayed stuck to me, talking into my face, crowding my vision like a bad conscience. I couldn't move. He tripped at my feet. I tried to walk off fast but he kept coming in front of me, making me change direction until I was walking in a circle. And I was beginning to cry. 'Me no hackle. Me no hackle no one.' He looked so pleadingly into my face I wondered for a split second if I was wrong. 'Me no t'ief. Two dollar. American. Two dollar. Me get di bag. Me bring di bag. Two dollar. Me no hackle, me no t'ief.' He kept touching my arm, my shoulders, grabbing my wrist. 'Two dollar, me bring di bag, me no t'ief.'

I grabbed for the purse in my bag and opened it. The man became quiet but stood close by me, looking around, shaking his hand up and down waiting for the money. He tried to look in the open purse. 'Me have change, me have change, gimme. Two dollar. Me have change.' There was a little bundle of American dollars ready to exchange for Jamaican ones as soon as I could.

The man became impatient, 'Come, come, come. Two dollar, gimme, me have change.' I grabbed for a note, it was a five-dollar bill. The man snatched it and walked off. His pink back wriggling through the crowds. Within seconds he had disappeared. And for a moment I wondered whether he might, after all, come back with my bag. It was then that I cried. In the middle of the arrival lounge at Kingston airport, clutching my open purse and thinking of Mum's words: 'Everyone should know where they come from.'

Then a woman's voice said, 'You must shut up that purse.' I nearly pushed the woman who stood in front of me. I nearly knocked her to the ground. But then I recognised her from the plane — 'oh boy, women fly Jamaican planes!' — and I collapsed forward onto her.

'Come, darlin',' the woman said. I was leaning on her with one hand, grabbing her shoulder and sobbing into the damp fabric of her nylon blouse. She began to pat my back, like my mum used to when I'd fallen over. 'Come, darlin',' she said again, soft and low, and she patted my back like she'd known me for ever.

'Your first time in Jamaica.' I had to straighten up and look in her face to find out whether that was a question or an all too obvious fact.

'I thought so,' she said, even though I had said nothing. She smiled. 'I said to Errol. I said Errol, that young girl is her first time in Jamaica, her first time. And you know how I know?' She took my hand and folded it around my purse, then

206

pushed my purse and hand into my bag. She indicated at something on my face using her own face for demonstration. I began to wipe my cheek as she carried on.

'You know how I know?' she giggled. 'You waitin' by the luggage ramp.' She giggled some more. 'Twenty years I been coming home and me bag never come with me once. Not once. One time,' she went on, picking a hair off the shoulder of my jumper, 'it end up in Thailand. I ask you. In Thailand or some such place.' She leant forward and closed the zipper on my bag. 'I said to Errol, I said, Errol, it's a shame the suitcase can't speak, we could listen to tales from all over the world.' She laughed and sniffed loudly. 'You see Errol,' she said, touching my arm then pulling me forward a little so I could get a better view. Errol was waiting in a long queue with the blank expression of a very patient man. 'You see he has a bag. We put everything we need for two days in that bag and we take it on the plane. Because we know,' she said pointing through the crowds to the bag at Errol's feet, 'we know it gonna take two, three days for our suitcases to finish it holiday.' Errol leant down and shunted the small bag another few inches as the queue began to go down.

'A man just said he could find my bag,' I said. The woman looked at me dropping her head down and pouting her lips.

'You give him money?' she asked. I didn't answer but the woman said, 'T'ief' anyway. She sucked her teeth for a very long time and moved her head slowly from one side to the other. 'T'ief everywhere.' She grabbed my arm, 'Come, darlin', we must get in the queue.' She pulled me over to the lost luggage queue whilst explaining, 'I see you from over there and I said to Errol, that young girl never been here before. I must get her before t'ief does.'

She stood by me at the back of the queue and called out, 'Errol, soon come.' She pulled me forward a little so Errol could see me. 'I just helping this young girl because t'ief get her already.' She folded her arms and looked at me. Other people in the queue turned and stared at me and started mumbling to companions as Errol waved his hand, nodded and rolled his eyes all in one movement. I looked at my feet.

'The only thing that come on the plane is boxes for higglers,' the woman began saying. I nodded. 'Higglers are a nuisance,' she went on. 'Mark you, they only trying to make a living and the Lord knows that that is hard enough. But higglers everywhere now.'

I didn't know what a higgler was. But I thought I should. I was after all the daughter of two Jamaicans. I thought I should know what a higgler is and I should know when someone is trying to rob me. If not by experience then in my genes. I stayed looking at my feet. Everyone should know where they come from.

'You see the sign?' the woman said nudging me. I looked up at the fading sign that said Lost Luggage. 'You wait here and the woman will give you a bit of paper which you must keep. Then you can get your bag when it comes.' She smiled at me, her full cheeks stretching to smooth capacity.

'Thank you,' I said, 'you've been really nice.' She waved her hand and frowned to quiet me.

'I said, that girl never been here before. I could tell, you know. You look sort of . . . ' she searched for the right word, 'sort of . . . innocent.'

I laughed.

'Someone meeting you?' she asked quickly.

'My aunt — I hope.' I shuddered. What if I stepped onto the Jamaican soil outside and there was no one there who knew me? I had never met my aunt before. She was a face in a photograph. A young woman smiling in front of a bungalow, wearing a small hat and carrying a handbag and Bible. For as long as I could remember I had pointed to that photograph and Mum had said, 'That's your Auntie Coral.' And lately she had begun adding, 'Of course, she's a bit older now.' Mum had told me to take the photo with me. I felt around for it in my bag — ready to whip it out and match it up to any strangers I saw.

'Of course Coral will know you,' Mum had assured me. But I could imagine Auntie Coral clutching one of my baby photos, with me a little toddler in a ruched swimming costume with wild hair, playing in a paddling pool on the beach at Eastbourne.

I had written to my aunt asking her if I could stay with her and she had replied enthusiastically, saying, 'Yes come. At last, a child of Mildred coming to Jamaica. We were beginning to think we would never see the day. Come.' It was followed by a list of all the things I must bring with me. Aspirin and Vitamin E capsules. Drugs from the chemist — some that I bought over the counter, some that the pharmacist shook his head at and told me to get a prescription. I had to bring the *All Saints Family Hymn Book* for piano. 'Just one copy for Vincent,' my aunt explained in the letter. 'His copy here falling apart and it's hard to get it in Jamaica.' And then, 'Oh yes and six descant recorders — for the children. Thank you.'

All the items were packed in the suitcase along with several packages and presents my mum and dad had given me. These caused me some difficulty when boarding the plane, as I could not, with my hand on my heart, say that I knew what everything was that was packed in my suitcase.

'What if there is no one there to meet me?' I said, to the woman at Kingston airport.

'Don't look so feared, darlin',' the woman said, placing her hand on my arm. 'Did they say they be there?' I didn't answer before she said, 'If they said they'd be there — they'd be there. You see.'

Errol had reached the head of the queue. He picked up their bag. 'Sugar,' he called out and Sugar said to me, 'I must go now. It was nice talking to you. You have a good time in Jamaica.' She smiled then her face became serious. 'But see you stay away from t'ief.' She joined Errol, taking the bag out of his hand — she slapped his arm whilst she waved to me until Errol, reluctantly, waved too.

★ ★ ★

I came out of the airport terminal clutching the bit of paper from the lost luggage. I had not understood everything the woman behind the desk had told me to do. But after I had asked her once to repeat herself I began to hear tuts and teeth being sucked behind me in the queue. I took the paper hoping that soon everything in Jamaica would be clearer to me.

There were lots of people waiting outside the airport. Waiting behind a barrier like a football crowd. Every time the doors opened, necks stretched and heads waggled trying to get a better view of the person walking out. Every face keen with anticipation — Jamaicans wondering whether you belonged to them.

I walked along the gangway having to exhibit myself like a piece of luggage. I looked into the crowd for someone that might be familiar — the young woman in a hat with a Bible. As I neared the end of the ramp I began to wonder what would happen if I was not claimed. If no one whistled to me, no one rushed through the crowds to hug me, no little child came running to me shouting 'Auntie, Auntie.' Would I have to walk the gangway again? Parading myself but this time from a different angle — 'This is Faith Columbine Jackson, from England. Parents left in 1948. Come to visit relations. Please step up if she's yours.'

Any Jamaican family could have claimed me and taken me home to talk about my mum and dad and what had happened to them in the

211

'Mother Country'. And my hosts would know it as a familiar story. It could be days before we realised that although familiar our photographs did not match up, our dates of births and deaths did not tally, our mix of genes was not quite the same. Until we finally had to admit that we were not, after all, kin.

Then I saw someone jumping and waving in my direction. I looked behind me. I expected to see someone waving and jumping there but there was no one. I walked slowly forward, staring at the commotion and then heard a faint, 'Faith,' being called. I began to wave. As I got closer I could see a man in a beige shirt smiling and crossing his outstretched arms in the air like he was directing a plane to land. 'Faith,' I heard again as I wondered who this man was going to be. I got closer and the man ran through the crowd and crushed me into his chest before I had time to see his face and work out if he was anyone from the photo album. Everything went black as I was held against him smelling lavender and sweat and listening to, 'It's good to meet you, Faith, after all this time,' coming in vibrations through his chest. When he finally let me out of his embrace I looked into his face, smiling my broadest, most excited, most welcoming grin as I tried to work out who he could be.

'I'm Vincent, your cousin Vincent,' he smiled back. Vincent turned me round, 'And this,' he said, 'is your auntie.'

I recognised her but not from any photograph. 'Coral,' I said, 'Auntie Coral.' She was an old woman, small and frail with greying hair and a dress that hung on her like it was designed for a larger frame. But she was unmistakably my mother's sister. Even though my mum was fat with hair that bottles of black dye did not allow to go grey, when Auntie Coral smiled her eyes creased into the same small slits, with little lines that radiated round them like the dials round a clock. And her lips were the same: 'too thin, to be thoroughbred African lips'. And when she tilted her head and said, 'Mildred's daughter,' I thought I heard my mum.

My aunt took both my hands in hers then moved my arms open and looked at me up and down. 'You skinny,' she concluded with a laugh. I laughed too then leant forward to hug her. She was angular and brittle like a bag of crisps and I didn't use my full force in the hug for fear of crushing her.

'I was scared you wouldn't be here,' I said with a smile. One of my aunt's eyebrows rose alarmingly on her forehead and her lips tightened into a thin line as she pierced Vincent with a stare. Vincent looked at his mother then at me and laughed, 'Of course we here.' Auntie Coral sucked her teeth quietly as Vincent asked, 'Where's your bag?' I explained about the luggage as my aunt looked up into my face, her expression softening as she started muttering, 'Mildred's daughter — little Mildred's daughter — I never thought I'd see the day.' And Vincent sucked his teeth at the inefficiency of Jamaican airports.

I sat in the back seat of Vincent's car and my

213

aunt sat in the front straining her body round so she could look at me. Vincent drove whilst explaining Jamaica like a guide on a tourist bus.

'You see the airport is on a bit of land that sticks out into the sea. The plane must land carefully or it would just miss the runway and there would be a terrible problem.' I sat forward in my seat resting my chin on my hand, watching the back of Vincent's head wiggling and nodding, his ears making tiny movements as he spoke. My aunt smiled at me and occasionally said, 'That's right,' or 'umm umm,' to Vincent's commentary. I was pleased he was talking so much as I could think of nothing to say to my new family — my mind a blank any Buddhist would have been proud of.

But as we drove into Kingston I sat back in my seat and looked out of the window. It was dark. Down in the midst of the jewel I had seen from the air, palm trees swayed. Their thick trunks loomed over us in the moonlight, like giant's legs waiting at the side of the road. Then along the streets the shacks began to appear. The buildings had no details in the night light except where a small fire showed up their flimsy wooden construction or a streetlight cast a glow over the scene. Black people were everywhere. Sitting by the shacks, walking along the road, in the road, standing, talking, gesturing in conversation, calling across to others. Eating food, watching the traffic going by. Bending over to small children. Children that ran and played, darting around in a game.

The smell of woodsmoke pervaded the car.

The dark brown smell reminded me of Guy Fawkes' night as I watched the women in their hair curlers and headscarves talking to men in scruffy shirts that were open to the waist.

'The roads are bad in Jamaica,' Vincent was saying, while the people, the fires and the shacks went by unexplained. 'Holes everywhere. You have to drive very carefully.'

'Vincent is a good driver, Faith,' Auntie Coral butted in.

'But people drive badly — they have no respect for the rules.' As Vincent spoke a car overtook us and pulled in front of us so quickly that he had to brake. The tyres screeched on the road. But nobody from the shacks looked up at the sudden noise as if it was anything unusual.

'You see what I mean,' Vincent cursed, 'idiots.' He changed gear, crunching the gearstick into place with a rasping sound. The car lurched forward and I had to put my hand out to stop myself knocking my forehead against the back of Vincent's neck. 'They drive like madmen especially round here,' Vincent said, as Coral sucked her teeth.

The car straightened up round a bend and the streetlights revealed empty streets. The people had gone. Suddenly there were large houses like mansions. Some bathed in floodlight, others with tall iron fences and gates. Some smaller with huge white satellite dishes resting in the front gardens, picking up the moonlight in their bowls. And there were black shadows from large dogs that walked slowly across the front paths.

'So tell me, Faith,' I heard Vincent say. I had to shake my head to bring myself back into the car, away from the astonishing strangeness of the life outside it. 'How you like Jamaica so far?'

18

'You see, Faith, there is good in everything,' my cousin Vincent proclaimed. 'At least we have no bag to bring in.' He giggled to himself as he stopped the car in front of my aunt's house.

Aunt Coral said, 'Amen.'

The house was surrounded by fences. Even in the dark I could see the web of impenetrable metal grilles that wrapped the property — around the garden, over the windows, across the door. My aunt undid the tall gate in front of the house and Vincent carefully manoeuvred the car into a small carport. Then Coral locked the gate behind us. As I got out of the car a large black dog walked slowly up to me and nuzzled its head onto my hand. I quickly raised my hands up into the air. Rabies! I'd read about it — the Third World is full of it. A death by rabies is horrible — scared of water and dying for a drink. Vincent shooed the dog away playfully. 'Get away, Hobo, she doesn't like you.'

Coral unlocked more gates that let us into the house — a lacework of metal triangles that went from the floor to the roof. She fiddled with her bunch of keys, tutting and mumbling, 'Keys! Keys! Keys!' then finally unlocked the front door.

The house was not like I expected.

'Come in, Faith — you must be tired out from that long journey.' It was a bungalow — like something you would retire to in Bexhill-on-Sea.

'I'll get you a drink. Would you like something to drink, Faith? Yes, I'm sure you would.' I don't know what I was expecting but somewhere in my mind was an image of a mud hut with a pointy stick roof and dirt floors.

'You look a bit hot, Faith. You want to take off that jumper?' But here was a front room that looked so familiar. A brown velour three-piece suite. A cupboard with ornaments — a woman with a sheep, a little bird on a branch.

'Would you like something to eat, Faith?' There was an electric lamp in the corner with a large pink shade.

'I can make you a sandwich. Would you like a sandwich?' There was a coffee table with a glass top, pink and red plastic flowers in a bowl, net curtains. 'Are you all right, Faith? You don't say much.' There was a television and a record player with a stack of records by its side.

'I expect it's all a bit different for you.' And a portrait of Jesus on the wall. 'You'll soon get used to us.'

It reminded me of home.

The kitchen had formica worktops. Formica worktops! I was expecting a black cast-iron range with a cooking pot permanently bubbling with something made from goat. The cooker was big and looked like the front of an American car, and the fridge was nearly as tall as me. The floor was not made of mud and straw — it was solid and covered with a geometric-print lino. And up on a high shelf above the kitchen cupboard was a food liquidiser. My mum didn't have a liquidiser.

'Would you like a little ice in your drink, although it's nice and cold?' All the familiarities made everything more strange. But then I sipped my drink and it was different to anything I had ever tasted. 'It's sorrel juice,' my aunt said. It was sweet and sticky with a spiky aftertaste. 'You like it? I make it meself.' And through the air vents in the brickwork of the kitchen wall I could faintly hear the rhythmic rasping of cicadas.

'So what you think of Jamaica?' Vincent asked again. Then he laughed like a schoolboy — behind his hand. He had a broad nose and lips that looked as if they were permanently pouting. His skin was the colour of caramel and when he smiled his cheeks became creaseless and smooth like toffee. He kept tapping his hand on the arm of his chair. And although he talked politely — 'It's nice to meet a cousin from England after all this time. We were wondering if we would ever see you,' — I knew he wanted to be somewhere else. He reminded me of someone. He reminded me of Carl.

Vincent suddenly stood up. He pulled on the hem of his shirt and flicked out his trousers until they once again covered his shoes. I was saying, 'Well, it's really nice to be here,' and Vincent was nodding at me. He left a polite pause after I had finished speaking then said, 'I must be going now, Mummy.'

'You off now, son?'

Vincent blew out breath. 'I have few errands to do before I can get to my bed.'

Coral held up a hand, 'Wait nah. I have something for you.'

'Come, Mummy, I am late,' Vincent said, as Coral shuffled into the kitchen singing, 'Soon come, soon come.' Vincent rolled his eyes and smiled at me. We both listened to the rustling in the kitchen and then smiled at each other again. Coral came back carrying a full plastic bag.

'It's just some bits and pieces, son.' Vincent took the bag without comment like I used to when Mum handed me my school packed lunch. He saluted me as he left and said, 'Tomorrow.'

'That was your cousin Vincent.' Coral locked the gates behind him and sat opposite me. 'His wife doesn't eat meat. And a man needs meat. That's what I give him — some chicken. He loves his chicken.' And the way she tilted her head and folded her arms under her breasts reminded me of Mum.

'He likes me soups when I use a ham bone. He loves ham and he can't get it at home.' But there were other ways in which she reminded me of Mum — ways that I could not describe or point to. She had the aura of kin. Perhaps if I had had a tape measure it would have been in the length of her lips as she grinned.

'I mean, Gloria, his wife, is a nice woman — it's just that she doesn't eat meat.' Or maybe it was the angle that she sat, the timbre of her voice or her accent — a lilting Jamaican cadence that relaxed me like a comfort blanket. 'And Vincent has always, always loved his meat.'

Coral's arms were bare. Her elbows had shrivelled into walnuts and her upper arms were flabby and wobbled around like a bloodhound's jowls. I never saw my Mum's bare arms — they

220

were always wrapped in thermal vests and blouses and jumpers — even in the summer, even when she would fan herself because she was too hot.

'Your mummy wrote me about you,' Coral was saying.

'What did she say?'

Coral fixed me with a look — a little tilt of the head and a tiny smile. She knew everything about me. Everything. I was sure of it. But she didn't say a word. Her slippers were maroon velour with pink flowers. I never thought they'd have slippers like that in Jamaica.

'Your mummy told me,' Coral at last began. I took a deep breath. 'She told me that you work for the television. That must be interesting.' And I laughed with a sort of relief.

'Ahh, that's better,' Coral said, 'you lookin' more relax now.' My fists unclenched and my shoulders dropped at least six inches. 'So, what did your mummy tell you about Jamaica?' I wasn't sure whether Aunt Coral really wanted an answer. But she sat quietly looking at me. Then I wasn't sure what answer to give her. 'Nothing much,' I shrugged.

'Nothing?'

'Mum and Dad didn't really talk about Jamaica. They were always very busy,' I added as an afterthought.

Coral sucked her teeth with frightening aggression. I quickly adjusted, 'Mum told me a bit about you and Eunice when you were little. The three sisters.'

'Oh yes.' Coral sat forward interested — looking like an adolescent about to hear what their best friend really thinks of them.

I had to carry on. 'She said you used to fight sometimes.'

Coral tipped her head back and laughed. 'Sometimes!' she hollered. She sat forward quickly and fixed my eyes with a stare. 'That mother of yours was a pest to me. She was so lazy. All day all she dream about is goin' to England. She just spend all day dreaming of Trafalgar Circus and lookin' in the mirror.'

I was about to say that that was what Mum said about her, but Coral carried on.

'Eunice wasn't much better. But at least Eunice did what you ask her. But your mother — nobody could tell her a thing. Not one thing.' She suddenly began to laugh and shake her head with the memory of it. 'Ohh that Mildred — little Mildred.' She jumped up from her seat and ran across the room. 'I tell you somethin' funny. You see this seat?' She was pointing at an old brown leather chaise longue that was under a window. 'You ask your mummy about this seat.' She sat down on it. 'I've had this seat for years. This seat used to be in our house at home. That's how old this seat is. And you know what? Mildred, your mother, used to sit on this seat — sit on this seat all day. All day!'

She began pulling some of the stuffing through a hole that was worn in the leather on the back of the chair. She sucked her teeth loudly. 'It's your mother that make this hole. She lie here and get a broom and jus' push the broom back and forth near the chair. Then she tell everyone she done the sweeping up.' Coral leant back on the chair like a madam and mimed how my mum would sweep. 'Back and forth on the same spot.' She laughed again. 'Ohh, she was a pest.' And I wasn't sure if the memory of it was good or bad.

Coral then cried out, 'Oh you,' so loudly that I jumped. She got down on her hands and knees beside the chair. 'Faith, look at this,' she said.

I was about to get up when Coral began pulling out a small dog from deep under the chair. It was little and tan brown and it was rolled up as if it was still asleep — as if it was not being pulled by its collar. Coral yanked it further into the room but the dog stayed curled and stiff.

'Look at this.' Coral now had the dog almost off the ground but it did not move a limb. 'He's meant to be guarding the house.'

The little dog then gave up its pretence at sleep and stood on four shaky legs, looking up sorrowfully at Coral with big black eyes.

'What you doin' under there?' Coral dragged the dog to the door. 'He's meant to be out at night,' she told me. 'But he gets scared with all the bangs and everythin'. I'm always finding him all over the place. Me neighbour left him for me, you see. But he's a very scared little dog. And I can't just turn him out. Him a sweet little thing. But he's a pest.'

The dog began to walk out of the door, his legs shaking like a newborn foal. 'Go, go and sit with Hobo.' Coral pointed the way for the dog.

223

He looked like he was about to pee himself. But Coral insisted, 'Go out and guard the house!'

★　★　★

I lay in bed on my first night in Jamaica not really knowing what day it was. 'You must have lost some time somewhere,' Coral had said as she'd shown me to the room. 'You can't leave England and come all that way without losing some bit of you.' I felt like I had been to an all-night party — soft-headed, with pieces of grit behind my eyes that kept them from closing.

The room had a dressing table with a dressing-table set. A brush with mother-of-pearl-effect blue plastic on the back, a matching mirror, a matching comb and two matching pots that should have contained face cream. They were laid out at angles to one another on the wooden chest, carefully placed for that womanly respectability. The room also had a fitted wardrobe made from an alcove, a table with a fan and a double bed. A double bed!

'These are shutters.' Coral pointed to the window. 'I don't suppose you have these in England.' She went over to the wooden shutters to demonstrate their use. 'It too hot to shut the window so . . . '

As she opened the shutters I could see directly into the neighbours' house. The sound of their television suddenly filled the little room — mechanical laughter from a sitcom. There was a woman dressed in yellow standing with her back to us. Her body was shaking with a

224

laugh. She had the biggest bottom I had ever seen. A circular padded pouffe of a bottom that seemed to be almost half of her. It was laughing too. Then she was gone. 'Television all day with them,' my aunt tutted as she shut the shutter. She pulled a net curtain across the window.

'Is that to keep out the mosquitoes?' I asked.

'Mosquitoes? We don't have mosquitoes. I never bothered by mosquitoes.'

My aunt turned on the fan which started up like a propeller of an old plane. 'You can leave that on to keep you cool,' she shouted above the noise. She mouthed something at me next. I turned the fan off and she repeated, 'You have all your things?'

'No, everything was in my suitcase.'

'What, you have no night things or comb? Cha. These people they don't know how they inconvenience. Wait.' Coral left the room and came back with a nightdress. A winter-warmer passion-killer of a nightdress — full-length with a frill of lace at the neck. 'You can wear this.' I began to sweat just holding it over my arm.

There was a shower unit over the bath and the toilet flushed. Coral explained how to light the gas geyser that heated the hot water. 'And then you get a match like this and you strike it hard against the box and you see it lights. Then you put it in this little hole and turn on this tap and you see . . . Come closer, Faith. You see how the little light appears. Then you can use it.'

'We used to have one of these at home,' I told her but she took no notice and started to go through the whole procedure again, this time

225

using mime. Coral brushed my cheek with her hand as I went to shut the door of the bedroom. 'You favour me sister,' she said. Then she slapped her hands together, 'Okay, little one — I leave you to get on.'

The room was dark but too noisy to sleep. The television from next door and faint titters of laughter that every now and then became raucous howls. Music coming from somewhere — a repetitive bass beat, rhythmic clapping. Dogs' sporadic piercing barks. Woof. Cicadas — criss, criss, criss. Laughing. A car horn. Boom, boom, boom. And in the little room there was a faint smell of woodsmoke — wafting past the mint toothpaste and the sweet-jasmine-scented soap.

Soon most of the sounds disappeared leaving only traffic noise. The crescendo and diminuendo of cars passing the house at the bottom of the garden. A distant noise — comforting — reminding me of my bedroom in London. Then suddenly there was revving and screeching as a car skidded, a high-pitched whine that ended in a dull thud and smashing glass. A crash! I sat up in bed waiting for the sounds of sirens. Ambulance, police, the fire brigade. But no sirens came. Nothing.

After a while I put my head back on the pillow. There was buzzing in my left ear. The persistent hum of a flying insect. I flicked my hand and the sound stopped for several seconds. Then it was back again — closer, louder. A whispered purr in my ear. A Jamaican mosquito had found me and it was rubbing its hands together and licking its lips.

Coral's Story told to me by Coral

When my Aunt Coral was a little girl she was 'free as a bird.' She played by the river, floating paper canoes into the water, she drank milk straight from the cow, she picked flowers and sang hymns as she walked to school in the hot sunshine. But as Coral grew older she became more responsible. 'You see, I had to feed the chickens and the goats and help Mummy all around the house and still find the time to sew dolls' clothes for my sisters. I was always working but I did not complain.' Coral was the oldest of three sisters. Four daughters had been born to her parents, William and Grace Campbell. There was Coral, Eunice, Muriel and Mildred.

Her sister Muriel died of pneumonia when she was only twelve. Muriel was 'a lovely sister — so kind and pretty and always a good word for everyone'. But she had anaemia all her short life and was always ill with one thing or another. Coral used to look after her sister Muriel: 'Well, I was expected to — I was the oldest — that's how things were in those days.' While Eunice and Mildred, evidently, did absolutely nothing: 'They

227

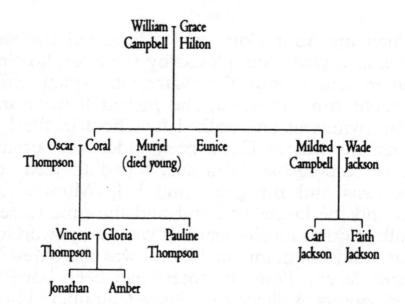

Family tree diagram:

William Campbell — Grace Hilton

Their children:
- Oscar Thompson — Coral
- Muriel (died young)
- Eunice
- Mildred Campbell — Wade Jackson

Oscar Thompson and Coral's children:
- Vincent Thompson — Gloria
- Pauline Thompson

Vincent Thompson and Gloria's children:
- Jonathan
- Amber

Mildred Campbell and Wade Jackson's children:
- Carl Jackson
- Faith Jackson

were useless, those two sisters. Useless.' The day before Muriel died she had asked Coral to tell her what heaven was like. 'She was always asking that — what is heaven like? She used to ask Daddy and Mummy from when she was small girl. It was like she knew she would be going there soon.'

Muriel died when Coral was away visiting her grandmother. 'It's funny, Faith, but when I left that day the sky was blue but as I walked a cloud came into the sky so black I thought the world was coming to an end. And I had a feeling then I would never see me sister again.' Muriel was buried in the garden of their house.

Coral went to the same school as Mildred. 'Your mummy's school but I left long before it burn down.' She worked very, very hard at school and was liked by all her teachers and was the most popular girl in the class. When she left the headmistress 'had tears in her eyes — she wanted me to come and work in the school. I was her favourite'. But Coral wanted to become a nurse. 'I liked the uniform. So clean.'

So she began training as a nurse at a hospital in Kingston. 'Yes, it was the same hospital your mummy was at. But I started there long before her. She always follow in me feet.' She enjoyed the training — she worked very, very hard and was liked by all the staff and was the most popular girl in her group. 'They sort of look up to me. They were pleased to have someone like me.'

Coral worked at the hospital for a few years. 'I don't remember how many.' And it was there that she met Oscar, her husband. 'Now how did I meet him? You want to know everything, Faith.'

Oscar Thompson drove a van for a living. His own van that had been bought with money his dad had left him when he died. He used to hire himself out to farmers on the island and take their produce to the market or the docks or wherever they wanted their produce taken. He worked with his younger brother Winston.

One day Winston cut his head getting into the van. 'The man was always busting up himself — he was a fool.' His head was bleeding so much that Oscar took him to the hospital. 'I can still remember — the way the man cry out, you think someone had slice off his head.' Coral had to dress his wound. 'There was nothing there, just a little cut but the noise he make. Cha.' It was while she was bandaging Winston's head with gentle care that Oscar noticed her. He smiled. 'He had such a smile — cheeky — like him just done something bad. But he never had. No, never. Not my Oscar.'

That evening Oscar waited outside the hospital for Coral to finish work. He did not know what time she would be leaving. He just sat outside for hours. 'He was like that, Oscar — patient. He could sit and wait for fruit to drop from trees.' When Coral came out she saw him and even though he walked up to her and said hello, Coral just walked by. 'Leave a man to wait, that's what my mother always told me. If he's interested he'll be back.' Oscar came to the hospital every day for a week before Coral talked to him. 'I say hello, I think, or something like that. Not too forward.' But eventually Coral let Oscar take her home in his van. Then she let him take her to Blue Mountain Peak where they held hands and looked out over the view. And after that Oscar and Coral went on other trips — Fern Gully and Dunn's River Falls, Hope Gardens and Mona Heights. 'I saw more of Jamaica then than any time since. It was lovely.'

Then one day a woman came up to Coral as she was leaving church on Sunday. She told her that the man she was seeing, Oscar, had a baby by another woman. 'She was a busybody — into everybody's business.' By that time Coral liked Oscar very much. 'Oh, I cried — you see he never said anything to me.' She refused to talk to Oscar for three weeks even though he came to the hospital every day. 'I just walk straight past him.' Then one day as Coral walked along the street Oscar jumped down out of a tree and landed in front of her. 'I nearly jumped out me skin. Suddenly he is standing before me, his black hair all curly and shinin' in the sun and that cheeky grin on his face. Ohh, Oscar.' He told Coral about the baby boy and how the boy's mother had run off just after the baby was born to live in Montego Bay with a Scotsman. 'You must understand, Faith, most men would have nothing to do with the child but Oscar knew his responsibilities.' The boy, Errol, lived with Oscar's aunt.

Oscar's mother was not pleased when Oscar and Coral decided to get married. 'She didn't like me — not at first.' Oscar had a lighter skin than Coral. 'You see his mother thought he

231

could do better. I was too dark. You must understand, Faith, that was how it was in those days.' But the wedding went ahead.

On the day, the church was full up with people. But neither Mildred nor Eunice were there because by that time they had both moved away. Only Coral's mum and dad came. Oscar's whole family filled the church with relations from all over the island. 'If I hadn't been there I don't think some of them would have noticed.' There were lots of speeches but the food — the chicken and rice, the curried goat, the cake and rum punch — ran out before everyone had got some. 'Some of them had three helpings before others had got to their feet. Some people! And Faith, they all think they so high-class because they have light skin. Cha. Sipping their drinks with their little fingers in the air. It was comical.'

Coral and Oscar rented a house in Kingston — a house with six rooms and a garden. They had two children. Pauline was born first and had a light skin like her father. Vincent was darker. 'But I love him all the same. He's my son.' Oscar worked very, very hard and was loved by all his children and family. 'You know, some days Oscar would come home and get everybody and we'd go for a drive in the van. Up into the hills or sometimes over to Ocho, to sit on the beach and watch the sun. And the children would play and be so happy. He'd say to the children, 'Who coming out to play?' and they'd jump up laughing and he'd lift them into the van. Happy days.'

But then Oscar's business started to do badly.

The van kept breaking down. 'He could fix it but it was the parts you see. We had no money. And every day it was something else.' Winston, Oscar's brother, left Jamaica and moved to New York. He wrote to Oscar and Coral telling them how much work there was in America, how much money they could make in America. How they needed drivers and how they needed nurses in America. Coral and Oscar talked it over. 'We always talk about everythin', me and Oscar. Some men don't, you know.'

They decided to go and live in New York. Coral got a job as a nurse and Oscar got a job driving a van for a furniture store. And the children started school. The only apartment they could get was in the Bronx. It was a small apartment and all four of them had to share a bedroom. 'Oh God, that place. Three locks on the door and all you could see out of the window was more windows. And some of the children running around with no shoes and poor, poor!' Coral could not stand to see Pauline and Vincent stuck in the little flat all the time. 'But I was scared to let them out. It was so rough.' And Pauline and Vincent missed Jamaica; the sun and the trees and the beach and the air and the food. So Coral sent them back to live with her mother in St Mary.

'Yes, Oscar and me stayed in New York. You must understand, we had to stay, Faith, to get the money. Pauline and Vincent were happy in Jamaica — they had trees and fresh air. But we had to stay in America, we had to work or else we would not have been able to make ends meet.

We would not have been able to provide for them. Pauline and Vincent were with their grandparents — they were happy. They were being well looked after. They were better off in Jamaica. We write them all the time and ask them about school work and everything. And we worked to give them the best. There was nothing else we could do, Faith. Nothing.'

Oscar and Coral sent money home every week. 'Vincent and Pauline had the best of everything, Faith; best shoes, best clothes. Those two children wanted for nothing.' After a few years Oscar and Coral had enough money to buy a house in Kingston and as often as they could they came home to be with their children. 'Every chance we get we come home. Every chance! It was all we could do.' And Pauline and Vincent grew strong and healthy and happy and did very, very well at school and were loved by everyone.

But by the time Coral and Oscar came back to Jamaica to live Pauline and Vincent were grown-up. 'Sometimes, Faith, sometimes I regret it. Sometimes I wish I watched them growing up. But what else could we do?'

When Oscar and Coral came back to Jamaica, Oscar became ill. 'We had been working so long, he was just tired out. I remember looking at Oscar asleep one day. He looked so grey and old like he was dead. It frighten me. I had to wake him up.' Oscar died of lung cancer a few years after they returned. 'He didn't know what to do with himself when he wasn't working. And the children they knew him, but . . .'

Coral cried and cried at the funeral. 'I thought

I'd never be able to stop. And you know, I still miss him. But life must go on. I'm happy. I have me garden and me dogs and church and ... Pauline married a lovely man — educated — a teacher. She lives in Canada, you know, and she has three children — all boys. She has her hands full. And Vincent comes to see me every day. And there is his family ... My cup is full, Faith. No time to regret. So here I am now. You know all about me, Miss-want-to-know-everything-from-England.'

19

Coral was standing over me when I opened my eyes. She was wearing a black hat that had a wide brim with a black and white chequered band round it, like the Metropolitan Police wear. 'Oh good, you're awake. I didn't want to have to wake you. You sleepin' so peacefully.'

It was still dark in the room but her white satin blouse glowed. It had a tie at the neck that formed into a huge floppy bow. 'What time is it?' I asked, convinced I had slept through the whole of my first day.

'It's late, but I didn't want to wake you. You sleepin', sleepin', sleepin''. Coral went to the window. 'It's eight o'clock or thereabouts.' She pulled open the shutters and a perfect rectangle of brilliant blue appeared at the top of the window. The sky. I could hear birds.

'It's morning!' I said.

Coral laughed. 'Of course it's morning and a lovely morning the Lord has sent you for your first day in Jamaica.' Her skirt was a bright grass green with mechanical pleats that would never need ironing. And there was lipstick on her lips and little neat pearl earrings in her ears.

'Church!' she exclaimed, smiling at me. 'You comin' to church?'

'Is it Sunday?'

'Of course it's Sunday, little one. The Lord's day and we'll be late if you don't hurry yourself.

236

'I'll leave you to get ready.'

I hadn't been to church for a long time. Mum used to plead with Carl and me to go once in a while so the Lord didn't forget us. But Carl stopped believing in God when he realised that the communion wine was red Hirondelle, and that our old vicar was regularly found pissed on the blood of Christ. He said he was an atheist. He could say it without ducking — without thinking he would be struck down by lightning or a thunderbolt for his blasphemous words. I was not so brave. I told Mum I was an agnostic — which had that maybe-maybe-not quality that hedged my bets nicely. But I was in Jamaica and careful not to offend.

My jeans felt damp and sweaty and my tee-shirt was no longer pure white but I had to wear them again. I had nothing else. But I left my jumper over the back of the chair — it was early morning and pleasantly warm in the room but I could sense how hot the day would soon become. I sat on the bed and tried to use the dressing-table set to do my hair. The brush was useless with soft bristles that glided over my head making no impression and the comb had tiny tightly spaced teeth made for fine flyaway blonde locks. A 'honky' comb, Carl would have called it and I wondered if there was anyone on this island who could actually use it.

My aunt looked appalled and slightly scared when she saw me. 'Is this all you've got?' she asked. I looked down at my clothes and then at my aunt. I was going to church. I had forgotten the hats, the white gloves, the shiny shoes, the

237

clean socks, the crisp ironed blouses, the neat creaseless skirts and the hair ribbons of my younger Sunday-best church days.

'I'm afraid all my clothes are in my suitcase. Everything, even my comb.' I patted at my hair and Coral let out a long sigh that gently slapped my face. 'Come,' she said sternly. She pulled me through the house to her bedroom.

Her wardrobe smelt like the old trunk my parents had at home — the trunk that held the old brown photo album, a white christening shawl and several of my little ballet tutus — a waft of mothballs and memories.

'You can't go to church dressed in pants, Faith.' Coral shook her head as she looked through her clothes. She pulled out a blue dress. 'Ahh here. I wore this to Pauline's wedding.' She held it up against me. 'It might be a little big but try it.' It had a white pointed collar, a pattern of sequins falling down one side of the bodice and puff sleeves that Princess Anne made fashionable — briefly, very briefly — with her wedding dress. And it was huge — size eighteen at least. I could have wrapped it round me and tied it with a belt without having to get into it.

'I think it might be a little big, Auntie.'

'Oh you think so?' she said. 'Maybe.' She carried on looking. Satin, crêpe and nylon dresses with collars and frills and spots and twirls and tassels and pleats. Henry would have loved to describe these. I kept shaking my head and trying to think of an excuse why I could not wear the item. I'm allergic to pink. But she didn't seem to want to give up. Her wardrobe

238

was a time machine of middle-aged fashion and we were heading for the early nineteen sixties when I said, 'Coral, you better leave me here — I think you're going to be late. I can come next Sunday, when I've got my own clothes.'

'You think so?' she said, defeated. 'I can leave you here? You have everything? I don't like to leave you on your first day. You think I can leave you? Your mummy won't think I abandon you?'

'No — I'll be fine.'

'I won't be gone long.' She hurried round collecting her handbag and a little scarf, then made her way to the door. As she stepped outside a woman from the next-door house looked over the wall. 'Auntie C — your niece come?'

'I'm just on me way to church, Sybil. But Faith, come meet Sybil.' It was the woman with the large bottom. I could tell, even though that part of her was hidden by a low concrete wall, because her face went with her behind — big round cheeks, broad and flat like they were pressed against a pane of glass. She put her hand out for me to shake. My aunt ushered me forward, and I had to stand on a bed of plants to reach the woman.

'She come from England?' Sybil asked my aunt but stayed smiling at me.

'Last night,' my aunt said. 'Vincent and me fetch her from the airport. But her bag get lost.' Both women sucked their teeth.

'She stayin' long time, Auntie C?'

'Couple weeks. Tell me, Sybil — you know me sister?'

239

'Is Mildred you talking of, Auntie C?'

'Um-hmm,' Coral sang. 'Mildred wantin' to come home.'

'Ya don't say.'

'I tell her it's changed.'

'Change, change, change.' Sybil shook her head and smiled at me.

'She want to get a place in Ocho.'

'Noooooo,' Sybil said, half-impressed, half-disdainful.

Coral nodded. 'You see, when me sister young she always sayin' she going to have a place in Ocho one day. And I said, don't go gettin' ideas. But now she been to England she say, see Coral, I can come back and get a place.'

'I didn't know that,' I said, surprised. Both women looked at me as if they had forgotten I was there but then began to nod their heads slowly.

'I'm off to church,' Coral said.

'You off to church, Auntie C?' Sybil responded.

'And I'm late.'

'I'm waitin' for me son or else I would go but . . . ' They started to talk about Sybil's son who evidently had just got a job as a mechanic and was having to work long hours. Long, long, long, hours. And if my aunt had been late for church when she woke me up, the service would now surely have been over.

'I must be gone. They wonder what happen to me,' Coral eventually said.

Sybil left the wall. 'It was nice to see your niece, Auntie C.' As she opened the door of her house I heard the television.

'Television night and day with her,' Coral whispered into my ear. 'And always wantin' to know me business. She's a pest.'

Coral locked the gates of the house behind her, leaving me inside. Hobo looked like a shadow on the ground — motionless, flat and black. He watched me with one eye as I walked up the side of the house. A little alleyway shaded by plants — lush green plants. Some with delicate leaves like ferns or jasmine. Others, like palms with leaves as big as plates. There were branches hanging with delicate berries and bushes with yellow and white flowers. And reds, so many reds — dark, pale, light, bright. Some plants I recognised from England where they could only live in the simulated tropics of central heating. Poinsettia, with vivid red spiky leaf flowers, grew like weeds. But most of the plants looked foreign and exotic to me.

At the back of the house, the path opened out into the scruffy yard. The concreted floor was breaking up, cracked and flaking and there was an old table and an upturned wheelbarrow lying abandoned. But surrounding and overhanging the yard were trees that hung with fruit. A lemon tree with dark green leaves and a few yellow drops dangling heavy ready for picking. Another with fruits the shape of stars that looked like they were moulded in pale translucent yellow plastic. And banana trees. Huge flat, fat green leaves with an obscene prong that had a red flower with a dark mauve centre sitting at the end and several hands of little bananas up the stem

241

varying in size and colour — from green to pale yellow — looking as if they were already displayed for a fruit shop. If I had had to draw the scene, my colouring pencils would have been worn to small stubs by now.

The heat from the sun began to physically push me into the shade. Hot fingers prodding me to move inside. There was one place laid out on the kitchen table — a plate, a knife, a spoon and an empty glass, with a bowl of fruit sitting next to it. Two bananas, an orange and three of the star-shaped fruits from the tree in the garden.

As I walked into the silent front room, the tail of the little tan dog quickly disappeared under the chaise longue. I bent down and saw the dog's wide eyes glinting from his hidey-hole. 'You can stay there,' I told it. There were photographs in frames on the open shelves of the cupboard that ran along one wall. I recognised a younger Vincent sitting in a gown, smiling, proud, holding a diploma tied with a blue ribbon. And Vincent again, this time with his arm round his sister Pauline. She looked like a white woman next to her darker brother. She was smiling and holding down her dark straight hair as it blew in the wind. Then Pauline dressed in her wedding dress and Pauline with a crumpled pink baby.

I gaped when I saw the framed picture of Carl and me. It had been taken at school — me with no front teeth and gravity-defying hair. We had the same picture at home but I took it out of our sitting room and buried it in a drawer. Underneath this photo were two fat photograph albums. I looked around me. To pull them out I had to take all the photographs off the shelf and carefully lift out the books. I felt like a burglar. As I picked up the first album I heard a fast scratching and scrabbling. A gekko stood on the wall in front of me. The tiny prehistoric-looking lizard stood on three legs, motionless — staring but not quite at me. I thought I was going to scream. Jamaica is a land of crawly things — things that bite, sting and kill you. Scorpions, tarantulas and wiggly-wiggly things. But this tiny lizard looked as startled as I did, so I just carried on my rummaging and heard it scuttle away.

The first page of the album was full of photographs of me, my brother and my mum and dad. Pictures I don't remember being taken. Carl by one of his vans dressed in white trousers with flares so stiff that they made him look like he was wearing two upturned funnels. Mum and Dad on holiday surrounded by a lot of smiling white people. The front of our house. Me on a bike — I never had a bike. The back of our house. Carl in a suit outside church. Me in my confirmation white, looking very sweet. Carl in his school uniform with his cap that would never stay on his springy-haired head. Me in my school uniform — summer edition with one sock round my ankle. Dad and Mum by Dad's van — 'Wades' Painting and Decorating of the Highest Quality' — with their feet missing and Dad looking anxiously towards the photographer. And Noel! Noel was here standing by the van with a bucket.

My family took up nearly half the album. The

243

rest of the pages were full of people I didn't recognise. Young, old, middle-aged and everything in between. Black and white photographs, brown photographs, coloured snaps with thumbs in the corner. People standing stiff and formal or on a beach or larking around somewhere lush. In front of buildings with snow on the ground or sitting in sunny gardens. Some of them had names and dates written on the back. Eunice, Mummy, Daddy, Auntie Matilda, Uncle Edmund, Grandma, Grandpa, Oscar, Mildred. Mildred! My mum in a studio picture — hand-tinted — a glamorous young woman with definable cheekbones, who looked much paler than I knew she was.

I slowly turned all the pages of the albums and stared into all the faces.

20

By the time my aunt came back from church — by the time I heard a car pulling into the house, keys jangling, my aunt calling, 'Hello, Faith. We're all here. Hello,' I was surrounded by photographs. Loose pictures that had fallen out of the albums — spilling onto the floor and fanning out across the little table. I was fumbling, nervous, as I hurried to put everything back in its place.

Suddenly a little girl was standing watching me. Vincent's daughter. She stared silently as I arranged the framed photos back on the shelf. And only when I had finished did I say, 'Hello, what's your name?' She didn't answer. I pointed to the picture of Vincent. 'Is that your dad?' She didn't answer. Her hair was combed into several long little bunches sprouting out of her head at different angles. They were held in place by bands fastened with small brightly coloured balls. And in between the bunches and the balls were lots of colourful slides and clips with hearts and flowers and tiny bunnies. 'I like your hair,' I said. She blinked slowly and parted her lips but didn't say a word. Then a young boy appeared. He looked like a shrunken man — dressed in a dark blue suit with a white shirt and an almost shaved head of hair. But the shirt was hanging half in and half out of the trousers, which were drooping dangerously low on his hips and his shoelaces were both undone.

'Youmeauntie?' he said, in what sounded like patois.

'Pardon?'

'Youmeauntie?'

'Oh! Am I your auntie?' I was pleased I had understood. 'No, I'm your cousin. My name's Faith. I'm your cousin, I think.' They both stared at me. 'Second cousin actually,' I began to muse when Vincent came in the room.

'There,' he said effusively. He spread his arms out to demonstrate me to his children. 'There, what did I tell you? There is your auntie. You must call her Auntie Faith. Say hello to Auntie Faith.'

'Youmeauntie,' the boy told me. I obviously was.

'Jonathan!' Vincent was exasperated. 'Speak properly to your auntie. Say, Hello. Auntie. Faith. My. Name. Is. Jonathan.' Vincent looked over their heads and rolled his eyes at me. Jonathan wriggled as he hitched up his trousers using his elbows, then said quickly, 'Hello, Auntie Faith, me name Jonathan.' Then he smiled and two dimples appeared in his cheeks.

The little girl's name was Amber but she stuck her head into her mother's waist and turned her back on me as I was introduced. Her mother was Gloria, Vincent's meatless wife. Gloria stared at me for a long time. Fixedly looking into my face, assessing each feature in turn, before she said, 'It is so nice to have you with us, Faith, even if it is only for a short while. I hope you enjoy your stay in Jamaica and will remember us to your family

246

when you return.' She delivered it like a
rehearsed speech — slowly and precisely — as I
stood smiling like an idiot waiting for her to
finish.

'Grandma, me wan drink,' Jonathan shouted.

'Oh, you want a drink, little one,' Coral said.
She took her hat off and undid the bow at the
neck of her blouse and let the ties hang loose
down her front.

'Don't say 'me wan drink', Jonathan,' Vincent
shouted. 'How many times must I tell you? Ask
your grandma for the drink politely.'

Vincent sucked his teeth and Gloria, still
staring at me, said, 'They get into such bad ways.
It's the other children. They rough, you see,
Faith, and they teach their bad ways to everyone.
Even those from decent homes.' Gloria's nose
was flat and broad and her hair, which was
straightened, was round and curly on her head.
She had very dark skin. A rich dark blue-black
that had no highlights of paler colour. She
reminded me of the Black and White Minstrels.
Those white people made up to look black
— caricatured with thick dark make-up and
woolly hair — that I used to watch on Saturday
night television, singing and dancing and
entertaining the British. I was ashamed of the
thought and lowered my eyes away from her.

'Come, Amber,' Coral was saying, 'come see
what I have for you.'

'Go with Grandma, nah,' Gloria said, gently
pushing her daughter who started to cling
tighter. Gloria began to peel her off starting with
an arm then pushing at her shoulder. 'She's shy

with new people. She'll be all right soon. You won't know her soon. But at first . . .'

'Come, children,' Coral sang from the kitchen.

Jonathan was now lying on the floor, with only one shoe on, pushing round a toy car and making toy car noises. 'You hear your grandma, Jonathan?' Vincent said. Jonathan took no notice. Vincent spoke again but this time his voice had lowered several octaves. 'Jonathan,' it thundered, 'go to your grandma, now,' it roared, 'and take your sister with you. I will not tell you again!' It put the fear of God in me. Jonathan looked at his father then quickly jumped to his feet and grabbed his sister by one of her bunches on the way to the kitchen.

Vincent and Gloria flopped down onto chairs when the children had left the room, with Vincent sighing, 'That boy! That boy can be such a little . . . What can we do with him?'

'I not frettin' today,' Gloria said, with a shrug. 'He never listens to me — but I not frettin' today.' Gloria looked back at me. 'So, how is Auntie?' I wasn't sure who she meant. 'Auntie Mildred,' she carried on. 'Your mummy,' she finally had to say.

'She sends her love. She's fine. Do you know her?'

'Oh yes. I have corresponded with her. I used to live near your grandparents, you see.' She became coy and giggly, 'That's how I met Vincent.' She looked up at her husband playfully but he took no notice — he was reading the paper. Gloria stared at him for a while then turned back to me. 'And Eunice. I know your

Auntie Eunice a little better because I stayed with her in America when I was a young woman. Do you know Auntie Eunice?'

I was ashamed to say no — that I had never met her nor really knew anything about her. 'Well, she and your mummy had a quarrel, I think. Vincent, what did Auntie Mildred and Auntie Eunice quarrel over?' Vincent shrugged. 'I can't recall now, but she is a lovely woman, Auntie Eunice,' Gloria went on. 'You see, I have travelled to America but I have never been to England. One day, God willing, I would like to visit with Auntie Mildred. We would like to go to England, wouldn't we, Vincent?' Vincent gave an unconvinced tip of his head as Gloria asked, 'Have you been to America, Faith?'

Gloria looked pleased when I said no. She began to tell me about all the things you could get in America but not in Jamaica. The clothes, the food, the films, the books, the cars. I nodded and was still nodding when her expression changed — she sneered ferociously. 'I hear your bag is lost. That always happens in this country. We can't organise, you see. These sort of things don't happen in America or England.' I muttered that they did and was about to tell her about Gatwick, a bag and a flight back from Greece but she wasn't listening. 'It's the trouble with this country, no one is willing to work and work hard so that things run smoothly.'

She then told me that Vincent would need to phone the airport for me to check that they have my bag. I told her I could do it but she shook her head and gave a little laugh. 'No, Vincent will understand how the phone works. You see this is a Third World country and things don't go smoothly like they do in America.'

At which point Coral came back in the room saying, 'I have no trouble.'

'Yes, Mummy,' Gloria replied, 'but you don't use the phone frequently.' And Coral's lips tightened to a small dash under her nose.

'We can take you to get the bag from the airport if it is there. Can't we, Vincent?'

Vincent said, 'Oh yes,' then went back to his paper.

'The children are looking forward to seeing the planes. Aren't they, Vincent?'

But Coral said, 'Amber is not coming — the planes will frighten her.'

'Don't be ridiculous, Mummy,' Gloria said without looking at Coral. 'Amber will like the planes.'

'No, I have asked the child and she does not want to see the planes. She would like to stay here with me,' Coral said.

'Of course she wants to see the planes. Vincent, tell Mummy. Of course she want to see the planes,' Gloria insisted.

'Let the child stay with Mummy, Gloria. She'll be frightened by the noise and start with her frettin'.'

'Amber will like the planes!'

'No, she will not. She can stay with Mummy.'

Gloria went to protest but Vincent held up his hand. It was final. Coral smiled then suddenly called into the kitchen, 'Sit down!' And Vincent and Gloria shouted together, 'Jonathan!'

Vincent took the little bit of paper I had been given at the lost luggage counter at the airport. He sat down on the chair by the telephone. He dialled several times banging down the receiver between each go. At which Gloria nodded her head and said how typical it was of Jamaica, while Coral insisted that it didn't happen to her when she used the phone and that Vincent must be doing something wrong.

'Let me try, son,' Coral eventually said. And Gloria told Auntie Coral that it wasn't Vincent that was at fault but the phone, the phone company, the phone company's workforce, Jamaica and the Third World.

'It's ringing! See I have it,' Coral said triumphant. She handed the phone back to Vincent to do the business, while she told Gloria that all she needed was some patience and a little faith.

'They have the bag,' Vincent said. 'It's waiting for us.' Coral clapped her hands together. 'So all we have to do is go and get it,' Vincent told me and Gloria sucked her teeth.

'Thank you. Are we going now?' I asked.

'Straight away,' Vincent replied. I looked round for my handbag. But then Vincent added, 'We'll just sit down and have the soup that Mummy has made for us and then we'll be going straight away.'

Eunice's Story told to me by Coral

'Eunice always said that she was the prettiest of we three sisters because of her nose. Cha.' Eunice had a straight nose like her father and long hair that was black, wavy and manageable. And she had a slender body and legs that a preacher had once told her were the finest in the district.

Eunice left Jamaica before either of her two sisters. She left to live with Great Aunt Myrtle in America — in New York. 'I think Great Aunt Myrtle was me grandmother's sister although she might have been her cousin. No ... wait ... well, we called her Auntie Myrtle.'

Auntie Myrtle had been living in America for a very long time. She was older than their grandmother, so the three sisters, Coral, Mildred and Eunice, did not know Aunt Myrtle personally — they had never met her. 'All we heard was Myrtle this and Myrtle that from Grandma and every Christmas a cardigan each.'

Great Aunt Myrtle had left Jamaica to marry a man, a black American who lived in midtown

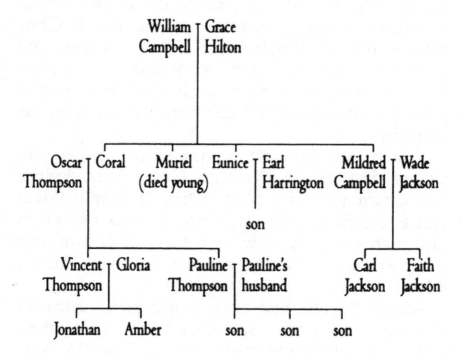

1st husband ⌐ Myrtle
2nd husband ⌐

William ⊤ Grace
Campbell | Hilton

Oscar ⊤ Coral   Muriel   Eunice ⊤ Earl   Mildred ⊤ Wade
Thompson | (died young) | Harrington   Campbell | Jackson
                                         son

Vincent ⊤ Gloria   Pauline ⊤ Pauline's   Carl   Faith
Thompson | Thompson | husband   Jackson Jackson

Jonathan   Amber   son   son   son

Manhattan. 'I'm sorry, I don't remember his name.' But the marriage was not a good one. 'She hardly knew him before she got married. She was only young — a girl. I think she got a bit of a shock. You see he was a gambler and a good-for-nothing who only wanted this young girl to look after all his needs.' It was not long before Myrtle and her husband separated. 'If I being honest, Faith, he walk out on her to live with another woman but hush.' Myrtle then had to decide whether to stay in America or go back to Jamaica. She stayed. She found a job working in service to a childless white couple who lived in a house on the Upper East side of the city. 'Oh, she worked for them for many years. And when the wife died Auntie Myrtle continued to look after the man until he became quite old.' The man came to rely on Myrtle for everything. 'All I am saying, Faith, is he was good to her and she was good to him.' The old man died in his bed just before the Wall Street crash of 1929. 'And you know what, he left Auntie Myrtle money in his will. Not a lot of money but enough so that when everyone else was starvin' and worryin' for a job, my auntie was sitting pretty.'

Myrtle bought a house in Harlem. 'You see she get it cheap because no one else could afford a thing at that time.' Myrtle moved to her new home and opened it as a respectable rooming house for men who worked on the railroad. 'Oh, she worked hard.'

After many years her husband, whom she had never divorced, became ill. 'He had tuberculosis.' He moved into Myrtle's house — 'typical of that sort of man,' — and she nursed him until he died. Myrtle stopped taking in lodgers after her husband's death. 'She did not like the look of the men that had started coming to her for rooms — they were becomin' too rough.' Myrtle was getting old — she had no children, she was on her own and lonely. So she wrote to her sister — 'That's your great-grandmother, Faith,' — asking if Coral would like to come and live with her in New York. 'She asked for me because I was the most sensible.'

But Coral did not want to go. She had a job in Jamaica and had just met Oscar and was planning to get married. Next, Aunt Myrtle asked for Mildred. But Mildred wanted to go to England not America. 'Your mother did not like America. Only England would do with her.' When Aunt Myrtle finally got round to asking for Eunice — 'She was her last choice,' — Eunice agreed.

When Eunice got to New York, she found that Aunt Myrtle wanted someone to fetch and carry and generally look after her. At first Eunice was very unhappy and wanted to go home. She did not want to spend her time with a finicky old lady. An old lady who liked her meals served at precisely the same time each day and who insisted on having the tablecloth on the kitchen table hanging an even six inches all the way round. But Aunt Myrtle promised that if Eunice stayed with her, she would inherit everything that her aunt had. 'A sorta bribe.' This was, by that time, the house in Harlem. 'A run-down place.' Its entire contents. 'Rubbish mostly.' And

256

money. 'She kept it in the floorboards under the bed.' So Eunice stayed because, 'it was quite a lot for those days'.

Eunice began to enjoy New York. 'Her head was turned.' She liked the music — she liked jazz and swing and would go to see Louis Armstrong's All Stars and Nat King Cole at the Apollo Theater. She liked to stay out late, drinking bourbon at Small's then onto the Savoy ballroom to dance. And she had lots and lots and lots of male admirers. 'She was wild — oh boy.'

Aunt Myrtle began to find Eunice quite a handful. Sometimes Eunice would not come home for days or she'd sleep and sleep and tell Aunt Myrtle to leave her alone. This was not what Aunt Myrtle had wanted. So Myrtle sent letters to her sister complaining about Eunice — she was lazy, she was useless, she wore red lipstick, she smoked cigarettes and she always had liquor on her breath. Her sister, 'my grandmother', told Eunice's mother about her daughter's wayward behaviour. Her mother would write to Eunice and tell her to be good to her great-aunt, who had so kindly taken her under her wing. And Eunice would get the letters and laugh. 'Eunice didn't care — she was young — she was living the high life. And there was nothing anyone could do about it.'

Then a strange thing happened, Aunt Myrtle met a man. She met a man who ran a local hardware store and was ten years younger than her. 'I can't remember his name either.' At the age of seventy-two, Aunt Myrtle fell in love and got married. She then told Eunice that she would have to leave — that she was not welcome in her house. She also told Eunice that she was no longer leaving any of her money or belongings to her — that everything she owned would now go to her new husband. 'He was a gold-digger — what else could we think — him with this run-down shop. And it was the last we hear from her.'

Eunice's mum 'your grandmother, Faith', — wanted Eunice to come back to Jamaica. But she was used to life in a city, life in America and did not want to go back to Jamaica and the countryside to live with her parents. And Eunice, by this time, had a job as a seamstress. 'Sounds good, but it just sewing up other people's clothes.' So instead of returning to Jamaica Eunice found lodgings in Harlem in the home of a woman called Honeysuckle Bird.

It was not long before Eunice met a young man — a friend of Honeysuckle's called Earl Harrington. She met him one night when Honeysuckle was cold-straightening Earl's hair in her room. Honeysuckle was called away as she began to apply the white paste to Earl's head. She asked Eunice to take over from her. Eunice did not really know what to do but she continued applying the corrosive paste until Earl began to scream that it was burning his scalp. As Eunice washed the paste off with buckets of cold water, a relieved Earl asked her if she would like to go out with him. Earl took Eunice to the Clique Club where Miles Davis was playing his 'Cool' jazz. 'And even though poor Earl was picking scabs out of his head for weeks, he still fell for me sister.'

Earl was also from Jamaica but he had moved to New York with his whole family many years before. Earl had been in the air force during the war and returned to New York full of hope for a new life and a new deal for black ex-servicemen. Earl was an aspiring musician. 'Musician! Any black man who could tap his foot say he's a musician.' After only a few months of courtship Earl and Eunice got married. 'She just write and tell Mummy she married a musician. I ask you. She was wild.'

Earl played trumpet in a jazz band when he could but during the day he worked as a carpenter and labourer. One night Earl got into a fight and was punched in the mouth. It bled and had to be stitched. After that he could no longer play his trumpet as he used to. It was also getting more difficult for him to find jobs as a carpenter and labourer. Things had not changed as he had hoped. Eunice and Earl spent one winter in Harlem without being able to afford proper heating. 'Auntie Myrtle would have nothing to do with Eunice and her financial problems. In the end Mummy had to send them money and she did not have it to give.'

So one spring day Earl and Eunice packed up their old car with all their belongings — 'It's beds and chairs I'm talking about as well as everything else, Faith,' — and drove all the way across America to California to start a new life. 'At least there they could be poor and warm.'

They settled in Los Angeles. Earl found a

good job as a carpenter working for the city. While Eunice took in sewing. But Eunice wanted to have children. She had three miscarriages then became pregnant again. This time the baby went to term and was born — a son. 'I don't think she named him.' He died two days later. 'That sort of knock the wind out of me sister.'

It was not long after that that Eunice began to train as a schoolteacher. 'She always wanted to be a teacher when she was little — always playing schools with her dolls. But she seemed more interested in beating the dolls than teaching them. Ahh, Eunice.' Eventually Eunice finished her training with distinction, — 'Or so she said.' She became the teacher of a class of small children. 'Only coloured children — she could only teach coloured children.' Eunice stopped wanting children of her own, as she declared that she now had all the children that she needed.

Earl and Eunice lived a quiet life in Los Angeles. 'You can ask Gloria what it was like — she stayed with them.' According to Gloria they lived in a lovely house, in a lovely part of the city even though everyone was coloured. It had a front and back yard and friendly neighbours who were always bringing over apple pies for them to eat. All the phones worked and the electricity never went off. Earl and Eunice had two big cars, both Chevrolets, that never went wrong. Three big colour televisions — one in the bedroom — with lots and lots of stations. A big fridge that you could almost sit in, an automatic washing machine, a fitted kitchen with all the latest equipment including a coffee percolator. Eunice had heated hair curlers and Earl had a tank with tropical fish that were worth a lot of money. And their toilet seat was made of bright blue inflated plastic that was hygienic and never cold to sit on. They wanted for nothing, nothing at all. But they also worked for the church and were very well respected.

Earl's mother then came to stay with them. She was old and frail and needed to get away from the New York climate. Eunice and Earl looked after her. But then Earl had a mild heart attack and had to retire. 'He was weak after that.' Eunice had to give up work to look after both him and his mother. Earl died after a second stronger attack which happened as he was feeding his fish. 'Faith, you have an uncle that was killed by fish.'

Eunice still lives in Los Angeles, 'taking care of Earl's mother. Me sister writes me how this woman is old and finicky and how she likes her meals to be served at the same time each day and how she is driving her mad. You see, Faith, the Lord move in mysterious ways. Eunice was meant to look after an old woman when she was young, but she preferred the high life. But it has come full circle. Now, after all that time, she end up looking after an old woman. Ahh, the wheels of God grind slow but grind exceeding small.'

21

Little boys take up too much room. I had to share the back seat of the car with Jonathan as we drove out to the airport. He sat sometimes with his legs wide open — swinging them and knocking his heels on the underside of the seat. 'Jonathan, stop that banging, nah.' Or he would have his legs on the seat, kicking me as he fidgeted and turned. I would push his feet off, while smiling at him, and he'd start knocking his heels on the underside of the seat again. 'Jonathan, stop that banging.'

Gloria handed him a plastic bag full of bits of sugar cane cut into small pieces. This was to shut him up — to stop him from saying, 'Daddy, why is the sky blue? . . . Daddy, are we near the planes? . . . Daddy, when is Tuesday? . . . Daddy, can I swim in the sea? . . . Daddy, how does a plane fly? . . . Daddy . . . Daddy . . . ? He was told to offer me a piece of cane and I told him that I had never eaten cane before. 'You never eat cane, Auntie Faith? Daddy, Auntie Faith never eat cane. Mummy, Auntie Faith never eat cane. There no cane in England, Auntie Faith? What you eat in England, Auntie Faith?' And Gloria told Jonathan that he should show his Auntie Faith how to eat cane.

For some moments he was quiet — his face serious and responsible. He took a piece of the cane from the bag and held it up in front of his face, making sure I was paying attention by hitting at my thigh. He placed it in his mouth with the exaggeration of a fire-eater. He clamped his mouth around the pale brown cane and began chomping his teeth up and down on it. He then opened his mouth to say, 'You suck all the juice, Auntie Faith.' Several strings of saliva and cane juice trickled from the corners of his mouth and down his front. He wiped his face with the back of his hand, he wiped his shirt front, his trousers and the seat. He pointed again to the cane in his mouth, 'You suck it.' Then he looked through the bag pulling out pieces of cane then putting them back, fingering them with his sticky fingers as he twisted them in the air, looking for the perfect one to give to me for my initiation into cane sucking. Eventually he found it and jabbed the piece of cane at my lips. Thank you. As I placed it in my mouth Jonathan tipped out the mangled chewed fibres of his spent cane into his hand and leant forward to Vincent. 'Finish, Daddy.'

'Jonathan, can you not see that I am driving the car and that I don't want your dirty rubbish?' Jonathan then handed the debris to Gloria instead, who said, 'I not frettin' today,' and threw the mess out of the window.

The cane was hard like balsa wood but as I bit down onto it, the sticky glutinous sweetness trickled into my mouth and slid effortlessly down my throat. But then it became horrible. A bitter sponge of sharp fibres that coated my mouth in woodchip wallpaper and started to soak up my saliva. I pulled the strands out of my mouth and held them in my hand. I was trying to study my first daylight view of Jamaica out of the window of the car. 'You like the cane, Auntie Faith?' Everything was like the night before — the women in hair curlers, the children, the dogs, the shacks, the woodsmoke, the men with their open shirts — but with more colour, with more detail. People in their Sunday best walking on the road carrying Bibles. Bicycles and cars. Higglers selling wares from boxes spread out on the road. Buses full to overflowing with people precariously hanging out of the doors and pressed up against the windows. And traffic lights and crossings and shops with mannequins, awnings and metal grilles. Sunlight and shadows in brilliant colours. In daylight everything did not look so strange. 'Auntie Faith, you like the cane?'

'Yes, it was very nice, sweet.' The palm trees looked as they should for such a hot day in a hot place.

'You like another piece, Auntie Faith?'

'No, thank you.'

But there were too many derelict houses. Along every road were houses like the ones I recognised from the photo albums of my family. The ones with proud relatives standing in the garden with the house in the background, maybe posing with a chair or with children lined up against a gate or sitting on the grass in front of the porch with pots of exotic plants blooming in black and white. Single-storey, pastel-painted houses in blues and pinks and lavenders. Houses with verandas and three steps up to the front door and shuttered windows all round looking

264

out onto the gardens.

But now those houses were shells. Like a dead tortoise, just the hardest parts were left. The soft bits — the beds, the chairs, the kitchens, the sitting rooms, the lives — were gone. Scooped out by time. And the houses looked like they had been left in a hurry. No time to sell or demolish. Just plenty of time to decay. Some of them were being reclaimed by animals and plants. Others by people so poor that the only sign of them were fires in the yard and lines of washing.

'Auntie Faith, do you live in a big house? Auntie Faith, do you have a car?'

'Oh Jonathan,' Vincent said. 'Stop asking so many questions, you're making me head ache.'

Vincent was a teacher and as we drove along he pointed out different schools and told me what was particular about them. 'And this school over there — you see it, Faith, behind the trees — this is the best school in Jamaica. Everyone want to go to this school and the competition is fierce.'

'Me goin' that school,' Jonathan told me.

'Well, you will have to work very hard, young man. And you will have to say, 'I am going to that school.' But, Faith, look over on this corner, this school is very run-down . . . '

Gloria, however, worked for a doctor as his receptionist and nurse. Her commentary was quite different. 'Faith, you see that corner over there? A while ago a bus turn over there. A car hit it and the bus turn over and thirty-six people died. Thirty-six!' Gloria pointed out the sight of several fatal road accidents before Vincent said,

265

'Gloria, Faith will be frightened to move listening to you. Now there is another school over the road and I don't know if you can see it . . .'

We drove down a road which a rich white lady had had built to avoid having to pass by the big house of a rich black man. We passed a red dusty bauxite mine.

'Auntie Faith, are you JLP or PNP?'

'Jonathan, what you know about that? What you know about politics?'

'I'm PNP, Daddy.'

Then we were driving by the sea — a dark flat navy sea — with Kingston in the distance and the Blue Mountains rising behind the city like a protective hand. As I watched the clouds parted and a soft shaft of sunlight briefly lit Kingston silver on the horizon. And Jonathan jabbed at my lips with another piece of cane saying, 'Open, Auntie Faith. Open.'

★ ★ ★

The airport was closed, except to people like me. People with bits of pale blue paper who stood at the door of the terminal building waiting to reclaim their luggage. There were very few planes taking off or coming into land at the airport because it was Sunday. Jonathan was disappointed. He cried with an open-mouthed 'waaahhh' that made his parents wince then promise to find a plane for him to see.

They left me with a small group of people huddling round double glass doors, shifting from

266

foot to foot in the heat as we all fanned ourselves with the bits of paper. More people joined us and we began mumbling and rolling our eyes. I looked for Sugar in the little crowd — 'Oh boy, women fly Jamaican planes.' All of the faces were black but unfamiliar. It was not long before there was a communal sucking of teeth — the baroque tutting going off at different points in the crowd, like air escaping from balloons, until finally a man in a uniform opened the door. He held us back with an outstretched arm as he checked inside the building, then said a conspiratorial, 'Come,' as if he was the lookout and we were the burglars.

I rushed through the door with the spirit of the January sales and was halfway into the terminal before I realised everyone else was taking it nice and slow. For a moment I was alone in the empty building which was quiet and still — unrecognisable as the scene of the cacophony and chaos of the night before. 'Me no t'ief, me no t'ief.' It was now just a vast room with a desert of concrete floor. The lost luggage was in a small room which was in a corner across the expanse. But I suddenly stopped walking boldly through the centre of the terminal and moved over to the edges.

It took a while to get my bag. I was first but was soon joined by the same small group that had formed outside. We all began to shift from foot to foot, fan ourselves, mumble, roll our eyes and eventually suck our teeth as we waited. The room was filled from floor to ceiling with a medley of luggage — suitcases, bags and shabby old brown boxes. Several officials wandered through the room holding our bits of paper which we had had to hand in. 'Oldest trick in the book that,' I mumbled to someone near me, who nodded. I began to complain. 'Excuse me. Excuse me, we have all been here a very long time. Will you be much longer? Excuse me.' Several people in my crowd said, 'Um-uhmmm' to that. But I was ignored until I spotted my blue and grey bag resting between a pushchair and something that looked like an ornamental elephant. 'Excuse me. Excuse me.'

'Wait. We're just getting your bag now, miss. Someone has just gone to get it,' a woman assured me. I pointed, 'It's over there.' The woman looked overjoyed to see it and pulled it out and handed it to me with no apparent bureaucracy. Someone in my crowd clapped and someone else slapped me on the back like I'd just won my luggage. And I said thank you to everyone as I left.

The wheels on my case squeaked and I stopped every few steps like a cautious rodent. The piercing sound drew saliva from the back of my cheeks. I had to go through Customs — I had to enter Jamaica again, this time with my bag.

The man at the Customs desk was a broad-nosed, thick-lipped, dark black man. Like men I only seemed to see working in kitchens in England or waving trains off at Underground stations. He wore a uniform with a peaked cap that sat back on his head so the stiff patent peak pointed upwards. I had nothing to declare. I stood beside him and smiled. His head turned slowly through ninety degrees to look at me. His eyes lifted briefly up to meet mine, blinked, then lowered again. His head then retraced its trajectory back to look straight ahead. He breathed in slowly, his brass chest buttons rising up and catching the light. Then he let the breath out through his mouth with the force of a bored sigh. I thought he was going to speak but he inhaled again, this time letting the breath out down his nose. He looked down at my bag with a flick of his eye then back at his own knees. He sucked his teeth quietly then said, 'Passport.'

'Oh right, yes, of course. Sorry.' I had to rummage around in my handbag to find it. 'It's in here somewhere . . .' I giggled to the man but he just stared into the distance. 'Here it is. Sorry.' I handed him the book which he took without looking. He opened the passport slowly at the page with my photo. His eyes shifted in my direction, then he sucked his teeth.

I held out my hand to get it back but he did not give it to me. We were both quiet again for several minutes before the man's lips parted and without any movement he asked, 'What you have in the bag?'

'In the bag? Oh, just clothes and things.'

He breathed in, he breathed out, he sniffed. 'What . . . things?' I was being interrogated. And he had already broken down my resistance. He was good. He was very good, because for some reason I looked at him and said, 'Oh, you know . . . drugs.'

I meant of course the things my aunt had

asked me to bring her, the paracetamol, the diarrhoea tablets, the Lemsips. But at that moment I could think of no other word to describe the items in my toilet bag except drugs. He did not look at me. His face remained blank as I began breathlessly to explain. 'Not drugs . . . not actual drugs . . . I mean aspirin and that sort of thing . . . for tummy upsets . . . vitamins . . . stuff you mix with hot water when you get a cold.' I stopped. The Customs man looked at me for the briefest moment. And I had never in my life felt so English.

I smiled while he breathed out and rolled his eyes in one lingering movement. Then his arm began to gradually move off his lap. I caught it out of the corner of my eye as it levitated up into the air, picking up my passport as it went. It hovered momentarily at shoulder level before the hand flicked the passport upwards.

'Can I go?' I asked, and his chin twitched yes.

Out in the car park I could hardly see. The sun was so bright the tarmac shimmered like glass. I waited by Vincent's car as my eyes steadily adjusted to the light. But I was still squinting when a van drove past me. On the side of it was a huge advertising poster. A picture of happy faces — drawn not photographed. People waving, some just saying 'hi', smiling, laughing. A representation of the people of Jamaica — Chinese, Indian, black with light skin, black with dark. And underneath the faces in bold red letters were the words, 'Have you been nice to a tourist today?'

Grace's Story told to me by Coral

'Now, Faith, what you want to know about your grandmother? Well, her name was Grace and she was a good mother to us all,' Auntie Coral told me. 'What, you want to know more?'

Grace Hilton was brought up in a little house in the north of the island, near Port Maria. She lived with her mother Cecelia and her sister Hester. Her father, Benjamin Nelson Hilton, worked in Cuba and she did not see him often as he was very rarely at home. Her sister was several years younger and she was her mother's 'eyeball'. 'That's what we say when we mean favourite, Faith.' Hester had a fair skin, her nose was straight and her lips were thin. Grace was dark with a broad nose and bottom lip that stuck out and made her look like she was sulking. On the occasions when their father would come home, people remarked how Hester looked like her daddy. Those same people then looked at Grace, squinted their eyes and said nothing. 'Different fathers! What put that idea in your head, Faith? What has your mummy been telling

271

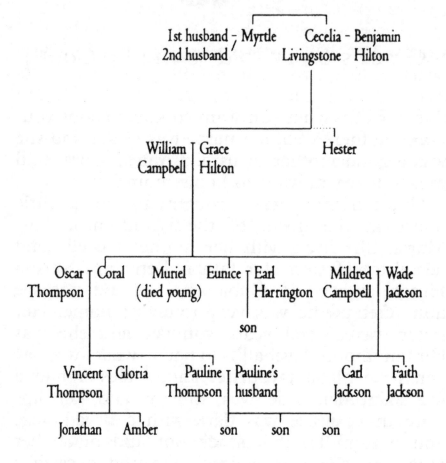

you? Just remember, in those days things were not as they are now.'

Grace learnt to read and write at a small school run by the Wesleyan Church. She had to walk several miles to go to school. On her way back she would play by the river with the other children. The girls lifting their skirts to paddle in the water while the boys threw in sticks and stones. But if she got dirty her mother would beat her. She would break off a switch from a tree and whip it against her daughter's back and legs. 'They were brought up strict in those days.'

Grace had to help around the house. She had to feed chickens, grind corn into meal, pick fruit, cook and wash. She had to sew and mend and she had to teach her sister Hester to do the same. But Hester had no patience and would not listen to her big sister and Grace would get beaten for it. 'Ah, sisters.' So Grace did all the sewing and told her mother that Hester had done this piece of embroidery or had patched this piece of dress and her mother would praise Hester. 'I don't think Grace had much time for her sister. Whenever anyone mention her, she just sort of tut.'

Grace knew a boy. 'Now if I tell you this, Faith, it's to go no further, you hear me?' His name was Nathaniel and he lived with his grandmother in a tiny house near to Grace. Nathaniel and Grace had known each other since they were little children. They used to play together by the river when she met him on her way from school. It was Nathaniel that taught her to climb trees and it was Nathaniel's fault that Grace got beaten for ripping the sleeve of her dress. 'I don't think your mummy knows this so don't go tellin' her . . . ' Nathaniel asked Grace to marry him and she said that she would. But Grace's mother did not approve of the match. She said that Nathaniel's family were only cane cutters. That he was too rough, too poor, too dark, too ignorant, for her daughter. Her mother told Grace that she must never see Nathaniel again. But they met in secret and Nathaniel gave Grace a ring that he made from an old coin. It didn't fit on her finger so she kept it in her pocket. 'I saw it once — big ugly thing.'

Then Nathaniel volunteered to join the army and fight in the First World War. He told Grace that the 'Mother Country' was calling him, that the 'Mother Country' needed him, that he must fight for his 'Mother Country'. He joined up into the British West Indies Regiment. Grace cried when he left. 'No, I don't think she did, Faith — she was never really one to show emotion, my mother. She liked to keep herself quiet.' But she promised that when he got back from the war, she would marry him. 'You see she thought that he would mostly cook and wash for everyone while he was there, but they made him fight!'

It was after Nathaniel had been away for about a year that Grace met another man — William Philip Campbell. William was the son of a woman Grace's mother knew from church. A decent woman. He came to the house to fix the roof and some fences and to dig holes on the land. 'I don't know what the holes were for, Faith, I just know he had to dig some holes.'

William had worked on the Panama Canal and had the gold watch that proved it. Grace's mother liked William because, she said, he was educated enough to be able to tell the time from this watch. She also liked him because he was trustworthy and hardworking. And, because he had a light skin the colour of caramel and black curly hair. 'Handsome.'

At first, Grace would have nothing to do with William, even though he made a point of saying good morning and good afternoon to her. But Grace gradually began to warm to William. She liked to listen to him sing as he worked. She liked the way he made the hammer's bang keep time for him as he sang his hymns. 'You see in Jamaica when the men were building, they used to have a man sing and all the other men work to the rhythm of the music. Quite clever.'

It was not long before William asked Grace to marry him. But at first she didn't want to. 'Thinking of the promise she made to Nathaniel, I expect.' But her mother insisted. She said that William was a good catch, that he would make a good husband, that he would work hard, make a good home for her and that she should marry him before a fine man like that changed his mind. So they were married.

Grace settled down to life as a married woman. She helped her husband tend and plant the small plot of land they had. She fed chickens, ground corn into meal, picked fruit, cooked, washed, sewed and mended. While William built her a house — a small wooden house with three

275

steps up to a veranda and rooms enough for a family to grow.

She stopped going to the Wesleyan Church and became a Baptist. But she found the congregation a little boisterous and noisy. So she became a Seventh Day Adventist. But the Saturday services did not suit her. She wanted to try the Anglicans — the Church of England, but she thought them too fair-skinned, too rich to accept her. So she returned again to being Wesleyan — a Methodist. 'My mother was always reading her Bible — always reading her Bible.'

Grace gave birth to Coral on a hot Sunday afternoon in the bedroom of her house, tended by her mother who told Grace she had never screamed when she had given birth. For six weeks Grace kept the baby Coral in a box by her bed until William finally had time and built a crib that rocked.

William started a small shop on the land in front of their house. By the time Coral was taking her first steps, William had bought another plot of land which was a little way from the house. William and Grace christened it Amity. And on the Sunday after William first broke the soil of that land, Grace put on her best hat and went to the Anglican Church for the first time.

'Oh, I remember those days — they were lovely. Let me tell you one of the things she did.'

Grace would make chocolate to sell in the shop. Beautiful, slender, brightly dressed young black women — 'You'd never see a fat one,'

276

— would come down from the hills. They carried baskets on their heads, cushioned by cotters and piled high with cocoa pods. Grace would buy the small, prune-like cocoa seeds and put them in a pig iron. 'You know what that is? A big heavy pot.' The pig iron with the seeds would then be put over the fire and parched. 'Sort of roasted, I suppose.' Grace would then take the roasted seeds and put them into a big pestle and mortar. Then she would stand and grind and crush and beat the seeds. 'All day Mummy would beat them, beat them, beat them. And I would watch and try to help but at that time I was only small. But when I got older that was one of my jobs.' The oil would begin to run out of the roasted seeds. Grace then collected the oil and left it in a cool place. When it was soft like butter she would roll it into long thin cigar shapes. And it was this cigar-shaped chocolate that she sold in the shop. 'After that, you see, you would grate the chocolate and have it as a drink. I liked it sweet with sugar. I had a lot of chocolate in those days.'

Nathaniel returned to Jamaica after the war and went to look for Grace. He eventually found her — with a child, and a husband who had a house and a shop and land that were bought with Panama Canal wages. Nathaniel's left hand was missing — his arm ended in a stump below his elbow and he walked with a limp.

Nathaniel came to the house to speak to Grace. She told him she was married with a child and a house and a shop and land and that he should go away. But he wouldn't. He cried.

'Well, he was crying and carrying on. And shaking. I remember him shaking. But you know what that sort of man is like.' When Nathaniel saw William he attacked him. He jumped the three steps of the veranda and pushed William to the ground and punched him with his good hand. 'Or it was Daddy who hit him. No one could tell in the confusion. But they roll on the ground fightin' and it not like Daddy to fight.' Eventually William managed to chase Nathaniel away. He waved his machete at him and threatened to kill him if he returned. 'It was the last Mummy heard of Nathaniel. Funny story really. But don't go tellin' Mildred. No one but me knows about that. And I am not a gossip.'

Grace became pregnant again, first with Muriel: 'Poor Muriel.' Then Eunice: 'Cry, cry, cry.' Then Mildred: 'Nothing but trouble. And oh boy, then the work began.' Grace looked after her children and the house and the shop and the chickens and the corn and the chocolate and the fruit. 'Mummy work all the hours the Lord sent. She always said that women should work hard.'

On Mondays Grace did the family's washing. She took the white sheets and clothes and pounded them in water in the zinc tank at the back of the house. Then she lay the washing out flat on the ground and left it in the sun. It was Mildred's job to keep the washing moist by flicking water over all the items through the day. The sun lifted out dirt and stains as the water evaporated from the cloth and bleached sheets brilliant white again.

In the evening Grace sewed dresses to sell in

the shop. Small dresses for little girls to wear to church. It was Eunice's job to sew the buttonholes and buttons onto the back of each one. Coral looked after the chickens. But when they needed one to eat it was Grace who caught it. She chased the selected bird round the yard, following it with her old metal bucket. When she had cornered the chicken she slapped the bucket over the top of it. Then she began to hit the bucket with a large metal spoon. And the bucket and the spoon and the chicken would make a terrible noise. When the bucket was removed the chicken was bewildered, dopey and dazed. And it was then that Grace chopped off its head with a knife. 'I didn't like that bit. The chicken would run round without its head before it fall down on the ground. I could never watch.' But it was Coral's job to take out the chicken's insides and pluck all the feathers.

When Muriel was ill Grace sat by her bedside with rags dipped in cool water that she laid on her daughter's head. She made teas with herbs and cocoa leaves for Muriel, she made chicken soups and bought cod liver oil for her to take. 'Your grandmother, Faith, was not what you would call affectionate. But she loved us.' Grace never cuddled her children or praised them for things they did. 'Never. She always said pride comes before a fall.' But when Muriel died, she took her Bible to a far tree and sat reading it for a day and a night. She said it was her the Lord was punishing.

It was then that Grace left the Anglican Church and became a Methodist again.

Grace's daughters all moved away one by one. Eunice to New York: 'Mummy told her to be careful who she mix with, but she didn't listen.' Coral to Kingston to become a nurse: 'She was very proud of me, I think.' And Mildred to England: 'She didn't want her to go. She didn't want her to go so far.' Grace and William were left on their own for only a few years before Coral's children went to live with them. 'Mummy acted like it was a bother but she was lonely, she didn't have enough to do. I knew she wanted them to stay.'

Coral's children Pauline and Vincent enjoyed life on their grandparents' farm and Grace looked after them like a mother would. She made them clothes — she made Pauline frilly satin dresses with bows at the back that Pauline wore with show-off pride. She made Vincent his school pants out of old trousers that William no longer had use for. Vincent would write to Coral in New York to complain that the trousers his grandma made him wear were so baggy that he kept tripping over in them and falling down. 'But apart from the pants, they had no complaints.'

Except for one Christmas. It was the Christmas when Coral and Oscar could not get to Jamaica from New York because of bad weather — they had to stay in America. 'It was just one time, just that one time. All the other times we came home and had a lovely time with the children.' Grace went into town to buy Pauline and Vincent some presents for their Christmas gifts. But on her way back, in the dark, along the road to the house, she was robbed. A man jumped out at her and knocked her to the ground. He then stole everything she was carrying and ran off into the bushes. Grace was not hurt but she now did not have presents for Pauline and Vincent. 'You see, when we were young, Faith, we had no chimney like you do in England for Father Christmas to come down. So Mummy used to put a pot by the window. On Christmas morning she would say, 'You see, Father Christmas has been because the pot in the window is moved.' And we would all look at the pot and it would have moved a long way from the window. Then we would all get our presents. Every year it was the same. Father Christmas came through the window and left us our presents.'

But that year — the year that Coral and Oscar could not get back from New York and the presents had been stolen along the dark road — Grace did not move the pot on the window. She simply told Pauline and Vincent that Father Christmas had not come to the house. 'I was a little upset because after that Pauline and Vincent knew that there was no Father Christmas and they were only young. It spoiled it for them. They knew that it was only their grandmother who bought the presents and that there were no presents because she had been robbed. And you know they cried on Christmas Day — cried on Christmas Day! That was the only time I ever wish mummy was a little kinder. But the next year Mummy moved the pot again and told them Father Christmas was back and they believed her.'

Grace got fat as she got older. Very fat. 'Must have been all the chocolate — she loved her chocolate, and cane and mango and dumplings and bammy. Every mornin' bammy.' One day she developed a pain in her side. A pain that became so bad she could not open the shop, a pain that became so intense that she could not stand straight at her cooker to prepare William his soup. William got her to hospital where she was told that her appendix would have to be removed. The operation took six hours. The doctors could not find her appendix easily — they told William it was because she was too fat. 'She never really recovered from that.'

The operation made Grace weak. 'So weak she could not look after the children so we had to send them away to school in Kingston. But she missed them — I think it just made Mummy weaker.' The doctor could find no reason why Grace was not recovering well. They told William that she should rest and eat a good diet. So William looked after Grace — he cooked for her, he washed her, he sat by her bed reading the Bible to her. 'And Daddy went to all her churches — every one — to ask them to pray for her. But Mummy just got weaker and thinner. So thin. And then passed on. It was as if she just faded away.'

Grace was buried on a rainy Wednesday morning. 'I remember that day like it was yesterday. Daddy and me sang — standing there in this pouring rain we sang 'Abide with me'. Mummy loved that hymn. 'In life, in death, O Lord, abide with me.'' Grace was placed at the bottom of the garden, near her house, on her land, in sight of her shop, in the grave alongside her daughter Muriel. 'And I miss her to this day. She was a wonderful woman, your grandmother. Wonderful.'

22

I unpacked the suitcase in my little room and placed everything I had brought for my aunt in a pile on the bed. The Vitamin E capsules, the aspirin, the *All Saints Family Hymn Book*, the six descant recorders in gold felt pouches. The presents my parents gave me for Coral were a little battered — still brightly wrapped but with tatty dents and corners like toffees squashed in a pocket for too long. But I was not coming to Jamaica empty-handed. I had so much to give.

I expected a surprised gratitude from Auntie Coral. A misty-eyed tearful look perhaps. All these things she could not get easily in Jamaica.

'Thank you,' she said evenly. She looked at the aspirin and fingered a recorder. She fanned quickly through the hymn book then lifted one of the wrapped presents and said, 'And what's all this?'

'They're gifts from Mum and Dad.'

Coral sighed, 'Oh.' She held her head. 'Now I must get them something to take back,' she said, under her breath. I told her that she was not to worry, that they were just gifts for her and her family, that Mum and Dad were not expecting anything in return. But Coral just raised her eyes and stared silently into my face.

My room was hot and still. Even when I waved my hand in front of my face I could not feel a breeze. I changed my clothes. Out of my jeans and into a cotton blouse and a skirt that I could flap at my knees. I put sandals on my feet and pulled my hair back tight off my face and into a bun on the top of my head.

When Auntie Coral saw me, she gave me that look I had wanted before — the misty-eyed tearful look. She gasped, threw her hands into the air, clapped and shouted, 'Ahh, my Faith, but now you look like a Jamaican!'

William's Story told to me by Coral

' 'Without vision, the people perish.' Your grandad, my father, always said that, Faith. It's from the Bible. He didn't make it up — but it was his saying.'

William Philip Campbell was the son of James Campbell. 'A Scottish man, Faith. A Scottish man with flame-red hair. My daddy always said his daddy had a bush of red hair and a skin as white as chalk. I never saw him — he died. All we did was hear about him from Daddy. He talked about him all the time.'

James came from the north-west of Scotland. He came from a large family. They all lived in a small stone house, in a beautiful lush green glen, where evidently the sun shone all day, even through rain. They were farmers who raised crops and kept livestock enough for their needs. 'Like in Jamaica.' But James's family was evicted from their house and land. 'I don't know why.' They were evicted so that the landowner could graze more sheep in the area. 'Sheep! Are you sure that is why, Faith? They teach you that at school, that it was for sheep? Cha.' James's

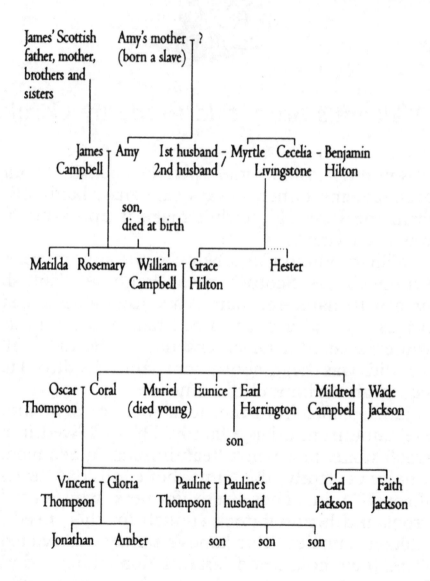

family was made to move from the lush green glen, out to the coastland where they had to stop farming and start fishing.

James was the second oldest boy. He fished with his father and his elder brother. But they could not catch enough fish to sell and feed a large, growing family. So in the summer months James would go to Glasgow and the Clyde Valley to try to find work. Any work. 'Mending, fixing, that sort of thing. He was the sort of man who could turn his hand to anything — just like my daddy.' At first he tried to return home during the winter months — to help with the fishing and bring money for food and rent. But the journey became too hard.

Then, in the city, James worked for a man who promised him a good job with good pay. The job was in Jamaica working on a sugar estate. There was a ship leaving — James was told the time, the date and the place. There were many other Scottish men on that ship that sailed for Jamaica. And they told each other how they were going to seek their fortunes in the Caribbean — how they were going to find a better life — and how, after a few years, they would return again to Scotland, triumphant. At the age of nineteen James Campbell boarded the ship for Jamaica and never saw his family again.

James was set to work on the estate, 'Mending, fixing, that sort of thing.' And fishing. He fished with men who were born slaves. Men who showed him how to make fishing pots from stripped bamboo. Men who taught him where to place the pots in the Jamaican waters, how

289

long to wait for them to fill, how to empty the pots and clean the fish and freshwater shrimps. Men who warned him of manatees and alligators. But men who worked under James's command. 'He was the white man — that's how it was, Faith.'

Amy — 'my father's mother,' — worked on the estate in the big house. She was a housemaid. She met James when he brought fish to the kitchen. They fell in love. 'Yes, I suppose so.'

Amy was 'Jamaican. You know . . . West Indian. Dark. But very pretty and very tall, I understand — although I never saw her.' She was the daughter of a woman who was born a slave. Her family had worked on the estate for many years — as slaves, as apprentices, and then as free men working in return for small plots of land and lodging. 'Maybe, maybe. To be honest with you, Faith, I don't know much about them. Daddy didn't talk about them.'

James and Amy had four children. 'Of course they were married. Of course! Of course!' The first-born was Matilda, then Rosemary was born almost exactly a year after her sister. Their next child, a son, died at birth. By the time William was born, he was the much-wanted son.

William was a pretty child who inherited his father's straight fine long nose. Rosemary's hair was red. And Matilda had a complexion that could have been mistaken for white. Amy used to show off her children to her family. She used to say that her husband, the white man, was one day going to take her and her children to Scotland to live in a small stone house, in a beautiful lush green glen where the sun shone all day, even through rain.

By the time William began school he could sign his own name — his mother taught him the alphabet at night by candle-light. William was the best pupil at his school and his teacher thought he could continue his education into secondary level. Amy did not want William to have to earn his living by working the land or fishing on the estate. But his father would not pay for William to have any more schooling. He did not believe education would help his son. His father said that it was time that William brought in money for his family, that William started to work. James taught his son all the trades he himself had learnt. 'He was a white man but he was not a rich man. He was richer than a black man. But still he was poor.'

James taught William to make the bamboo fishing pots. He showed him where to place them in the waters, how long to wait for them to fill, how to empty the pots and clean the fish and freshwater shrimps. He warned him of manatees and alligators and as William worked — his nimble young fingers wove the bamboo in and out fast and silent, 'like an old woman knitting,' — his father taught him hymns he had learnt in Scotland. And they sang together:

We have an anchor that keeps the soul
Steadfast and sure while the billows roll
Fastened to the rock which cannot move
Grounded firm and steady in the Saviour's love.

They began to sell the bamboo fishing pots to other fishermen. And James would take the money he had earned with his son and stow it away in a wooden box that he kept under their house. Every Sunday James would take out the money and wash the coins one by one. He'd carefully dry each coin, place them into neat piles then put them back in the wooden box and hide them until the next Sunday when he would wash the coins again. 'He did, Faith, he washed them! My father told me and my father was not a person to joke.'

William grew tall with broad shoulders. 'Handsome.' His face was angelic, 'slightly quizzical — like he has a question for you'. William was nineteen when his father told his son that he should find work on the construction of the Panama Canal. His father went with William down to the office in Kingston. William waited with all the other men — hundreds of men who crowded at the offices each day, jostling each other in the heat, hoping to be chosen for the dollar-a-day jobs. He got a job and when he told his father, James shook his son by the hand. 'You see, he didn't want to make it look like they were desperate. He didn't want to jump up and down like all the others. He was too proud.' But his mother cried on the quayside as the whole family lined up in their best clothes to watch William's ship set sail for Panama. His father gave William a leather case — the case he had carried on his sea journey from Scotland. 'My daddy kept that case for a long time. I remember it — beaten-up old thing.'

Because William could read and write, because he knew how to add and subtract and because he had a light skin, he was put to work in the stores. His job was to count in all the supplies of equipment and food, and then once in he had to count them out again. 'It was hard work though, Faith. A lot of men died.' William worked in a complex of buildings and it was here that William developed an interest in teeth. There was a lot of toothache in Panama. Men lined up in the complex for wages, food, news from home and to see the dentist. A little building had been set aside where the dentist visited, set up a chair and fixed the men's teeth. William watched as men paid good money from their wages to have the dentist pull out a tooth that was giving them pain. 'That's how he got the idea.'

When, a few years later, William returned to Jamaica from Panama he wanted to train as a dentist. But his father did not approve. William pleaded with him — he told his father that he knew there was money to be made in dentistry. He told him how dentists could drill and fill teeth to save them in the mouth, and how he had been told that in England they could take photographs that showed the inside of a tooth. Soon, he proclaimed, everyone in Jamaica would go to a dentist. 'Without vision, the people perish.' But his father thought money spent on education, any education, was a waste. He told William he should learn to fix shoes instead.

Then William's father died suddenly, not long after his son's return. James died of a fever that started in the evening and had killed him by the afternoon of the following day. In his delirium he had screamed tuneless hymns and begged for his mother to wash him. After James was buried, Amy returned to the estate house to work once again as a housemaid. William would not go back to working on the estate. He took jobs anywhere he could in the district and waited for land to come up for sale — land that he could purchase with his Panama Canal wages.

And then William met Grace. He would watch the two sisters, Hester and Grace, as they went about their jobs. He would look down on them from the roof he was fixing, watching them unseen for several minutes at a time. At first William had eyes for Hester with her fair skin and trim waist. But one afternoon he saw her kissing a man who had hidden in some bushes at the back of the house. They walked off together — the man with his arm resting around Hester's trim waist — and William began to like Grace.

'Mummy was not what you would call pretty.' But William liked the way Grace read her Bible under a tree and swatted away flies with a white handkerchief. He liked the fact that she was prim and shy. That when she offered him a bowl of water to wash in after he had dug some holes — 'I tell you already, Faith, I don't know what the holes were for,' — she lowered her eyes when he took it from her. He liked that she hummed as she ground corn and that her lips had a defiant curl when she called her sister to help. And when one day she looked William in the eye, he could feel her respect.

'Then, you see, Amy, my daddy's mother,

passed on. She was buried near her own people, so I understand — she was not buried with her husband. I don't know what she died of, but she must have been getting old. But, you see, after she passed on Daddy was free.'

It was a few days after William had signed the papers that proved he had purchased his own plot of land that he married Grace. He took his new bride and walked her through the bushes and over the stony soil of their property. William then employed young men from the district to help him build a house on the land. 'And they rob him. They took nails and wood — even the fruit from the trees. They would have taken the bread from his mouth if he had not watched them all day. Cha! Thieving is as old as time, Faith.' When the house was finished, William wanted to lift Grace up the three steps onto the veranda and into the house. But Grace would not let him. 'Mummy was not what you call playful.'

The land had trees — oranges, lemons and coconuts. And William planted bananas, an ackee and a tamarind tree. He dug the earth and sowed in sweet potatoes. He bought goats and chickens. He bought coffee beans that he roasted and ground himself and big bags of sugar that he scooped into smaller bags. And he built a shack at the front of the land — he built it himself without the help of the young men from the district. He opened it as a shop and stacked the shelves with everything he grew, ground and bagged. And on his other piece of land — the land they called Amity — he grew coconuts, yams and sweet potatoes and he kept cattle. He sold the milk from the cattle in the shop and the meat from the cattle to a butcher.

But some years the coconuts fell from the trees yellowing soft and smelling of a sweet decay. Or the sweet potatoes squelched and disintegrated to mud as he pulled them from the earth. The land was exhausted and produced banana trees with no fruit. And citrus trees where the fruit did not ripen but rotted where it fell.

At these times William had to find work in Kingston. 'My daddy would do anything for an honest living.' He worked in a large drapery shop. 'He was what you call a floorwalker.' He made sure the customers were happy and well served. But William hated the work. 'He didn't like being told what to do.' He didn't like being told what to do by people who were, evidently, darker than him. So it was then that he took his father's advice and began to mend shoes instead.

William mended shoes in the evening, setting himself up on a stool with his long legs splayed out and around the iron stand and shoe last that sat in front of him. He tipped up shoes onto the last, ripping off old soles and replacing them with new leather, which he split and pared with knives and skivers, tapping in nails in neat rows all along the sole edge. 'He was very neat — methodical.'

He pinned a notice in the shop, 'William Campbell Mends Shoes', and people came from a long way to have William mend their shoes. Soon William began making whole pairs of shoes for people. 'All leather. Good shoes. Not like the rubbish you get nowadays.' He bought calfskins in black and tan and alligator skins for special orders. He had wooden lasts for forming shoes: men's size six to eleven, boys' one to five and ladies' three to seven. He had steel hammers, needles, shoemaker's thread, pincers and wax, awl blades for piercing holes and eyelets in black and white for taking the leather laces. He stored all the small items during the day, in boxes that he put in a big trunk. But the lasts and wooden shoe stretcher were left neatly on shelves in a corner of the sitting room, in family rows of severed feet. 'And every evening, Faith, he sat tap, tap, tapping. I used to like to watch him. Tap, tap, tapping.'

William talked of opening a shop in town to sell his shoes. A shop where people would pay good money to slip their feet into 'William Campbell's All-Leather Shoes'. He talked of hiring people to help him. Backroom boys in leather aprons with palms permanently blackened with polish who'd help him make the shoes, and young women in frilly lace aprons who would sell them to willing customers. He thought that Grace and his daughters would soon be able to move to a big house with electricity and running water — that soon they would be able to live a life of ease.

But it did not happen. 'You know why, Faith? Canvas shoes!' William's shoe business collapsed when shoes made from canvas began to appear. The canvas shoes were inferior in every way to William's hand-crafted all-leather shoes. But they were much cheaper to buy because they were much cheaper to make. All around him William saw people who had used his services for many years turn to wearing the flimsy canvas shoes instead.

William left the shoe business convinced that the reason all these people preferred canvas shoes was because they were thieves. Thieves, he said, could not sneak up on anyone in his shoes. The good-quality leather shoes he made squeaked. But in canvas shoes any thief could come right up to your back — come right up to your house and you would not know they were there. 'It's true, Faith. It's true!'

William continued to work his land and some days he took his growing daughters with him down to Amity. 'Lovely days.' They would help him pick fruit, dig up the sweet potatoes and yams and clear the land of branches and twigs blown down by the high Jamaican winds. William would build a fire with the wood and as the sun set they would throw sweet potatoes into the flames, roast the tubers black and then eat them. 'Just like that, with no butter or anything. But they were the nicest fluffiest sweet potato I have ever eaten. Ahh, lovely.'

But William was a strict father. 'Oh boy. He was strict. He had an old belt he would lash us with if we answer him or Mummy back or we didn't do our jobs or we were late from school. And I always knew when Daddy was going to give one of us a licking because the chickens would fly into the trees like they knew he was on the warpath. He could be fierce. Even to this day the sound of chickens flappin' make me nervous.'

William did not like his daughters to mix with anyone who was darker than they were. 'That's how it was. Even though Mummy was dark she wasn't as dark as some people.' Sometimes William would turn friends of his daughters away from the house, telling them that children of his did not mix with people like them. 'But we had to make friends with the people we lived with. But Daddy did not understand this.' He wouldn't let them swim with other children. 'He thought it was indecent for us to take off our clothes in front of other people.' And he never ever let them talk to boys. 'That wasn't why we left, Faith. No, no. We had to find work.'

One by one his daughters went away. But it was Mildred going to England that upset William the most. 'He said it was too far.' But Mildred had had her head turned. After the Second World War a lot of newly-wed white English women came to Jamaica. They came with their black Jamaican husbands — men who had been stationed in England, in the army and RAF during the war. Some of the women found jobs in department stores and shops, some worked as teachers. Mildred loved the way they dressed and curled their hair and she loved to listen to the women speak. She would go down to the department store and listen to them talking in their English accents. 'She loved those women.' Mildred spent hours in front of the mirror reciting, 'What beautiful weather for the time of year,' over and over. 'She was mad! She would practise walking like them and trying to curl-up her hair like them.'

One day William came home with a woman who had recently returned from a six-month trip to England. 'That was not like Daddy — he did not have what you would call friends. But he sat this woman down with Mildred and the woman began.' She told Mildred how it was cold in England. How England had been badly bombed. How the housing was bad and the food and clothes were rationed. How it was grey in England, how it rained in England. There was fog, there was snow. And how the people were unfriendly in England. 'But it didn't make one bit of difference to Mildred. It was like a calling.'

Mildred told her father that she was not going to England for long and that she would return to the island with money. William just laughed. 'Well, not laughed. Daddy didn't really laugh, he was a serious man — he sort of raised his eyes.' But Mildred promised that she would one day come back. And she looked William in the eye and said, 'Daddy. Without vision the people perish.'

William lived for only six months after Grace died. In those months he began to go to church. He was a Baptist. 'Daddy never went to church while I knew him. He just read his Bible at night and whistled his hymns during the day. He didn't have time for the church.' William went to church twice on Sundays. On Saturdays he opened the church and cleaned it ready for weddings. And on weekday evenings he spent his time paving a path up from the road to the

300

church doors and planting beds of flowers around the walls.

It was on his land called Amity that William had a stroke. He was found at sunset, his fingers still clutching a spade — he had been digging a hole. 'Poor Daddy. Just like that. One day there, the next day gone. It was a shock.' He was buried in the garden alongside Grace and Muriel. And the small congregation of mourners at the funeral sang, *We have an anchor that keeps the soul, steadfast and sure while the billows roll*. 'And you know a funny thing, Faith — as soon as we began singing that hymn, as soon as we lift up our heads to sing . . . all the chickens flew up into the trees.'

23

Coral visited her friend Violet Chance on the third Saturday of every month. She had been doing it for eight years. 'You come, Faith — I have a little surprise for you.' Vincent drove us. He had an 'errand' to do in Ocho Rios. He had to deliver bag juice to vendors in the seaside port. Bag juice was sugary water, brightly coloured and packed in plastic. Vincent bought large amounts of the liquid in bags and because Gloria did not like Vincent to put them in her ice compartments, he put them in his mother's freezer. When they were iced hard and snowy Vincent delivered them to people who sold them on the streets — to tourists or to anyone who wanted to be cooled by frozen juice. 'It makes a little extra money,' Vincent told me.

'I thought you were a teacher,' I said.

And Vincent sighed, 'Faith, I teach in school, I teach piano at home, I play organ for the choir, I teach the Sunday children scripture, I take the children to school and run errands for my wife. I pick you up from the airport and I take Mummy to Violet in St Mary. And . . . I deliver bag juice, all over the island. I must be wicked because there is no rest for me.'

The car groaned and slipped down several inches as Vincent loaded the boot with the bulky frozen juices. Vincent puffed all the way out of Kingston saying, 'Mummy, you make me late.'

While Coral sat panting in the front seat, complaining, 'Always rushin' me. Cha.'

Vincent stopped the car on a road out of Kingston at a long line of stalls that curled round with the bend. Open shacks like open-fronted shops, with smoke being fanned out of the dark interiors into the sun.

'The best jerk pork in Jamaica,' Vincent declared.

'Oh no — we stopped?' Coral moaned.

All the stalls were selling food, all had battered white rusting freezers outside, lines of mottled green oranges hanging from hooks on string and plastic baskets of green-pink paw paw. Women in dirty pastel dresses with tight headscarves cut meat or leant on the freezers talking and laughing and peeling oranges. Children played around in the road wheeling hula hoops along the ground and chasing dogs. While the customers stood fanning themselves as they ate greasy meat and rice in any shade they could find.

Vincent chose 'Maxie's Hot Spot' with its Pepsi-Cola signs and soup for sale. A young girl was standing over a barbecue in the vapour of white smoke cooking chicken and pork. Turning the pieces over on the fire, she stopped only to stir a pot of soup and wipe her forehead with the inside of her bare arm. An old fat woman sat in the darkness at the back of the shack with her legs splayed, fanning herself with a banana leaf and sipping Pepsi-Cola from a bottle.

'I am going to have some jerk pork. I can't pass without getting any. You must have jerk pork

303

in Jamaica — and this is the best. You want some, Faith?'

I said yes but Coral complained, 'Don't make her eat this food, Vincent. She not used to it. She from England.'

'Oh Mummy, don't fuss,' Vincent said. 'Have some of the soup, Mummy?'

Coral gave a disgusted no, and stayed sitting in the car motionless as Vincent and I ate paper platefuls of jerk pork with festival bread. The meat was spiced and crisp, hot with pimento, nutmeg and thyme and the cakey bread soaked up the meat juices and coated my fingers in salty fried dough.

Vincent drank the soup. 'Mummy, you sure you won't have some? It's lovely.'

'No.'

He winked at me and whispered, 'Eight years we been coming here — eight years and she never had it once.' He held the paper cup with his pinky out like a vicar sipping tea. Coral was staring straight ahead with her hands resting neatly on her lap until I went over to the bin to throw away my Pepsi-Cola bottle. Her arm lunged out of the car window and grabbed an urgent handful of my skirt and buttock. 'Wait!' she yelled, like she was saving me from jumping off a cliff. Vincent took the bottle from me and put it in the boot of the car. 'You get money for these bottles, Faith. These are valuable bottles. Never throw away these bottles.'

We drove off the main road, onto smaller roads where the car swerved and swayed as Vincent avoided holes I could have jumped in up to my knees. We meandered along the edge of cane fields — a looming wall of straggly thick poles that looked anything but sweet, overhanging the road with unruly pointed leaves that sometimes brushed the car as we went along. And every man I saw carried a machete and every woman looked expressionlessly into the car as we drove past.

Vincent finally stopped the car in front of a low bungalow. Coral gathered up her handbag and signalled to me, 'Come.' The windows on the house were all closed up with metal shutters.

'This is where I drop you off, Faith,' Vincent said. The front gate was made of ornate wrought iron showing two birds swooping. And there were three steps up to a veranda.

'Meet us at Violet's,' Coral instructed Vincent through the car window.

'Mummy, is eight years I been bringin' you here. I know, Mummy, I know!'

Coral called 'Yoo hoo!' and took my hand as she opened the gate. A solitary brown chicken stopped pecking at the ground and looked at us. But no one called back and Coral said, 'Good.' I followed her into the garden of the empty house. Past two wooden chicken coops that had turned grey and flaky in the sun. Past a line of corrugated-iron fencing with panels blown over at odd angles and rusting oil drums full of wood. The land crunched under my feet — stony, parched, with grass browning in patches. Banana trees with no fruit poked up through the grass like weeds — the ends of their leaves brown and ragged. Coral stopped by a small mound of earth; a tiny hillock on the flat of the garden. I put my foot on the mound ready to climb but Coral held me back.

'Have some respect, Faith,' she said. 'This is where your grandmother and grandfather are buried.'

I thought we were at the house of Violet Chance.

'No, this is where your mummy and me grew up. This used to be our land.'

I had been to Blenheim Palace and stared transfixed at the romper suit Winston Churchill wore when he was planning his strategies for war. I had been to Hampton Court and listened for the screams in the long gallery. I had sat in the seat where Shakespeare courted Anne Hathaway. And drunk in the pub where Dick Turpin was captured. But . . .

'Here?!' I shouted at Coral. 'This is where you grew up? This is where Mum grew up . . . ?'

'Hush, Faith — don't shout.'

This was the land bought with Panama Canal wages. Where women with cotters on their heads sold cocoa pods for chocolate. And where chickens flew up into the trees when Nathaniel and William rolled in the dirt. This was the land with a house that had three steps up to a veranda.

'No, this is a different house, Faith. The one your mummy and me lived in was pulled down long ago. But calm down, child — it's nothing to be excited about.'

This was where my mum grew up and kept a goat called Columbine — on this land! It was so far from Crouch End clock tower, Dunn's bakery and the W3 bus.

'No, Faith, we can't go in the house. There is no one here. They are all in Florida.' I put my ear to the trunk of a lemon tree.

'Stop that, child. What are you doing? Have you gone mad?' I opened the doors of the chicken coops and peered behind the corrugated fence.

'Come, we must go now, Faith. You can't behave. This is someone else's land now.'

The grass went brown along a straight line. 'Yes, Faith, this is where the old house was. But come, we must go.' I followed it balancing on the edge, along the wall of a room in the house that my grandfather built.

'Oh child, you are trying my patience . . . It's the kitchen, I think — I don't remember now. Is a long time ago.' I ran to another spot, 'What room was this, Coral?'

'No, Faith, come,' she demanded. Coral looked all around her, flustered and embarrassed as if there was someone watching. 'Come now or they will not let me come back.'

'Can we see the grave again?' I asked. I had not looked properly. All I had seen was the disturbed rounded earth. I had not knelt and pressed my ear to the ground. I had not laid flowers. I had not told them I was their granddaughter from England. I had not left my respect. Coral flapped her hands, 'No! Child. Please come!' She shook her head, pointed a finger at me and shouted deliberately, 'Come now or I will tell your mummy that you cannot behave.'

Cecelia's Story told to me by Vincent

'I always understood that our great-grandmother Cecelia was a miserable woman,' Vincent told me. 'The sort of woman that has the weight of the world on her shoulders. Her name used to be Livingstone before it was changed to Hilton. Did you know that? Did Mummy tell you that? Cecelia Livingstone. Livingstone like the great explorer of Africa. When I was a boy I used to wonder if I was related to him. But I never liked to explore — I did not have the time and I preferred to read books. So I'm not sure that we are related. But you like to explore, don't you, Faith? I must look into it again.'

Cecelia and her older sister Myrtle were the daughters of Katherine Livingstone. Nobody except Katherine knew who fathered the two girls. 'No, you have me there, Faith. I do not know that. Katherine could have been forced into a liaison. Or she could have fallen for some smooth-tongue man — a West Indian or Englishman, Irish, Scottish, Indian or Welshman. We had them all on these shores so who can tell?'

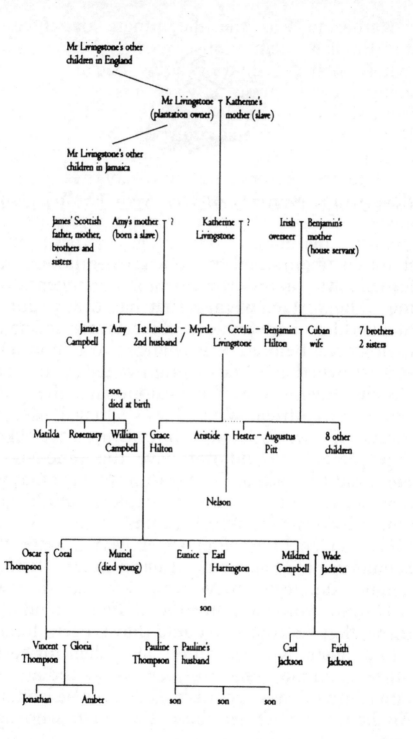

Katherine was the illegitimate daughter of an English plantation owner. Her mother, 'whose name I do not know because we are going back in time now!' gained her freedom from slavery when she gave birth to Katherine. Rumour had it that this English plantation owner — 'Mr Livingstone I presume,' — fathered several hundred children by the slave women on his estate. 'Well, it was plenty anyway, Faith.' After the women gave birth the English plantation owner gave them their freedom from slavery. Consequently he ran into serious debt after he had freed nearly all the female childbearing slaves and found himself left with only a few elderly toothless males. 'Sometimes I think these people were not very bright. What you think?' He sold the plantation and went back to England where he started a foundation for the rehabilitation of fallen women. 'As God is my witness, Faith, that is true. But I can't remember who told me now — I may have read it or Mummy may have said but . . . but where was I? Oh yes, Katherine.' Katherine had died giving birth to Cecelia. The two motherless girls were brought up by their grandmother, 'whose name I do not know'.

However, the girls were left to fend for themselves when their grandmother died suddenly from Denghie fever. Cecelia was only thirteen and Myrtle fourteen. Myrtle soon left Jamaica to marry a man and start a new life in America — in New York. Cecelia stayed and worked as a housemaid for the new owners of the plantation that her grandfather, the English-man, had sold.

Cecelia then became pregnant. 'To cut a long story short, Faith — this is the thing your Auntie Coral would never tell you. Oh no, Mummy would never tell you — this is why I am telling you because I have more of an open mind on that time in our history.' At the age of fourteen Cecelia gave birth to Grace — 'your grand-mother, Faith,' — but nobody ever knew who Grace's father was. 'She was illegitimate, this is what I think, although Mummy would never say herself. You see, Cecelia could have been forced into a liaison. Or she could have fallen for some smooth-tongue man — a West Indian or Englishman, Irish, Scottish, Indian or Welshman perhaps. But I don't think it was someone Chinese because Grandma did not have that look about her.' Cecelia continued to work as a domestic servant, carrying Grace with her to work and hiding the little baby in cupboards and cellars and under beds, as she went about her duties.

Then one day as Cecelia was standing on a chair and stretching up to pick tamarinds from a tree with her baby strapped to her back in an old curtain, she slipped and was caught by a man. The man was Benjamin Nelson Hilton. 'Your great-grandfather. But when my mummy tells that story there is no baby, no curtain — nothing is strapped to a back.'

Benjamin Hilton was the son of an Irishman who was an overseer on an estate. His mother, a black woman, was in service but left when she

312

started having children by the Irish overseer. She had eight boys and two girls and Benjamin was the oldest. The Irish overseer built Benjamin's mother a house in which to bring up his children. 'The house was of a box construction, Faith. It was two layers of wood with a cavity that today would be filled with wires and things. It was a very good house, with three bedrooms, a parlour, dining room, even a small nursery.' Benjamin and his brothers and sisters grew up in the box house and then moved all over the world — four brothers to America, a sister to Canada, another to Cuba, two brothers to the banana plantations of Costa Rica and another brother to a whaling fleet that fished the Pacific waters. 'I don't know what happened to the Irish overseer — went to America probably. I never really heard much about him.'

Benjamin Nelson Hilton got a job in service in Cuba, working for a Spanish family who owned a large sugar estate that employed many Jamaicans. Benjamin became fluent in Spanish and was the favourite servant of the family. Some said it was because he could cook *bacalao* with spiced sweet potatoes, peppers, eggs and black olives better than any Spanish cook. He was provided with a good house and land in Cuba and he was in charge of all the domestic staff. 'I heard he was a lovely man — much older than Cecelia though. Mummy only met him once but she said he could make chickens' eggs come out of your ears.'

When Benjamin's mother died he inherited the box house but because he worked in Cuba he left the house and the land in the charge of three men who lived not in the box house but in a smaller house on the land. 'today we would call it a shed.' He paid them to care for the house and land and he also supplied them with a plot of land to cultivate for their own needs. He called them his estate managers.

It was not long after Cecelia fell from the tree into Benjamin's arms that she became pregnant by him. He moved her and Grace into the box house and told his managers that they now worked for her. 'And to cut a long story short, he became Grace's father from then on.'

Cecelia changed her name to Hilton, telling everyone that she had married Benjamin. 'But they were not married, Faith. And I will tell you why all in good time.' Benjamin then had to return to his position in Cuba. By the time he returned again to Jamaica, Cecelia had given birth to twin boys. They lived for only a few minutes before their lips turned blue as they gulped for air and died. They were buried in the garden. By the time Benjamin left for Cuba again Cecelia was once more pregnant. This time Benjamin came back from Cuba to see his child born — lifeless and stiff. 'This went on for a long time — he would come to Jamaica, get Cecelia pregnant and the baby would die. Four children she lost, born dead, and one she miscarry. Terrible. No wonder she was miserable.' Grace, meanwhile, was growing into a healthy young girl — playing by the river, feeding the chickens, learning to read and write. Happy when her daddy visited from Cuba with the gift of a doll or a brightly painted wooden horse. But her mother seemed to resent Grace her life.

Then Benjamin came from Cuba with a gift for Cecelia. Wrapped in a shawl, dressed in a white cotton tunic with a tiny lace bonnet, was a baby girl. 'He brought her a baby. Yes, Faith, it's a shock. This is a shocking story.' Benjamin had another family in Cuba — he was married. His wife was part-Spanish, part-African. Benjamin and his Cuban wife had eight children. 'She was Catholic and so was he . . . well, when he was in Cuba.' When his wife was distressed that she was pregnant for the ninth time, Benjamin told her that he knew a woman who could bring up the child. His wife agreed. Benjamin took his two-month-old daughter over to Jamaica and gave her to Cecelia. 'Cecelia told everyone that this baby was her lucky, healthy, seventh-born child. But Grace knew differently.' The baby had a beautiful fair complexion with dark eyes and black hair and she looked like Benjamin. Her name was Anna-Maria Consuela del Pilar Andrade de Garcia Hurtade Hilton but Cecelia changed it to Hester. 'And Hester became her mother's eyeball.'

Hester was taken care of by Grace, while her mother looked on and appreciated this beautiful child who grew to look so like her absent husband. Hester went to Wesleyan Church School with Grace. 'But Grandma once told me that her sister was not very clever at school. She would get all the letters in words jumbled up and round the wrong way. In those days they were beaten for it but now in my school I think we

315

would say she was dyslexic.' But Hester could dance — swirling in the yard dressed in her mother's long skirt. Hester could sing — any hymn, like a bird. She could swim faster than all the boys in the district and climb trees higher. When her father came to visit he sat her on his knee and taught her Spanish — *Buenos Dias, Adios, Hoy el tiempo es muy bueno*. He brought dresses for the two girls — hand-me-downs from the children of his other family. 'And as I understand, Hester's clothes always fitted perfectly but the ones for poor Grace needed several adjustments.'

When Hester was fourteen she pleaded with her mother that she wanted to learn to play the piano. 'Her mother could not afford to buy her a piano, they were expensive things, but this girl just nag at her.' So Cecelia arranged for Hester to go to the house of the Baptist Minister on Monday mornings and play the piano there while the Minister and his wife were away teaching at their school for girls. 'Grandma said Hester was not very good on the piano either. Although she could only practise by banging down her fingers at the kitchen table because she had no instrument of her own and you cannot learn the piano like that. Cha. Grandma did not have one good word for her sister.'

It was while Hester was trying to plot out the tune to 'Away in a manger' that she met Aristide. Aristide was a piano tuner. 'This man used to travel round Jamaica and all the other small islands tuning up the instruments. And where there were no pianos to tune he worked as a

316

carpenter. He was from Martinique, a Creole, they called them, a mulatto — mind you, he said he was a Frenchman.' He had black hair, black eyes and a complexion as soft as pale brown silk.

'Grandma met him. He came to the house and spoke with Cecelia. He was Cecelia's age — not a young man. Cecelia gave him a drink of milk. She thought he was a very fine man with his French accent and *bonjours* and *au revoirs*. That is of course before she realise what he was doing with Hester.'

Hester would smuggle Aristide into the Minister's house. He taught her duets on the piano. Duets where Hester only had to bang out two chords as Aristide provided the melody. The housemaid told Cecelia how much better Hester's playing had become. But then they stopped playing the piano. Aristide would wait for Hester near her house, crouching down in the bushes until Hester could get away, then they would walk together down to the river. 'To cut a long story short, Faith, by the time Hester was fifteen she was pregnant by this man and him just run.' Aristide left the district to go to Kingston and was never heard of again.

Hester gave birth to a rosy-cheeked son who was christened Nelson. But Hester had no time for her baby. She would carry on going for walks by the river and playing the piano at the Minister's house, leaving her son with Cecelia. 'Cecelia had to feed the baby on milk from the cow because she could never find Hester to come feed him. She used to call out for her and everyone in the district would know it was time for the baby's feed, everyone except Hester. And of course because she was not feeding the baby, Hester's . . . you know . . . Hester's . . . you know, Faith . . . ' Hester's breasts dried of milk before they should.

As Hester wandered back from the market one day after buying two bags of rice for her mother, a young man who was sleeping under an ackee tree jumped up and offered to carry the bags of rice for her. The young man was Augustus Pitt. Augustus told Hester that he was a carpenter who had worked in many great houses and built some of the finest cabinets in the whole of the island. Augustus told Cecelia that his grandmother had a shop and land in St Anne's that he would one day inherit. He told them both that his mother worked in Cuba demonstrating new kitchen equipment to fine wives of rich men and that his father was an officer in the American army. 'Basically, Faith, the man was a liar and a lazy good-for-nothing.'

Hester married Augustus and the newly-married couple lived with Cecelia. But Augustus soon began to spend his days sitting round the house expecting Hester and Cecelia to wait on him. 'And you know what the man start to say? He say his American father die suddenly. He say his mother had married again in Cuba and was not returning home. He say his grandmother had to sell her shop. You know the sort of man I mean? And when Cecelia ask him for his help around the place with the chickens, the goats, the mango trees, he say he was a carpenter and not brought up to work on the land. And then he tell her that he has a bullet in his leg from the war in France and that is why he has to rest up. Cha!' Then one day Cecelia caught him beating the four-year-old Nelson — 'beating him with his fist until the little boy's nose ran with blood. All because he had not brought Augustus the drink he had asked for. There is never any call for that. It was then Cecelia told him to take his bony backside and find somewhere else to live.'

Augustus left, taking Hester with him. 'Cecelia did not want Hester to go, just this man who was a pest to her. But Hester just turn her back on her mother and leave the house with this sit-down-on-his-bottom man.' Hester and Augustus went to Cuba. 'And I always wonder whether she ever met her real family — we'll never know. No one ever saw Hester again. You could not mention Hester in my grandmother's house.'

Benjamin stopped coming home to Jamaica. He wrote to Cecelia that his health was getting bad — that some days he could not remember his way home, or the faces of his children. He continued to send Cecelia money but never again returned to Jamaica. 'As I understand it and I am not sure how I know this, Faith, so don't bother asking me, he died an old man in Cuba. But he gave Cecelia the box house and was happy to do so. He was a kind man.'

Cecelia was left to bring up Nelson on her own. And Nelson became his grandmother's eyeball. 'That boy, so Mummy would tell me, could do no wrong.' Evidently when Mildred — 'that is your mummy, Faith,' — was a young girl she had to go to her grandmother's house nearly every day. Cecelia's house was near to the school she attended and at lunchtimes her grandmother would feed her. But Cecelia was never nice to Mildred. Mildred complained to her sisters that her grandmother never took her on her lap like she did to Nelson. She never smiled at her like she did to Nelson. She never took her to the market or for trips into town. She just sat her at the table, got out the jug of milk and cut her some bread or sometimes a piece of fruit. 'She treated Mildred as if she were just any child. Your mummy did not like to go to her grandmother's. And Nelson used to tease her — push her in the river, throw stones at her, that sort of thing.'

One day Nelson took a pencil and scribbled all over the pages of Mildred's schoolbook. 'Mildred knew she would get a beatin' from her teacher so she went to her grandmother and show her what the boy had done. But her grandmother just look on the book then on Mildred's face like she could not hear what she was saying. So Mildred ask her grandmother if she is deaf. And, oh, the carry-on!' Cecelia complained to Grace and William that their child was ungrateful, that their child was rude, that their child was greedy, unruly and that their child had scribbled in her good schoolbooks. 'And, so I understand, Mildred got one licking from her daddy for cheeking her grandmother. All because of Nelson. In my experience young boys can be very difficult. Cha.'

But Nelson grew into a handsome young man

with dark eyes and wavy hair like his mother and a straight back that stood him erect and tall. Cecelia decided to use the money Benjamin gave her to send Nelson to a private school in St Mary — a school that was run by the Catholic Church for the children of 'decent' families. 'It was one of the best schools in Jamaica. In England you would call it a public school.' Nelson was accepted by the school. His uniform was bought and the fees for the year paid by Cecelia. But before Nelson started the head of the school called Cecelia to him. 'And this headmaster told her there had been complaints about Nelson joining the school — that some white parents did not want their child mixing with someone from Nelson's background. Nelson was illegitimate, this man said. Cecelia's husband was only a domestic servant, he told her, and Cecelia's grandmother was born a slave. I ask you!' When Cecelia told Nelson that he could not go to the school after all he took a knife and slashed his new uniform into strips. 'He was so humiliated. You see how it was, Faith? They would not let him through the doors of the school even though he had the money and the complexion. No — now he was the wrong class!'

Nelson left his grandmother's house to work as an office boy for a newspaper in Kingston. And after six months in Kingston he left Jamaica to work in America. He promised his grandma that he would soon send back money for her and one day make her a wealthy woman. Nelson went to Washington and regularly wrote to his grandma about his newspaper job, about his lodgings and the people he met. On two occasions he returned to Jamaica dressed in a suit, with an American accent and money in his pocket to spend on his totally deaf grandmother.

Then Cecelia received a letter from Nelson informing her that he was getting married. 'And although Cecelia was not a young woman she start to make plans to go to this wedding. Oh, she would go to America and see her sister, she said. Oh, she and her sister would watch her Nelson walking up the aisle with his bride. Oh, she would be so proud, she said. She had a hat made. Straw with a band made of little English cherries. I know this hat because my grandma had it in her cupboard.' But Cecelia never got to wear the hat with little English cherries.

'Now listen to this, Faith.' When Nelson wrote to his grandmother again the letter said that the woman he was marrying was white. That the woman he was marrying was from a good family in America. He told his grandmother that the woman he was marrying did not know that he was black. She understood Nelson to be a white man. 'And this letter carry on to say that if this woman ever found out that his family were coloured, negro — if anyone ever found out that his grandmother had a black skin and was related to slaves — then this fiancée of his would not marry him. Because in America, Faith, no matter how white you look, if you are descended from slaves then you are black.' Nelson did not want his grandmother at his wedding. 'He did not want this coloured woman sitting in the church in her fine hat, shaming him. He told

322

Cecelia never to contact him again under any circumstances. He cut off that whole side of his family, that whole side of his past. And that was the last anyone hear of him. And good riddance I say!'

And Cecelia? 'Oh, she just carry on, sort of shrug it off, so I understand. That is what I was told. She just got on with her life.' But she took Nelson's photograph from the shelf where it had always sat and she buried it in the garden of the house and marked it with a cross. 'And she never really smiled after that.'

Cecelia never saw Hester, Nelson, or Benjamin again before she died. But Grace, her daughter, was with her at the end. She cooked for Cecelia and washed and combed her hair before Cecelia passed away one hot day in June in the bedroom in the box house. 'Your great-grandmother, Faith, was a miserable woman.'

24

The road up to where Violet Chance lived was rutted like it had been freshly shelled by artillery. The sky was overcast but still the heat was a weight to carry, eased only by an occasional puff of cool air from the 'Jamaica breeze'. A little girl came skipping up the road. Her hair was braided — neat and flat. She wore a school uniform — a pale blue cotton tunic with a pleated skirt and a crisp white blouse. She was holding a bunch of leaves and grass and singing, 'Oh we have a friend in Jesus' in a voice as beautiful as a bird. She said, 'Good morning, Auntie,' to us as we passed her. Coral said, 'Well, good morning to you, little one.' And the girl skipped on up the road, losing leaves from her bunch as it waved in her hand.

Coral walked slowly. I would take two steps then stand and wait for her to catch me up. I tried to walk to her pace but felt like a tightrope walker losing my balance as I placed my feet down carefully in front of one another. So I walked and waited, walked and waited. Until Coral asked, 'Why you walk so fast, child? You will fall down.'

Violet Chance lived in a shop. It took Coral and me twenty minutes to walk the few hundred yards to the small wooden cabin that sat on a corner at a junction where four roads met. It looked no bigger than an English country bus shelter: a wooden open-fronted shed that fitted the description of the little shop that my grandparents had run. 'Is this your parents' old shop, Coral?' I said reverently. Coral's still tight 'Faith, you cannot behave' lips gradually began to smile. 'Child, all these places look the same. Nothing much changes.'

The shop had been painted once. Pale green paint still clung on to the dark brown splintered wood in distressed patches. There was a serving counter with a protective mesh screen that ran to the ceiling like in a bank. The shelves around the walls were crowded with brightly coloured packets, boxes and tins — the yellows, reds, blues and oranges dazzling and gaudy in the shade of the shop. Washing powder, biscuits, breakfast cereals, instant coffee, tea, sugar, drinking chocolate, cigarettes, bottles of rum. Uniform factory-packed goods with no space between each item. Striped plastic shopping bags hanging from hooks, shoelaces and ribbons. Straw hats and rows of oranges on string. Hair curlers and hairnets and flip-flop sandals. A department store in a box.

Coral called, 'Yoo hoo!' through the mesh screen. A little door among the shelves opened. The shop wobbled. And a tiny woman walked through. She was wizened, shrunken, a raisin woman. Her head was topped with a bun of fine straight white hair, but her jaw was clenched so tight that her lips were a drooping line of cartoon sadness. She did not look up to see who had called out but tutted and fussed as she sorted through a jailor's bunch of keys. She unlocked a door in the mesh grille and then glanced upwards.

'Oh Coral, you so old,' she said. 'Am I as old as you? Look at you — you an old woman.' Coral moved through the mesh gate, giggling as she caught my arm, 'Come, Faith, hurry yourself now.'

The back of the shop was like a museum 'experience': the sights, the sounds, the smells of life in a small Jamaican shop at the turn of the century. No imagination was needed. It was very dark inside — my eyes had to adjust. It was lit by a small window that was opaque with dirt and bird droppings. There was a narrow single bed made up with a sheet and pillow, a wooden chair with two slumping cushions on the seat and back, a footstool with a tatty embroidered cover and a small wooden table. There was a radio with a cloth front and large dials — a wireless. And a telephone — a Bakelite phone that looked like it had to be hand-cranked before use. There was no colour in the room — it was sepia. Except for a floral dress that was hanging on the wall — it had a faint hint of turquoise. And the sandal shoes that were placed neatly below it were white.

The three of us filled the room. Violet told us to sit. The two older women stuck out their bottoms and lowered themselves down, confident they would reach something to sit on. Coral took the bed and Violet the chair. I sat on the footstool and looked up.

'This is me niece — she's . . . ' Coral began but Violet cut her off.

'Did you bring me the things you say? Is today you said you'd bring me me things, Coral.'

'I have it! I have it, Violet, but you want to know me niece first . . . '

'Me feet been very bad. Painin' me. Bad pain, Coral. Some days I can hardly stand. And the doctor he said I must rest up. I say to him, 'Doctor, how can I rest up?' I tell him I have a shop and I have no husband any more.' Violet looked at me for the first time. 'Him run off, you see,' she explained, her eyes squinting slits. 'Him run off one day. Him say he's gone to get something and that was the last I see him. Him never come back. And he leave me not knowing if him dead or alive. But I have to get on.' She sucked her teeth.

Coral sat forward to speak but Violet went on. 'He's not my first husband — not the first one, oh no.' Coral sat back. 'Oh no, not the first. The third. He's the third. The first one die — Lord rest his soul. He was weak. The second one him run off with a young girl with a big batty and wiggle-wiggle hips. Canada. You know is Canada they run to, Coral? I divorce him. And I marry Winston. Two years and him gone to get something in Ocho and I never see him again. How many years he been gone? I don't know. Eight, ten, long time. And I have to get on. Enough crosses with this shop but now me feet playin' me up. Painin' me.' There was the briefest pause. 'Did you bring the stuff for me feet, Coral? Is today you say you bring it.'

'Violet, stop with your chat,' Coral began. 'This is Faith, she is . . . '

'I know who this,' Violet said, waving her hand. 'Mildred's daughter. I can see she favour Mildred. You have any brother and sister?'

'I have a brother, Carl.'

'Him younger or older?'

'Older.'

'But tell me, you know your daddy, child?'

'Violet!' Coral sucked her teeth.

'Hush, Coral.'

'My father's Wade Jackson.'

Violet sat back on her chair and let out a long 'ohh'. 'He's your daddy. They still married?'

'Violet, hush up!' Coral said but Violet did not. 'I didn't think that would last. Them marry so quickly, then off — whoosh — to England like them somethin' to hide. And I said he would not stay around.' Violet tapped Coral's arm, 'I know is your sister but she was my friend. And is England and them black men in England they run off with the first white woman who wiggle her backside at them.'

'Oh Violet, not that again,' Coral huffed.

'Men are like that. She was lucky. They still married. I remember I gave them a valuable little horse for a weddin' present. But me say no more. It is not my business. The child say she know her daddy. She has a brother. If she say so . . .'

Coral began to search through her bag, 'Come, let me give you somethin' for your foot. Is Faith brought this from England.' She brought out a bottle of Vitamin E capsules while Violet said, 'Come, child, get off that stool, I need that for me foot.' I stood up and accidentally kicked the wireless. 'Watch where you standin', child! That is a valuable thing. Me husband buy me that radio.'

I was huge in the room — I had too many arms and legs. Which husband? And nowhere to sit. I apologised and sat next to Coral, budging her gently along the bed. She was cutting the end off a capsule and squeezing the oil onto her hand.

Violet lifted her leg up onto the stool. Her foot was under my nose. It was misshapen — the toes slanted like they'd fallen over. A bone stuck out with a purple knobbly end. There were red round bits and yellow pussy bits and loose flapping skin. The heel of her foot was leather and her toenails looked like large cashew nuts — curled and brown.

'I have terrible trouble with me feet.' She pointed out some of the bigger blisters which I was trying to avoid looking at. 'You see this hard skin,' she tapped her leather heel. 'Painin' me. And this here. No, here, child, look just here, you see it? Doctor say it the worst he seen. And I am on my feet all day. Coral said Vitamin E oil will help. I say I don't know anything can help. Coral, you ready with that yet? I have no husband now him run off. No help. No husband. And me on my feet all day.'

Coral began to rub Violet's feet. 'That feel nice, Violet?'

'I feel nothing, Coral. Is hard skin. I feel nothing.'

The oil was odourless — her feet were not. I stood up. 'I need the toilet,' I said. Violet sucked

329

her teeth. 'I can't take her now, I have to see to me foot. Is too much pain to take her now. You don't know about pain, you young. I can't take you now . . .'

'Come, I'll take her,' Coral said. She gave Violet the broken capsules with instructions, 'Squeeze out the oil and rub it on your feet.'

'I can't reach, Coral. Come soon. Take her and come.' Violet gave Coral her keys and Coral pulled me out through the shop as Violet shouted, 'And see you lock up or thief will take everything I have.'

'She's old,' Coral whispered to me, then added, 'Mark you, she's younger than me.'

'Does she live in that shop?'

Coral nodded. 'Oh yes, all day in that little place.'

'She must be very poor,' I said. Coral laughed. And at that moment I saw sitting through the trees in dappled light, a huge house. A grand house. A single-storey house with stunted doric pillars at the front gate and matching pillars on either side of the main door.

'You still want the toilet, Faith?' The house was sitting in grounds that stretched in every direction that I looked and it took Coral and me several minutes to get from the gate to the front porch.

It was Violet's house. Bought and paid for by her first husband and left to Violet in his will. The two acres of land that surrounded the house were bought by her second husband. Planted and cultivated by him with citrus trees, coconut, paw paw, bananas, bougainvillea and hibiscus.

And given to Violet by a judge when he ran off to Canada with a big batty woman. Her third husband had decorated the house — painting it with the colours that Violet loved — pale pink with lilac paintwork. He had fitted the tall front gates and had the pillars copied from a book called *In Search of the Ancient World*. The pillars were to have been topped with two lions leaping but he disappeared with the money before they were installed.

But Violet thought the house was too big. She had no children, she had no husband. She preferred the room at the back of the shop. And although Violet used a bucket and a gully for her toilet, her guest had to use the house. 'What toilet you want?' Coral laughed as we went through the door. There were three bathrooms and six bedrooms. Coral beckoned me to a closed door. 'Look in there, Faith.' I opened the door and in front of me was an ornate carved four-poster bed draped in a white mosquito net.

'Cinderella!'

Coral patted my head and gave me the bunch of keys. 'Now lock all the locks like you see me do. You mustn't forget any or she'll be frettin'. I'll go back so she can finish with her moanin' and you can stay here for a little. Cinderella.'

All the beds in the house were made up ready for occupation. Violet used to have lodgers in these rooms — travelling salesmen who would stay for one or two nights before moving on to Ocho Rios or Kingston. But she found it too much work with the shop and the land. So the house stayed empty. Occasionally someone would come and stay and they would have the house to themselves. And roam the rooms imagining how they would live if it was their house. If they had lived in St Mary in a house with six bedrooms and three bathrooms, in two acres of land with fruit trees and flowers. Which room would they choose for themselves? The one with the four-poster bed or perhaps one of the smaller rooms with a narrow single bed but yellow hibiscus growing at the window.

The kitchen table sat in the middle of a fitted kitchen with turquoise units and a matching fridge as big as a wardrobe. The sitting room had an L-shaped sofa big enough for a family — big enough for Carl's long legs. And a large-screen television that Dad would like and a set of shelves to take the ornamental ceramic fruit and Mum's collection of little glass creatures.

But the mosquito net around the four-poster bed had holes I could put my fingers through and the sheets of the bed were tatty and grey. All the flowers inside the house were plastic, faded and covered in dust. The fridge was turned off — warm inside and growing several varieties of mould — it smelt like a rubbish bin.

I sat down on the sofa and looked at the magazine that lay casually on the coffee table — it was seven years out of date. Then I heard a fluttering behind me like a bird. I saw a sparrow caught in the room — hitting itself against the window. Banging itself with a regular beat against the glass. But then I realised it was not a small bird but a giant moth. A black furry moth. A moth so big it could have eaten a cardigan whole and spat out the buttons. It flew round the room in slow deliberate circles. I could feel the wind of its wings. I ducked and crouched to get to the window. But the window was locked and gridded up with grilles designed to keep things out. Another moth swooped past me. Past my left ear with a soft whoosh. While the first moth banged its wings, frantic against the window. The front door was stiff and stuck. I pulled and pushed and kicked. The black shadows flew into the room, sweeping round each other, their wings flapping a soft sound like flesh on flesh. I stood still for a lifetime until they settled on the walls — one on either side of the room, their wings open and so dark they looked like moth-shaped holes. I pulled at the door again and it opened, letting a startling bright light into the room. The two moths fluttered over my head and the three of us escaped.

★ ★ ★

'Coral, I think I feelin' somethin',' Violet said. Sitting back in the little room behind the shop, I watched my aunt hunched over her friend's foot, slowly massaging tiny capsule-sized amounts of oil deep into her heels.

'No. Wait. Yes. Yes, yes, I feel somethin' just then.' Violet's face gathered the faint trace of a smile as she turned towards me.

'Your mummy and me used to play together. You know that? You know that child?' Violet told me. 'Oh yes. She was my friend, we went to school together. She was clever, your mummy.

333

She could recite all her tables before anyone. But I would get a licking from the teacher. In those days they hit you hard. It's true, Coral, huh? They hit you hard. They beat you. They beat you for any little thing, with a stick. Ehh, Coral? With a stick they beat you. Ehh, Coral? What you say, Coral?'

'Is a long time ago, I like to forget all that.'

'We used to run up the road your mummy and me. She and that goat. She loved that goat. Stinking, smelly thing with some damn-fool name. It used to eat up everything. One time it eat my shoe and I got such a beatin'. 'Where is the good shoe — that was a good shoe.' That was my mummy — shoutin'. All the time, shoutin'. She long dead now, in peace at last and the Lord rest her soul. But she had her crosses to bear. Oh my mummy, she knew trouble . . . '

I quickly asked, 'Have you lived here all your life, Violet?'

Violet frowned. 'Here?' she repeated. 'No . . . no . . . no.' She descended a scale as she spoke. She began to laugh. She hit Coral's arm. 'The child ask me if I have always lived here.' She descended the scale with, 'No . . . no . . . no.' She pointed towards the little window, 'I used to live over there.'

I stretched to see where she was pointing. I expected to see the corrugated iron rooftops of a village in the distance or a panoramic vista with a horizon of blue sea. But all I could see was across the road to the opposite corner. 'I grew up over there. On that corner — behind the tree. You can't see now but we used to have a house

334

there. But it burn down. I only came over here,'
Violet pointed at the spot she was sitting in now,
'after I got married. For the first time. To my first
husband. Who was taken by the Lord. No, I grew
up over there. At first I did not like it over here.
I said to my first husband that I did not like it
— that I wanted to go back. But now I am used
to it and I don't think I would like to go back
over there. What you think, Coral?'

Coral tapped my leg and secretly winked at
me. 'It's nicer here,' Coral said and I nodded.

'I knew your daddy too,' Violet said.

Coral shifted on the bed beside me. 'Oh, not
all that chat again. Come, Violet, I think I hear
someone in the shop.'

'What he do now, your daddy?' Violet carried
on.

'He has his own business.'

'Really. They let black man have business in
England?'

'Painting and decorating.'

Violet was shocked. 'But Wade was a
bookkeeper. Coral, Wade was a bookkeeper. He
used to have a good job here. Sums and money
and keeping everything just so. That was your
daddy. It's true. Coral, tell me me not losing me
mind. Wade used to do sums. What they call
them? What they call them?'

'Accountant?' I said.

'There's someone in the shop, Violet,' Coral
said.

'Let them wait, Coral. Let them wait, nah. I
am talking to the child about her daddy.'

Wade's Story told to me by Violet

'Your daddy was the son of people who were friends with my daddy. No, wait. Now I think, I think your daddy's daddy was a cousin of my mummy's cousin. No, no. Your daddy's daddy was the son of my daddy's cousin's uncle or was it his aunt? No, I think it was his uncle. But no. Wait, wait . . . ' Evidently, my dad's parents were showy people. 'All show, always showing off. They had no more than anyone else but they like to show off and carry on like they some high-class people. And it all show.'

My grandfather was Obadiah Jackson. His father was a white man. 'Or so they say. No one ever saw him. They had a picture but anyone can have a picture.' He was a doctor who worked in Mandeville. 'I think they say him name Cecil . . . no, wait, Cedric . . . no, Seymour . . . I don't know. They say him Dr Jackson. All show.'

He married a West Indian woman, a black woman called Mary. 'Marry! Him no marry her. Cha.' Mary had a lot of children by Dr Jackson. 'And plenty other men — so I hear.' The doctor however had another family in England. 'That's

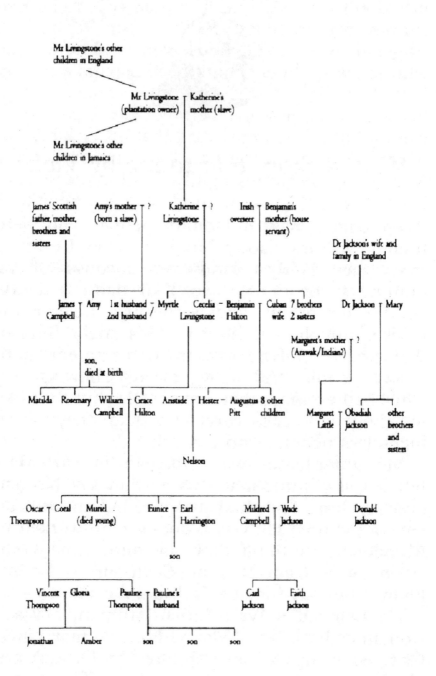

how it was. They have pickney everywhere. They just don't care. All the little half-breed children runnin' round. And then them run off back to England. To some big house with a white woman who know nothing. Think her husband sittin' in Jamaica pinin' on her. And him chasing the first black batty him see! Doctor or no doctor, men cannot hold their urges. And that is black man or white.' Dr Jackson went back to England leaving Mary to bring up his family. 'And he must have been a guilty man because she had money. I heard she had plenty money. Oh, she had money.'

Obadiah, my grandfather, was the eldest in his family. He was tall and skinny with thin legs. 'Look like them could snap and land his backside on the ground.' He left Mandeville at the age of eighteen and travelled to Kingston. There he made an unsuccessful attempt to extend his education so he could become a lawyer. 'He was not a clever man, him just have big ideas.' After a year he gave up on the law. 'Child, it was the law give up on him!' Obadiah needed another occupation. One hot Sunday at church Obadiah noticed how many women wore ribbons in their hair, on their clothes. Little girls, teenagers, young women, all wearing different coloured ribbons. Evidently, the Lord put the idea in Obadiah's head that he should buy and sell ribbon. 'Child, I am just tellin' you what I have been told. But if you think you know better then go ask your daddy and I will hush me mouth.'

Obadiah began to import ribbons. He bought

339

them from an American man who sent Obadiah the finest-quality ribbons in Kingston. Silk ribbon — grosgrain and watered. Satin ribbon — plain, brocaded and striped. Obadiah then sold them to shops. After a while he added lace — torchon, Chantilly and fine silk chiffon — gentlemen's collars and cuffs, embroidery silks, sewing silks, cotton thread on spools and the occasional bolt of novelty gingham cloth.

He met Margaret Little, my grandmother, in one of the shops he supplied. She worked at the back of the shop as a seamstress. 'Although she say she was dressmaker. No one know the difference but her. But she stick up her nose and say dressmaker not seamstress, if you please. All show.'

Margaret Little did not know her father, he died when she was a baby — 'Or so she say.' He was, according to Margaret, part French and part Arawak. 'Some days he was part-Indian and part-Spanish. Other times I have known him to be part-Irish and the other part-Indian Maharaja who was at the court of Queen Victoria.' Her mother was Arawak and Indian. 'Listen, child, to what I am tellin' you. Your grandmother would say her parents were anything — they were descended from anywhere where the skin is darker than a white man. Anywhere except Africa. Oh no. Your grandmother would not utter the word African or West Indian.'

Margaret's mother married again when Margaret was twelve years old. She married a West Indian man, a black man who worked as a printer in Kingston. Her mother had five other children by the West Indian man. She became frail and ill and unable to look after the children or her husband. Margaret was expected to take over all her duties. 'You understand what I'm saying, child — *all* her duties.' If she complained she was beaten by her stepfather. 'Oh, she hated that man, hated him.' When she was sixteen she ran away from him and the family. Her stepfather found her and brought her back home but Margaret ran away again. By the time her stepfather found her for the second time, Margaret had met Obadiah. She did not return home with him as she was by then engaged to be married. She was seventeen.

Obadiah fell in love with Margaret, a vulnerable orphaned girl who was, he thought, the only daughter of a Portuguese sea captain and an Arawak princess. Obadiah and Margaret were married and they had two sons — Wade and Donald. 'And even when her sons born with picky-picky head, big lip, broad nose, she still say is no West Indian, no African in them. Cha, the woman and her pickney were black as peppercorn but she still think she nice.'

Wade and his brother grew up in St Andrew. 'Everyone else say it St Mary but no, their mummy and daddy say to tell everyone they live in St Andrew. Cha!' Wade and Donald both went to a good school, paid for by Obadiah. They sang *God save the King* and followed the teacher's baton as it tripped across the map pointing at all the pink lands of the British Empire. They learnt the Kings and Queens of England, reciting the wives of Henry the Eighth — 'divorced, beheaded, died, divorced, beheaded, survived'. They learned their times tables and the square on the hypotenuse. In English they learnt the past tense, the past imperfect and to speak with the King's English, where the rain fell on the plain in Spain. And at that school they learnt to write with a copperplate script.

But Wade was left-handed. His schoolteacher was an Englishwoman — Miss Honeychurch. She would not allow Wade to use his left hand. Every time he used it — to write legibly, to draw a straight line — she hit him across the knuckles with a ruler. 'I hear sometime him hand swell up like a balloon. Red and bleedin'.' Wade was beaten on his left hand until he learnt to use his right. It was at this time that Wade also developed a stutter. He could not say his words quickly. But if he took too long with a word, if his face contorted and his lips trembled before he spoke, then Miss Honeychurch would beat him. Wade became very quiet. 'He was very shy at that time, your daddy. He would say nothin'. That teacher beat sound out of him. But one time, I heard, after your daddy left the school, someone see him on the road with menace in his eye. They say, Wade, where you go? Him say, to see his teacher. They say, Wade, what for you go — to thank her for teaching you? You know what him say? You know what your daddy say? Him say, No, I go to kill her!'

The family liked to mix in Jamaican high society. 'High society! Cha! They say they high society people, but they were all show. They had parties in their yard and they call them garden parties. All the servants done up in white uniform, handing tea and what have you on silver trays. And all the guests standing up with their fingers sticking out like they taking tea with the Queen. But only light skin and white people. Only light skin and white could come through their door. Oh yes! If you were black you were cleaning plates and getting a whippin' from Margaret for slacking and cheeking up her guests.' Obadiah used these occasions to strike deals and make contacts. 'And every Friday night these people have dances. All the light skin and white people dancing with each other. And there is Margaret and Obadiah acting like they one of them, doing foxtrot and waltz. I know these dances, I did them with my first husband and they are not fun. But these people think they so fine. Every Friday night dancing round in circles. Cha! And talking business. That's why they make up all this past — all this Arawak-French-I-don't-know-what-Maharaja-and-so-on t'ing — because those sort of people — those high society sort of people they mixed with don't know you if they think you black.'

Wade and Donald always accompanied Margaret and Obadiah to parties. They stood a few feet behind their parents smiling politely. It was expected that the two young men would mix with the children of white people and light-skinned people — of people who would be beneficial to the business. 'They dress them boys up fine and make them slick-up their hair and teach them to bow and speak like an Englishman. But for the money. Everything was

343

money with them. Money, money, money, that's all they talk about.'

Obadiah once commanded Wade to take a girl out — the daughter of a man who was about to open a chain of haberdasher's shops in Spanish Town, Savannah-la-Mar and Port Antonio. But Wade did not like the girl. 'Him tell me she was ugly with teeth all black-up and rotting from too much cane and a waist so big him arm could not get round and when him dance with her she crush him up and squeeze him so he could not breathe. So he say no. Him say no to his daddy.' Wade refused to ask the girl to go for a walk with him and Obadiah beat him — badly. 'Is no the strap and a little tappin' with him. No, Wade had black eye and puffy cheek and bruise on his arm and leg. Are you hearin' me, child? And all his mummy say is he should obey his father. Is cruel, not strict. Child, are you listening to me? My daddy was strict but him no beat me till me face all puff and bloody. Them cruel. They was cruel. Ehh, child, ehh, child? Cruel?'

After that Donald joined the air force. 'You know why him join up for the war? Because he so feared of his daddy. Some people say him still wet-up himself in the night, even as a grown man.' He signed up in secret, not even telling Wade what he was about to do. He knew his father and mother would not approve, but he wanted to get away from Jamaica, away from his parents. 'Him rather go halfway across the world and get shot by some German bullet and lie down dying in mud in some field with his inside hanging out and spreading on the ground before him, than stay with his daddy.'

Donald thought he would be able to leave Jamaica secretly — he thought he would not have to tell anyone of his plans. But his mother found out. 'And she make fuss. I hear she made one fuss. You never see anything like the fuss that woman make. She faint and fall down and she tell everyone how ungrateful her son is — how he should repay her for all the sacrifice she made for him but no, him turn his back on them. And she grab her heart and say she dyin'. Carrying on and fussing and falling down like she some delicate thing and she as strong as an ox.'

Wade's hand was slapped down onto a Bible — he was made to promise in front of God, on his mother's life, on fear of punishment that he would not volunteer to join the air force, that he would not join the army, that he would not, of his own free will, leave Jamaica like Donald. 'Oh, the carry-on.'

Wade spent the war working as a bookkeeper for Tate & Lyle. 'This is what I am sayin' to you, child, your daddy was sums and keeping everything just so. Him spend his time travelling the island to sugar estates, counting and things. While his brother was in England writing to him, 'Come Wade, come out — leave them and come out to England,' like the devil sittin' on his shoulder.' Wade read Donald's letter in secret, sitting high above Kingston harbour watching supply boats pulling into the dock surrounded by convoys of warships. He spent hours looking out over the horizon before he wrote the letters back that told Donald that he had promised to stay in Jamaica.

Wade's father eventually made him give up his job at Tate & Lyle. He wanted Wade to work for him. 'They nag him. They go on to him about how he should be helping them. How they getting old and need someone to look after everything. And they go on and on at him. But he had a good job and plenty people want to work for Tate & Lyle. But they go on and on until him just say 'Stop'.' Wade left Tate & Lyle to work for Obadiah. But Obadiah was as strict a boss as he was a father. He would shout at Wade, he would shout at him in front of anyone. He expected Wade to work at any hour of the day, sometimes waking Wade in the night to ask about a sum of money or deliveries due. Wade's parents watched everything he did. 'He became very secret, your daddy. When you meet him, him lookin' around like someone about to pounce on him. I feel sorry for him. He look sort of . . . scared.'

Then Wade met Eunice. 'No, child! Listen to me what I am tellin' you. Wade, your daddy, met Eunice, your mummy's sister.' Wade met Eunice at a dance run by the church. He travelled up to St Mary to see Eunice. 'Him say he come to see my daddy on some business although why he need to see my daddy — my daddy grow sugar and citrus fruit — he have nothing to do with buttons and bows. I was courting my first husband who died, God rest his soul. But you see, child, Wade came to be near Eunice.'

Wade took Eunice out for a walk. 'But Eunice

had plenty boyfriends — she was not that sweet on Wade. When him want to see her again she say, 'Oh, I don't know,' and she make up some half-bake story why she cannot see him concerning some Auntie Myrtle.'

It was two days later that Wade met Mildred standing at a bus stop with Violet. 'I forget where we were going now, child. But him come up and smile. Him always polite and I introduce him — I did not know he was sweet on Eunice.' Wade and Mildred talked. 'Him say, 'Is hot today.' And I say, 'Wade, you don't know what heat is if you think it hot — it is not hot.' And Mildred say, 'Oh yes, I agree Wade, it is very hot.' And it was not hot but she agree with him because she like the look of him. Cha.'

Wade arranged to meet Mildred again — to go for a walk with her. He liked Mildred, he liked her determination to leave Jamaica and go to England. But he did not know that she was Eunice's sister. 'And then the trouble start. Oh boy! Eunice see Wade walking with Mildred. She come up to them and Wade thought she was vex with him. But she shout at Mildred. She shout, 'What you doing with him?' Is then Wade see they sisters. And him can't speak. Him stutter come back and the two sisters lookin' 'pon him for an explanation. The poor man just look at the two women and nearly pass out. Him run to me to fix up the situation.'

Violet talked to Eunice who told her that she did not care for Wade — she thought him too shy, too quiet. And anyway, she told Violet, she was going to America, to the land of the free.

Mildred told Violet that she thought Wade was a very nice young man. 'And that is how it came about. But Eunice always say her sister stole him from her and your mummy say Eunice lead him on. But . . . No . . . Wait. You tell me they still not speaking? Cha! I am thankful I have no brothers and sisters — nothing but trouble. Ehh? Ehh? Nothing but trouble?'

Obadiah and Margaret did not like Mildred — she was too dark. When Wade told them that he and Mildred were getting married Margaret hired a man to investigate Mildred's family background. She wanted to know was Mildred a quadroon, an octoroon, a half-breed or just black. The investigator consulted documents kept at the records office in Spanish Town, he spoke to people who had dealings with the family and spent several hours hiding outside Mildred's home waiting to catch sight of her mother and father. Margaret eventually told Wade that Mildred had too much African in her blood. 'And there is she, as black as night. Cha.'

Wade and Mildred got married without his parents' consent. His mother fainted and fell down and told everyone how ungrateful her son was, she clutched at her heart and said she was dying. And neither Obadiah nor Margaret went to the wedding where everyone agreed, it rained all day.

'And then they 'whoosh' off to England.' A few months later Wade and Mildred Jackson sailed to England on a banana boat. 'Are you cryin', child? What is there to cry about? Cha! We all have our crosses to bear. Stop with your snivellin', I am not finished yet.'

★ ★ ★

Donald received a letter from his father a month after Mildred and Wade arrived in England. Obadiah wanted Donald to return to Jamaica. 'Oh, he said to him that his mummy is sick. That she is dying, that she could not get up from her bed since she lost both her sons to England. It was killing his mother to have two ungrateful sons. Oh, the carry-on! Cha! He got letter after letter beggin' him, 'Come home and we will give you the business to run and money and all sorts. Come home, Donald, leave Wade and we will give you everything.' And this foolish boy believe them.' Donald decided to return to Jamaica even though Wade pleaded with him not to go. But Donald was tired of England — of the cold, of living in one room, of emptying dustbins and sweeping floors for a living. And of people shouting 'Sambo!' and 'Jungle Bunny!' at him in the street. So Donald returned.

'But then you know what? Obadiah die — suddenly.' Margaret and Obadiah were expecting guests at the house and Margaret ordered that the floor be polished. 'She liked her floors to shine. You could see your batty in her floors.' The floor shone like glass and as Obadiah came in the door he slipped on it. He broke a rib which punctured his stomach and he died three days later in hospital of internal bleeding.

Donald took over the business but soon

349

realised it was all show. That his father's business had debts, not money. That his mother was in fact poor. 'She end her life penniless. She had to beg and borrow from everyone.' Donald then disappeared. 'Nobody knew what happen to him. Some say him living as a hermit in the mountains with long beard and shaggy-shaggy clothes. Others say him killed by people wanting money from his daddy and lying in some ditch. I hear him a rich man in America and change him name. But no one knows.'

Margaret went to live with one of her nieces, a West Indian woman, a black woman of African descent. She lived with her niece for many years. Her niece looked after Margaret into old age and buried her alongside Obadiah when she died. 'But till the day she died she never talked of Wade. And your daddy . . . you know him send regular money to her. He never say it was from him but everyone know except her. Him never miss, so I heard. Never miss. He was a better son than she deserved. Cha. All show. And him still married to Mildred? You sure?'

25

Gloria's oldest sister Carmen was getting married, for the second time, to a Jamaican man who had a job with good prospects in the United States of America.

'Of course you must come, child,' Coral had said. 'You are family now. And you can't stay in the house on your own. You must come. She must come, ehh, Gloria?'

And Gloria had said, 'My sister and I would be happy if you would come to her wedding. A cousin of my husband is always welcome at our family celebrations. So, yes, Mummy, please feel that you can invite Faith.'

Gloria arrived to collect Coral and me with spectacular hair rollers in her hair. Fat pink plastic tubes undulating over the top of her head in a neat logjam. Pale green rollers graduating down the back and a regiment of tiny blue rollers finishing off the short stray hair at the nape of her neck. 'I have been at me friend's all morning. She do up me hair nice. No one can do it like her.'

Coral was wearing a blue floral headscarf which covered the unmistakable ripples of several hundred tiny hair curlers. 'You not covering up your head, Gloria?' Coral asked.

'Yes, Mummy, but I am waiting until I get in the car.'

'I like to cover up me head straight away. I

351

don't like to look . . . rough.'

Amber had three tiny pink hair rollers at the front of her hair and a headscarf.

'Ahh,' Coral said, 'Look at me little girl, she covers up her head nice.'

Gloria patted my hair. 'I am sorry, Faith, I should have thought about your hair. But you'll have to have it just plain today — there is no time to fix it up now.'

One of the headlights on Vincent's car was broken — smashed. Vincent knelt down in front of it while Jonathan — hands on knees, pensive frown — stood behind him looking at the man's work his daddy was doing. Vincent taped an old plastic bag round the light to stop water getting in.

The light was lost on the way back from Violet's. We were driving along a road that was dark. People were walking at the side of the road but we could only see their black silhouettes faintly before the headlights picked up their form and briefly showed colours in their clothes. Suddenly a dog was in the beam of the headlight — a small black dog. It seemed to run under the car. Vincent swerved the car which went up and down in a pothole and bounced us out of our seats. Then there was a dull thump. The car stopped suddenly and I was thrown forward onto Vincent. Coral shouted, 'What 'appen!' Vincent cursed a loud, 'Bloody . . . ' and was then silent.

The dog was at the side of the road, lying down at twisted angles, panting. 'Oh no,' I said. I ran to the dog but stopped. It raised itself up onto shaky legs but kept its head low — one of its ears was up, the other flopped limp over its face and its black eyes looked pathetic at me. I took another step saying, 'All right, doggy, all right.' The dog whimpered and limped off into the bushes.

Vincent and Coral were inspecting the damage to the car.

'I think the dog's hurt,' I said. 'It was limping — it went in the bushes.' And Vincent said, 'Good. Bloody thing mash up me light.'

And I asked, 'Aren't we going to help the dog?'

My aunt and cousin both looked at me like I had just fallen to earth — incredulous, slightly frightened. 'Faith, the dog bash up me car. You know how much it going to cost to get a new light? If I can get one at all! And on top of everything else I have to do. And this damn wedding and everyone having to go in the car. You want me to worry for a dog?' Vincent shook his head as Coral said, 'Come, son, look, we can put a little tape on it here . . . and here . . . and then it will look like new.'

'Mummy, the light is gone — little bit of tape goin' to do nothin'. And I must have two lights or I am in violation of the law. Cha! Next time a dog hit me car I make sure I kill it.' We carried on the rest of the journey in silence, with only one headlight that picked up nothing in its beam.

Gloria's head kept squashing against the roof of the car as we drove to the wedding — the pink hair rollers compressing down to ovals every so often. 'Vincent, we need a bigger car,' she said, as she crouched and slumped in the front seat. And Coral said, 'Oh — we are having no trouble in the back.'

There was a small crowd gathered round Gloria's parents' house when we arrived. People sat on chairs in the shade of the veranda, fanning themselves and drinking a pale brown liquid from frosted glasses. Others stood up in the sun shading their eyes from the light — chatting and laughing in small groups. Children ran round between people's legs — chasing one another and screaming, 'No you, no you!' Until a grown-up caught one of them by the arm and told them to 'stand still and behave, nah'. Then they stopped running for a moment, sheepishly looked around until no one was watching, then ran off again.

Gloria guided Amber into the house and called out for Jonathan, who was busy eyeing the children playing. 'Jonathan, come now, you must get changed.' He hitched up his trousers using his elbows and kicked at the ground as he walked to the door of the house. Vincent was accepting a cup of steaming mannish water which he held with his pinky out as he told a little group that he had no time to chat, that he was in a rush because he had to get to the church to play the organ. Coral patted my shoulder, — 'You all right little one?' — as a grey-haired woman caught her arm — 'Coral, we are waitin' on you,' — and pulled her away to a group of elderly women who sat round a table under a tree stringing flowers into tiny bouquets.

No one noticed me. I smiled at anyone who

looked in my direction. But no one did. I was blending in. I was just one of the crowd. I was just another guest. It was wonderful. The sun was past its midday incendiary heat but still I was sticky. My nicely ironed silk top pressed against my back and the trousers stuck to my legs turning a darker shade in sweaty patches. I shook them loose. And no one watched me. All around me was chattering in that soothing Jamaican lilt, broken only when someone laughed loud or shrieked at a child to 'stop messing up the good clothes'. And no one stared at me or whispered, 'Who is she?'

And I thought . . . I will visit Jamaica regularly. I thought . . . I could even live here. Work in Jamaican television. Who, on this Caribbean island, would care how slowly I walked? In Jamaica I would be told to slow down, to take it nice and easy. No problem. I could be a director, a producer. In Jamaica I could be anything. Irie.

Jonathan was dressed in a suit with a wine-coloured cummerbund and a frilly shirt. And Amber in a lemon-yellow satin dress with white lace trim. Coral wore a hat with a small bouquet of feathers on one side that looked like the debris from a cat's prey. She took my elbow. 'Come, we will all walk to the church together on this fine Jamaican day.' A hummingbird flew next to an open flower on an orange hibiscus. Its wings were a blur as its head, still and precise, stuck its beak into the flower's nectar. A breeze blew through my clothes and gently moved leaves through shades of green. And I walked slowly — at Coral's pace. It was easy. Ah my, but

355

you look like a Jamaican now, Faith.

Vincent was already at the church. Organ music drifted from the open doors. 'Listen to me son,' Coral said. Vincent was playing the sort of music I heard at church in England when we would go as a family. Thumping chords with twiddly bits in between. Nothing you could hum, nothing you could even remember but music that sounded majestic, religious, because it came out of an organ.

The church had doors all the way round that opened letting in the outside. At the main doors Coral and me were handed a service order and a hymn book. Jonathan complained that he had not been given anything. He stuck out his bottom lip, folded his arms and refused to move until I had given him mine. Then he smiled with dimples and said, 'Thank you, Aunie Faith.'

People were already sitting in the pews. The church was almost full and it was shimmering with satin. Grass-green, sunshine-yellow, powder-pink, baby-blue — bright, gaudy, psychedelic satin with bows, frills, lace, white gloves, white hats, white socks, patent-leather shoes. Even the men were bright in their suits with frilly shirts. My two-piece silk trouser outfit was in an understated navy blue, which was very chic in North London.

I stepped into the church after my aunt, Amber and Jonathan. I was gazing at the wooden beams in the ceiling and the stained glass in the main window. When I looked to see where my aunt had sat down, I saw a young woman examining me. She was staring at my legs. She nudged the woman beside her and whispered, 'Pants.' The woman beside her nudged another woman who nudged someone else. Other people looked up, twisting round, stretching to get a better look. Soon all I could hear in the church was the ripple of the word 'pants' as it passed from the lips of everyone in the congregation that noticed I was wearing trousers in church. Everyone stared. Little girls hid their laugh behind their hands, men shook their heads and old women sucked their teeth. I walked down the centre aisle to my aunt with the congregation's gaze following me like I was the bride.

My aunt had told me, 'Pants should be all right for a wedding. It's for the Sunday service when that sort of thing is not done.' My aunt did not seem to notice the excitement that my entrance had caused. I slipped in the row beside her, as the Pastor, in his red robes, stood by a lectern waggling his head to get a better look at the foreigner as I sat down in my pants.

The bride was late. The congregation were fanning themselves with the order of service sheets. Vincent played the same music over and over again until I could almost hum along and every few minutes he turned around to see if the bride was arriving.

It began to get windy. The wind came in through the open doors and riffled Bibles and hymn books open and rolled some order of service sheets along the floor. Amber was asleep on the pew — curled up sucking her thumb.

Jonathan was being held down by Coral's hand as he wriggled and said, 'Grandma, when is the bride comin'? . . . Is she comin' now, Grandma? . . . How long will it be, Grandma?'

We had been waiting an hour. Coral began to suck her teeth. The wind was now fierce. When two women near the doors lost their hats — which were then chased round the pews by an usher and Jonathan — the doors around the edge of the church were closed. Vincent kept huffing, his shoulders rising up to his ears then falling, as he changed the music on the organ's stand. And Coral said, 'Cha, when is the child coming? Me son must be tired. You think I should take him a little somethin' to eat?' Eventually a man across the church nodded and held up his thumb and Vincent began to play 'Ave Maria'.

Vincent had been moaning on the way back from Violet's, just before he hit the dog, that Gloria's sister wanted to walk up the aisle to 'Ave Maria' but he did not know which one.

'There are lots of 'Ave Maria's', I tell her. Which one you want? So she starts hummin' up this tune sayin', 'This one, Vincent'. And the woman could have been singing 'Jingle Bells' or 'God Save the Queen'. And I am sayin' to her, 'I do not hear a tune.' She sing me one more time and I say, 'You must get me the music, Carmen.' And she is sucking on her teeth tellin' me she doesn't have the time. Cha.'

But now he was playing it. 'Oh my love, my love, it will surely be, that some day you'll walk down the aisle with me.' I sang along as the congregation were instructed to stand by the Pastor, raising his two arms dramatically into the air. There were a lot of creaking bones and a long 'ohhh' as Coral stood up. Amber was woken by Jonathan's gentle punch and got up, rubbing her eyes. Vincent had been through the verses and the chorus but still there was no bride. Then a man walking backwards came down the aisle. He was videoing — crouching down low as he held the camera up to his face with one hand and directed the bride and her bridesmaids with the other — forward, stop, left a bit, okay, walk.

The bride walked up the aisle on her own — there was no one giving her away. She was dressed in white lace — covered in it from head to toe with a veil that hung down over her face. Behind, her bridesmaids — Gloria and two younger women — were in identical long tangerine dresses with tangerine hats, tangerine gloves and tangerine shoes. Jonathan shouted, 'There is Mummy,' and Coral hushed him with a stare. The procession began to move up the aisle. The bride took two steps forward and then one step back and the bridesmaids followed the movement. Two steps forward and one step back — two steps forward and one step back — two steps forward and one step back. The church was big, the aisle was long, the music was slow and Coral said loudly, 'Lord, we goin' to be here all day.'

Vincent had played 'Ave Maria' at least thirty times before the bride had even passed the pulpit. He was muttering to himself — his lips moving in silent curses each time he started the song again. Several of the older and larger women had given up standing and were sitting

359

down fanning themselves. An old man in front of me had his eyes shut and his head slumped back like a corpse. Amber was back asleep on the pew and Jonathan was being held by Coral in a gentle half-nelson, by the time the bride finally reached her groom. And it was with an audible relief that the Pastor finally told the congregation to 'Please be seated.'

'We are gathered together today to witness . . .' the Pastor began. The wind started to rattle at the doors and windows. We sang 'All things bright and beautiful', as the wind began to howl and whistle through cracks. 'Do you, Carmen Beverly Benson, take this man . . .' The wind whacked and buffeted against the doors. It crashed at the windows. It bounced against the roof. It boomed. It roared. It pummelled the walls. The church felt like a box made of sticks as the wind huffed and puffed. But no one except me seemed to care. Everyone else was staring towards the happy couple — looking around for anyone who objected to the marriage — smiling as the bride's voice croaked, 'I do' — saying 'ahh' when the groom took the bride's hand in his. Even the children just sat slumped against grown-ups, kicking their legs against the pews. Only I turned round every time the wind crashed at a door like a stampede of bulls. Only I jumped when it rumbled like thunder. In England, a wind like this would be on the evening news — a wind like this would be honoured with plaques in several woods around the country. But here only my eyes opened wide. Only I ducked. Only I gasped. Only I muttered, 'Jesus Christ!' This hurricane would be called Faith — because only I noticed it.

The old man in front of me picked his nose as the choir sang 'Ave Maria' once more. The bride and groom signed the register and the church swayed. After the ceremony the Pastor spoke. 'Perhaps due to the little bit of wind we are experiencing, we should gather together inside the church and not outside as planned. From here, after the photographs and greeting of friends and relations, we can make our way over to the hall where the celebration will be held.'

Vincent got up from the organ and joined Coral and me, moaning, 'You see how long the bride take to get to the altar? I play that damn tune a hundred times. One time I look up and the bride going backwards. Cha! I thought I was losing me mind.'

Dresses were blown up — flapping round women's shoulders, hats grabbed onto heads, branches tumbled along the ground, bouquets lost their petals, ties whipped in the air, small children were held down by firm hands, as everyone walked to the hall at a slant — head first into the wind — muttering, 'Oh, there is a little bit of breeze today.'

The bride, the groom and the bridesmaids were sitting at the top table under an archway that was decorated with a tangle of green leaves dripping with yellow, orange and pink flowers the size of melons. The guests were ushered in to seats that were laid out in rows in front of the archway — but only the women and children sat down. The men, including Vincent, stood round

361

the doorway with their hands in their pockets, chatting and rocking on the balls of their feet. There was a line of tables at the back of the room covered in pristine white table cloths that held the wedding feast. Huge silver bowls of goat curry, lines of paper cups for mannish water, oval platters with fried chicken, fish and dumplings, bowls of salad and hillocks of rice and peas rising every few feet along the table. And four waitresses in black uniforms with couldn't-care-less expressions leant on the wall behind the tables and watched the guests.

The Pastor was invited to give a speech. He coughed and began, 'Marriage is a bond between a man and a woman sanctified in the presence of God and blessed with children . . . ' The audience called, 'Praise be,' 'Umm-umm,' and 'Yes, sir.' After a few minutes the speech became peppered with, 'We know the bride and groom will have plenty to do tonight . . . the groom is looking forward to rising for the occasion of his wedding . . . I'm sure the groom will know all about rockets tonight . . . the groom should go easy on the rum punch because he will need all his strength for the favourite of God's work . . . ' while the groom grinned, the audience laughed and the bride looked down at her lap.

After half an hour the Pastor was still talking. 'And I could not leave this occasion without first telling you of my own wedding, but forgive me if I do not tell you of my wedding night — my wife likes to keep that pleasure to herself.' Guests began to fidget. Little children began running around the hall. And Coral started looking to the table of food.

'Faith, you sure people not getting food while I am sitting listening to this man?' She wanted a ripe banana. 'I just need a little banana to tide me over. Just a little banana.' When the Pastor finally finished — 'I must not keep everyone from the fine food or the bride and groom from what comes naturally,' — Coral got halfway out of her seat. But the best man stood up saying, 'Thank you, Pastor, and I would now like to add a few words.' Coral sat down groaning, 'Not another one.' The best man's and the groom's speech were short. When Gloria's father eventually told everyone that the party should begin, I looked round to ask Coral if she wanted me to get her a banana. But she was already on her way to the table of food with a speed that even in England would be called fast.

The Pastor smiled in my direction. He began to walk through the crowd and I realised he was coming to me. He kept his eyes fixed firmly on my face as he negotiated the guests.

'So,' he said when he reached me. He stared at me as if we had been talking before and had been interrupted. I didn't know what to say. He carried on.

'You are from?'

'England,' I said.

He took in every inch of my face without blinking. 'Oh, England. And you are here with?'

'I'm staying with my aunt.'

'And that is your aunt who?'

'Aunt Coral.'

'And that is Coral who?'

'Thompson.'

'Oh, the Thompsons. So, you are related how?'

'I'm her niece.'

'Her niece. The daughter of who?'

'Of Coral's sister, Mildred.'

'Oh.' He momentarily took his eyes off me and I swallowed.

'So, you must be the cousin of Gloria and Vincent. So your name is?'

'Faith.'

'And that is Faith what?'

'Faith Jackson.'

'Oh.' He gazed up to the ceiling. 'You are the daughter of Mildred Jackson. And your father is?'

'Wade Jackson.'

'Wade.' He frowned and wiped his tongue round the inside of his mouth. He parted his lips but said nothing for a moment then, 'And you live in?'

'England,' I said.

'Yes. And that is where in England?'

'London.'

'Ahh, London.' He sounded like I had said something important. 'Do you know Delores Foot? She lives in London. She went to London to be with her mother who had left Jamaica several years earlier but was taken ill and was in hospital with cancer. We all prayed for her of course but she was an old woman and she was taken to a better place by the Lord. Delores stayed on in London however and took up residence in a place called Streatham.' He pronounced it like a cured meat — streat ham. 'Have your paths crossed . . . ?'

I was suddenly grabbed by the shoulders, spun round and my head pressed in between two flabby sweating bosoms that were pungent with BO. I pushed away and looked up into the face of my mother — but my mother with a white skin.

'Eunice's daughter!' The woman screamed so loud that the Pastor flinched.

'Excuse me,' he said as he left.

'Eunice's daughter!' The woman raised her arms to the heavens. Coral was behind her.

'Is *Mildred's* daughter I say, Constance — not Eunice.' And the woman without hesitation changed her invocation to, 'Mildred's daughter — Mildred's daughter!'

'This is your Auntie Constance, Faith,' Coral said evenly, her lips slowly forming into the tight line. The woman held my shoulders again and pressed her face so close to mine I could see the open pores on her nose and the freckle of brown liver spots on her cheeks. She whispered, 'I am your mummy's cousin. I am Afria. You must call me Auntie Afria.' And Coral sucked her teeth.

Her resemblance to my mum was remarkable. She was the same size, she was the same height and her face had the same fat cheeks that bulged like smooth plums and eyes that smiled into small slits. But that was where it stopped. Constance was wearing a yellow, orange and black headscarf, tied up like an African headdress in high complicated folds. Her dress

365

matched. It was tied around her, elaborately swooping over her breasts and wrapping her hips so her bottom stuck out like a shelf. She could have been an African queen but for the fact that her skin was white and her eyes were the palest blue.

'You know me? You know me?' she sang. Her accent was pure Jamaican. 'Afria, your Auntie Afria. And you are Mildred's little daughter. Come, give me a hug, little Grace.'

Coral butted in. 'Constance, I tell you the child's name is Faith. You no listening to me?'

'Faith, you know me — Faith. I am your Auntie Afria. Your mummy's cousin.'

Coral tutted.

'Now come, tell me how is your mummy?' Afria pulled me onto a seat, sat down beside me and immediately began to cry. She pulled a small handkerchief out from the folds of her dress and dabbed at her eyes. 'You must not mind me. But to see Eunice's daughter and you looking just like her. Just like Eunice.'

'Mildred,' I said.

'Just like Mildred. Just like her.'

'You look like her as well,' I told her. Afria's mouth opened wide. She made a quiet wailing sound like she was in pain, her body shuddered and she sobbed. She squashed me once more against her chest. She pulled me away and wiped my eyes with her handkerchief, although I was not crying.

'Call me Afria, Afria,' she said, wiping my chin and neck.

'Your name is not Constance, then?' I asked.

Afria stopped dabbing me, stopped crying and in a quiet, clipped, controlled voice said, 'I have not been Constance for a long time, but your Auntie Coral does not seem to hear. To her I am always Constance.' She stared into my eyes for a long moment — her pupils fixed black dots. She threw her arms into the air, 'Mildred's daughter. Mildred's little daughter.'

When she stood up to dance, she danced like a woman whose name was Afria. She stood in the middle of the dancers on the floor with her arms raised above her head. She tilted her hips from side to side with a precision that made her bottom look disconnected from her body. She waggled her head in time with the motion and stamped her feet. Her eyes were closed — she was in a world of her own.

'Oh, look at her,' Coral said.

'She's enjoying herself,' I said.

'That is what is worrying me.'

'Why?'

Coral looked full into my face. 'Child, you are young, you are from England, you don't know.'

As Afria danced her headdress began to slip to one side of her head. It wobbled and shook. Every few minutes she took a small plastic bottle from out of the folds of her dress and tipped up the contents into her mouth as she waved through the other dancers on the floor.

'Mummy,' Gloria said to Coral urgently. 'Are you ready for when Auntie Constance goes?' I looked at them puzzled but they ignored me.

'Ah, maybe she won't today,' Coral sighed.

Gloria sucked her teeth. 'Me sister does not want the same trouble as I had at my wedding — she ruin me dress, Mummy, with the rum and goat's blood.'

'I know, I was there. But she has changed. I have given her a little talking-to . . . '

Just as Coral said that, Afria took a large bulbous-cheek mouthful of the drink in the plastic bottle. She shook her arms then sprayed the fine mouthful of spray onto the bride who was dancing with her groom. The droplets rose from her mouth in an arc and sprinkled down like confetti all over the bride's hair and the front of her dress. The bride screamed. Coral was on Afria. 'No, Constance! Don't start with all that juju rubbish again. I have told you!' Afria pulled away from Coral and sprayed again — this time at the groom. Gloria grabbed at the bottle, wrestling it from Afria's grip as Afria screamed in a high-pitched wail, 'It's for good luck . . . they will fear no white man in America. Fear no white man!'

Vincent joined his mother and held Afria by the arm. 'They will fear no white man,' she kept screeching as Vincent said, 'Auntie, they fear no white man already without you messing up their clothes with your rum.'

The three of them pulled and pushed and poked Afria on to a bench at the edge of the room. I went and sat by her. Her headdress was tilting dangerously to one side and the folds of her tunic were unravelling. I asked, 'Are you all right, Auntie?' She looked at me sternly, 'I am no longer Constance. I am Afria. I am Afria. They must call me Afria.' She shut her eyes and slumped slowly over onto my shoulder. She was asleep with her rum-scented mouth wide open and a loud, rhythmic snoring rattling from her throat.

Constance's Story told to me by Coral

'Your cousin Constance? She callin' herself Afria now. Stupidness! What sort of name is that? Well, I cannot tell you of Constance without tellin' you of me aunties first. You see, Constance is the only daughter of my Auntie Matilda, who was the eldest sister of my daddy. So you must know me aunties before you will understand anything about Constance Noble.'

William Campbell had two sisters, Matilda and Rosemary, who were born within a year of each other. Matilda was the one born with raven-black hair and skin as white as eggshell — except for the patch of brown on the thigh of her left leg that her mother said was in the shape of an angel. Her mother, Amy, was as dark as chocolate and when she took her daughter around the district she was thought to be her nanny — merely someone who looked after this English child. 'And that is how her mother treat her — she spoil her like she some precious thing.' Her mother would cuddle, cosset and preen Matilda because she could not believe that someone as dark as she could produce such a

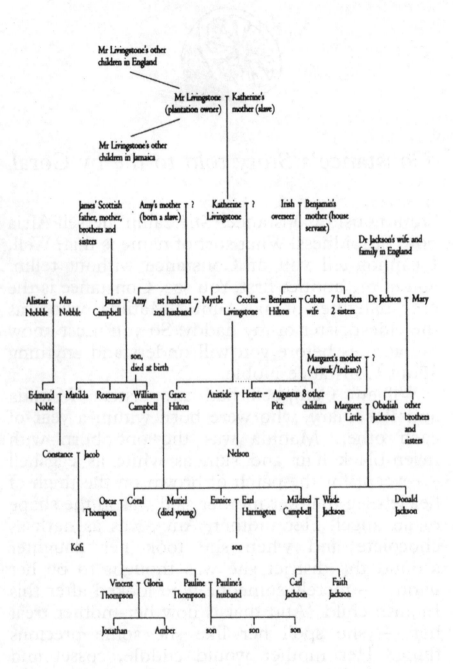

fair child — a pass-for-white child. Matilda's sister Rosemary was as dark as her mother, with a broad nose, lips like a pinched kiss and a head of thick, frizzy, red hair that was so long she could sit on the plait that ran down her back like a length of ship's rope. Rosemary could not pass for white but her black eyes sparked and flashed with life.

The two sisters were very close. 'Oh, they were thick — they went everywhere together. Where one went, the other follow.' The sisters were so much in each other's company that even though they looked so different people began to think of them as twins. They sat together in the church school and though there was a year between them they learnt to read and write at the same pace. They sat side by side in church and could recite the twenty-third psalm in perfect unison as if only one voice were speaking. They played together — they made baskets from leaves and sent straw dolls sailing off down the river. They dressed the baby goat in shawls and a bonnet and carried it in a bucket as their naughty little child. They cooked, mended, washed, sewed and could gut fish with such speed and skill that their father would tell them they would make him his fortune when one day they all returned to Scotland.

After their father died the two sisters left the countryside and went to Kingston to work in a department store. 'I understand they were put in different departments at this store — Rosemary worked in the household bit while Matilda worked in ladies' fashion.' They stayed in the house of a Miss Reeside — an Englishwoman who took as lodgers the unmarried daughters of respectable families. 'She was one of them English people who thought herself a good person. Always doing work for the poor and the coloured people, as they call us. Always smiling on you and saying, 'Good day'. But let me tell you, Faith, them look down their nose at everyone.'

And it was at this time that the two sisters began to grow apart. Rosemary went wild. 'Oh boy, wild just like Eunice and the same thing — men.' Rosemary with her flashing black eyes was very popular at the department store. Young men would wait for Rosemary outside the shop in the evenings. Deliverymen, store hands, men who brought produce to the store from the docks. 'They were rough men — so my daddy told me.' They were evidently men who gambled, men who drank, men who thought nothing of getting several women pregnant at one time. 'You know the sort of man I mean, Faith. Cha!' And Rosemary was a woman who liked to dance, who liked to laugh, who liked the attention of all these young men. 'So my daddy said.'

Rosemary tried to persuade her sister to go with her to dances in St Andrew, to have early evening walks with her in Hope Gardens or join in the excitement with her at Kingston race track. But Matilda refused. Matilda thought it was all beneath her. Matilda worked in the day and in the evening she sat with Miss Reeside, read her Bible and sewed. She told her sister that Miss Reeside had said that she, Matilda, should never mix with black men. Miss Reeside said that she, Matilda, should have pride because of her fair skin and save herself for an Englishman who was educated and had a house. She turned away one young man because Miss Reeside found out that his mother was only a housekeeper. Another she shook her head at because half of him was Jewish. And as Rosemary got ready to go out in the early evenings — as she wound her hair up on top of her head and rubbed her skin with cocoa butter and white lilac scent — she warned her sister to be careful of all the advice. She warned her in case she, Matilda, should wind up an old maid like Miss Reeside.

It was not long before Rosemary came excited to her sister, twirling and dancing around the room as she told her that she had met a man — that she was in love. The man, she told Matilda, the man she was going to marry was a painter.

When Matilda met the man, all she saw were the chippings of paint, dirty and rough under his fingernails. She watched him scoop up a large piece of the cake she had baked, stuff it through bloated thick lips and chew it with his mouth open. She saw him take an orange from the plate without asking, peel it with his black fingers and wipe the juice from his chin with the back of his hand. Matilda asked the man politely what he had been painting. 'And she is expecting this man to say he has been painting a chicken coop or a wall. And you know what him say? The man say he has been painting the birth of Christ! It's true, Faith. Me auntie nearly fall down faint. The birth of Christ.' The man Rosemary was going to marry was an artist. He wanted Rosemary to leave Jamaica, to live in New York with him, because Rosemary was, he said, his muse.

'Then there was trouble.'

Matilda made William come to Kingston to talk sense to their sister. Then the two of them told Rosemary that being an artist was not a job for a man like that. Rosemary told them that he had already sold a painting that now hung in a house in Mandeville where it was admired by white people and ministers of the church. William and Matilda told Rosemary that a man like that would soon abandon her in New York and leave her to a life of destitution in a country where coloured people were treated as badly as dogs. And she told them that he had been offered rent-free lodgings by people who admired his work. It was an adventure, she said, a new life. They told her he was too black. She told them, but so was she.

So William went to see the young man. 'And I don't know what he did to frighten that young man. But oh boy, Daddy could be fierce.'

A few days later Rosemary received a parcel from the man she was going to marry, delivered to her by a young boy who stood in the doorway without shoes. The parcel contained a painting and a note. The note said that he had decided to go to New York on his own. He told her that she would still be his muse because he loved her but that she should stay in Jamaica with her sister Matilda who needed her. The painting was of a white woman and a black woman sitting at a tea table with cake and oranges. It was called *Rosemary and Matilda — the Jamaican sisters.*

Rosemary went to her room and took a pair of scissors to her hair. She cut off her long plait and wound it round into a box, covered it with a cotton cloth and placed it in a drawer. She wanted to put the painting on the wall but Matilda would not let her. Matilda did not like the painting — she said he had made Rosemary look like a negro. She ripped it up and burnt it, telling her sister that it was better if she forgot all about the man.

Rosemary became very quiet after that — 'Pining on him, I suppose.' She stopped going out in the early evenings but stayed home with Matilda and Miss Reeside and embroidered white cotton runners with trailing flowers and butterflies. 'And, you know, the funny thing is, Faith — that man became quite famous. He went to New York, to Harlem, and he paint lots of pictures. And they were sold for a lot of money. And Rosemary saw a picture of him in *The Daily Gleaner* some years later. He was in Kingston being entertained by high-up people. He was a respected black artist in America. I hear he had money. But it was too late then. Funny, ehh? A man like that — who'd have thought it?'

Then Matilda met her Englishman — she met him at a house dance that she attended with Miss Reeside. His name was Edmund Noble. Edmund had come to Jamaica to teach at the teacher training college in Kingston. He was a small man — 'Very small and very thin,' — only five feet six inches tall. 'Him look like him been shrivelled up by the heat. With this blonde hair that always sticking on his forehead with sweat.' But Matilda liked him; she said that Edmund was a man of intellect, a man of theories. 'And his face was always red and shinin'-up. Look like him taken by fever. And he had a little squeaky-squeaky voice.' Evidently, Edmund was teaching teachers to teach although he had never taught in a school himself.

Matilda fell in love with him — 'Yes, I suppose so. Well, he was an Englishman.' So Matilda became Mrs Noble. 'Ah, let me tell you, Faith. When him first came to Jamaica his name was Edmund Nobble. Nobble — like the thing you find on your cardigan or on the end of a stick. Him spend all his time telling people to pronounce it *noble*. Noble, he tell them — something that is admirable — noble, call me noble. But everyone keep calling him the Nobble-man. So he take out one of the 'B's. It's true, Faith . . . so I heard.'

The newly-wed couple moved into a house near the college and Rosemary moved with them. 'He did well, he got two wives to wash and cook and sew for him.' Matilda wanted a child but everyone shook their heads because she had married a small Englishman — a man of intellect, a man of theories and a man who'd developed chronic bronchitis. 'He spend all his evenings sitting in a chair on the veranda rocking and coughing — he did not look capable of reproducing.'

Matilda was in her thirties before she became pregnant. 'And everyone wondered who the father was. We used to laugh about that, your mummy and me.' Matilda, as everyone commented, was quite old to be having her first child. The doctor and the midwives told her — 'Or so Matilda said,' — that she should spend a lot of time resting in bed. Matilda rested while Rosemary gave up her position at the department store to look after her sister. Matilda's baby was born late one Sunday evening. Rosemary held her sister's hand through the whole twelve-hour labour while Edmund, evidently, held his head over a bowl of steaming eucalyptus water. The baby was christened Constance. And Rosemary, her aunt, would say to everyone she met, 'The child that is born on the Sabbath day is bonny and blithe and happy and gay.'

Matilda was extremely proud of Constance with her blue eyes the colour of ice and her curly hair that was as pale as sand. She would let no one but her or Rosemary look after her child. Rosemary adored Constance. She would plait her hair and tell her stories of men being swallowed by whales and teach her to dance the Charleston as they laid out the washing. If Constance woke in the night she would call Rosemary's name. If she fell in the yard she would run to Rosemary. 'And I think Matilda was jealous because she began to treat her sister bad.' Matilda began to treat Rosemary as if she were her servant. When people called in from the college Matilda would make Rosemary bring in the tea and cakes. She made Rosemary cook and clean, telling her that her husband was paying for Rosemary to live with them so it was the least she could do to repay the kindness. And while Rosemary worked Matilda rested or took Constance around the town. 'She not only looked like a white woman, she began to act like one — with her house and her English husband and her blue-eyed child.'

William would occasionally send Coral, Eunice and Mildred to stay with his sisters in Kingston. 'When Daddy came to the city we liked to go with him and we would stay with our aunties . . . oh, and Uncle Edmund.' Matilda insisted that Coral, Eunice and Mildred called her daughter not Constance but Miss Constance. She told the girls that Miss Constance was of a better class than they were and that they should acknowledge this by addressing her with respect — by addressing her as Miss. 'I ask you. I could not believe my ears when I first hear this. Every time we say the child's name, Auntie Matilda would tell us off and say we must have some respect and call this little child — who was younger than us — Miss Constance.'

Matilda took it on herself to teach her nieces manners — the ways of the English. At teatime she sat them at the table and made them eat lemons. They ate lemons with sugar and a tiny spoon. She assured her small nieces, as they grimaced and sucked in their cheeks, that that was how the English eat lemons. 'And the thing bitter no matter how much sugar you put on it. It make me mouth water just thinking of it. But she make us all and Constance — Miss

Constance — eat off the lemon saying all the time this is what the English do. Everything was what the English do.' She made them eat mango, banana, papaya with a knife and fork. 'Like the English.' She taught them to drink tea — to pour tea into china cups and add milk. 'Like the English. She had sugar in little cubes and I liked that. We were to plop them in the tea and stir it. But we were only allowed two lumps. But when she was not looking we would drop more lumps in our cups till we could hardly get the spoon to move.' Constance grew up with cousins who called her Miss Constance when sitting at a tea table with her mother and squeezed and teased her and called her 'Red Ant' and 'Glass Eye' when left to play by themselves.

When Constance was eleven she was sent to England to receive a better education. Rosemary cried night and day in the weeks before Constance left Jamaica but Matilda assured her sister that it was what the English did. Constance travelled out on a ship chaperoned by a woman returning to Kingston-on-Thames. She was met at Tilbury docks by Edmund's father and mother — her grandparents. They drove her to their home in the English countryside. 'I think it was Hampshire. Or it could have been Buckinghamshire. No, it was Herefordshire. Cha. All I know is that it was a shire because Auntie Matilda always sayin' that although she's missing her daughter, she is getting a good education in a shire. And nobody sure what the woman was talking about.'

Edmund's parents, Mr and Mrs Alistair

Nobble, were nervous of the child their son would send from Jamaica. But when they saw Constance they were delighted. She was so pretty, so fair, so polite, with only a few strange habits — like eating lemons and insisting on spelling their noble name only with one *b*.

Constance went to a private school as a day girl — a school where her grandfather used to be a principal. She did well in all her lessons — top in English, top in history, captain of the house netball team. She had elocution lessons after school that taught her to speak with rounded vowels. Her grandparents would send letters and photographs of Constance back to her mother, father and aunt. 'And we would have to look at these when we visit. Every time we visit it was Constance this, Constance that, Constance, Constance, Constance.'

But then Germany invaded Poland and war was declared in Europe. England went to war with Germany. 'Oh, Faith. All the children in England being sent away to escape the bombs and there is my auntie sendin' her precious Miss Constance into the war. In Jamaica we just have a little inconvenient blackout and she is in England being shot at and bombed. We should not have laughed but sometimes we sisters did.'

Constance could not safely come back to Jamaica. She stayed in England all through the war. She sent letters to her Aunt Rosemary pleading for her to send some bananas. 'In every letter she ask for eating bananas — wanting Rosemary to put a couple hands of them in the parcel. I ask you.' They were on rationing in

England — there was not enough for her to eat in England. She had to wear old clothes in England and share her belongings with two little boys who had been evacuated from the East End of London — who said 'ain't' and 'blimey', sniggered at her bra on the washing line and used the cups as target practice for their catapults. 'Poor Constance.'

By the time the war was over and it was safe for Constance to return to Jamaica she was at university studying English. So she stayed in England until she took her degree and then went back to Jamaica.

Constance returned to Kingston to her family home. But Jamaica had changed. Her beloved Aunt Rosemary was dead. She died a few months before Constance was to return. She died at her brother William's house in St Mary of cancer — a tumour that grew on her spine and invaded her bones. She had been visiting the family with photographs — Constance in a mortar board and gown, Constance in the garden of a house smelling a rose — when she found she was unable to stand up. Her legs would not support her. She was put to bed. 'And Mummy look after her.' She was paralysed, could no longer walk or lift a cup to her mouth. Almost overnight she became too weak to move — her legs as skinny as a bird — and she could not return home. 'She died quickly. She must have had it for a long time. But she was in pain. Oh, terrible pain, so Mummy said.' She was buried in the garden of the house alongside Muriel.

Matilda, Constance's mother, had grown old. Her hair was white and her face had become mottled with pale brown liver spots, like the one on the thigh of her left leg, which gave her the appearance of a much darker woman. Constance's father, Edmund, was very frail. He had lost all his hair and had a bald head which he kept covered with a khaki cotton hat to prevent it from turning red in the sun. Ill health had made him give up working and he now spent all day in a chair on the veranda, sipping weak English tea. But Matilda was pleased finally to have her daughter home. She invited people to the house. She liked Constance to talk — to tell everyone in her impeccable English of life in the shires. She liked Constance to serve the tea — to show everyone her faultless English manners. But occasionally, although she did not admit it to her, Matilda found it hard to understand what her daughter was saying.

Constance got a job — a good job — with a firm of solicitors. The two elderly lawyers were impressed with her education, her nicely rounded vowels and her knowledge of RAF fighter aircraft. She ran the office filing and typing documents and the two elderly lawyers promised that one day she would be able to learn all about the law.

Mildred, — 'your mummy', — began to spend a lot of time with Constance. 'Oh, they became thick. Like . . . like . . . I would say sisters but they were more friendly.' Mildred listened as Constance told her stories about England — about coal fires, about winter icicles that hung

384

from roofs and frost on the inside of window panes in lacy opaque patterns. Stories about university — of libraries stuffed from floor to ceiling with leather-bound books on any subject you could think of. About her teacher who had danced with Hitler before the war and how as she stepped with him he had told her that he would one day kill all Jews because a Jew had cheated his family. Mildred followed Constance like a shadow. 'She said she wanted to be like Constance Noble.' And Constance stayed by Mildred trying to learn again the ways of Jamaican life. Trying to lose her rounded vowels and speak once more like a Jamaican. Because Constance found that the people of Jamaica had changed.

'That was the biggest shock to her.' Before she had left Jamaica she was Miss Constance — everyone admired her fair hair, her blue eyes, her pale skin. But now people sucked their teeth at her in the street. 'Oh, you think you're nice because you white. Oh, you think you white,' a black woman shouted after her one day. She would get ignored in shops, served last, treated rudely. And on two occasions someone spat at the ground in front of her feet.

Constance started to change. She visited her Aunt Rosemary's grave. And then the grave of her grandfather James. 'At this time we thought nothing of it.' But Constance then wanted William to tell her where her grandmother Amy was buried. William did not know. So Constance visited the estate Amy had worked on — the plantation where her grandmother was born and brought up. She wanted to find Amy's grave. 'She have this damn-fool notion to dig her up and bury her again in the garden. We all say she mad.' Constance wanted Amy buried in William and Grace's garden alongside Auntie Rosemary and Muriel. 'She got so vex. Oh boy. She tell everyone that we did not care about her grandmother — *her* grandmother, she say to me — because she was black. Oh, she tell me, Marcus Garvey say this and Marcus Garvey say that. And I say to her, I do not care what the man say, I am not diggin' up bones!'

Her mother, Matilda, told Constance that she did not have to bother with all that sort of business. That she did not have to bother with all that side of her family. She was fair-skinned, she was educated, she should not worry herself about those people. But Constance told her mother that she was proud of her black race. 'Her mother nearly fall down. She burn Constance books and things — which I thought was going too far — but she make a fire in the yard and she burn all these books that she said was turning her daughter's head.'

It was then that Constance met a Rastafarian man called Jacob. 'Oh Faith, you should have seen him. Him look like a tramp.' Constance left her good job to live with a small group of Rastafarians. 'It nearly killed her mother!' Her mother tried to persuade Constance to return to England. Her English grandparents wrote to Constance pleading with her to come back to the shire. But Constance called England Babylon — a place of sin where the evil white man lived

— and swore she would never return. Her mother wept. Constance stopped combing her hair, sat in the sun, wiped her skin with cocoa butter. And told everyone she was letting her black inside out. 'I ask you.'

Just before Constance announced that she was having a baby for Jacob, Edmund, her father, died. 'He sort of just expired — gone — of a cold or something. Her mother said thank God he was not alive to hear about the baby — but I don't think he would have noticed.'

Constance did not cry at her father's funeral and suggested to her mother that his headstone should have the words 'Forgive me' inscribed, because, she explained, he had come to Jamaica to oppress the black man. It was then that Matilda turned her back on her daughter and had no more to do with her. 'Matilda died an old woman — ninety-six. And you know she wanted to be buried by her sister Rosemary but we had sold the land because Daddy had died many years earlier and there was nothing we could do. So we bury her in Kingston Parish Church by her husband.'

Constance gave birth to a son whom she called Kofi. Her son was born with caramel-coloured skin and a head of frizzy hair the colour of sand. Jacob had lots of children by different women and he saw his son only twice. On both occasions he commented to Constance that this child of his did not look like an African. Constance left her Rastafarian home. She had inherited money from her father and used it to take her baby to Africa. Constance travelled to

Sierra Leone with a small group of Jamaicans. They were people who wanted to visit Africa to trace their ancestry — the exiled Maroons and runaway slaves. But Constance heard them calling her 'Bakkra' and 'white woman' behind her back. 'It's then she start to dress in all these African clothes and what have you.' When Constance returned to Jamaica she insisted that everyone call her Afria.

She moved out to the countryside — bought a house with some land. She grew bananas, made wood carvings of masks she had seen in Africa and raffia baskets with 'Jamaica' woven on the side in florid colours which she sold to tourists in the market. She told tourists she was an obeah woman who could cure disease and make people love them. 'She tell me that when she was young she had these gifts — she could see the future, she tell me. She say she told Mildred that she would go and live in England. But me sister practically had her ticket at the time. I could have told her that. Cha. Poor Constance — she searching for something.'

When her son was fourteen she took him to Kingston to see Haile Selassie. They joined the crowds of followers in the rain as they jostled to get a look at the Messiah, the King of Kings, the Lion of Judah. She told her son that one day they would both return to their homeland of Africa.

But when Kofi was seventeen he left home. He cut off his waist-length dreadlocks and moved to the United States where he changed his name to Edmund. He joined the US Navy and then on his discharge he studied law. 'And now he is a big lawyer in Chicago and sends his mother money but never comes back to Jamaica.' And Constance evidently used to send herbs to Edmund every Christmas — herbs that were meant to keep him successful. Until Edmund begged her to stop, as one year, they were seized by US Customs and Edmund was kept under suspicion of drug smuggling until it was discovered that the consignment was a mixture of thyme, chilli and ground chicken bones.

And now Constance lives on her own in the small wooden house, where she keeps chickens and goats and tends her weed garden. She still sits in the sun, 'to keep herself dark. And that is what has gone to her head.' And she wears African clothes and tells everyone on family occasions that they must remember that she is called Afria.

'But she is quite happy, Faith — quite happy . . . until of course she drinks too much rum. Cha. Poor Constance.'

26

'So soon!' Coral kept saying, 'You only just come. Tell me you're not goin' back so soon. Tell me it's not two weeks already.' I was going home to my mum and dad, to Carl and Ruth, to Mick, Marion and Simon, I was going home to England. 'But that time just fly by.' I had to return to the rest of my life. 'You sure it's so soon?' Only when she had read the plane ticket for herself — holding it at arm's length and running reading glasses like a magnifying glass across the tiny print — did she stroke my cheek and say, 'But you'll be back, little one — Jamaica is in your blood.'

I had learnt to adapt to Jamaican ways. I had told Vincent that my flight was an hour earlier than it actually was. I was not frettin' as I packed my suitcase for my return. Soon come, I thought to myself as Vincent did not appear at the stated time and Coral thought she could 'just have a little shut-eye' before we left for the airport.

My suitcase should have had more room in it — there were no descant recorders, no family hymn books, Vitamin E capsules or bright battered packages. But I was taking much more back from Jamaica than I could ever have brought with me.

I was taking back the gift of tee-shirts. White tee-shirts with 'Jamaica' emblazoned on the front in gold, green and black. 'Irie' in vivid pink. 'No problem' in thick black handwriting, back and front. 'Don't worry — be happy' sparkling in blue surrounded by the smiling faces of happy black people dancing in the sun. Big tee-shirts — one size fits all.

I had bought them at the beach near Ocho Rios and Dunn's River Falls. I had sat digging my toes into the sand of the white beach that stretched down to the edge of a turquoise sea that was as clear and still as a pond. This was where the sea sloped gently to let tourists swim or skid along raucously riding on the back of giant bananas or flip like fish, snorkelled and flippered on the surface. But further out the sea changed dramatically to a dark blue — a line so abrupt it looked to be drawn across the water. This navy sea was deep. It let the boats, the yachts, the liners cruise along the island's edge and disgorge their foreigners into the hands of traders.

The Caribbean Sea is like no other. I swam in its warm clear bath as tiny silver fish darted around my legs. I looked up at a blue sky and then along at the line of coconut palms that bent down, bowing their giant leaves to the beach. Paradise.

On the beach scruffy women wandered in bare feet clutching green leaves that oozed aloe vera. They offered massage to the white-skinned tourists who stretched out in the sun like slabs of uncooked chicken. Or they would take fine straight European hair and plait it neat and pretty into acceptable African dreadlocks that were tipped with colourful plastic beads that clacked with every move. Men followed behind, alert, looking around as vigilant as truants, asking anyone who did not belong if there was anything they could get them. 'You from England, sister?' they had said to me. 'I know England, sister — Notting Hill, you know it? You have a dollar? You wan' me get you somethin' nice, sister?'

When the sun set it dropped behind the horizon so quickly it left a trace of green in my vision. The night sky was dense, black, pock-marked with silver with a moon that was strange to me — an upturned crescent, like a smile in the sky.

Coral assured me that Mum and Dad would like the heavy, large, cumbersome, square chopping board I was taking back for them. 'Me sister can cut up her yams and things on it.' She told me it was worth the extra weight to take back such a good all-Jamaican product. It was made from squares of different coloured woods. Dark wood, light wood, white wood packed into a solid mosaic.

I had bought it from a shop in the grounds of Devon House — a yellow and white great house built by a rich black Jamaican man at the time that my grandparents were taking their first breaths. This rich black man constructed his house in the classical style — with pillars, sweeping stairways, driveways and landscaped gardens.

Coral and me had wandered the grounds of the house one hot Wednesday afternoon. The beautiful gardens kept pristine for tourists, with flowers of every colour and shade opening to the sun. Climbing trees winding through the woodwork of the veranda creating dappled shade where black businessmen and tourists sat sipping Blue Mountain cappuccino and espresso, eating stuffed *roti* at tables with starched white linen, served to them by straight-backed waiters in white jackets who walked between the tables with swift efficiency and deferential stoops.

We ate ice cream, walking in the shade of overhanging palms. Jamaican ice cream — paw paw, pineapple with rum, coconut, almond, chocolate, coffee, mocha. I took three licks of mango and banana flavour — creamy and so cold it shivered in my head and I had agreed with my Auntie Coral as she insisted, 'Faith — Jamaican ice cream is the best in the world and let no one tell you otherwise.'

I placed a flat grey stone in my suitcase. I had picked it up at Fort Charles in Port Royal. A stone that could have been lying on that ground for several hundred years. That could have been kicked by the young Horatio Nelson as he strutted the fort, protecting the island from 'foreign' invasion. It was near the grave of Nelson's wife. I was told by the guide — a woman of my age who sucked a length of grass and pointed over her shoulder, nonchalantly reciting her fixed text while looking at no one — that it was not the wife of my English history lessons. No, this was Nelson's Jamaican wife, she had said as she picked the grass from her teeth — his black wife who nursed and tended him in ill health. After that I had walked giddy into the

Giddy House — a sunken room, sloping into the earth at an abrupt angle — the product of an earthquake. And although I had been standing upright, I looked to be leaning, falling and unsteady.

I packed a bag full of red coffee berries intending, when I got to London, to pluck out the familiar beans from inside and roast them as my grandfather used to do and make at least a mouthful of the famous brew. I had picked the handful of berries myself from a stranded bush high up in the Blue Mountains. Vincent's car had cursed and grumbled its way up the rutted, winding mountain roads. And Gloria had cursed and grumbled, 'Faith — Jamaican roads are the worst in the world and let no one tell you otherwise.' Jonathan, Amber and I played cat's cradle in the back of the car — each of us in turn twisting the looped string until it was a tangle of knots. We bumped up tracks lush with the green vegetation of ferns, rubber trees, yucca, juniper, eucalyptus, and looked down the valleys where the dense green was broken by whiffs of white woodsmoke that puffed like ghosts up into the air.

We left the car and bought five bottles of Coca-Cola from a windowless bar that was painted on the outside with scenes from the life of Andy Capp and Flo. Bleached by the sun and far from home those cartoon characters argued round the front and side of the building. On foot, we had followed Vincent up a winding path through undergrowth, over stones and rubble as Gloria fussed, 'This is stupidness. Where are we going, Vincent?' And Jonathan and Amber giggled at the adventure. Vincent told us we were nearly there as he called at a house that grasped the side of the sloping hill. A boy came out — gangly and shy. He looked no one in the eye and mumbled about dogs as he led us further up, swiping at plants and leaves with a stick. We left our Coca-Cola bottles hidden by a rock on a path that looked too deserted to have thieves. Three black dogs ran, barking. The boy pacified them and they hung their heads, growling and slathering on the ground, as he held them back so we could pass.

And then high up in the mountain there was a house. It overlooked Kingston, where the city looked no more than a mottled grey pattern stretching out to the sea. The house was pretty pink and white, with delicate wooden filigree fretwork surrounding the veranda in low vaulting archways. The grey slate roof sloped like a country church and the windows were tall and elegantly glazed with squares of glass like fine Georgian houses in England.

Jonathan had pressed his nose up against the window and excitedly pointed at everything he could see inside. Family pictures on a brown wooden table. Sofas, chairs, bookshelves and cabinets that could be antiques. 'We can't go in, Jonathan . . . we don't have a key . . . the boy does not have a key to the house, Jonathan . . . someone lives in the house, Jonathan . . . they are away at the moment . . . I don't know where they have gone . . . Child, how am I to know when they are coming back?'

But what Vincent had wanted me to see was around at the back of the house. It was a shed. It had an opening for the door and two windows that had no glass. It was made of wood that was shaped like slates in overlapping squares gone grey in the sun. And I walked into this unprotected place — past the oil drum that acted as a door. Inside were wooden bunks like three large shelves up a wall. Slave quarters, Vincent had told me.

'No. Slave quarters would have fallen down long ago,' Gloria had insisted. Preserved, Vincent had explained, from when this was a great house of a coffee plantation. 'They don't preserve things like that. Who want to preserve a thing like that,' Gloria had said. But Vincent told me again that this was where the slaves of the plantation lived and worked. This tiny wooden shed was home for slaves. 'Come, Jonathan, come, Amber, look here nah . . . come and look, it's not just a shed . . . it's nothing to be feared of . . . no, no slaves are in there now . . . why don't you want to look?'

From the bottom bunk, past the brown slatted wood in the window holes, across the dirty oil drum and past the debris at the door, I had looked out and seen the pretty pink slave-owner's house and beyond that the sky and the panoramic view of one of the most beautiful islands on earth. I had picked the handful of coffee berries from a bush I had strained to reach on land that sloped magnificently down away from the house, as the boy led us back down the hillside. The dogs resumed their guarding. The Coca-Cola bottles had gone.

As I packed my bag I told Auntie Coral that before I came to Jamaica I knew nothing about my family. And my auntie said, 'Well, now you know a little, Faith. But there is more. There is always more.' I thought my history started when the ship carrying my parents sailed from Jamaica and docked in England on Guy Fawkes' night. But I was wrong. As my aunt twisted on her seat in the shade searching for the right word, as Vincent licked his fingers and filled his mouth with jerk pork, and as Violet scowled and chided me to listen, they laid a past out in front of me. They wrapped me in a family history and swaddled me tight in its stories. And I was taking back that family to England. But it would not fit in a suitcase — I was smuggling it home.

'You see,' Auntie Coral explained to me as I sat on my case, 'Jamaica used to be part of the British Empire.' A childlike smile came into her eyes, she playfully tipped her head. 'When I was a girl — a little girl — I used to be so proud that we were part of the British Empire. England was our Mother Country. That's what we called it. My teacher at school used to say, 'England is the Mother Country and we . . . ' and she would run her finger round the room pointing at every one of us . . . 'we are all the Mother Country's children.'

'You know, Faith, in those days we did not learn about Jamaica in lessons. Oh no. I knew everything about England and nothing about Jamaica — the place I lived. Funny really. You know what we learn, Faith? We learn to recite the

Kings and Queens of England. We had to learn all their names by heart and then stand up in front of the teacher and say them off.' My aunt began to skip on her toes like she was a girl once again. She held her cheeks and looked up into the air. 'Okay now. Richard Two, Henry Four, Henry Five and Henry Six. Now wait . . . wait . . . Henry Seven . . . no . . . Edward. Now which Edward was this?' I watched my aunt trying to remember. Laughing to herself, waving her hands in front of her face, stepping lightly and saying, 'Now who was next? I knew this all once.' I looked at her black skin that wrinkled round her eyes and her lips that were too thin to be thoroughbred African lips. I watched her as she remembered the Mother Country. The country where I live, among people so unaware of our shared past that all they would see if they were staring at my aunt would be a black woman acting silly.

Let those bully boys walk behind me in the playground. Let them tell me, 'You're a darkie. Faith's a darkie.' I am the granddaughter of Grace and William Campbell. I am the great-grandchild of Cecelia Hilton. I am descended from Katherine whose mother was a slave. I am the cousin of Afria. I am the niece of Coral Thompson and the daughter of Wade and Mildred Jackson. Let them say what they like. Because I am the bastard child of Empire and I will have my day.

★ ★ ★

By the time Vincent finally arrived I was frettin'. He called 'Yoo hoo!' as he came through the door. I was sitting on the bed looking into the house next door at Sybil, the woman who lived there, as she stood with her ample back to the window and her right hand in a large bowl squeezing and kneading a grey gooey mixture while she chuckled along to her television.

'Right, shall we go?' I said, getting up.

'Wow!' Vincent laughed. 'Oh, you are in a hurry.' He sat down on the bed beside me. He frowned as he looked in at Sybil. 'What she making there? Look like cake. That reminds me, I must see if Mummy is steeping her fruit.' Then he remembered me. 'Now first, Faith, I have greetings from Gloria who says she is sorry she cannot come an' see you off but she has to work. And this,' he rummaged in his pocket and handed me a hair grip with a tiny ladybird on it, 'is a gift from Amber for your hair. And this,' he handed me a folded sheet of paper from an exercise book, 'is from your friend Jonathan.' It was a drawing done in red, yellow and blue felt-tip pen of a car with spectacular wings and the words 'for Auntie Faith' written in black over the top.

'It's meant to be a car, I think,' Vincent said. I nodded. 'Oh, you can see that, can you?' he added pensively. 'Now where is Mummy?'

'Asleep.'

'Good, then I have time to go and pick up the light for my car. I know a man who says he has one.'

I could see my plane in the shimmering heat

haze, slowly taxi-ing the runway without me. I wanted to beg Vincent not to leave now he had come. No, Vincent, no! I thought of grabbing for his ankles, wrestling him to the floor as I watched him leave the room. But instead I followed him out to his car with my suitcase squeaking along beside me. 'I'll come with you,' I said, 'I'll put the case in the boot.' I intended to hurry him up.

We drove out to a strip of derelict land. Scrub grass parched in the sun, strewn with the litter of boxes, cans, plastic bags, rusting parts of cars. At the end of the lane that ran through the land was a garage. A wooden shack that leant dangerously — as if one gentle prod could tip it onto the ground. Vincent went into the shack as I waited, sitting on the bonnet of the car looking at my watch. Vincent and a mechanic, dressed in overalls the colour and texture of an oil slick, came out just a few minutes later. I was relieved until the mechanic said, 'I just have to do a little errand for Mummy and I will get the light on the way back. Soon come.' The mechanic waved at Vincent and me from the open window of his car as he sped away trailing dust, exhaust and a thumping reggae bass.

'We can wait. We still have a little time before your plane,' Vincent said. And I cursed that little black dog for running into Vincent's car and hoped it died a bloody and painful death in the bushes. Vincent took a bag juice for each of us out of the car. We sat in the shade made by the leaning shack and squeezed at the juice. Mine was green but tasted pink.

'Now, when we have finished here we must hurry and get Mummy or you will miss this plane. And then Auntie Mildred would be vex with us. Where is me daughter, she would say? I send out me little daughter and what have you done with her?' Vincent chuckled then he looked at me. 'Tell me, Faith, you know that your mummy sent you here?'

'Well, Mum and Dad thought I could do with a holiday.'

'Yes, I know that. But what I am asking you is, did you know they send you here?' I was confused. 'Your mummy never told you, did she, Faith?'

'Told me what?'

'She never told you that she ring her sister and beg her to take you. She never told you that. Auntie Mildred keep ringin' and sayin', 'Oh, Faith is havin' trouble.' She beg Mummy to take you in. She say, 'Please take her in and show her Jamaica.''

And as we sat in the shade, on derelict land strewn with rubbish, sipping warm bag juice, waiting for a mechanic, on my last day in Jamaica, Vincent told me the story.

'Auntie Mildred and Uncle Wade' had told Coral that I was in big trouble in England. Not drugs, Vincent assured me, I was not in trouble with drugs. I was, according to my mother, far too sensible ever to smoke any of that ganja or weed. No, my problem was that I was running around like one of my grandmother's headless chickens.

Evidently, I had left college with big ideas

401

— big ideas, way, way, way above my station. I was going to be some sort of big-shot-textile-fashion-and-thing designer. Oh, I was going to do this and I was going to do that. Then to everyone's surprise I got a good job with travel and all sorts. But then what happened — what happened? Of course I lost the job. And worse. When I lost the job I tried to hide it from my parents because evidently, I think of them as some fool people who just got off a boat — people so silly they could not tell that their only daughter was skipping out the house and sitting with her friend all day. But they said nothing. Nothing. They said absolutely nothing because they are not the sort of parents to pry. They are the sort of parents who let their children make their own mistakes.

And oh boy, what mistakes, what mistakes I made, my mum and dad had told Coral. First I left home. I left the nice comfortable home of my parents to go and live in some broken-down house, where the walls were painted dark green — a green that would turn the stomach of any sensible person. Second, I had said I was living with some nice girls from good homes but it turned out that I moved in with men. Grown men who would, no doubt, expect me to wait on them. But worse, much worse, I was also living with the girl whom my parents suspected of having intimate relations with several men outside of marriage.

But you see, my mum and dad had explained to all my Jamaican relatives, part of my problem was that everyone I lived with was white. Not

402

that there was anything wrong with them being white — because in England we all live with one another — black or white, it doesn't matter. Thank the Lord — it's not like America. No. It was just that these white people were not brought up as I was. They did not go to church on Sunday. They dressed in sloppy clothes that were unpressed and ill-fitting, which was not what looks nice on me. And they all had hair that was straight and lank like a drink of water and because I wanted to fit in, I was not looking after my hair as I should. All these people I lived with were people who did not want to get on in life — musicians and ne'er-do-wells whom my parents suspected drank a lot of alcohol. I was different to them — I had not been brought up like that. But who was to say my head would not be turned.

And I was not getting enough to eat.

Then there was my brother. Oh, there was my brother. So sensible. So steady. Carl could take care of himself. He was not a worry to them at all. Sometimes they wished they had had two boys. Carl was happy. Carl was settled. Carl had a girlfriend. Mark you, she had some strange ideas but she kept her hair very neat. Carl was not a worry to them at all.

Then, praise be, their prayers were answered. I got a job. A very good job in television. They were not quite sure what I did at work but they knew I was meeting all manner of famous people. Oh, they were so proud. Perhaps now I would settle down, they hoped. Maybe with a nice young man — like the young man who worked with my dad — Noel. A lovely, sensible man who went to church and worked hard. They tried to bring us together — not so that I would notice — they were, evidently, very subtle. But no, I had other ideas. I was not interested even though the young man would be a good catch for any young woman.

Then I lost that good job because I would not get out of bed. And if the young man from the house — who turned out to be very nice, clean, respectable and actually trained in the law — had not had the good sense to visit them at home and tell them what was happening, I would still be in that bed today. And the sink in the house was filthy and blocked.

I was a problem to them, they had told Vincent. I could not settle down, they'd confided in Gloria. And what could they do? Because, they'd told Coral, they were thinking, only thinking, mind, just thinking that maybe one day they might come to Jamaica themselves — to live. Just thinking, mind, no plans, just thinking. But they could not leave England until I was settled, until I was happy with a nice home and a husband maybe.

They had no regrets. Oh, they had given me a better life in England, better than I could have had in Jamaica. They had no regrets. But when they first came to England it was a different story — when they first came to England they had had trouble. Oh boy, they had big trouble! Everyone called them 'Wog' and 'Darkie'. Everyone told them they were from the jungle. Nobody wanted them to live in their house, or even in their street. They laughed at their food, at their clothes, at the way they spoke. But they knew they were Jamaican. They knew where they came from and they knew where they wanted to go. They just got on with it. They learnt to get along with people. They learnt to smile and laugh and all the while just quietly make the life they wanted. And they have had a good life. But me, I was born in England and I knew nothing else.

Evidently, I had never in my life shown even the slightest interest in my parents' life before they came to England. I never asked where they lived, what life was like for them. I never wanted to know about any of my Jamaican relatives. I never asked my mother about her parents and I had never asked my father about his upbringing. And even though I was named after a lovely goat I never questioned my mother about the animal. I was not interested. According to my parents, my eyes would roll in my head when they began to speak about the place they had once called home. No. I, like all the other young people in England, thought my parents were some fool people who knew nothing. I, like all the other young people in England, was only interested in my friends, the opposite sex and staying out as late as possible.

So now, according to my parents, I had no job, no proper home and everywhere I looked I saw people trying to hold me back. Everywhere I looked I saw people trying to keep me down because I am black. I was just running around like there is something missing. They were at their wits' end, they did not know what to do with me.

'But then,' Vincent told me, 'Uncle Wade had a good idea.' The good idea my dad came up with was to send me to Jamaica.

They thought, maybe if I knew a little about Jamaica, maybe if I knew a little about that life . . . So they asked my Auntie Coral to take me in.

'When you sent your letter,' Vincent carried on, 'Mummy answer it like it out of the blue. Oh yes, she say, what a surprise. Come to Jamaica.' Then I arrived late at night at Kingston airport. 'Mummy was scared you would be one of those punky people with spiky hair.' But when Vincent and Coral first saw me, walking slowly along the ramp that led from the airport terminal, they thought I looked . . . lost.

Everyone, evidently, was relieved.

Coral kept asking Vincent, 'What am I supposed to tell the child that she does not know already?' But then after I had been in Jamaica for a few days my Auntie Coral complained to Vincent instead, 'What did my sister talk to her child about — the weather? The child knows nothing!' Coral was surprised at my ignorance. She was surprised at how little of my past had been carried on that banana boat to England. 'That sister of mine is a pest,' Coral concluded. 'I have had to do all her work since I was a girl, and she is not done with me yet. Cha.'

Vincent finished his story, slurped his last mouthful of bag juice, rubbed his hands

406

together, shook out his legs and said, 'So.' He looked at me and I stared back at him. Then he asked slowly, 'Are you surprised to learn what your mummy and daddy say?' I shook my head. He leant closer to me, 'But, Faith, you know your mouth is hangin' open?' I slapped my dry lips together. I was, I thought, putting my hands on my hips. I thought I was saying to Vincent, my bloody parents are so interfering — I am so humiliated that my parents did that — I am so embarrassed they did that to you and Coral. I thought I was turning crimson. But I realised when I looked in Vincent's face, that I was smiling. I just smiled.

The mechanic came back — his car screeching to a halt in the dust — as Vincent covered my hands with his and said, 'But what I just told you we will keep a little secret, ehh, Faith? Between you and me. A family secret.' He tapped his nose then jumped up. 'He's back — time flies when you have a story to tell, ehh?' He skipped over to the car. The mechanic was grinning so much he looked to be in pain. He took out a light from the boot of his car. He took it proudly over to Vincent's car. Vincent rubbed his hands together saying, 'Good.' They put the light up to the hole. And it was two inches too big.

'No problem,' the mechanic said. 'I can just poke it here and push it in a little there.'

'How can you poke and push at metal and glass? If it doesn't fit, it doesn't fit. Me cousin has a plane to catch to England and I am sittin' wastin' me time waitin' on you. Cha.'

'Come tomorrow,' the mechanic said, nonchalantly. 'Me brother has another one that will fit.
Come tomorrow. No problem. No problem.'

★　★　★

We arrived at the airport with time to spare. We
had collected Coral. Vincent had had two
bowlfuls of ham bone soup. The little dog had
been pulled out from under the brown leather
chaise longue three times and made to sit at the
front gate. I had had to open my suitcase several
times to place in a wooden wall plaque with
patois words and meanings, a ceramic ackee that
said 'Jamaica' along one leaf and a brown
cardboard box that contained six well-wrapped
drinking glasses that Coral had insisted I took
home for Mum, instructing me to tell the
busybody man at Customs to mind his business
if he wanted to know what was in the box.

I waved to my suitcase as it was taken from me
at the airport terminal and thrown into a pile
with all the other bags. The terminal was as
chaotic as when I arrived. There were people
moving around me everywhere — jostling,
pushing, standing in line to check in, wandering
lost, holding bits of paper, eating, waving,
hugging people goodbye. Talking, shouting,
screeching. Coral and Vincent were waiting for
me in a corner of the terminal. I saw them from
afar — standing quite still. A fixed point in the
bustle.

I cried as I hugged my Auntie Coral. Fat tears
rolling down my cheeks. Coral gently wiped my

face with her handkerchief and said, 'You must always remember us, little one.'

'What are you crying for?' Vincent asked. He hugged me hard into his chest so my nose flattened and I could not breathe. 'I thought you were pleased to be going home.'

I saw them looking for me from a viewing platform on top of the airport building. My aunt had her arms folded in front of her and Vincent was shielding his eyes from the sun and looking around for the right plane. As my plane taxied along the runway and got ready for take-off I waved at them through the window — but I don't think they saw me.

Part III

England

27

I noticed them after the plane had landed in England. Bright sparks of colour in the distance. Breaking up the black of the night sky. Green, yellow, red, gold, silver, blue — bursting pocks of colour from this side, from that side, from all around. Fireworks. Fireworks in the night sky over England.

At first I thought it may be a welcome home for me. The distant horizon briefly lit gold by a shower of sparks like an electric dandelion. I thought it may be a welcome for me having travelled so far and England needing me. A fluorescent green spiral that whizzed upwards and was gone. But I knew I couldn't be right. A crack and three red sparks floated slowly down and out. I knew I couldn't be right and I wasn't. A brief fizzing green arc that turned gradually to silver-blue. No. I knew this was England, November the fifth. There are always fireworks on November the fifth. It was Guy Fawkes' night and I was coming home. I was coming home to tell everyone . . . My mum and dad came to England on a banana boat.

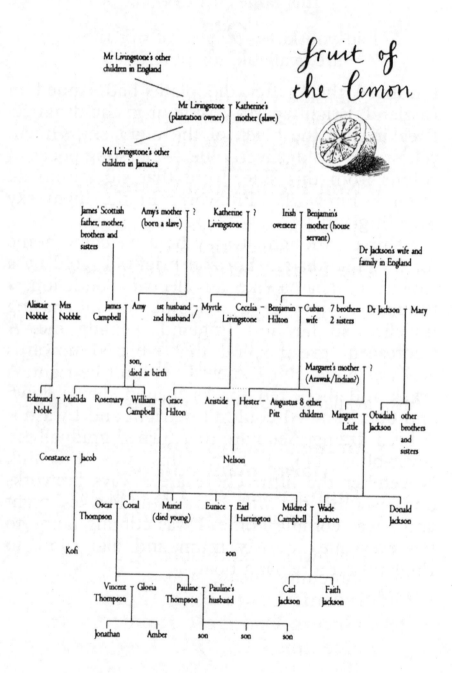

fruit of the lemon

We do hope that you have enjoyed reading this large print book.

Did you know that all of our titles are available for purchase?

We publish a wide range of high quality large print books including:
Romances, Mysteries, Classics
General Fiction
Non Fiction and Westerns

Special interest titles available in large print are:
The Little Oxford Dictionary
Music Book
Song Book
Hymn Book
Service Book

Also available from us courtesy of Oxford University Press:
Young Readers' Dictionary
(large print edition)
Young Readers' Thesaurus
(large print edition)

For further information or a free brochure, please contact us at:
Ulverscroft Large Print Books Ltd.,
The Green, Bradgate Road, Anstey,
Leicester, LE7 7FU, England.
Tel: (00 44) 0116 236 4325
Fax: (00 44) 0116 234 0205

Other titles published by
The House of Ulverscroft:

SMALL ISLAND

Andrea Levy

It is 1948 and England is still shaken by war.
At 21 Nevern Street, London, Queenie Bligh
takes in lodgers who have recently arrived
from Jamaica. She feels she has no choice.
Her husband, Bernard, did not return from
the war. What else could she do? Among her
tenants are Gilbert and his new wife,
Hortense. Gilbert Joseph was one of the
thousands of Jamaican men who joined the
RAF to fight against Hitler. He finds himself
treated very differently now that he is no
longer in a blue uniform. It is desperation
that makes him remember a wartime
friendship with Queenie and knock at her
door. Queenie's neighbours do not approve
of her choice of tenants. England may be
recovering from a war but at 21 Nevern
Street it has only just begun.

NEVER FAR FROM NOWHERE

Andrea Levy

Olive and Vivien were born in London to Jamaican parents and brought up on a council estate. They go to the same grammar school. Vivien's life becomes a chaotic mix of friendships, youth clubs, skinhead violence, A-levels, discos and college. But Olive, three years older and her skin a shade darker, has a very different tale to tell . . .

THE MEMORY OF RUNNING

Ron McLarty

Smithson Ide's life so far has led him nowhere. He's forty-three years old, weighs too much, and keeps himself numb with food and alcohol. His only emotional ties are to his parents and to the memory of his older sister, Bethany, who has been missing for twenty years. Then his parents die in a car crash and he learns of Bethany's death in LA County. Drunk and bereft, he takes his old Raleigh bicycle and starts cycling. Once he starts, he finds he can't stop and then he's riding across America to recover his sister. Along the way he meets all sorts of people who help or hinder him. Smithy's ride is an extraordinary quest, to rediscover the past and memories of Bethany, but it's also his journey back to life and love.

A MAN OF HIS TIME

Alan Sillitoe

In 1887, twenty-one-year-old Ernest Burton leaves his parents' home in a village near Nottingham, to work as a journeyman blacksmith in the coalfields of South Wales. Boldly, recklessly, Ernest stands up to his superiors and seduces young girls. Realising that everyone must settle down sometime, he returns to his childhood village and marries his sweetheart, eventually becoming a master blacksmith. A tyrannical father of eight, he instils in his sons and daughters a mixture of fear and hatred of him. But Ernest also has an effortless charm and magnetic attraction, and a softer, more tender heart than anyone would ever know. And when an unforeseen tragedy destroys what he holds most dear, this soft side threatens to overwhelm him.

THE SERGEANTS' TALE

Bernice Rubens

It is 1947, and in the British Mandate of Palestine the political pressure is rising. Jewish immigrants are arriving from Europe in their thousands, smuggled ashore past the armed patrols. The Wertman family, like the Jewish community, is divided: Avram is a member of the Irgun, a terrorist group fighting to end the occuption; his daughter Hannah works for the Haganah, peacefully campaigning for a Jewish state. David Millar and Will Griffiths are two English sergeants, reluctant conscripts, who transfer to Intelligence. Half-Catholic, half-Jewish, David has mixed feelings about his work, more so when he becomes close to Hannah. Will, meanwhile, is finding trouble at the Jerusalem jazz bar where he plays his saxophone . . .